Kelly Link is the author of the collections *Stranger Things Happen, Magic for Beginners* and *Pretty Monsters*. She and Gavin J. Grant have co-edited a number of anthologies, including multiple volumes of *The Year's Best Fantasy and Horror* and, for young adults, *Monstrous Affections*. She is the co-founder of Small Beer Press. Her short stories have been published in *The Magazine of Fantasy & Science Fiction, The Best American Short Stories,* and *Prize Stories: The O. Henry Awards.* She has received a grant from the National Endowment for the Arts. Link was born in Miami, Florida. She currently lives with her husband and daughter in Northampton, Massachusetts.

www.kellylink.net

By Kelly Link

Get in Trouble

Pretty Monsters

Magic for Beginners

Stranger Things Happen

GET IN TROUBLE

KELLY LINK

CANONGATE
Edinburgh · London

This paperback edition first published by Canongate Books in 2016

First published in Great Britain in 2015 by Canongate Books Ltd,
14 High Street, Edinburgh EH1 1TE

www.canongate.tv

1

First published in the United States by Random House,
an imprint and division of Random House LLC,
a Penguin Random House Company, New York.

"The Summer People": Originally published in *Tin House* (fall 2011).
"I Can See Right Through You": Originally published in *McSweeney's* (fall 2014).
"Secret Identity": Originally published in *Geektastic: Stories from the Nerd Herd*,
edited by Holly Black and Cecil Castellucci (Little Brown, 2009).
"Valley of the Girls": Originally published in *Subterranean Online* (summer 2011).
"Origin Story": Originally published in *A Public Space* (winter 2006).
"The New Boyfriend": Originally published in *A Public Space* (fall 2014).
"Two Houses": Originally published in *Shadow Show: All-New Stories in Celebration
of Ray Bradbury*, edited by Mort Castle and Sam Weller (HarperCollins, 2012).
"Light": Originally published in *Tin House* (fall 2007).

British Library Cataloguing-in-Publication Data
A catalogue record for this book is available on
request from the British Library

ISBN 978 1 78211 385 0

Book design by Caroline Cunningham

Printed and bound in Great Britain by Clays Ltd, St Ives plc.

For Henry William Link III

Year after year
On the monkey's face
A monkey face
                    —Basho, trans. Robert Hass

Contents

Contents

GET IN TROUBLE

The Summer
People

✕ ✕ ✕

F ran's daddy woke her up wielding a mister. "Fran," he said, spritzing her like a wilted houseplant. "Fran, honey. Wakey wakey."

Fran had the flu, except it was more like the flu had Fran. In consequence of this, she'd laid out of school for three days in a row. The previous night, she'd taken four NyQuil caplets and gone to sleep on the couch while a man on the TV threw knives. Her head was stuffed with boiled wool and snot. Her face was wet with watered-down plant food. "Hold up," she croaked. "I'm awake!" She began to cough, so hard she had to hold her sides. She sat up.

Her daddy was a dark shape in a room full of dark shapes. The bulk of him augured trouble. The sun wasn't out from behind the mountain yet, but there was a light in the kitchen. There was a suitcase, too, beside the door, and on the table a plate with a mess of eggs. Fran was starving.

Her daddy went on. "I'll be gone some time. A week or three.

Not more. You'll take care of the summer people while I'm gone. The Robertses come up this weekend. You'll need to get their groceries tomorrow or next day. Make sure you check the expiration date on the milk when you buy it, and put fresh sheets on all the beds. I've left the house schedule on the counter and there should be enough gas in the car to make the rounds."

"Wait," Fran said. Every word hurt. "Where are you going?" He sat down on the couch beside her, then pulled something out from under him. He showed her what he held: one of Fran's old toys, the monkey egg. "Now, you know I don't like these. I wish you'd put 'em away."

"There's lots of stuff I don't like," Fran said. "Where you off to?"

"Prayer meeting in Miami. Found it on the Internet," her daddy said. He shifted on the couch, put a hand against her forehead, so cool and soothing it made her eyes leak. "You don't feel near so hot right now."

"I know you need to stay here and look after me," Fran said. "You're my daddy."

"Now, how can I look after you if I'm not right?" he said. "You don't know the things I've done."

Fran didn't know but she could guess. "You went out last night," she said. "You were drinking."

"I'm not talking about last night," he said. "I'm talking about a lifetime."

"That is—" Fran said, and then began to cough again. She coughed so long and so hard she saw bright stars. Despite the hurt in her ribs, and despite the truth that every time she managed to suck in a good pocket of air, she coughed it right back out again, the NyQuil made it all seem so peaceful, her daddy might as well have been saying a poem. Her eyelids were closing. Later, when she woke up, maybe he would make her breakfast.

"Any come around, you tell 'em I'm gone on ahead. Ary man tells you he knows the hour or the day, Fran, that man's a liar or a fool. All a man can do is be ready."

He patted her on the shoulder, tucked the counterpane up around her ears. When she woke again, it was late afternoon and her daddy was long gone. Her temperature was 102.3. All across her cheeks, the plant mister had left a red, raised rash.

On Friday, Fran went back to school. Breakfast was a spoon of peanut butter and dry cereal. She couldn't remember the last time she'd eaten. Her cough scared off the crows when she went down to the county road to catch the school bus.

She dozed through three classes, including calculus, before having such a fit of coughing the teacher sent her off to see the nurse. The nurse, she knew, was liable to call her daddy and send her home. This might have presented a problem, but on the way to the nurse's station, Fran came upon Ophelia Merck at her locker.

Ophelia Merck had her own car, a Lexus. She and her family had been summer people, except now they lived in their house up at Horse Cove on the lake all year round. Years ago, Fran and Ophelia had spent a summer of afternoons playing with Ophelia's Barbies while Fran's father smoked out a wasps' nest, repainted cedar siding, tore down an old fence. They hadn't really spoken since then, though once or twice after that summer, Fran's father brought home paper bags full of Ophelia's hand-me-downs, some of them still with the price tags.

Fran eventually went through a growth spurt, which put a stop to that; Ophelia was still tiny, even now. And far as Fran could figure, Ophelia hadn't changed much in most other ways: pretty, shy, spoiled, and easy to boss around. The rumor was her family'd moved full-time to Robbinsville from Lynchburg after a teacher caught Ophelia kissing another girl in the bathroom at a school dance. It was either that or Mr. Merck being up for malpractice, which was the other story, take your pick.

"Ophelia Merck," Fran said. "I need you to come with me to see Nurse Tannent. She's going to tell me to go home. I'll need a ride."

Ophelia opened her mouth and closed it. She nodded.

Fran's temperature was back up again, at 102. Tannent even wrote Ophelia a note to go off campus.

"I don't know where you live," Ophelia said. They were in the parking lot, Ophelia searching for her keys.

"Take the county road," Fran said. "129." Ophelia nodded. "It's up a ways on Wild Ridge, past the hunting camps." She lay back against the headrest and closed her eyes. "Oh, hell. I forgot. Can you take me by the convenience first? I have to get the Robertses' house put right."

"I guess I can do that," Ophelia said.

At the convenience, Fran picked up milk, eggs, whole-wheat sandwich bread, and cold cuts for the Robertses, Tylenol and more NyQuil for herself, as well as a can of frozen orange juice, microwave burritos, and Pop-Tarts. "On the tab," she told Andy.

"I hear your pappy got himself into trouble the other night," Andy said.

"That so," Fran said. "He went down to Florida yesterday morning. He said he needs to get right with God."

"God ain't who your pappy needs to get on his good side," Andy said.

Fran pressed her hand against her burning eye. "What's he done?"

"Nothing that can't be fixed with the application of some greaze and good manners," Andy said. "You tell him we'll see to't when he come back."

Half the time her daddy got to drinking, Andy and Andy's cousin Ryan were involved, never mind it was a dry county. Andy kept all kinds of liquor out back in his van for everwho wanted it and knew to ask. The good stuff came from over the county line, in Andrews. The best stuff, though, was the stuff Fran's daddy made. Everyone said that Fran's daddy's brew was too good to be strictly natural. Which was true. When he wasn't getting right with God, Fran's daddy got up to all kinds of trouble. Fran's best guess was that, in this particular situation, he'd promised to supply something that God was not now going to let him deliver. "I'll tell him you said so."

Ophelia was looking over the list of ingredients on a candy wrapper, but Fran could tell she was interested. When they got back into the car Fran said, "Just because you're doing me a favor don't mean you need to know my business."

"Okay," Ophelia said.

"Okay," Fran said. "Good. Now mebbe you can take me by the Robertses' place. It's over on—"

"I know where the Robertses' house is," Ophelia said. "My mom played bridge over there all last summer."

The Robertses hid their spare key under a fake rock just like everybody else. Ophelia stood at the door like she was waiting to be invited in. "Well, come on," Fran said.

There wasn't much to be said about the Robertses' house.
There was an abundance of plaid, and everywhere Toby Jugs and
statuettes of dogs pointing, setting, or trotting along with birds in
their gentle mouths.

Fran made up the smaller bedrooms and did a hasty vacuum
downstairs while Ophelia made up the master bedroom and
caught the spider that had made a home in the wastebasket. She
carried it outside. Fran didn't quite have the breath to make fun
of her for this. They went from room to room, making sure there
were working bulbs in the light fixtures and that the cable wasn't
out. Ophelia sang under her breath while they worked. They
were both in choir, and Fran found herself evaluating Ophelia's
voice. A soprano, warm and light at the same time, where Fran
was an alto and somewhat froggy even when she didn't have the
flu.

"Stop it," she said out loud, and Ophelia turned and looked at
her. "Not you," Fran said. She ran the tap water in the kitchen
sink until it was clear. She coughed for a long time and spat into
the drain. It was almost four o'clock. "We're done here."

"How do you feel?" Ophelia said.

"Like I've been kicked all over," Fran said.

"I'll take you home," Ophelia said. "Is anyone there, in case
you start feeling worse?"

Fran didn't bother answering, but somewhere between the
school lockers and the Robertses' master bedroom, Ophelia
seemed to have decided that the ice was broken. She talked
about a TV show, about the party neither of them would go to
on Saturday night. Fran began to suspect that Ophelia had had
friends once, down in Lynchburg. She complained about calculus homework and talked about the sweater she was knitting.

She mentioned a girl rock band that she thought Fran might like, even offered to burn her a CD. Several times, she exclaimed as they drove up the county road.

"I'll never get used to it, to living up here year round," Ophelia said. "I mean, we haven't even been here a whole year, but . . . It's just so beautiful. It's like another world, you know?"

"Not really," Fran said. "Never been anywhere else."

"Oh," Ophelia said, not quite deflated by this reply. "Well, take it from me. It's freaking gorgeous here. Everything is so pretty it almost hurts. I love morning, the way everything is all misty. And the trees! And every time the road snakes around a corner, there's another waterfall. Or a little pasture, and it's all full of flowers. All the *hollers*." Fran could hear the invisible brackets around the word. "It's like you don't know what you'll see, what's there, until suddenly you're right in the middle of it all. Are you applying to college anywhere next year? I was thinking about vet school. I don't think I can take another English class. Large animals. No little dogs or guinea pigs. Maybe I'll go out to California."

Fran said, "We're not the kind of people who go to college."

"Oh," Ophelia said. "You're a lot smarter than me, you know? So I just thought . . ."

"Turn here," Fran said. "Careful. It's not paved."

They went up the dirt road, through the laurel beds, and into the little meadow with the nameless creek. Fran could feel Ophelia suck in a breath, probably trying her hardest not to say something about how beautiful it was. And it was beautiful, Fran knew. You could hardly see the house itself, hidden like a bride behind her veil of climbing vines: virgin's bower and Japanese honeysuckle, masses of William Baffin and Cherokee roses overgrowing the porch and running up over the sagging roof. Bumblebees, their legs armored in gold, threaded through the meadow grass, almost too weighed down with pollen to fly.

"It's old," Fran said. "Needs a new roof. My great-granddaddy ordered it out of the Sears catalog. Men brought it up the side of the mountain in pieces, and all the Cherokee who hadn't gone away yet came and watched." She was amazed at herself: next thing she would be asking Ophelia to come for a sleepover.

She opened the car door and heaved herself out, plucked up the poke of groceries. Before she could turn and thank Ophelia for the ride, Ophelia was out of the car as well. "I thought," Ophelia said uncertainly. "Well, I thought maybe I could use your bathroom?"

"It's an outhouse," Fran said, deadpan. Then she relented: "Come on in, then. It's a regular bathroom. Just not very clean."

Ophelia didn't say anything when they came into the kitchen. Fran watched her take it in: the heaped dishes in the sink, the pillow and raggedy quilt on the sagging couch. The piles of dirty laundry beside the efficiency washer in the kitchen. The places where tendrils of vine had found a way inside around the windows. "I guess you might be thinking it's funny," she said. "My pa and me make money doing other people's houses, but we don't take no real care of our own."

"I was thinking that somebody ought to be taking care of you," Ophelia said. "At least while you're sick."

Fran gave a little shrug. "I do fine on my own," she said. "Washroom's down the hall."

She took two NyQuil while Ophelia was gone and washed them down with the last swallow or two of ginger ale out of the refrigerator. Flat, but still cool. Then she lay down on the couch and pulled the counterpane up around her face. She huddled into the lumpy cushions. Her legs ached, her face felt hot as fire. Her feet were ice cold.

A minute later Ophelia sat down beside her.

"Ophelia?" Fran said. "I'm grateful for the ride home and for the help at the Robertses', but I don't go for girls. So don't lez out."

Ophelia said, "I brought you a glass of water. You need to stay hydrated."

"Mmm," Fran said.

"You know, your dad told me once that I was going to hell," Ophelia said. "He was over at our house doing something. Fixing a burst pipe, maybe? I don't know how he knew. I was eleven. I don't think I knew, not yet, anyway. He didn't bring you over to play after he said that, even though I never told my mom."

"My daddy thinks everyone is going to hell," Fran said from under the counterpane. "I don't care where I go, as long as it ain't here and he's not there."

Ophelia didn't say anything for a minute or two and she didn't get up to leave, either, so finally Fran poked her head out. Ophelia had a toy in her hand, the monkey egg. She turned it over, and then over again.

"Give here," Fran said. "I'll work it." She wound the filigreed dial and set the egg on the floor. The toy vibrated ferociously. Two pincerlike legs and a scorpion tail made of figured brass shot out of the bottom hemisphere, and the egg wobbled on the legs in one direction and then another, the articulated tail curling and lashing. Portholes on either side of the top hemisphere opened and two arms wriggled out and reached up, rapping at the dome of the egg until that, too, cracked open with a click. A monkey's head, wearing the egg dome like a hat, popped out. Its mouth opened and closed in ecstatic chatter, red garnet eyes rolling, arms describing wider and wider circles in the air until the clockwork ran down and all of its extremities whipped back into the egg again.

"What in the world?" Ophelia said. She picked up the egg, tracing the joins with a finger.

"It's just something that's been in our family," Fran said. She stuck her arm out of the quilt, grabbed a tissue, and blew her nose for maybe the thousandth time. "We didn't steal it from no one, that's what you're thinking."

"No," Ophelia said, and then frowned. "It's just—I've never seen anything like it. It's like a Fabergé egg. It ought to be in a museum."

There were lots of other toys. The laughing cat and the waltzing elephants; the swan you wound up, who chased the dog. Other toys that Fran hadn't played with in years. The mermaid who combed garnets out of her own hair. Bawbees for babies, her mother had called them.

"I remember now," Ophelia said. "When you came and played at my house. You brought a silver minnow. It was smaller than my little finger. We put it in the bathtub, and it swam around and around. You had a little fishing rod, too, and a golden worm that wriggled on the hook. You let me catch the fish, and when I did, it talked. It said it would give me a wish if I let it go."

"You wished for two pieces of chocolate cake," Fran said.

"And then my mother made a chocolate cake, didn't she?" Ophelia said. "So the wish came true. But I could only eat one piece. Maybe I knew she was going to make a cake? Except why would I wish for something that I already knew I was going to get?"

Fran said nothing. She watched Ophelia through slit eyes.

"Do you still have the fish?" Ophelia asked.

Fran said, "Somewhere. The clockwork ran down. It didn't give wishes no more. I reckon I didn't mind. It only ever granted little wishes."

"Ha ha," Ophelia said. She stood up. "Tomorrow's Saturday. I'll come by in the morning to make sure you're okay."

"You don't have to," Fran said.

"No," Ophelia said. "I don't have to. But I will."

When you do for other people (Fran's daddy said once upon a time when he was drunk, before he got religion) things that they could do for themselves, but they pay you to do it instead, you both will get used to it.

Sometimes they don't even pay you, and that's charity. At first, charity isn't comfortable, but it gets so it is. After some while, maybe you start to feel wrong when you ain't doing for them, just one more thing, and always one more thing after that. Might be you start to feel as you're valuable. Because they need you. And the more they need you, the more you need them. Things tip out of balance. You need to remember that, Franny. Sometimes you're on one side of that equation, and sometimes you're on the other. You need to know where you are and what you owe. Unless you can balance that out, here is where y'all stay.

Fran, dosed on NyQuil, feverish and alone in her great-grandfather's catalog house, hidden behind walls of roses, dreamed—as she did every night—of escape. She woke every few hours, wishing someone would bring her another glass of water. She sweated through her clothes, and then froze, and then boiled again.

She was still on the couch when Ophelia came back, banging through the screen door. "Good morning!" Ophelia said. "Or maybe I should say good afternoon! It's noon, anyhow. I brought oranges to make fresh orange juice, and I didn't know if you liked sausage or bacon so I got you two different kinds of biscuit."

Fran struggled to sit up.

"Fran," Ophelia said. She came and stood in front of the sofa, holding a cat-head biscuit in each hand. "You look terrible." She brushed her knuckles over Fran's forehead. "You're burning up! I knew I oughtn't've left you here all by yourself! What should I do? Should I take you down to the emergency?"

"No doctor," Fran said. "They'll want to know where my daddy is. Water?"

Ophelia scampered back to the kitchen. "You need antibiotics. Or something. Fran?"

"Here," Fran said. She lifted a bill off a stack of mail on the floor, pulled out the return envelope. She plucked out three strands of her hair. She put them in the envelope and licked it shut. "Take this up the road where it crosses the drain," she said. "All the way up." She coughed. Dry things rattled around down inside her lungs. "When you get to the big house, go round to the back and knock on the door. Tell them I sent you. You won't see them, but they'll know you come from me. After you knock, you go in. Go upstairs directly, you mind, and put this envelope under the door. Third door down the hall. You'll know which. After that, you oughter wait out on the porch. Bring back whatever they give you."

Ophelia gave her a look that said Fran was delirious. "Just go," Fran said. "If there ain't a house, or if there is a house and it ain't the house I'm telling you 'bout, then come back and I'll go to the emergency with you. Or if you find the house, and you're afeared and you can't do what I asked, come back, and I'll go with you. But if you do what I tell you, it will be like the minnow."

"Like the minnow?" Ophelia said. "I don't understand."

"You will. Be bold," Fran said, and did her best to look cheerful. "Like the girls in those ballads. Will you bring me another glass of water afore you go?"

Ophelia went.

Fran lay on the couch, thinking about what Ophelia would see. From time to time, she raised a curious sort of spyglass—something much more useful than any bawbee—to her eye. Through it she saw first the dirt track, which only seemed to dead-end. Were you to look again, you found your road crossing over the shallow crick, the one climbing the mountain, the drain running away and down. The meadow disappeared again into beds of laurel, then trees hung all over with climbing roses, so that you ascended in drifts of pink and white. A stone wall, tumbled and ruint, and then the big house. The house, dry-stack stone, stained with age like the tumbledown wall, two stories. A slate roof, a long slant porch, carved wooden shutters making all the eyes of the windows blind. Two apple trees, crabbed and old, one laden with fruit and the other bare and silver black. Ophelia found the mossy path between them that wound around to the back door with two words carved over the stone lintel: BE BOLD.

And this is what Fran saw Ophelia do: having knocked on the

door, Ophelia hesitated for only a moment, and then she opened it. She called out, "Hello? Fran sent me. She's ill. Hello?" No one answered.

So Ophelia took a breath and stepped over the threshold and into a dark, crowded hallway with a room on either side and a staircase in front of her. On the flagstone in front of her were carved the words: BE BOLD, BE BOLD. Despite the invitation, Ophelia did not seem tempted to investigate either room, which Fran thought wise of her. The first test a success. You might expect that through one door would be a living room, and you might expect that through the other door would be a kitchen, but you would be wrong. One was the Queen's Room. The other was what Fran thought of as the War Room.

Fusty stacks of magazines and catalogs and newspapers, encyclopedias and gothic novels leaned against the walls of the hall, making such a narrow alley that even lickle tiny Ophelia turned sideways to make her way. Dolls' legs and silverware sets and tennis trophies and mason jars and empty matchboxes and false teeth and still chancier things poked out of paper bags and plastic carriers. You might expect that through the doors on either side of the hall there would be more crumbling piles and more odd jumbles, and you would be right. But there were other things, too. At the foot of the stairs was another piece of advice for guests like Ophelia, carved right into the first riser: BE BOLD, BE BOLD, BUT NOT TOO BOLD.

The owners of the house had been at another one of their frolics, Fran saw. Someone had woven tinsel and ivy and peacock feathers through the banisters. Someone had thumbtacked cut silhouettes and Polaroids and tintypes and magazine pictures on the wall alongside the stairs, layers upon layers upon layers; hundreds and hundreds of eyes watching each time Ophelia set her foot down carefully on the next stair.

Perhaps Ophelia didn't trust the stairs not to be rotted through. But the stairs were safe. Someone had always taken very good care of this house.

At the top of the stairs, the carpet underfoot was soft, almost spongy. Moss, Fran decided. They've redecorated again. That's going to be the devil to clean up. Here and there were white and red mushrooms in pretty rings upon the moss. More bawbees, too, waiting for someone to come along and play with them. A dinosaur, needing only to be wound up, a plastic dime-store cowboy sitting on its brass-and-copper shoulders. Up near the ceiling, two armored dirigibles, tethered to a light fixture by scarlet ribbons. The cannons on these zeppelins were in working order. They'd chased Fran down the hall more than once. Back home, she'd had to tweeze the tiny lead pellets out of her shin. Today, though, all were on their best behavior.

Ophelia passed one door, two doors, stopped at the third door. Above it, the final warning: BE BOLD, BE BOLD, BUT NOT TOO BOLD, LEST THAT THY HEART'S BLOOD RUN COLD. Ophelia put her hand on the doorknob, but didn't try it. Not afeared, but no fool neither, Fran thought. They'll be pleased. Or will they?

Ophelia knelt down to slide Fran's envelope under the door. Something else happened, too: something slipped out of Ophelia's pocket and landed on the carpet of moss.

Back down the hall, Ophelia stopped in front of the first door. She seemed to hear someone or something. Music, perhaps? A voice calling her name? An invitation? Fran's poor, sore heart was filled with delight. They liked her! Well, of course they did. Who wouldn't like Ophelia?

She made her way down the stairs, through the towers of clutter and junk. Back onto the porch, where she sat on the porch swing, but didn't swing. She seemed to be keeping one eye on the house and the other on the little rock garden out back, which ran up against the mountain right quick. There was even a waterfall, and Fran hoped Ophelia appreciated it. There'd never been no such thing before. This one was all for her, all for Ophelia, who'd opined that waterfalls are freaking beautiful.

Up on the porch, Ophelia's head jerked around, as if she were afraid someone might be sneaking up the back. But there were only carpenter bees, bringing back their satchels of gold, and a woodpecker, drilling for grubs. There was a ground pig in the rumpled grass, and the more Ophelia set and stared, the more she and Fran both saw. A pair of fox kits napping under the laurel. A doe and a fawn teasing runners of bark off young trunks. Even a brown bear, still tufty with last winter's fur, nosing along the high ridge above the house. While Ophelia sat enspelled on the porch of that dangerous house, Fran curled inward on her couch, waves of heat pouring out of her. Her whole body shook so violently her teeth rattled. Her spyglass fell to the floor. Maybe I am dying, Fran thought, and that is why Ophelia came here.

Fran went in and out of sleep, always listening for the sound of Ophelia coming back down. Perhaps she'd made a mistake, and they wouldn't send something to help. Perhaps they wouldn't send Ophelia back at all. Ophelia, with her pretty singing voice, that shyness, that innate kindness. Her curly hair, silvery blond.

They liked things that were shiny. They were like magpies that way. In other ways, too.

But here was Ophelia, after all, her eyes enormous, her face lit up like Christmas. "Fran," she said. "Fran, wake up. I went there. I was bold! Who lives there, Fran?"

"The summer people," Fran said. "Did they give you anything for me?"

Ophelia set an object upon the counterpane. Like everything the summer people made, it was right pretty. A lipstick-sized vial of pearly glass, an enameled green snake clasped round, its tail the stopper. Fran tugged at the tail, and the serpent uncoiled. A pole ran out the mouth of the bottle, and a silk rag unfurled. Embroidered upon it were the words DRINK ME.

Ophelia watched this, her eyes glazed with too many marvels. "I sat and waited, and there were two little foxes! They came right up to the porch and went to the door and scratched at it until it opened. They trotted right inside! Then they came out again and one came over to me with the bottle in its jaws. It laid down the bottle right at my feet and they went trotting down the steps as easy as you please and into the woods. Fran, it was like a fairy tale."

"Yes," Fran said. She put her lips to the mouth of the vial and drank down what was in it. She coughed, wiped her mouth, and licked the back of her hand.

"I mean, people say something is like a fairy tale all the time," Ophelia said. "And what they mean is somebody falls in love and gets married. Happy ever after. But that house, those foxes, it really is a fairy tale. Who are they? The summer people?"

"That's what my daddy calls them," Fran said. "Except when he gets religious, he calls them devils come up to steal his soul.

It's because they supply him with drink. But he weren't never the one who had to mind after them. That was my mother. And now she's gone, and it's only ever me."

"You take care of them?" Ophelia said. "You mean like the Robertses?"

A feeling of tremendous well-being was washing over Fran. Her feet were warm for the first time in what seemed like days, and her throat felt coated in honey and balm. Even her nose felt less raw and red. "Ophelia?" she said.

"Yes, Fran?"

"I think I'm going to be much better," Fran said. "Which is something you done for me. You were brave and a true friend, and I'll have to think how I can pay you back."

"I wasn't—" Ophelia protested. "I mean, I'm glad I did. I'm glad you asked me. I promise I won't tell anyone."

If you did, you'd be sorry, Fran thought but didn't say. "Ophelia? I need to sleep. And then, if you want, we can talk. You can even stay here while I sleep. If you want. I don't care if you're a lesbian. There are Pop-Tarts on the kitchen counter. And those two biscuits you brung. I like sausage. You can have the one with bacon."

She fell asleep before Ophelia could say anything else.

The first thing she did when she woke up was run a bath. In the mirror, she took a quick inventory. Her hair was lank and greasy, all witchy knots. There were circles under her eyes, and her tongue, when she stuck it out, was yellow. When she was clean and dressed again, her jeans were loose and she could feel all her bones. "I could eat a whole mess of food," she told Ophelia. "But a cat-head and a couple of Pop-Tarts will do for a start."

There was fresh orange juice, and Ophelia had poured it into a stoneware jug. Fran decided not to tell her that her daddy used it as a sometime spittoon.

"Can I ask you some more about them?" Ophelia said. "You know, the summer people?"

"I don't reckon I can answer every question," Fran said. "But go on."

"When I first got there," Ophelia said, "when I went inside, at first I decided that it must be a shut-in. One of those hoarders. I've watched that show, and sometimes they even keep their own poop. And dead cats. It's just horrible.

"Then it just kept on getting stranger. But I wasn't ever scared. It felt like there was somebody there, but they were happy to see me."

"They don't get much in the way of company," Fran said.

"Yeah, well, why do they collect all that stuff? Where does it come from?"

"Some of it's from catalogs. I have to go down to the post office and collect it for them. Sometimes they go away and bring things back. Sometimes they tell me they want something and I get it for them. Mostly it's stuff from the Salvation Army. Once I had to buy a hunnert pounds of copper piping."

"Why?" Ophelia said. "I mean, what do they do with it?"

"They make things," Fran said. "That's what Ma called them, makers. I don't know what they do with it all. They give away things. Like the toys. They like children. When you do things for them, they're beholden to you."

"Have you seen them?" Ophelia said.

"Now and then," Fran said. "Not so often. Not since I was much younger. They're shy."

Ophelia was practically bouncing on her chair. "You get to look after them? That's the best thing ever! Have they always been here?"

Fran hesitated. "I don't know where they come from. They aren't always there. Sometimes they're . . . somewhere else. Ma said she felt sorry for them. She thought maybe they couldn't go home, that they'd been sent off, like the Cherokee, I guess. They live a lot longer, maybe forever, I don't know. I expect time works different where they come from. Sometimes they're gone for years. But they always come back. They're summer people. That's just the way it is with summer people."

"Like how we used to come and go," Ophelia said. "That's how you used to think of me. Like that. Now I live here."

"You can still go away, though," Fran said, not caring how she sounded. "I can't. It's part of the bargain. Whoever takes care of them has to stay here. You can't leave. They don't let you."

"You mean, you can't leave, ever?"

"No," Fran said. "Not ever. Ma was stuck here until she had me. And then when I was old enough, I took over. She went away."

"Where did she go?"

"I'm not the one to answer that," Fran said. "They gave my ma a tent folds up no bigger than a kerchief. It sets up the size of a two-man tent, but on the inside, it's teetotally different, a cottage with two brass beds and a chifferobe to hang your things up in, and a table, and windows with glass in them. When you look out one of the windows, you see wherever you are, and when you look out the other window, you see them two apple trees, the ones in front of the house with the moss path between them?"

Ophelia nodded.

"Well, my ma used to bring out that tent for me and her when my daddy had been drinking. Then Ma passed the summer people on to me, and on a morning after we spent the night in that tent, I woke up and saw her climb out that window. The one that shouldn't ought to be there. She disappeared down that path. Mebbe I should've followed on after her, but I stayed put."

"Where did she go?" Ophelia said.

"Well, she ain't here," Fran said. "That's what I know. So I have to stay here in her place. I don't expect she'll be back, neither."

"She shouldn't have left you behind," Ophelia said. "That was wrong, Fran."

"I wish I could get away for just a little while," Fran said. "Maybe go out to San Francisco and see the Golden Gate Bridge. Stick my toes in the Pacific. I'd like to buy me a guitar and play some of them old ballads on the streets. Just stay a little while, then come back and take up my burden again."

"I'd sure like to go out to California," Ophelia said.

They sat in silence for a minute.

"I wish I could help out," Ophelia said. "You know, with that house and the summer people. You shouldn't have to do everything, not all of the time."

"I already owe you," Fran said, "for helping with the Robertses' house. For looking in on me when I was ill. For what you did when you went up to fetch me help."

"I know what it's like when you're all alone," Ophelia said. "When you can't talk about stuff. And I mean it, Fran. I'll do whatever I can to help."

"I can tell you mean it," Fran said. "But I don't think you

know what it is you're saying. If you want, you can go up there again one more time. You did me a favor, and I don't know how else to pay you back. There's a bedroom up in that house and if you sleep in it, you see your heart's desire. I could take you back tonight and show you that room. And anyhow, I think you lost a thing up there."

"I did?" Ophelia said. "What was it?" She reached down in her pockets. "Oh, hell. My iPod. How did you know?"

Fran shrugged. "Not like anybody up there is going to steal it. Expect they'd be happy to have you back up again. If they didn't like you, you'd know it already."

Fran was straightening up her and her daddy's mess when the summer people let her know they needed a few things. "Can't I have just a minute to myself?" she grumbled.

They told her that she'd had a good four days. "And I surely do appreciate it," she said, "considering I was laid so low." But she put the skillet down in the sink to soak and wrote down what they wanted.

She tidied away all of the toys, not quite sure what had come over her to take them out. Except that when she was sick, she always thought of Ma. There was nothing wrong with that.

When Ophelia came back at five, she had her hair in a pony-tail and a flashlight and a thermos in her pocket, like she thought she was Nancy Drew.

"It gets dark up here so early," Ophelia said. "I feel like it's Halloween or something. Like you're taking me to the haunted house."

"They ain't haints," Fran said. "Nor demons nor any such

thing. They don't do no harm unless you get on the wrong side of 'em. They'll play a prank on you then, and count it good fun."

"Like what?" Ophelia said.

"Once I did the warshing up and broke a teacup," Fran said. "They'll sneak up and pinch you." She still had marks on her arms, though she hadn't broken a plate in years. "Lately, they been doing what all the people up here like to do, that reenacting. They set up their battlefield in the big room downstairs. It's not the War Between the States. It's one of theirs, I guess. They built themselves airships and submersibles and mechanical dragons and knights and all manner of wee toys to fight with. Sometimes, when they get bored, they get me up to be their audience, only they ain't always careful where they go pointing their cannons."

She looked at Ophelia and saw she'd said too much. "Well, they're used to me. They know I don't have no choice but to put up with their ways."

That afternoon, she'd had to drive over to Chattanooga to visit a particular thrift store. They'd sent her for a used DVD player, riding gear, and all the bathing suits she could buy up. Between that and paying for gas, she'd gone through seventy dollars. And the service light had been on the whole way. At least it wasn't a school day. Hard to explain you were cutting out because voices in your head were telling you they needed a saddle.

She'd gone on ahead and brought it all up to the house after. No need to bother Ophelia with any of it. The iPod had been lying right in front of the door.

"Here," she said. "I brought this back down."

"My iPod!" Ophelia said. She turned it over. "They did this?"

The iPod was heavier now. It had a little walnut case instead of pink silicone, and there was a figure inlaid in ebony and gilt.

"A dragonfly," Ophelia said.

"A snake doctor," Fran said. "That's what my daddy calls them."

"They did this for me?"

"They'd embellish a bedazzled jean jacket if you left it there," Fran said. "No lie. They can't stand to leave a thing alone."

"Cool," Ophelia said. "Although my mom is never going to believe me when I say I bought it at the mall."

"Just don't take up anything metal," Fran said. "No earrings, not even your car keys. Or you'll wake up and they'll have smelted them down and turned them into doll armor or who knows what all."

They took off their shoes when they got to where the road crossed the drain. The water was cold with the last of the snow-melt. Ophelia said, "I feel like I ought to have brought a hostess gift."

"You could pick them a bunch of wildflowers," Fran said. "But they'd be just as happy with a bit of kyarn."

"Yarn?" Ophelia said.

"Roadkill," Fran said. "But yarn's okay."

Ophelia thumbed the wheel of her iPod. "There's songs on here that weren't here before."

"They like music, too," Fran said.

"What you were saying about going out to San Francisco to busk," Ophelia said. "I can't imagine doing that."

"Well," Fran said, "I won't ever do it, but I think I can imagine it okay."

When they got up to the house, deer were grazing on the green lawn. The living tree and the dead were touched with the last of the daylight. Chinese lanterns hung in rows from the rafters of the porch.

"You need to come at the house from between the trees," Fran said. "Right on the path. Otherwise, you don't get nowhere near it. And I don't ever use but the back door."

She knocked at the back door. BE BOLD, BE BOLD. "It's me again," she said. "And Ophelia. The one who left the iPod."

She saw Ophelia open her mouth and went on hastily, "Don't. They don't like it when you thank them. It's poison to them. Come on in. *Mi casa es su casa.* I'll give you the grand tour."

They stepped over the threshold, Fran first.

"There's the pump room out back where I do the wash," she said. "There's a big ole stone oven for baking in, and a pig pit, though why I don't know. They don't eat meat. But you prob'ly don't care about that."

"What's in this room?" Ophelia said.

"Hunh," Fran said. "Well, first, it's a lot of junk. They just like to accumulate junk. Way back in there, though, is what I expect is a queen."

"A queen?"

"Well, that's what I call her. You know how in a beehive, way down in the combs, you have the queen and all the worker bees attend on her?

"Far as I can tell, that's what's in there. She's real big and not real pretty, and they are always running in and out of there with food for her. I don't think she's teetotally growed up yet. For a while now I've been thinking on what Ma said, about how maybe these summer people got sent off. Bees do that, too, right? Go off and make a new hive when there are too many queens?"

"I think so," Ophelia said.

"The queen's where my daddy gets his liquor, and she don't bother him none. They have some kind of still set up in there, and every once in a while when he ain't feeling too religious, he goes in and skims off a little bitty bit. It's awful sweet stuff."

"Are they, uh, are they listening to us right now?"

In response came a series of clicks from the War Room.

Ophelia jumped. "What's that?" she said.

"Remember I told you 'bout the reenactor stuff?" Fran said. "Don't get spooked. It's pretty cool."

She gave Ophelia a little push into the War Room.

Of all the rooms in the house, this one was Fran's favorite, even if they dive-bombed her sometimes with the airships, or fired off the cannons without much thought for where she was standing. The walls were beaten tin and copper, scrap metal held down with twopenny nails. Molded forms lay on the floor representing scaled-down mountains, forests, and plains where miniature armies fought desperate battles. There was a kiddy pool over by the big picture window with a machine in it that made waves. There were little ships and submersibles, and occasionally one of the ships sank, and bodies would go floating over to the edges. There was a sea serpent made of tubing and metal rings that swam endlessly in a circle. There was a sluggish river, too, closer to the door, that ran red and stank and stained the banks.

The summer people were always setting up miniature bridges over it, then blowing the bridges up.

Overhead were the fantastic shapes of the dirigibles, and the dragons that were hung on string and swam perpetually through the air above your head. There was a misty globe, too, suspended in some way that Fran could not figure, and lit by some unknown source. It stayed up near the painted ceiling for days at a time and then sunk down behind the plastic sea according to some schedule of the summer people's.

"I went to a house once," Ophelia said. "Some friend of my father's. An anesthesiologist? He had a train set down in his basement and it was crazy complicated. He would die if he saw this."

"Over there is a queen, I think," Fran said. "All surrounded by her knights. And here's another one, much smaller. I wonder who won, in the end."

"Maybe it's not been fought yet," Ophelia said. "Or maybe it's being fought right now."

"Could be," Fran said. "I wish there was a book told you everything that went on. Come on. I'll show you the room you can sleep in."

They went up the stairs. BE BOLD, BE BOLD, BUT NOT TOO BOLD. The moss carpet on the second floor was already looking a little worse for wear. "Last week I spent a whole day scrubbing these boards on my hands and knees. So of course next thing they go and pile up a bunch of dirt and stuff. They won't be the ones have to pitch in and clean it up."

"I could help," Ophelia said. "If you want."

"I wasn't asking for help. But if you offer, I'll accept. The first door is the washroom," Fran said. "Nothing queer about the toilet. I don't know about the bathtub, though. Never felt the need to sit in it."

She opened the second door.

"Here's where you sleep."

It was a gorgeous room, all shades of orange and rust and gold and pink and tangerine. The walls were finished in leafy shapes and vines cut from all kinds of dresses and T-shirts and what have you. Fran's ma had spent the better part of a year going through thrift stores, choosing clothes for their patterns and textures and colors. Gold-leaf snakes and fishes swam through the leaf shapes. When the sun came up in the morning, Fran remembered, it was almost blinding.

There was a crazy quilt on the bed, pink and gold. The bed itself was shaped like a swan. There was a willow chest at the foot of the bed to lay out your clothes on. The mattress was stuffed with the down of crow feathers. Fran had helped her mother shoot the crows and pluck their feathers. She thought they'd killed about a hundred.

"Wow," Ophelia said. "I keep saying that. Wow, wow, wow."

"I always thought it was like being stuck inside a bottle of orange Nehi," Fran said. "But in a good way."

"I like orange Nehi," Ophelia said. "But this is like outer space."

There was a stack of books on the table beside the bed. Like everything else in the room, all the books had been picked out for the colors on their jackets. Fran's ma had told her how once the room had been another set of colors. Greens and blues, maybe? Willow and peacock and midnight colors? And who had brought the bits up for the room that time? Fran's great-grandfather or someone even further along the family tree?

Who had first begun to take care of the summer people? Her mother had doled out stories sparingly, and so Fran had only a piecemeal sort of history.

Hard to figure out what would please Ophelia to hear anyway, and what would trouble her. All of it seemed pleasing and troubling to Fran, in equal measure after so many years.

"The door you slipped my envelope under," she said, finally. "You oughtn't ever go in there."

Ophelia looked interested. "Like Bluebeard," she said.

Fran said, "It's how they come and go. Even they don't open that door very often, I guess." She'd peeped through the keyhole once and seen a bloody river. She bet if you passed through that door, you weren't likely to return.

"Can I ask you another stupid question?" Ophelia said. "Where are they right now?"

"They're here," Fran said. "Or out in the woods chasing nightjars. I told you I don't see them much."

"So how do they tell you what they need you to do?"

"They get in my head," Fran said. "It's hard to explain. They just get in there and poke at me. Like having a really bad itch or something that goes away when I do what they want me to."

"Oh, Fran," Ophelia said. "Maybe I don't like your summer people as much as I thought I did."

Fran said, "It's not always awful. I guess what it is, is complicated."

"I guess I won't complain the next time my mom tells me I have to help her polish the silver. Should we eat our sandwiches now, or should we save them for when we wake up in the middle of the night?" Ophelia asked. "I have this idea that seeing your heart's desire probably makes you hungry."

"I can't stay," Fran said, surprised. She saw Ophelia's expression and said, "Well, hell. I thought you understood. This is just for you."

Ophelia continued to look at her dubiously. "Is it because there's just the one bed? I could sleep on the floor. You know, if you're worried I might be planning to *lez out* on you."

"It isn't that," Fran said. "They only let a body sleep here once. Once and no more."

"You're going to leave me up here alone?" Ophelia said.

"Yes," Fran said. "Unless you decide you want to come back down with me. If you're afraid."

"If I did, could I come back another time?" Ophelia said.

"No."

Ophelia sat down on the golden quilt and smoothed it with her fingers. She chewed her lip, not meeting Fran's eye.

"Okay. I'll do it." She laughed. "How could I not do it? Right?"

"If you're sure," Fran said.

"I'm not sure, but I couldn't stand it if you sent me away now," Ophelia said. "When you slept here, were you afraid?"

"A little," Fran said. "But the bed was comfortable, and I kept the light on. I read for a while and then I fell asleep."

"Did you see your heart's desire?" Ophelia said.

"I saw it," Fran said, and then said no more.

"Okay, then," Ophelia said. "I guess you should go. You should go, right?"

"I'll come back in the morning," Fran said. "I'll be here afore you even wake."

"Thanks," Ophelia said.

But Fran didn't go. She said, "Did you mean it when you said you wanted to help?"

"Look after the house?" Ophelia said. "Yeah, absolutely. You really ought to go out to San Francisco someday. You shouldn't have to stay here your whole life without ever having a vacation or anything. I mean, you're not a slave, right?"

"I don't know what I am," Fran said. "I guess one day I'll have to figure that out."

Ophelia said, "Anyway, we can talk about it tomorrow. Over breakfast. You can tell me about the suckiest parts of the job and I'll tell you what my heart's desire turns out to be."

"Oh," Fran said. "I almost forgot. When you wake up tomorrow, don't be surprised if they've left you a gift. The summer people. It'll be something they think you need or want. But you don't have to accept it. You don't have to worry about being rude that way."

"Okay," Ophelia said. "I will consider whether I really need or want my present. I won't let false glamour deceive me."

"Good," Fran said. Then she bent over Ophelia where she was sitting on the bed and kissed her on the forehead. "Sleep well, 'Phelia. Good dreams."

Fran left the house without any interference from the summer people. She couldn't tell if she'd expected to find any. As she came down the stairs, she said rather more fiercely than she'd meant to: "Be nice to her. Don't play no tricks." She looked in on the queen, who was molting again.

She went out the front door instead of the back, which was

something she'd always wanted to do. Nothing bad happened, and she walked down the hill feeling strangely put out. She went over everything in her head, wondering what still needed doing that she hadn't done. Nothing, she decided. Everything was taken care of.

Except, of course, it wasn't. The first item was the guitar, leaned up against the door of her house. It was a beautiful instrument. The strings, she thought, were silver. When she struck them, the tone was pure and sweet and reminded her—as it was no doubt meant to—of Ophelia's singing voice. The keys were made of gold and shaped like owl heads, and there was mother-of-pearl inlay across the boards like a spray of roses. It was the gaudiest gewgaw they'd yet made her a gift of.

"Well, all right," she said. "I guess you don't mind what I told her." She laughed out loud with relief.

"Why everwho did you tell what?" someone said.

She picked up the guitar and held it like a weapon in front of her. "Daddy?"

"Put that down," the voice said. A man stepped forward out of the shadow of the rosebushes. "I'm not your damn daddy. Although, come to think of it, I would like to know where he is."

"Ryan Shoemaker," Fran said. She put the guitar down on the ground. A second man stepped forward. "And Kyle Rainey."

"Howdy, Fran," said Kyle. He spat. "We were lookin' for your pappy, like Ryan says."

"If he calls I'll let him know you were up here looking for him," Fran said.

Ryan lit up a cigarette, looked at her over the flame. "It was your daddy we wanted to ask, but I guess you could help us out instead."

"It don't seem likely somehow," Fran said. "But go on."

"Your daddy was meaning to drop off some of the sweet stuff the other night," Kyle said. "Only, he started thinking about it on the drive down, and that's never been a good idea where your daddy is concerned. He decided Jesus wanted him to pour out every last drop, and that's what he did all the way down the mountain. If he weren't a lucky man, some spark might've cotched while he were pouring, but I guess Jesus don't want to meet him face-to-face just yet."

"And if that weren't bad enough," Ryan said, "when he got to the convenience, Jesus wanted him to get into the van and smash up all Andy's liquor, too. Time we realized what was going on, there weren't much left besides two bottles of Kahlua and a six-pack of wine coolers."

"One of them smashed, too," Kyle said. "And then he took off afore we could have a word with him."

"Well, I'm sorry for your troubles, but I don't see what it has to do with me," Fran said.

"What it has to do is we conferred some about it. Seems to us your pappy could provide us with entrée to some of the finest homes in the area. I hear summer people like their tipples."

"So then," Fran said, "if I have this right, you're hoping my daddy will make his restitution by becoming your accessory in breaking and entering."

"Or he could pay poor Andy back in kind," Ryan said. "With some of that good stuff."

"He'll have to run that by Jesus," Fran said. "I 'spect it's a better bet than the other, but you might have to wait till he and Jesus have had enough of each other."

"The thing is," Ryan said, "I'm not a patient man. And it may be so that your pappy is out of our reach at present moment, but here you are. And I'm guessing you can get us into a house or two."

"Or you could point us in the direction of your daddy's private stash," Kyle said.

"And if I don't choose to do neither?" Fran asked, crossing her arms.

"Here's the kicker, so to speak, Fran," Kyle said. "Ryan has not been in a good mood these last few days. He bit a sheriff's deputy on the arm last night in a bar. Which is why we weren't up here sooner."

Fran stepped back. "Wait up. Okay? I'll tell you a thing if you promise not to tell my daddy. Okay? There's an old house farther up the road that nobody except me and my daddy knows about. Nobody lives there, and so my daddy put his still up in it. He's got all sorts of articles stashed up there. I'll take you up. But you can't tell him what I done."

"Course not, darlin'," Kyle said. "We don't aim to cause a rift in the family. Just to get what we have coming."

And so Fran found herself climbing right back up that same road. She got her feet wet crossing the drain but kept as far ahead of Kyle and Ryan as she dared.

When they got up to the house, Kyle whistled. "Fancy sort of ruin."

"Wait'll you see what's inside," Fran said. She led them around to the back, then held the door open. "Sorry about the lights. The power goes off more than it stays on. My daddy usually brings up a flashlight. Want me to fetch one?"

"We got matches," Ryan said. "You stay right there."

"The still is in the room over on the right. Mind how you

go. He's got it set up in a kind of maze, with the newspapers and all."

"Dark as hell at the damned stroke of midnight," Kyle said. He felt his way down the hall. "I think I'm at the door. Sure enough, smells like what I'm lookin' for. Guess I'll just follow my nose. No booby traps or nothing like that?"

"No, sir," Fran said. "He'd've blowed himself up a long time before now if he tried that."

"I might as well take in the sights," Ryan said, the lit end of his cigarette flaring.

"Yes, sir," Fran said.

"And might there be a pisser in this heap?"

"Third door on the left, once you go up," Fran said. "The door sticks some."

She waited until he was at the top of the stairs before she slipped out the back door again. She could hear Kyle fumbling toward the center of the Queen's Room. She wondered what the queen would make of Kyle. She wasn't worried about Ophelia at all. Ophelia was an invited guest. And anyhow, the summer people didn't let anything happen to the ones who looked after them.

One of the summer people was sprawled on the porch swing when she came out. He was whittling a stick with a sharp knife.

"Evening," Fran said and bobbed her head.

The summer personage didn't even look up at her. He was one of the ones so pretty it almost hurt to peep at him, but you couldn't not stare, neither. That was one of the ways they cotched you, Fran figured. Like wild animals when someone shone a light at them. She finally tore her gaze away and ran down the stairs like the devil was after her. When she stopped to look back, he was still setting there, smiling and whittling that poor stick down.

She sold the guitar when she got to New York City. What was left of her daddy's two hundred dollars had bought her a Greyhound ticket and a couple of burgers at the bus station. The guitar got her six hundred more, and she used that to buy a ticket to Paris, where she met a Lebanese boy who was squatting in an old factory. One day she came back from her under-the-table job at a hotel and found him looking through her backpack. He had the monkey egg in his hand. He wound it up and put it down on the dirty floor to dance. They both watched until it ran down. *"Très joli,"* he said.

It was a few days after Christmas, and there was snow melting in her hair. They didn't have heat in the squat, or even running water. She'd had a bad cough for a few days. She sat down next to her boy, and when he started to wind up the monkey egg again, she put her hand out to make him stop.

She didn't remember packing it. And of course, maybe she hadn't. For all she knew, they had winter places as well as summer places. She would bet they got around.

A few days later, the Lebanese boy ran off, no doubt looking for someplace warmer. The monkey egg went with him. After that, all she had to remind herself of home was the tent that she kept folded up like a dirty handkerchief in her wallet.

It's been two years, and every now and again while Fran is cleaning rooms in the pension, she closes the door and sets up the kerchief tent and gets inside. She looks out the window at the two apple trees, the dead one and the living. She tells herself that one day soon she will go home again.

I Can See Right Through You

When the sex tape happened and things went south with Fawn, the demon lover did what he always did. He went to cry on Meggie's shoulder. Girls like Fawn came and went, but Meggie would always be there. Him and Meggie. It was the talisman you kept in your pocket. The one you couldn't lose.

Two monsters can kiss in a movie. One old friend can go to see another old friend and be sure of his welcome: so here is the demon lover in a rental car. An hour into the drive, he opens the window of the rental car, tosses out his cell phone. There is no one he wants to talk to except for Meggie.

(1991) This is after the movie and after they are together and after they begin to understand the bargain that they have made. They are both, suddenly, very famous.

Film can be put together in any order. Scenes shot in any order of sequence. Take as many takes as you like. Continuity is independent of linear time. Sometimes you aren't even in the scene together. Meggie says her lines to your stand-in. They'll splice you together later on. Shuffle off to Buffalo, gals. Come out tonight.

(This is long before any of that. This was a very long time ago.)

Meggie tells the demon lover a story:

Two girls and, look, they've found a Ouija board. They make a list of questions. One girl is pretty. One girl is not really a part of this story. She's lost her favorite sweater. Her fingertips on the planchette. Two girls, each touching, lightly, the planchette. Is anyone here? Where did I put my blue sweater? Will anyone ever love me? Things like that.

They ask their questions. The planchette drifts. Gives up nonsense. They start the list over again. Is anyone here? Will I be famous? Where is my blue sweater?

The planchette jerks under their fingers.

M-E

Meggie says, "Did you do that?"

The other girl says she didn't. The planchette moves again, a fidget. A stutter, a nudge, a sequence of swoops and stops.

M-E-G-G-I-E

"It's talking to you," the other girl says.

M-E-G-G-I-E H-E-L-L-O

Meggie says, "Hello?"

The planchette moves again and again. There is something animal about it.

H-E-L-L-O I A-M-W-I-T-H-Y-O-U I A-M-W-I-T-H-Y-O-U A-L-W-A-Y-S

They write it all down.

M-E-G-G-I-E O I W-I-L-L L-O-V-E-Y-O-U A-L-W-A-Y-S

"Who is this?" she says. "Who are you? Do I know you?"

I S-E-E Y-O-U I K-N-O-W Y-O-U W-A-I-T A-N-D I W-I-L-L C-O-M-E

A pause. Then:

I W-I-L-L M-E-G-G-I-E O I W-I-L-L B-E-W-I-T-H-Y-O-U A-L-W-A-Y-S

"Are you doing this?" Meggie says to the other girl. She shakes her head.

M-E-G-G-I-E W-A-I-T

The other girl says, "Can whoever this is at least tell me where I left my sweater?"

Meggie says, "Okay, whoever you are. I'll wait, I guess I can wait for a while. I'm not good at waiting. But I'll wait."

O W-A-I-T A-N-D I W-I-L-L C-O-M-E

They wait. Will there be a knock at the bedroom door? But no one comes. No one is coming.

I A-M W-I-T-H Y-O-U A-L-W-A-Y-S

No one is here with them. The sweater will never be found. The other girl grows up, lives a long and happy life. Meggie goes out to L.A. and meets the demon lover.

W-A-I-T

After that, the only thing the planchette says, over and over, is Meggie's name. It's all very romantic.

(1974) Twenty-two people disappear from a nudist colony in Lake Apopka. People disappear all the time. Let's be honest: the only thing interesting here is that these people were naked. And that no one ever saw them again. Funny, right?

(1990) It's one of the ten most iconic movie kisses of all time. In the top five, surely. You and Meggie, the demon lover and his monster girl; vampires sharing a kiss as the sun comes up. Both of you wearing so much makeup it still astonishes you that anyone would ever recognize you on the street.

It's hard for the demon lover to grow old.

Florida is California on a Troma budget. That's what the demon lover thinks, anyway. Special effects blew the budget on bugs and bad weather.

He parks in a meadowy space, recently mowed, alongside other rental cars, the usual catering and equipment vans. There are two gateposts with a chain between them. No fence. Eternal I endure.

There is an evil smell. Does it belong to the place or to him? The demon lover sniffs under his arm.

It's an end-of-the-world sky, a snakes-and-ladders landscape: low emerald trees pulled lower by vines; chalk and apricot ant-hills (the demon lover imagines the bones of a nudist under every one); shallow water-filled declivities scummed with algae, lime and gold and black.

The blot of the lake. That's another theory: the lake.

A storm is coming.

He doesn't get out of his car. He rolls the window down and watches the storm come in. Let's look at him looking at it. A pretty thing admiring a pretty thing. Abandoned site of a mass disappearance, muddy violet clouds, silver veils of rain driving down the lake, the tabloid prince of darkness, Meggie's demon lover arriving in all his splendor. The only thing to spoil it are the bugs. And the sex tape.

(2012) You have been famous for more than half of your life. Both of you. You only made the one movie together, but women still stop you on the street to ask about Meggie. Is she happy? Which one? you want to ask them. The one who kissed me in a movie when we were just kids, the one who wasn't real? The one who likes to smoke a bit of weed and text me about her neighbor's pet goat? The Meggie in the tabloids who drinks fucks gets fat pregnant too skinny slaps a maître d' talks to Elvis's ghost ghost of a missing three-year-old boy ghost of JFK? Sometimes they don't ask about Meggie. Instead they ask if you will bite them.

Happiness! Misery! If you were one, bet on it the other was on the way. That was what everyone liked to see. It was what the whole thing was about. The demon lover has a pair of gold cuff links, those faces. Meggie gave them to him. You know the ones I mean.

(2010) Meggie and the demon lover throw a Halloween party for everyone they know. They do this every Halloween. They're famous for it.

"Year after year, on a monkey's face a monkey's face," Meggie says.

She's King Kong. The year before? Half a pantomime horse. He's the demon lover. Who else? Year after year.

Meggie says, "I've decided to give up acting. I'm going to be a poet. Nobody cares when poets get old."

Fawn says, appraisingly, "I hope I look half as good as you when I'm your age." Fawn, twenty-three. A makeup artist. This year she and the demon lover are married. Last year they met on set.

He says, "I'm thinking I could get some work done on my jawline."

You'd think they were mother and daughter. Same Viking profile, same quizzical tilt to the head as they turn to look at him. Both taller than him. Both smarter, too, no doubt about it.

Maybe Meggie wonders sometimes about the women he sleeps with. Marries. Maybe he has a type. But so does she. There's a guy at the Halloween party. A boy, really.

Meggie always has a boy and the demon lover can always pick him out. Easy enough, even if Meggie's sly. She never introduces the lover of the moment, never brings them into conversations or even acknowledges their presence. They hang out on the edge of whatever is happening, and drink or smoke or watch Meggie at the center. Sometimes they drift closer, stand near enough to Meggie that it's plain what's going on. When she leaves, they follow after.

Meggie's type? The funny thing is, Meggie's lovers all look like the demon lover. More like the demon lover, he admits it, than he does. He and Meggie are both older now, but the world is full of beautiful black-haired boys and golden girls. Really, that's the problem.

The role of the demon lover comes with certain obligations. Your hairline will not recede. Your waistline will not expand. You are not to be photographed threatening paparazzi, or in sweatpants. No sex tapes.

Your fans will: Offer their necks at premieres. (Also at restaurants and at the bank. More than once when he is standing in front of a urinal.) Ask if you will bite their wives. Their daughters. They will cut themselves with a razor in front of you.

The appropriate reaction is—

There is no appropriate reaction.

The demon lover does not always live up to his obligations. There is a sex tape. There is a girl with a piercing. There is, in the middle of some athletic sex, a comical incident involving his foreskin. There is blood all over the sheets. There is a lot of blood. There is a 911 call. There is him, fainting. Falling and hitting his head on a bedside table. There is Perez Hilton, Gawker, talk radio, YouTube, Tumblr. There are GIFs.

You will always be most famous for playing the lead in a series of vampire movies. The character you play is, of course, ageless. But you get older. The first time you bite a girl's neck, Meggie's neck, you're a twenty-five-year-old actor playing a vampire who hasn't gotten a day older in three hundred years. Now you're a forty-nine-year-old actor playing the same ageless vampire. It's getting to be a little ridiculous, isn't it? But if the demon lover isn't the demon lover then who is he? Who are you? Other projects disappoint. Your agent says take a comic role. The trouble is you're not very funny. You're not good at funny.

The other trouble is the sex tape. Sex tapes are inherently funny. Nudity is, regrettably, funny. Torn foreskins are painfully funny. You didn't know she was filming it.

Your agent says, That wasn't what I meant.

You could do what Meggie did, all those years ago. Disappear. Travel the world. Hunt down the meaning of life. Go find Meggie.

When the sex tape happens you say to Fawn, But what does this have to do with Meggie? This has nothing to do with Meggie. It was just some girl.

It's not like there haven't been other girls.

Fawn says, It has everything to do with Meggie.

I can see right through you, Fawn says, less in sorrow than in anger. She probably can.

God grant me Meggie, but not just yet. That's him by way of St. Augustine by way of Fawn the makeup artist and Bible group junkie. She explains it to the demon lover, explains him to himself. And hasn't it been in the back of your mind all this time? It was Meggie right at the start. Why shouldn't it be Meggie again? And in the meantime, you could get married once in a while and never worry about whether or not it worked out. He and Meggie have managed, all this time, to stay friends. His marriages, his other relationships, perhaps these have only been a series of delaying actions. Small rebellions. And here's the thing about his marriages: he's never managed to stay friends with his ex-wives, his exes. He and Fawn won't be friends.

The demon lover and Meggie have known each other for such a long time. No one knows him like Meggie.

The remains of the nudist colony at Lake Apopka promise reasonable value for ghost hunters. A dozen ruined cabins, some roofless, windows black with mildew; a crumbled stucco hall, Spanish tiles receding; the cracked lip of a slop-filled pool. Between the cabins and the lake, the homely and welcome sight of half a dozen trailers; even better, he spots a craft tent.

Muck farms! Mutant alligators! Disappearing nudists! The demon lover, killing time in the LAX airport, read up on Lake Apopka. The past is a weird place, Florida is a weird place, no news there. A demon lover should fit right in, but the ground sucks and clots at his shoes in a way that suggests he isn't welcome. The rain is directly overhead now, shouting down in spit-warm gouts. He begins to run, stumbling, in the direction of the craft tent.

Meggie's career is on the upswing. Everyone agrees. She has a ghost-hunting show, *Who's There?*

The demon lover calls Meggie after the *Titanic* episode airs, the one where *Who's There?*'s ghost-hunting crew hitches a ride with the International Ice Patrol. There's the yearly ceremony, memorial wreaths. Meggie's crew sets up a Marconi transmitter and receiver just in case a ghost or two has a thing to say.

The demon lover asks her about the dead seagulls. Forget the

Marconi nonsense. The seagulls were what made the episode. Hundreds of them, little corpses fixed, as if pinned, to the water.

Meggie says, You think we have the budget for fake seagulls? Please.

Admit that *Who's There?* is entertaining whether or not you believe in ghosts. It's all about the nasty detail, the house that gives you a bad feeling even when you turn on all the lights, the awful thing that happened to someone who wasn't you a very long time ago. The camera work is moody, extraordinary. The team of ghost hunters is personable, funny, reasonably attractive. Meggie sells you on the possibility: Maybe what's going on here is real. Maybe someone is out there. Maybe they have something to say.

The demon lover and Meggie don't talk for months and then suddenly something changes and they talk every day. He likes to wake up in the morning and call her. They talk about scripts, now that Meggie's getting scripts again. He can talk to Meggie about anything. It's been that way all along. They haven't talked since the sex tape. Better to have this conversation in person.

(1991) He and Meggie are lovers. Their movie is big at the box office. Everywhere they go they are famous and they go everywhere. Their faces are everywhere. They are kissing on a thousand screens. They are in a hotel room, kissing. They can't leave their hotel room without someone screaming or fainting or pointing something at them. They are asked the same questions again. Over and over. He begins to do the interviews in character. Anyway, it makes Meggie laugh.

There's a night, on some continent, in some city, some hotel room, some warm night, the demon lover and Meggie leave a window open and two women creep in. They come over the balcony. They just want to tell you that they love you. Both of you. They just want to be near you.

Everyone watches you. Even when they're pretending not to. Even when they aren't watching you, you think they are. And you know what? You're right. Eyes will find you. Becoming famous, this kind of fame: it's luck indistinguishable from catastrophe. You'd be dumb not to recognize it. What you've become.

When people disappear, there's always the chance that you'll see them again. The rain comes down so hard the demon lover can barely see. He thinks he is still moving in the direction of the craft tent and not the lake. There is a noise, he picks it out of the noise of the rain. A howling. And then the rain thins and he can see something, men and women, naked. Running toward him. He slips, catches himself, and the rain comes down hard again, erases everything except the sound of what is chasing him. He collides headlong with a thing: a skin horribly clammy, cold, somehow both stiff and yielding. Bounces off and realizes that this is the tent. Not where you'd choose to make a last stand, but by the time he has fumbled his way inside the flap he has grasped the situation. Not dead nudists, but living people, naked, cursing, laughing, dripping. They carry cameras, mikes, gear for ghost hunting. Videographers, A2s, all the other useful types and the not so useful. A crowd of men and women, and here is Meggie. Her hair is glued in strings to her face. Her breasts are wet with rain.

He says her name.

They all look at him.

How is it possible that he is the one who feels naked?

"The fuck is this guy doing here?" says someone with a little white towel positioned over his genitals. Really, it could be even littler.

"Will," Meggie says. So gently he almost starts to cry. Well, it's been a long day.

She takes him to her trailer. He has a shower, borrows her toothbrush. She puts on a robe. Doesn't ask him any questions. Talks to him while he's in the bathroom. He leaves the door open.

It's the third day on location, and the first two have been a mixed bag. They got their establishing shots, went out on the lake and saw an alligator dive down when they got too close. There are baby skunks all over the scrubby, shabby woods, the trails. They come right up to you, up to the camera and try like hell to spray. But until they hit adolescence, all they can do is quiver their tails and stamp their feet.

Except, she says, and mentions some poor A2. His skunk was an early bloomer.

Meggie interviewed the former proprietor of the nudist colony. He insisted on calling it a naturist community, spent the interview explaining the philosophy behind naturism, didn't want to talk about 1974. A harmless old crank. Whatever happened, he had nothing to do with it. You couldn't lecture people into thin air. Besides, he had an alibi.

What they didn't get on the first day or even on the second day was any kind of worthwhile read on their equipment. They have the two psychics—but one of them had an emergency, went back to deal with a daughter in rehab; they have all kinds of psychometric equipment, but there is absolutely nothing going on, down, or off. Which led to some discussion.

"We decided maybe we were the problem," Meggie says. "Maybe the nudists didn't have anything to say to us while we had our clothes on. So we're shooting in the nude. Everyone nude. Cast, crew, everyone. It's been a really positive experience, Will. It's a good group of people."

"Fun," the demon lover says. Someone has dropped off a pair of pink cargo shorts and a T-shirt, because his clothes are in his suitcase back at the airport in Orlando. It's not exactly that he forgot. More like he couldn't be bothered.

"It's good to see you, Will," Meggie says. "But why are you here, exactly? How did you know we were here?"

He takes the easy question first. "Pike." Pike is Meggie's agent and an old friend of the demon lover. The kind of agent who likes to pull the legs off of small children. The kind of friend who finds life all the sweeter when you're in the middle of screwing up your own. "I made him promise not to tell you I was coming."

He collapses on the floor in front of Meggie's chair. She runs her fingers through his hair. Pets him like you'd pet a dog.

"He told you, though. Didn't he?"

"He did," Meggie said. "He called."

The demon lover says, "Meggie, this isn't about the sex tape."

Meggie says, "I know. Fawn called, too."

He tries not to imagine that phone call. His head is sore. He's dehydrated, probably. That long flight.

"She wanted me to let her know if you showed. Said she was waiting to see before she threw in the towel."

She waits for him to say something. Waits a little bit longer. Strokes his hair the whole time.

"I won't call her," she says. "You ought to go back, Will. She's a good person."

"I don't love her," the demon lover says.

"Well," Meggie says. She takes that hand away.

There's a knock on the door, some girl. "Sun's out again, Meggie." She gives the demon lover a particularly melting smile. Was probably twelve when she first saw him on-screen. Baby ducks, these girls. Imprint on the first vampire they ever see. Then she's down the stairs again, bare bottom bouncing.

Meggie drops the robe, begins to apply sunblock to her arms and face. He notes the ways in which her body has changed. Thinks he might love her all the more for it, and hopes that this is true.

"Let me," he says, and takes the bottle from her. Begins to rub lotion into her back.

She doesn't flinch away. Why would she? They are friends.

She says, "Here's the thing about Florida, Will. You get these storms, practically every day. But then they go away again."

Her hands catch at his, slippery with the lotion. She says, "You must be tired. Take a nap. There's herbal tea in the cupboards, pot and Ambien in the bedroom. We're shooting all afternoon, straight through to evening. And then a barbecue—we're filming that, too. You're welcome to come out. It would be great publicity for us, of course. Our viewers would love it. But you'd have to do it naked like the rest of us. No clothes. No exceptions, Will. Not even for you."

He rubs the rest of the sunblock into her shoulders. Would like nothing more than to rest his head on her shoulder.

"I love you, Meggie," he says. "You know that, right?"

"I know. I love you, too, Will," she says. The way she says it tells him everything.

The demon lover goes to lie down on Meggie's bed, feeling a hundred years old. Dozes. Dreams about a bungalow in Venice Beach and Meggie and a girl. That was a long time ago.

There was a review of a play Meggie was in. Maybe ten years ago? It wasn't a kind review, or even particularly intelligent, and yet the critic said something that still seems right to the demon lover. He said no matter what was happening in the play, Meggie's performance suggested she was waiting for a bus. The demon lover thinks the critic got at something true there. Only, the demon lover has always thought that if Meggie was waiting for a bus, you had to wonder where that bus was going. If she was planning to throw herself under it.

When they first got together, the demon lover was pretty sure he was what Meggie had been waiting for. Maybe she thought so, too. They bought a house, a bungalow in Venice Beach. He wonders who lives there now.

When the demon lover wakes up, he takes off the T-shirt and cargo shorts. Leaves them folded neatly on the bed. He'll have to find somewhere to sleep tonight. And soon. Day is becoming night.

Meat is cooking on a barbecue. The demon lover isn't sure when he last ate. There's bug spray beside the door. Ticklish on his balls. He feels just a little bit ridiculous. Surely this is a terrible idea. The latest in a long series of terrible ideas. Only this time he knows there's a camera.

The moment he steps outside Meggie's trailer, a P.A. appears as if by magic. It's what they do. Has him sign a pile of releases. Odd to stand here in the nude signing releases, but what the fuck. He thinks, I'll go home tomorrow.

The P.A. is in her fifties. Unusual. There's probably a story there, but who cares? He doesn't. Of course she's seen the fucking sex tape—it's probably going to be the most popular movie he ever makes—but her expression suggests this is the very first time she's ever seen the demon lover naked or rather that neither of them is naked at all.

While the demon lover signs—doesn't bother to read anything, what does it matter now, anyway?—the P.A. talks about someone who hasn't done something. Who isn't where she ought to be. Some other gofer named Juliet. Where is she and what has she gone for? The P.A. is full of complaints.

The demon lover suggests the gofer may have been carried off by ghosts. The P.A. gives him an unfriendly look and continues to talk about people the demon lover doesn't know, has no interest in.

"What's spooky about you?" the demon lover asks. Because of course that's the gimmick, producer down to best boy. Every woman and man uncanny.

"I had a near-death experience," the P.A. says. She wiggles her arm. Shows off a long ropy burn. "Accidentally electrocuted myself. Got the whole tunnel and light thing. And I guess I scored okay with those cards when they auditioned me. The Zener cards?"

"So tell me," the demon lover says. "What's so fucking great about a tunnel and a light? That really the best they can do?"

"Yeah, well," the P.A. says, a bite in her voice. "People like you probably get the red carpet and the limo."

The demon lover has nothing to say to that.

"You seen anything here?" he tries instead. "Heard anything?"

"Meggie tell you about the skunks?" the P.A. says. Having snapped, now she will soothe. "Those babies. Tail up, the works, but nothing doing. Which about sums up this place. No ghosts. No read on the equipment. No hanky-panky, fiddle-faddle, or woo woo. Not even a cold spot."

She says doubtfully, "But it'll come together. You at this séance barbecue shindig will help. Naked vampire trumps nudist ghosts any day. Okay on your own? You go on down to the lake, I'll call, let them know you're on your way."

Or he could just head for the car.

"Thanks," the demon lover says.

But before he knows what he wants to do, here's another someone. It's a regular Pilgrim's Progress. One of Fawn's favorite books. This is a kid in his twenties. Good-looking in a familiar way. (Although is it okay to think this about another guy when you're both naked? Not to mention: who looks a lot like you did once upon a time. Why not? We're all naked here.)

"I know you," the kid says.

The demon lover says, "Of course you do. You are?"

"Ray," says the kid. He's *maybe* twenty-five. His look says: You know who I am. "Meggie's told me all about you."

As if he doesn't already know, the demon lover says, "So what do you do?"

The kid smiles an unlovely smile. Scratches at his groin luxuriously, maybe not on purpose. "Whatever needs to be done. That's what I do."

So he deals. There's that pot in Meggie's dresser.

Down at the lake people are playing volleyball in a pit with no net. Barbecuing. Someone talks to a camera, gestures at someone else. Someone somewhere smoking a joint. At this distance, not too close, not too near, twilight coming down, the demon lover takes in all of the breasts, asses, comical cocks, knobby knees, everything hidden now made plain. He notes with an experienced eye which breasts are real, which aren't. Only a few of the women sport pubic hair. He's never understood what that's about. Some of the men are bare, too. *O tempora, o mores.*

"You like jokes?" Ray says, stopping to light a cigarette.

The demon lover could leave; he lingers. "Depends on the joke." Really, he doesn't. Especially the kind of jokes the ones who ask if you like jokes tell.

Ray says, "You'll like this one. So there are these four guys. A kleptomaniac, a pyromaniac, um, a zoophile, and a masochist. This cat walks by and the klepto says he'd like to steal it. The pyro says he wants to set it on fire. The zoophile wants to fuck it. So the masochist, he looks at everybody, and he says, 'Meow?'"

It's a moderately funny joke. It might be a come-on.

The demon lover flicks a look from under his lashes. Suppresses the not-quite-queasy feeling he's somehow traveled back in time to flirt with himself. Or the other way round.

He'd like to think he was even prettier than this kid. People used to stop and stare when he walked into a room. That was

long before anyone knew who he was. He's always been someone you look at longer than you should. He says, smiling, "I'll
bite. Which one are you?"

"Pardon?" Ray says. Blows smoke.

"Which one are you? The klepto, the pyro, the cat-fucker, the
masochist?"

"I'm the guy who tells the joke," Ray says. He drops his cigarette, grinds it under a heel black with dirt. Lights another.
"Don't know if anyone's told you, but don't drink out of any of
the taps. Or go swimming. The water's toxic. Phosphorous, other
stuff. They shut down the muck farms, they're building up the
marshlands again, but it's still not what I'd call potable. You staying out here or in town?"

The demon lover says, "Don't know if I'm staying at all."

"Well," Ray says. "They've rigged up some of the less wrecked
bungalows on a generator. There are camp beds, sleeping bags.
Depends on whether you like it rough." That last with, yes, a leer.

The demon lover feels his own lip lifting. They are both wearing masks. They look out of them at each other. This was what
you knew when you were an actor. The face, the whole body,
the way you moved in it, just a guise. You put it on, you put it off
again. What was underneath belonged to you, just you, as long as
you kept it hidden.

He says, "You think you know something about me?"

"I've seen all your movies," Ray says. The mask shifts, becomes the one the demon lover calls "I'm your biggest fan." Oh,
he knows what's under that one.

He prepares himself for whatever this strange kid is going to
say next and then suddenly Meggie is there. As if things weren't

awkward enough without Meggie, naked, suddenly standing there. Everybody naked, nobody happy. It's Scandinavian art porn.

Meggie ignores the kid entirely. Just like always. These guys are interchangeable, really. There's probably some website where she finds them. She may not want him, but she doesn't want anyone else, either.

Meggie says, touching his arm, "You look a lot better."

"I got a few hours," he says.

"I know," she says. "I checked in on you. Wanted to make sure you hadn't run off."

"Nowhere to go," he says.

"Come on," Meggie says. "Let's get you something to eat."

Ray doesn't follow; lingers with his cigarette. Probably staring at their yoga-toned, well-enough-preserved celebrity butts.

Here's the problem with this kid, the demon lover thinks. He sat in a theater when he was fifteen and watched me and Meggie done up in vampire makeup pretend-fucking on a New York subway car. The A train. Me biting Meggie's breast, some suburban movie screen, her breast ten times bigger than his head. He probably masturbated a hundred times watching me bite you, Meggie. He watched us kiss. Felt something ache when we did. And that leaves out all the rest of this, whatever it is that you're doing here with him and me. Imagine what this kid must feel now. The demon lover feels it, too. Love, he thinks. Because love isn't just love. It's all the other stuff, too.

He meets Irene, the fat, pretty medium who plays the straight man to Meggie. People named Sidra, Tom, Euan, who seem to be in charge of the weird ghost gear. A videographer, Pilar. He's almost positive he's met her before. Maybe during his AA period? Really, why is that period more of a blur than the years he's spent drunk or high? She's in her thirties, has a sly smile, terrific legs, and a very big camera.

They demonstrate some of the equipment for the demon lover, let him try out something called a Trifield Meter. No ghosts here. Even ghosts have better places to be.

He assumes everyone he meets has seen his sex tape. Almost wishes someone would mention it. No one does.

There's a rank breeze off the lake. Muck and death.

People eat and discuss the missing P.A.—the gofer—some Juliet person. Meggie says, "She's a nice kid. Makes Whore-igami in her spare time and sells it on eBay."

"She makes what?" the demon lover says.

"Whore-igami. Origami porn tableaux. Custom order stuff."

"Of course," the demon lover says. "Big money in that."

She may have some kind of habit. Meggie mentions this. She may be in the habit of disappearing now and then.

Or she may be wherever all those nudists went. Imagine the ratings then. He doesn't say this to Meggie.

Meggie says, "I'm happy to see you, Will. Even under the circumstances."

"Are you?" says the demon lover, smiling, because he's always smiling. They're far enough away from the mikes and the cameras that he feels okay about saying this. Pilar, the videographer, is recording Irene, the medium, who is toasting marshmallows. Ray is watching, too. Is always somewhere nearby.

Something bites the demon lover's thigh and he slaps at it.

He could reach out and touch Meggie's face right now. It

would be a different story on the camera than the one he and Meggie are telling each other. Or she would turn away and it would all be the same story again. He thinks he should have remembered this, all the ways they didn't work when they were together. Like the joke about the two skunks. When Out is in, In is out. Like the wrong ends of two magnets.

"Of course I'm happy," Meggie says. "And your timing is eerily good because I have to talk to you about something."

"Shoot," he says.

"It's complicated," she says. "How about later? After we're done here?"

It's almost full dark now. No moon. Someone has built up a very large fire. The blackened bungalows and the roofless hall melt into obscure and tidy shapes. Now you can imagine yourself back when it was all new, a long time ago. Back in the seventies when nobody cared what you did. When love was free. When you could just disappear if you felt like it and that was fine and good, too.

"So where do I stay tonight?" the demon lover says. Again fights the impulse to touch Meggie's face. There's a strand of hair against her lip. Which is he? The pyromaniac or the masochist? In or Out? Well, he's an actor, isn't he? He can be anything she wants him to be.

"I'm sure you'll find somewhere," Meggie says, a glint in her eye. "Or someone. Pilar has told me more than once you're the only man she's ever wanted to fuck."

"If I had a dollar," the demon lover says. He still wants to touch her. Wants her to want him to touch her. He remembers now how this goes.

Meggie says, "If you had a dollar, seventy cents would go to your exes."

Which is gospel truth. He says, "Fawn signed a prenup."

"One of the thousand reasons you should go home and fix things," Meggie says. "She's a good person. There aren't so many of those."

"She's better off without me," the demon lover says, trying it out. He's a little hurt when Meggie doesn't disagree.

Irene the medium comes over with Pilar and the other videographer. The demon lover can tell Irene doesn't like him. Sometimes women don't like him. Rare enough that he always wonders why.

"Shall we get started?" Irene says. "Let's see if any of our friends are up for a quick chat. Then I don't know about you but I'm going to go put on something a little less comfortable."

Meggie addresses the video camera next. "This will be our final attempt," she says, "our last chance to contact anyone who is still lingering here, who has unfinished business."

"You'd think nudists wouldn't be so shy," Irene says.

Meggie says, "But even if we don't reach anyone, today hasn't been a total loss. All of us have taken a risk. Some of us are sunburned, some of us have bug bites in interesting places, all of us are a little more comfortable in our own skin. We've experienced openness and humanity in a way that these colonists imagined and hoped would lead to a better world. And maybe, for them, it did. We've had a good day. And even if the particular souls we came here in search of didn't show up, someone else is here."

The A2 nods at Will.

Pilar points the camera at him.

He's been thinking about how to play this. "I'm Will Gald," he says. "You probably recognize me from previous naked film roles such as the guy rolling around on a hotel room floor clutching his genitals and bleeding profusely."

He smiles his most lovely smile. "I just happened to be in the area."

"We persuaded him to stay for a bite," Meggie says.

"They've hidden my clothes," Will says. "Admittedly I haven't been trying that hard to find them. I mean, what's the worst thing that can happen when you get naked on camera?"

Irene says, "Meggie, one of the things that's been most important about *Who's There?* right from the beginning is that we've all had something happen to us that we can't explain away. We're all believers. I've been meaning to ask, does Will here have a ghost story?"

"I don't—" the demon lover says. Then pauses. Looks at Meggie.

"I do," he says. "But surely Meggie's already told it."

"I have," Meggie says. "But I've never heard you tell it."

Oh, there are stories the demon lover could tell.

He says, "I'm here to please."

"Fantastic," Irene says. "As you know, every episode we make time for a ghost story or two. Tonight we even have a campfire." She hesitates. "And of course as our viewers also know, we're still waiting for Juliet Adeyemi to turn up. She left just before lunch to run errands. We're not worried yet, but we'll all be a lot happier when she's with us again."

Meggie says, "Juliet, if you've met a nice boy and gone off to ride the teacups at Disney World, so help me, I'm going to ask for all the details. Now. Shall we, Irene?"

All around them, people have been clearing away plates of half-eaten barbecue, assembling in a half circle around the campfire. Any minute now they'll be singing "Kumbaya." They sit on their little towels. Irene and Meggie take their place in front of the fire. They clasp hands.

The demon lover moves a little farther away, into darkness. He is not interested in séances or ghosts. Here is the line of the shore. Sharp things underfoot. Someone joins him. Ray. Of course.

It is worse, somehow, to be naked in the dark. The world is so big and he is not. Ray is young and he is not. He is pretty sure that the videographer Pilar will sleep with him; Meggie will not.

"I know you," the demon lover says to Ray. "I've met you before. Well, not you, the previous you. Yous. You never last. *We* never last. She moves on. You disappear."

Ray says nothing. Looks out at the lake.

"I *was* you," the demon lover says.

Ray says, "And now? Who are you?"

"You charge by the hour?" the demon lover says. "Why follow me around? I don't seem to have my wallet on me."

"Meggie's busy," Ray says. "And I'm curious about you. What you think you're doing here."

"I came for Meggie," the demon lover says. "We're friends. An old friend can come to see an old friend. Some other time I'll see her again and you won't be around. I'll always be around. But you, you're just some guy who got lucky because you look like me."

Ray says, "I love her."

"Sucks, doesn't it?" the demon lover says. He goes back to the fire and the naked people waiting for other naked people. Thinks about the story he is meant to tell.

The séance has not been a success. Irene the medium keeps saying that she senses something. Someone is trying to say something.

The dead are here, but also not here. They're afraid. That's why they won't come. Something is keeping them away. There is something wrong here.

"Do you feel it?" she says to Meggie, to the others.

Meggie says, "I feel something. Something is here."

The demon lover extends himself outward into the night. Lets himself believe for a moment that life goes on. Is something here? There is a smell, the metallic stink of muck farms. There is an oppressiveness to the air. Is there malice here? An ill wish?

Meggie says, "No one has ever solved the mystery of what happened here. But perhaps whatever happened to them is still present. Irene, could it have some hold on their spirits, whatever is left of them, even in death?"

Irene says, "I don't know. Something is wrong here. Something is here. I don't know."

But *Who's There?* picks up nothing of interest on their equipment, their air ion counter or their barometer, their EMF detector or EVP detector, their wind chimes or thermal imaging scopes. No one is there.

And so at last it's time for ghost stories.

There's one about the men's room at a trendy Santa Monica

restaurant. The demon lover has been there. Had the fries with truffle-oil mayonnaise. Never encountered the ghost. He's not somebody who sees ghosts and he's fine with that. Never really liked truffle-oil mayonnaise, either. The thing in the bungalow with Meggie wasn't a ghost. It was drugs, the pressure they were under, the unbearable scrutiny; a *folie à deux;* the tax on their happiness.

Someone tells the old story about Basil Rathbone and the dinner guest who brings along his dogs. Upon departure, the man and his dogs are killed in a car crash just outside Rathbone's house. Rathbone sees. Is paralyzed with shock and grief. As he stands there, his phone rings—when he picks up, an operator says, "Pardon me, Mr. Rathbone, but there is a woman on the line who says she must speak to you."

The woman, who is a medium, says that she has a message for him. She says she hopes he will understand the meaning.

"Traveling very fast. No time to say good-bye. There are no dogs here."

And now it's the demon lover's turn. He says: "A long time ago when Meggie and I were together, we bought a bungalow in Venice Beach. We weren't there very much. We were everywhere else. On junkets. At festivals. We had no furniture. Just a mattress. No dishes. When we were home we ate out of take-out containers.

"But we were happy." He lets that linger. Meggie watches. Listens. Ray stands beside her. No space between them.

It's not much fun, telling a ghost story while you're naked. Telling the parts of the ghost story that you're supposed to tell.

Not telling other parts. While the woman you love stands there with the person you used to be.

"It was a good year. Maybe the best year of my life. Maybe the hardest year, too. We were young and we were stupid and people wanted things from us and we did things we shouldn't have done. Fill in the blanks however you want. We threw parties. We spent money like water. And we loved each other. Right, Meggie?"

Meggie nods.

He says, "But I should get to the ghost. I don't really believe that it was a ghost, but I don't not believe it was a ghost, either. I've never spent much time thinking about it, really. But the more time we spent in that bungalow, the worse things got."

Irene says, "Can you describe it for us? What happened?"

The demon lover says, "It was a feeling that someone was watching us. That they were somewhere very far away, but they were getting closer. That very soon they would be there with us. It was worse at night. We had bad dreams. Some nights we both woke up screaming."

Irene says, "What were the dreams about?"

He says, "Not much. Just that it was finally there in the room with us. Eventually it was always there. Eventually whatever it was was in the bed with us. We'd wake up on opposite sides of the mattress because it was there in between us."

Irene says, "What did you do?"

He says, "When one of us was alone in the bed it wasn't there. It was there when it was the two of us. Then it would be the three of us. So we got a room at the Chateau Marmont. Only it turned out it was there, too. The very first night it was there, too."

Irene says, "Did you try to talk to it?"

He says, "Meggie did. I didn't. Meggie thought it was real. I thought we needed therapy. I thought whatever it was, we were doing it. So we tried therapy. That was a bust. So eventually—" He shrugs.

"Eventually what?" Irene says.

"I moved out," Meggie says.

"She moved out," he says.

The demon lover wonders if Ray knows the other part of the story, if Meggie has told him that. Of course she hasn't. Meggie isn't dumb. It's the two of them and the demon lover thinks, as he's thought many times before, that this is what will always hold them together. Not the experience of filming a movie together, of falling in love at the exact same moment that all those other people fell in love with them, that sympathetic magic made up of story and effort, repetition and editing and craft and other people's desire.

The thing that happened is the thing they can never tell anyone else. It belongs to them. No one else.

"And after that there wasn't any ghost," he concludes. "Meggie took a break from Hollywood, went to India. I went to AA meetings."

It's gotten colder. The fire has gotten lower. You could, perhaps, imagine that there is a supernatural explanation for these things, but that would be wishful thinking. The missing girl, Juliet, has not returned. The ghost-hunting equipment does not record any presence.

Meggie finds the demon lover with Pilar. She says, "Can we talk?"

"What about?" he says.

Pilar says, "I'll go get another beer. Want one, Meggie?"

Meggie shakes her head and Pilar wanders off, her hand brushing against the demon lover's hip as she goes. Flesh against flesh. He turns just a little so he's facing away from the firelight.

"It's about the premiere for next season," Meggie says. "I want to shoot it in Venice Beach, in our old bungalow."

The demon lover feels something rush over him. Pour into his ears, flood down his throat. He can't think of what to say. He has been thinking about Ray while he flirts with Pilar. He's been wondering what would happen if he asked Meggie about Ray. Really, they've never talked about this. This thing that she does.

"I'd like you to be in the episode, too, of course," Meggie says.

He says, "I don't think that's a good idea. I think it's a terrible idea, actually."

"It's something I've always wanted to do," Meggie says. "I think it would be good for both of us."

"Something something closure," he says. "Yeah, yeah. Something something exposure something possible jail term. Are you *insane*?"

"Look," Meggie says. "I've already talked to the woman who lives there now. She's never experienced anything. Will, I need to do this."

"Of course she hasn't experienced anything," the demon lover says. "It wasn't the house that was haunted."

His blood is spiky with adrenaline. He looks around to see if anyone is watching. Of course they are. But everyone is far away enough that the conversation is almost private. He's surprised Meggie didn't spring this on him on camera. Think of the drama. The conflict. The ratings.

"You believe in this stuff," he says finally. Trying to find what will persuade her. "So why won't you leave it alone? You know what happened. We know what happened. You know what the story is. Why the fuck do you need to know more?" He's whispering now.

"Because every time we're together she's here with us," Meggie says. "Didn't you know that? She's here now. Don't you feel her?"

Hair stands up on his legs, his arms, the back of his neck. His mouth is dry, his tongue sticks to the roof of his mouth. "No," he says. "I don't."

Meggie says, "You know I would be careful, Will. I would never do anything to hurt you. And it doesn't work like that, anyway." She leans in close, says very quietly, "It isn't about us. This is for me. I just want to talk to her. I just want her to go away."

(1992) They acquire the trappings of a life, he and Meggie. They buy dishes and mid-century modern furniture and lamps. They acquire friends who are in the business, and throw parties. On occasion things happen at their parties. For example, there is the girl. She arrives with someone. They never find out who. She is about as pretty as you would expect a girl at one of their parties to be, which is to say that she is really very pretty.

After all this time, the demon lover doesn't really remember what she looked like. There were a lot of girls and a lot of parties and that was another country.

She had long black hair. Big eyes.

He and Meggie are both wasted. And the girl is into both of

them and eventually it's the three of them, everyone else is gone, there's a party going on somewhere else, they stay, she stays, and everyone else leaves. They drink and there's music and they dance. Then the girl is kissing Meggie and he is kissing the girl and they're in the bedroom. It's a lot of fun. They do pretty much everything you can do with three people in a bed. And at some point the girl is between them and everyone is having a good time, they're having fun, and then the girl says to them, Bite me.

Come on, bite me.

He bites her shoulder and she says, No, really bite me. Bite harder. I want you to really bite me. Bite me, please. And suddenly he and Meggie are looking at each other and it isn't fun anymore. This isn't what they're into.

He gets off as quickly as he can, because he's almost there anyway. And the girl is still begging, still asking for something they can't give her, because it isn't real and vampires aren't real and it's a distasteful situation and so Meggie asks the girl to leave. She does and they don't talk about it. They just go to sleep. And they wake up just a little bit later because she's snuck back into the house, they find out later that she's broken a window, and she's slashed her wrists. She's holding out her bloody wrists and she's saying, Please, here's my blood, please drink it. I want you to drink my blood. Please.

They get her bandaged up. The cuts aren't too deep. Meggie calls her agent, Pike, and Pike arranges for someone to take the girl to a private clinic. He tells them not to worry about any of it. It turns out that the girl is fifteen. Of course she is. Pike calls them again, after this girl gets out of the clinic, when she commits suicide. She has a history of attempts. Try, try, succeed.

The demon lover does not talk to Meggie again, because Pilar—who is naked—they are both naked, everyone is naked, of course—but Pilar is really quite lovely and fun to talk to and the camera work on this show is really quite exquisite and she likes the demon lover a lot. Keeps touching him. She says she has a bottle of Maker's Mark back in one of the cabins and he's already drunker than he's been in a while. Turns out they did meet once, in an AA meeting in Silver Lake.

They have a good time. Really, sex is a lot of fun. The demon lover suspects that there's some obvious psychological diagnosis for why he's having sex with Pilar, some need to reenact recent history and make sure it comes out better this time. The last girl with a camera didn't turn out so well for him. When exactly, he wonders, have things turned out well?

Afterward they lie on their backs on the dirty cement floor. Pilar says, "My girlfriend is never going to believe this."

He wonders if she's going to ask for an autograph.

Pilar's been sharing the cabin with the missing girl, Juliet. There's Whore-igami all over the cabin. Men and women and men and men and women and women in every possible combination, doing things that ought to be erotic. But they aren't; they're menacing instead. Maybe it's the straight lines.

The demon lover and Pilar get dressed in case Juliet shows up.

"Well," Pilar says, from her bunk bed, "good night."

He gets Juliet's bunk bed. Lies there in the dark until he's sure Pilar's asleep. He is thinking about Fawn for some reason. He can't stop thinking about her. If he stops thinking about her, he

will have to think about the conversation with Meggie. He will
have to think about Meggie.

Pilar's iPhone is on the floor beside her bunk bed. He picks it
up. No password. He types in Fawn's number. Sends her a text.
Hardly knows what he is typing.

I HOPE, he writes.

He writes the most awful things. Doesn't know why he is
doing this. Perhaps she will assume that it is a wrong number. He
types in details, specific things, so she will know it's not.

Eventually she texts back.

WHO IS THIS? WILL?

The demon lover doesn't respond to that. Just keeps texting
FILTHY BITCH YOU CUNT YOU WHORE YOU SLIME
etc. etc. etc. Until she stops asking. Surely she knows who he is.
She must know who he is.

Here's the thing about acting, about a scene, about a character;
about the dialogue you are given, the things your character does.
None of it matters. You can take the most awful words, all the
words, all the names, the acts he types into the text block. You
can say these things, and the way you say them can change the
meaning. You can say, "You dirty bitch. You cunt," and say them
differently each time; can make it a joke, an endearment, a cry
for help, a seduction. You can kill, be a vampire, a soulless thing.
The audience will love you no matter what you do. If you want
them to love you. Some of them will always love you.

He needs air. He drops the phone on the floor again where
Pilar will find it in the morning. Decides to walk down to the
lake. He will have to go past Meggie's trailer on the way, only he
doesn't. Instead he stands there watching as a shadow slips out of

the door of the trailer and down the stairs and away. Going where? Almost not there at all.

Ray?

He could follow. But he doesn't.

He wonders if Meggie is awake. The door to her trailer is off the latch and so the demon lover steps inside.

Makes his way to her bedroom, no lights, she is not awake. He will do no harm. Only wants to see her safe and sleeping. An old friend can go to see an old friend.

Meggie's a shape in the bed and he comes closer so he can see her face. There is someone in the bed with Meggie.

Ray looks at the demon lover and the demon lover looks back at Ray. Ray's right hand rests on Meggie's breast. Ray raises the other hand, beckons the demon lover closer.

The next morning is what you would predict. The crew of *Who's There?* packs up to leave; Pilar discovers the text messages on her phone.

Did I do that? the demon lover says. I was drunk. I may have done that. Oh God, oh hell, oh fuck. He plays his part.

This may get messy. Oh, he knows how messy it can get. Pilar can make some real money with those texts. Fawn, if she wants, can use them against him in the divorce.

He doesn't know how he gets in these situations.

Fawn has called Meggie. So there's that, as well. Meggie waits to talk to him until almost everyone else has packed up and gone; it's early afternoon now. Really, he should already have left. He has things he'll need to do. Decisions to make about flights, a new phone. He needs to call his publicist, his agent. Time for them to earn their keep. He likes to keep them busy.

Ray is off somewhere. The demon lover isn't too sorry about this.

It's not a fun conversation. They're up in the parking lot now, and one of the crew, he doesn't recognize her with her clothes on, says to Meggie, "Need a lift?"

"I've got the thing in Tallahassee tomorrow, the morning show," Meggie says. "Got someone picking me up any minute now."

" 'Kay," the woman says. "See you in San Jose." She gives the demon lover a dubious look—is Pilar already talking?—and then gets in her car and drives away.

"San Jose?" the demon lover says.

"Yeah," Meggie says. "The Winchester House."

"Huh," the demon lover says. He doesn't really care. He's tired of this whole thing, Meggie, the borrowed T-shirt and cargo shorts, Lake Apopka, no-show ghosts, and bad publicity.

He knows what's coming. Meggie rips into him. He lets her. There's no point trying to talk to women when they get like this. He stands there and takes it all in. When she's finally done, he doesn't bother trying to defend himself. What's the good of saying things? He's so much better at saying things when there's a script to keep him from deep water. There's no script here.

Of course, he and Meggie will patch things up eventually. Old friends forgive old friends. Nothing is unforgivable. He's wondering if this is untrue when a car comes into the meadow.

"Well," Meggie says. "That's my ride."

She waits for him to speak and when he doesn't, she says, "Good-bye, Will."

"I'll call you," the demon lover says at last. "It'll be okay, Meggie."

"Sure," Meggie says. She's not really making much of an effort. "Call me."

She gets into the back of the car. The demon lover bends over, waves at the window where she is sitting. She's looking straight ahead. The driver's window is down, and okay, here's Ray again. Of course! He looks out of the window at the demon lover. He raises an eyebrow, smiles, waves with that hand again, need a ride?

The demon lover steps away from the car. Feels a sense of overwhelming disgust and dread. A cloud of blackness and horror comes over him, something he hasn't felt in many, many years. He recognizes the feeling at once.

And that's that. The car drives away with Meggie inside it. The demon lover stands in the field for some period of time, he is never sure how long. Long enough that he is sure he will never catch up with the car with Meggie in it. And he doesn't.

There's a storm coming in.

The thing is this: Meggie never turns up for the morning show in Tallahassee. The other girl, Juliet Adeyemi, does reappear, but nobody ever sees Meggie again. She just vanishes. Her body is never found. The demon lover is a prime suspect in her disappearance. Of course he is. But there is no proof. No evidence.

No one is ever charged.

And Ray? When the demon lover explains everything to the police, to the media, on talk shows, he tells the same story over and over again. I went to see my old friend Meggie. I met her lover, Ray. They left together. He drove the car. But no one else supports this story. There is not a single person who will admit that Ray exists. There is not a frame of video with Ray in it. Ray was never there at all, no matter how many times the demon lover explains what happened. They say, What did he look like? Can you describe him? And the demon lover says, He looked like me.

As he is waiting for the third or maybe the fourth time to be questioned by the police, the demon lover thinks about how one day they will make a movie about all of this. About Meggie. But of course he will be too old to play the demon lover.

Secret Identity

*D*ear Paul Zell.

Dear Paul Zell *is exactly how far I've gotten at least a dozen times, and then I get a little further, and then I give up. So this time I'm going to try something new. I'm going to pretend that I'm not writing you a letter, Paul Zell, dear Paul Zell. I'm so sorry. And I am sorry, Paul Zell, but let's skip that part for now or else I won't get any further this time, either. And in any case: how much does it matter whether or not I'm sorry? What difference could it possibly make?*

So. Let's pretend that we don't know each other. Let's pretend we're meeting for the first time, Paul Zell. We're sitting down to have dinner in a restaurant in a hotel in New York City. I've come a long way to have dinner with you. We've never met face-to-face. Everything I ever told you about myself is more or less a lie. But you don't know that yet. We think we may be in love.

We met in FarAway, online, except now here we are up close. I could reach out and touch your hand. If you were really here.

Our waiter has poured you a glass of red wine. Me? I'm drinking a Coke. You're thirty-four. I'm almost sixteen.

I'm so sorry, Paul Zell. I don't think I can do this. Except I have to do this. So let's try again. (I keep trying again and again and again.) Let's start even further back.

Picture the lobby of a hotel. In the lobby, a fountain with Spanish tiles in green and yellow. A tiled floor, leather armchairs, corporate art, this bank of glass-fronted elevators whizzing up and down, a bar. Daddy bar to all the minibars in all the rooms. Sound familiar? Maybe you've been here before.

Now fill up the lobby with dentists and superheroes. Men and women, oral surgeons, eighth-dimensional entities, mutants, and freaks who want to save your teeth, save the world, and maybe end up with a television show, too. I've seen a dentist or two in my time, Paul Zell, but we don't get many superheroes out on the plain. We get tornadoes instead. There are two conventions going on at the hotel, and they're mingling round the fountain, tra la la, tipping back drinks.

Boards in the lobby list panels on advances in cosmetic dentistry, effective strategies for minimizing liability in cases of bystander hazard, presentations with titles like "Spandex or Bulletproof? What Look Is Right for You?" You might be interested in these if you were a dentist or a superhero. Which I'm not. As it turns out, I'm not a lot of things.

A girl is standing in front of the registration desk. That's me. And where are you, Paul Zell?

The hotel clerk behind the desk is only a few years older than me. (Than that girl, the one who's come to meet Paul Zell. Is it pretentious or pitiful or just plain psychotic the way I'm talking about myself in the third person? Maybe it's all three. I don't care.) The clerk's nametag says Aliss, and she reminds the girl I wish wasn't me of someone back at school. Erin Toomey, that's who. Erin Toomey is a hateful bitch. But never mind about Erin Toomey.

Aliss the hotel clerk is saying something. She's saying, "I'm not finding anything." It's eleven o'clock on a Friday morning, and at that moment the girl in the lobby is missing third-period biology. Her fetal pig is wondering where she is.

Let's give the girl in line in the hotel lobby a name. Everybody gets a name, even fetal pigs. (I call mine Alfred.) Of course it isn't like FarAway. I don't get to choose my name. If I did, it wouldn't be Billie Faggart. That ring any bells? No, I didn't think it would. Since fourth grade, which is when I farted while I was coming down the playground slide, everyone at school has called me Smelly Fagfart. That's because Billie Faggart is a funny name, right? Except girls like Billie Faggart don't have much of a sense of humor.

There's another girl at school, Jennifer Groendyke. Everyone makes jokes about us. About how we'll move to California and marry each other. You'd think we'd be friends, right? But we're not. I'm not good at the friends thing. I'm the human equivalent of one of those baby birds that falls out of a nest and then some nice person picks the baby bird up and puts it back. Except that now the baby bird smells all wrong. I think I smell wrong.

If you're wondering who Melinda Bowles is—the thirty-two-year-old woman you met in FarAway—no, you've never really met her. Melinda Bowles has never sent late-night e-mails to Paul Zell, not ever. Melinda Bowles would never catch a bus to New York City to meet Paul Zell, because she doesn't know Paul Zell exists.

Melinda Bowles has never been to FarAway.

Melinda Bowles has no idea who the Enchantress Magic EightBall is. She's never hung out online with the Master Thief Boggle. I don't think she knows what an MMORPG is.

Melinda Bowles has never played a game of living chess in King Nermal's Chamber in the Endless Caverns under the Loathsome Rock. Melinda Bowles doesn't know a rook from a writing desk. A pawn from a pwn.

Here are some things you know about Melinda Bowles that are true. She used to be married, but she got a divorce. She lives in her parents' house. She teaches high school. I used her name when I signed up for an account on FarAway. More about my sister, Melinda, later.

Anyway. Girl-liar Billie says to desk-clerk Aliss, "No message? No envelope? Mr. Zell, Paul Zell?" (That's you. In case you've forgotten.) "He's a guest here? He said he was leaving something for me at the front desk."

"I'll look again if you want," Aliss says. But she does nothing. Just stands there staring malevolently past Billie as if she hates the world and everyone in it.

Billie turns around to see who Aliss is glaring at. There's a regular-ish guy behind Billie; behind him, out in the lobby, there are all sorts of likely candidates. Who doesn't hate a dentist? Or maybe Aliss isn't crazy about superheroes. Maybe she's contemplating the thing that looks like a bubble of blood. If you were there, Paul Zell, you might stare at the bubble of blood, too. You can just make out the silhouette of someone/something inside.

Billie doesn't keep up with superheroes, not really, but she feels as if she's seen the bloody bubble on the news. Maybe it saved the world once. It levitates three feet above the marble floor of the atrium. It plops bloody drops like a sink faucet in hell. Maybe Aliss worries someone will slip on the lobby floor, break an ankle, sue the hotel. Or maybe the bubble of blood owes her ten bucks.

The bubble of blood drifts over to the Spanish-tiled fountain. It clears the lip, just barely; comes to a halt two feet above the surface of the water. Now it looks like an art installation, albeit kind of a disgusting one. But perhaps it is seeing a heroic role for itself: scaring off the kind of children who like to steal pennies from fountains. Future criminal masterminds might turn their energies in a more productive direction. Perhaps some will become dentists.

Were you a boy who stole coins from fountains, Paul Zell?

We're not getting very far in this story, are we? Maybe that's because some parts of it are so very hard to tell, Paul Zell. So here

I linger, not at the beginning and not even in the middle. Already it's more of a muddle.

Behind the desk, even Aliss has gotten tired of waiting for me to get on with the story. She's stopped glaring, is clacking on a keyboard with her too-long nails. There's glitter residue around her hairline and a half-scrubbed-off club stamp on her right hand. She says to Billie, "Are you a guest here? What was your name again?"

"Melinda Bowles," Billie says. "I'm not a guest. Paul Zell is staying here? He said he would leave something for me behind the desk."

"Are you here to audition?" Aliss says. "Because maybe you should go ask over at the convention registration."

"Audition?" Billie says. She has no idea what Aliss is talking about. She's forming her backup plan already: walk back to Port Authority and catch the next bus back to Keokuk, Iowa. That would have been a simpler e-mail to write, I see now. *Dear Paul Zell. Sorry. I got cold feet.*

"Aliss, my love. Better lose the piercing." The guy in line behind Billie is now up at the counter beside her. His hand is stamped, like Aliss's. Smudgy licks of black eyeliner around his eyes. "Unless you want management to write you a Dear John."

"Oh, shit." Aliss's hand goes up to her nose. She ducks down behind the counter. "Conrad, you asshole. Where did you go last night?"

"No idea," Conrad says. "I was drunk. Where did you go?"

"Home." Aliss says the word like it's a blunt instrument. She's still submerged. "You want something? Room need making up? Night-shift Darin said he saw you in the elevator around three in the morning. With a girl." *Girl* is a dagger.

"Entirely possible," Conrad says. "Like I said, drunk. Need any help down there? Taking out the piercing? Helping this kid? Because I want to make last night up to you. I'm sorry, okay?"

Which would be the right thing to say, but Billie thinks this guy sounds not so penitent. More like he's swallowing a yawn.

"That's *very* nice of you, but I'm *fine*." Aliss snaps upright. The piercing is gone and her eyes glitter with either tears or murder. "This must be for you," she tells Billie in a cheery desk-clerk robot voice. It's not much of an improvement on the stabby voice. "I'm *so* sorry about the confusion." There's an envelope in her hand.

Billie takes the envelope and goes to sit on a sofa beside a dentist. He's wearing a convention badge with his name on it and where he comes from and that's how she knows he isn't a superhero and he isn't Paul Zell.

She opens her envelope. There's a room key inside and a piece of paper with a room number written on it. Nothing else. What is this, FarAway? Billie starts to laugh like an utter maniac. The dentist stares.

Forgive her. She's been on a bus for over twenty hours. Her clothes smell like bus, a cocktail of chemical cleaners and other people's breath, and the last thing she was expecting when she went off on this quest, Paul Zell, was to find herself in a hotel full of superheroes and dentists.

It's not like we get a lot of superheroes in Keokuk, Iowa. There's the occasional flyover or Superheroes on Ice event, and every once in a while someone in Keokuk discovers they have the strength of two men, or can predict the sell-by date on cans of tuna in the supermarket with 98.2 percent accuracy, but even minor-league talents head out of town pretty quickly. They take off for Hollywood, to try and get on a reality show. Or New York or Chicago or even Baltimore, to form novelty rock bands or fight crime or both.

But, here's the thing: the thing is that under ordinary circumstances, Billie would have nothing better to do than to watch a woman with a raven's head wriggling upstream through the crowd around the lobby bar, over to the fountain and that epic bubble of blood. The woman holds up a pink drink, she's standing on tiptoes, and a slick four-fingered hand emerges from the bubble of blood and takes the glass from her. Is it a love story? How does a woman with a raven's beak kiss a bubble of blood? Paul Zell, how are you and me any more impossible than that?

Maybe it's just two old friends having a drink. The four-fingered hand orients the straw into the membrane or force field or whatever it is and the glass empties itself like a magic trick. The bubble quivers.

But: Paul Zell. All Billie can think about is you, Paul Zell. She has the key to Paul Zell's hotel room. Back before she met you, way far back in FarAway, Billie was always up for a quest. Why not? She had nothing better to do. And the quest always went like this: Find yourself in a strange place. Encounter a guardian. Outwit them or kill them or persuade them to give you the item they've been guarding. A weapon or a spell or the envelope containing the key to room 1584.

Except the key in Billie's hand is a real key and I don't do that kind of quest much anymore. Not since I met you, Paul Zell. Not since the Enchantress Magic EightBall met the Master Thief Boggle in King Nermal's Chamber and challenged him to a game of chess.

While I'm coming clean, here's a minor confession. Why not? Why should you care that besides the Enchantress Magic Eight-Ball I used to have two other avatars in FarAway? There's Constant Bliss, who's an elfin healer, and frankly kind of a pill, and there's Bearhand, who, as it turns out, was kind of valuable in terms of accumulated points, especially weapons class. There was a period, you see, when things were bad at school and worse at home, which I don't really want to talk about and anyway it was a bad period during which I liked running around and killing things. Whatever. Last month I sold Bearhand when you and I were planning all of this, for bus fare. It wasn't a big deal. I'd kind of stopped being Bearhand except for every once in a while when you weren't online and I was lonely or sad or had a really, really shitty day at school.

I'm thinking I may sell off Constant Bliss, too, if anyone wants to buy her. If not, it will have to be Magic EightBall. Or maybe I'll sell both of them. But that's part of the story I haven't gotten to yet.

And, yeah, I do spend a lot of time online. In FarAway. Like I said, it's not like I have a lot of friends, not that you should feel sorry for me, because you shouldn't, Paul Zell, that's NOT why I'm telling you all of this.

My sister? Melinda? She says wait a few years and see. Things get better. Of course, based on her life, maybe they do get better. And then they get worse again, and then you have to move back home and teach high school. So how exactly is that better?

And, yes, in case you're wondering, my sister, Melinda Bowles, is kind of stunning and all the boys in my school who despise me have crushes on her even when she flunks them. If you're still speaking to me after you read this, I'll be happy to make up a spreadsheet of character traits and biographical incidents. One column will be Melinda Bowles and the other will be Billie Faggart. There will be little checkmarks in either column—or both—depending. But the story about shaving off my eyebrows when I was a kid? That was true. I mean, that was me. And so was the thing about liking reptiles. Melinda? She's not so fond of the reptiles. But then, maybe you don't really have a chameleon named Moe and a tokay gecko named Bitey. Maybe you made up some stuff, too, except, yeah, okay, why would you make up some lizards? I keep having to remind myself: Billie, just because you're a liar doesn't mean the world is full of liars. Except that you did lie, right? You were at the hotel. You left me the key to your room at the hotel in an envelope addressed to Melinda Bowles. Because if you didn't, then who did?

Sorry. This is supposed to be me. Not me solving the big mysteries of the universe and everything. Except, here's the thing about Melinda, in case you're thinking maybe the person you fell in love with really exists. The *salient* thing. Melinda has a boyfriend. Also, she's super religious, like seriously born again. Which you're not. So even if Melinda's boyfriend got killed or something, which I know is something she worries about, it would never work out between you and her.

And one more last thing about Melinda, or maybe it's actually about you. This is the part where I have to thank you. Because:

because of you, Paul Zell, I think Melinda and I have become friends. Because all year I've been interested in her life. I ask her how her day was and I actually listen when she tells me. Because how else could I convince you that I was a thirty-two-year-old divorced high school algebra teacher? And it turns out that we actually have a lot in common, me and Melinda, and it's like I even *understand* what she thinks about. Because she has a boyfriend who's far away (in Afghanistan) and she misses him and they write e-mails to each other, and she worries about what if he loses a leg or something and will they still love each other when he gets back?

And I have you. I had this thing with you, even if I couldn't tell her about you. I guess I still can't tell her.

Billie gets into an elevator with a superhero and the guy who blew off Aliss. The superhero reeks. BO and something worse, like spoiled meat. He gets out on the seventh floor and Billie sucks in air. She's thinking about all sorts of things. For example, how it turns out she doesn't have a fear of heights, which is a good thing to discover in a glass elevator. She's thinking about how she could find a wireless café, go online and hang out in FarAway, except Paul Zell won't be there. She wonders if the guy who bought Bearhand is trying him out. Now that would be weird: to run into someone who used to be you. What would she say? She's thinking how much she wants to take a shower and she's wondering if she smells as bad as that superhero did. She's thinking all of this and lots of other things, too.

"Now that's how to fight crime," says the other person in the elevator. (Conrad Linthor, although Billie doesn't know his last name yet. Maybe you'll recognize it, though.) "You smell it to death. Although, to be fair, to get that big you have to eat a lot of protein and the protein makes you stinky. That's why I'm a vegetarian." The smile he gives Billie is as ripe with charm as the elevator is ripe with super stink.

Billie prides herself on being charm resistant. (It's like not having a sense of humor. A sense of humor is a weakness. I know you're supposed to be able to laugh at yourself, but that's pretty sucky advice when everyone is always laughing at you already.) She stares at Conrad Linthor blankly. If you don't react, mostly other people give up and leave you alone.

Conrad Linthor is eighteen or nineteen, or maybe a well-preserved twenty-two. He has regular features and white teeth. He'd be good-looking if he weren't so good-looking, Billie thinks, and then wonders what she meant by that. She can tell that he's rich, although again she's not quite sure how she knows this. Maybe because he pressed the penthouse floor button when he got on the elevator.

"Let me guess," Conrad Linthor says, as if he and Billie have been having a conversation. "You're here to audition." When Billie continues to stare at him blankly, this time because she really doesn't know what he's talking about and not just because she's faking being stupid, he elaborates: "You want to be a sidekick. That guy who just got off? The Blue Fist? I hear his sidekicks keep quitting for some reason."

"I'm here to meet a friend," Billie says. "Why does everyone keep asking me that? Are you? You know, a sidekick?"

"Me?" Conrad Linthor says. "Very funny."

The elevator door dings open, fifteenth floor, and Billie gets off.

"See you around," Conrad Linthor calls after her. It sounds more mocking than hopeful.

You know what, Paul Zell? I never thought you would be super handsome or anything. I never cared about what you might turn out to look like. I know you have brown hair and brown eyes and you're kind of skinny and you have a big nose. I know because you told me you look like your avatar, Boggle. Me, I was always terrified you'd ask for my photo, because then it would really have been a lie, even more of a lie, because I would've sent you a photo of Melinda.

My dad says I look so much like Melinda did when she was a kid, it's scary. That we could practically be twins. But I've seen pictures of Melinda when she was my age and I don't look like her at all. Melinda was kind of freakish looking when she was my age, actually. I think that's why she's so nice now and not vain, because it was a surprise to her, too, when she got awesome looking. I'm not gorgeous and I'm not a freak, either, and so that whole ugly duckling then knockout swan thing that Melinda went through probably isn't going to happen to me.

But you saw me, right? You know what I look like.

Billie knocks on the door of Paul Zell's hotel room, just in case. Even though you aren't there. If you were there, she'd die on the spot of heart failure, even though that's why she's there. To see you.

Maybe you're wondering why she came all this way, when meeting you face-to-face was always going to be this huge problem. Honestly? She doesn't really know. She still doesn't know. Except you said: Want to meet up? See if this is real or not?

What was she supposed to do? Say no? Tell the truth?

There are two double beds in room 1584, and a black suitcase on a luggage rack. No Paul Zell, because you're going to be in meetings all day. The plan is to meet at the Golden Lotus at six.

Last night you slept in one of those beds, Paul Zell. Billie sits down on the bed closest to the window. It's a damn shame housekeeping has already made up the room, otherwise Billie could climb into the bed you were sleeping in last night and put her head down on your pillow.

She goes over to the suitcase, and here's where it starts to get kind of awful, Paul Zell. This is why I have to write about all of this in the third person, because maybe then I can pretend that it wasn't really me there, doing these things.

The lid of your suitcase is up. You're a tidy packer, Paul Zell. The dirty clothes on the floor of the closet are folded. Billie lifts up the squared shirts and khakis. Even the underwear is folded. Your pants size is 32, Paul Zell. Your socks are just socks. There's a velvet box, a jeweler's box, near the bottom of the suitcase, and Billie opens it. Then she puts the box back at the bottom of the suitcase. I can't really tell you what she was thinking right then, even though I was there.

I can't tell you everything, Paul Zell.

Billie didn't pack a suitcase, because her dad and Melinda would have wondered about that. (But nobody's ever surprised when you go off to school and your backpack looks crammed full of things.) Billie takes out the skirt she's planning to wear to dinner and hangs it up in the closet. She brushes her teeth and afterward she puts her toothbrush down on the counter beside your toothbrush. She closes the drapes over the view, which is just another building, glass-fronted like the elevators. As if nobody could ever get anything done if the world wasn't watching, or maybe because if the world can look in and see what you're doing then what you're doing has to be valuable and important and aboveboard. It's a far way down to the street, so far down that the window in Paul Zell's hotel room doesn't open, probably because people like Billie can't help imagining what it would be like to fall.

All the little ant people down there, who don't even know you're standing at the window looking down at them. Billie looks down at them.

Billie closes the blackout curtain over the view. She pulls the cover off the bed closest to the window. She takes off her jeans and shirt and bra and puts on the Metallica T-shirt she found in Paul Zell's suitcase.

She lies down on a fresh white top sheet, falls asleep in the yellow darkness. She dreams about you.

When she wakes up her neck is kinked on an unfamiliar pillow. Her jaw is tight because she's forgotten to wear her mouthpiece. She's been grinding her teeth. So, yes, the teeth grinding, that's me. Not Melinda.

It's 4:30, late afternoon. Billie takes a shower. She uses Paul Zell's herbal conditioner.

The hotel where she's staying is on CNN. Because of the superheroes.

For the last three weeks Billie has tried not to think too much about what will happen at dinner when she and Paul Zell meet.

But even though she's been trying not to think about it, she still had to figure out what she was going to wear. The skirt and the sweater she brought are Melinda's. Billie hopes they'll make her look older, but not as if she is *trying* to look older. She bought a lipstick at Target, but when she puts it on it looks too Billie Goes to Clown School, and so she wipes it off again and puts on ChapStick instead. She's sure her lips are still redder than they ought to be.

When she goes down to ask about Internet cafés, Aliss is still on the front desk. "Guests can use their room keys to access the business center," Aliss tells her.

Billie has another question. "Who's that guy Conrad?" she says. "What's his deal?"

Aliss's eyes narrow. "His deal is he's the biggest slut in the world. Like it's any of your business," she says. "But don't think that he's got any pull with his dad, Little Miss Wannabe Sidekick. No matter what he says. Hook up with him and I'll stomp your ass. It's not like I want this job anyway."

"I've got a boyfriend," Billie says. "Besides, he's too old for me."

Which is an interesting thing for her to say, when I think about it now.

Here's the thing, Paul Zell. You're thirty-four and I'm fifteen. That's nineteen years' difference. That's a substantial gap, right? Besides the legal issue, which I am not trying to minimize, I could be twice as old as I am now and you'd still be older. I've thought about this a lot. And you know what? There's a teacher at school, Mrs. Christie. Melinda was talking, a few months ago, about how Mrs. Christie just turned thirty and her husband is sixty-three. And they still fell in love, and, yeah,

Melinda says everyone thinks it's kind of repulsive, but that's love, and nobody really understands how it works. It just happens. And then there's Melinda, who married a guy *exactly the same age that she was,* who then got addicted to heroin, and was, besides that, just all-around bad news. My point? Compared to those thirty-three years between Mr. and Mrs. Christie, nineteen years is practically nothing.

The real problem here is timing. And, also, of course, the fact that I lied. But, except for the lying, why couldn't it have worked out between us in a few years? Why do we really have to wait at all? It's not like I'm ever going to fall in love with anyone again.

Billie uses Paul Zell's room key to get into the business center. There's a superhero at one of the PCs. The superhero is at least eight feet tall, and she's got frizzy red hair. You can tell she's a superhero and not just a tall dentist because a little electric sizzle runs along her outline every once in a while as if maybe she's being projected into her too-small seat from some other dimension. She glances over at Billie, who nods hello. The superhero sighs and looks at her fingernails. Which is fine with Billie. She doesn't need rescuing, and she isn't auditioning for anything, either. No matter what anybody thinks.

For some reason, Billie chooses to be Constant Bliss when she signs into FarAway. She's double incognito. Paul Zell isn't online and there's no one in King Nermal's Chamber, except for the living chess pieces who are always there, and who aren't really alive, either. Not the ones who are still standing or sitting, patiently, upon their squares, waiting to be deployed, knitting or picking their noses or flirting or whatever their particular programs have been programmed to do when they aren't in combat. Billie's favorite is the King's Rook, because he always laughs when he moves into battle, even when he must know he's going to be defeated.

Do you ever feel as if they're watching you, Paul Zell? Sometimes I wonder if they know that they're just a game inside a game. When I first found King Nermal's Chamber, I walked all around the board and checked out what everyone was doing. The White Queen and her pawn were playing chess, like they always do. I sat and watched them play. After a while the White Queen asked me if I wanted a match, and when I said yes, her little board got bigger and bigger until I was standing on a single square of it, inside another chamber exactly the same as the chamber I'd just been standing in, and there was another White Queen playing chess with her pawn, and I guess I could have kept on going down and down and down, but instead I got freaked out and quit FarAway without saving.

Bearhand isn't in FarAway right now. No Enchantress Magic EightBall, either, of course.

Constant Bliss is low on healing herbs, and she's quite near the Bloody Meadows, so I put on her cloak of invisibility and go out onto the battlefield. Rare and strange plants have sprung up where the blood of men and beasts is still soaking into the ground. I'm wearing a Shielding Hand, too, because some of the plants don't like being yanked out of the ground. When my collecting box is full, Constant Bliss leaves the Bloody Meadows. I leave the Bloody Meadows. Billie leaves the Bloody Meadows. Billie hasn't quite decided what she should do next, or where she should go, and besides it's nearly six o'clock. So she saves and quits.

The superhero is watching something on YouTube, two Korean guys break-dancing to Pachelbel's *Canon in D*. Billie stands up to leave.

"Girl," the superhero says.

"Who, me?" Billie says.

"You, girl," the superhero says. "Are you here with Miracle?"

Billie realizes a mistake has been made. "I'm not a sidekick," she says.

"Then who are you?" the superhero says.

"Nobody," Billie says. And then, because she remembers that there's a superhero named Nobody, she says, "I mean, I'm not anybody." She escapes before the superhero can say anything else.

Billie checks her hair in the women's bathroom in the lobby. Melinda is always trying to get Billie to wear something besides T-shirts and jeans, and, sure, she looks different right now but Billie, looking in the bathroom mirror, suddenly wishes she looked more like herself, forgetting that what she needs is to look less like herself. To look less like a fifteen-year-old crazy liar.

Although apparently what she looks like is a sidekick.

The maître d' at the Golden Lotus asks if she has a reservation. It's now five minutes to six. "For six o'clock," Billie says. "For two. Paul Zell?"

"Here we are," the maître d' says. "The other member of your party isn't here, but we can go ahead and seat you."

Billie is seated. The maître d' pushes her chair in and Billie tries not to feel trapped. There are other people eating dinner all around her, dentists and superheroes and maybe ordinary people, too. Costumes are definitely superheroes, but just because some of the hotel guests aren't wearing costumes doesn't mean they're dentists. Although some of them are definitely dentists.

Billie hasn't eaten since this morning, when she got a bagel at Port Authority. Her first New York bagel. Cinnamon raisin with blueberry cream cheese. Her stomach growls.

People who aren't Paul Zell are seated at tables, or go to the bar and sit on bar stools. Billie studies the menu. She's never had sushi before. A waiter pours her a glass of water. Asks if she'd like to order an appetizer while she's waiting. Billie declines. The people at the table next to her pay their bill and leave. When she looks at her watch, she sees it's 6:18.

You're late, Paul Zell.

Billie thinks: maybe she should go back to the room and see if there are any messages. "I'll be right back," she tells the maître d'. The maître d' could care less. There are superheroes in the hotel lobby and there are dentists in the elevator and there's a light on the phone in room 1584 that would flash if there were any messages. It isn't flashing. Billie dials the number for messages just in case. No message.

Back in the Golden Lotus no one is sitting at the table reserved for Paul Zell, six o'clock, party of two. Billie sits back down anyway. She waits until 7:30, and then she leaves while the maître d' is escorting a party of superheroes to a table. So far none of the superheroes are ones that Billie recognizes, which doesn't mean that their superpowers are lame. It's just, there are a lot of superheroes and knowing a lot about superheroes has never been Billie's thing.

She rides the glass-fronted elevator and opens the door of Paul Zell's hotel room without knocking, which is okay because no one is there. She orders room service. This should be exciting because Billie's never ordered room service in her life. But it's not. She orders a hamburger. She drinks a juice from the minibar and watches the Cartoon Network. She waits for someone to knock on the door. When someone does, it's just a bellboy with her hamburger.

By nine o'clock Billie has been down to the business center twice. She checks e-mail, checks FarAway, checks all the chat rooms. No Boggle. No Paul Zell. Just chess pieces, and it isn't her move. She writes Paul Zell an e-mail; in the end, she doesn't send it.

When she goes upstairs for the last time, no one is there. Just the suitcase. She doesn't really expect anyone to be there. The jeweler's box is still down at the bottom of the suitcase.

The office building in the window is still lit up. Maybe the lights stay on all night long, even when no one is there. Billie thinks those lights are the loneliest things she's ever seen. Even lonelier than the light of distant stars that are already dead by the time their light reaches us. Far down below, ant people do their antic things.

Billie opens up the minibar again. Inside are miniature bottles of gin, bourbon, tequila, and rum that no one is going to drink unless Billie drinks them. What would Alice do, Billie thinks. Billie has always been a Lewis Carroll fan, and not just because of the chess stuff.

There are two beers and a jar of peanuts. Billie drinks all of the miniatures and both normal-sized cans of beer. Perhaps you noticed the charges on your bill.

Here is where details begin to be a little thin for me, Paul Zell. Perhaps you have a better idea of what I'm describing, what I'm omitting. Then again maybe you don't.

It's the first time Billie's ever been drunk, and she's not very good at it. Nothing is happening, that she can tell. She perseveres. She begins to feel okay, as if everything is going to be okay. The okay feeling gets larger and larger until she's entirely swallowed up by okayness. This lasts for a while, and then she starts to fade in and out, like she's jumping forward in time, always just a little bit dizzy when she arrives. Here she is, flipping through channels, not quite brave enough to click on the pay-for-porn channels, although she thinks about it. Then here she is, a bit later, putting that lipstick on again. This time she kind of likes the way she looks. Here she is, lifting all of Paul Zell's clothes out of the suitcase. She takes the ring out of the box, puts it on her big toe. Now there's a gap. Then: here's Billie, back again, she's bent over a toilet. She's vomiting. She vomits over and over again. Someone is holding back her hair. There's a hand holding out a cold, damp facecloth. Now she's in a bed. The room is dark, but Billie thinks there's someone sitting on the other bed. He's just sitting there.

Later on, she thinks she hears someone moving around the room, doing things. For some reason, she imagines it's the Enchantress Magic EightBall. Rummaging around the room, looking for important, powerful, magical things. Billie thinks she ought to get up and help. But she can't move.

Much later on, when Billie gets up and goes to the bathroom to throw up again, Paul Zell's suitcase is gone.

There's vomit all over the sink and the bathtub, and on her sister's sweater. Billie's crotch is cold and wet; she realizes she's pissed herself. She pulls off the sweater and skirt and hose, and her underwear. She leaves her bra on because she can't figure out how to undo the straps. She drinks four glasses of water and then crawls into the other bed, the one she hasn't pissed in.

When she wakes up it's one in the afternoon. Someone has left the Do Not Disturb sign on the door of room 1584. Maybe Billie did this, maybe not. She won't be able to get the bus back to Keokuk today; it left this morning at 7:32. Paul Zell's suitcase is gone, even his dirty clothes are gone. There's not a sock. Not even a hair on a pillow. Just the herbal conditioner. I guess you forgot to check the bathtub.

Not that Billie notices any of this, thinks about any of this for a while. Billie is almost glad her head hurts so much. She deserves much worse. She pushes one of the towels around the sink and the counter, mopping up crusted puke. She runs hot water in the shower until the bathroom smells like puke soup. She strips the sheets off the bed she peed in, and shoves them with Melinda's destroyed sweater and skirt and all of the puke-stained towels under the counter in the bathroom. The water is only just warm when she takes her shower. Better than she deserves. Billie turns the handle all the way to the right, and then shrieks and turns it back. What you deserve and what you can stand aren't necessarily the same thing.

She cries bitterly while she conditions her hair. She takes the elevator down to the lobby and goes and sits in the Starbucks. The first time she's ever been inside a Starbucks. What she really

wants is a caramel iced vanilla latte, but instead she orders a
double espresso. More penance.

Billie is pouring little packets of sugar into her double espresso
when someone sits down next to her. It isn't you, of course. It's
that guy Conrad. And now we're past the point where I owe you
an apology, and yet I guess I ought to keep going, because the
story isn't over yet. Remember how Billie thought the room key
and the bus ride seemed like FarAway, like a quest? Now is the
part where it starts seeming more like one of those games of
chess, the kind you've already lost and you know it, but you
don't concede. You just keep on losing, one piece at a time, until
you're the biggest loser in the world. Which is, I guess, how life
is like playing chess with someone better than you'll ever be.
Because it's not like you're ever going to win in the end, is it?

   Anyway. Part two. In which I go on writing about myself in
the third person. In which I continue to act stupidly. Stop reading if you want.

Conrad Linthor sits down without being asked. He's drinking
something frozen. "Sidekick girl. You look terrible."

   All during this conversation, picture superheroes of various
descriptions. They stroll or glide or stride purposefully past Billie's table. They nod at the guy sitting across from her. Billie
notices this without having the strength of character to wonder
what's going on. Every molecule of her being is otherwise engaged with processing a thousand lifetimes' worth of misery,

woe, self-hatred, heartbreak, shame, all-obliterating roiling nausea, and pain.

Billie says, "So we meet again." She can't help herself. It's the kind of thing you end up saying in a hotel full of superheroes. "I'm not a sidekick. My name's Billie."

"Whatever," Conrad Linthor says. "Conrad Linthor. So what happened to you?"

Billie swigs bitter espresso. She lets her hair fall in front of her face. Baby bird, she thinks. Leave me alone. Wrong smell.

But Conrad Linthor doesn't go away. He says, "All right, me first. Let's swap life stories. That girl at the desk when you were checking in? Aliss? I've slept with her a couple of times. When nothing better came along. She really likes me. And I'm an asshole, okay? No excuses. Every time I hurt her, though, the next time I see her I'm nice again and I apologize and I get her back. Mostly I'm nice just to see if she's going to fall for it this time, too. I don't know why. I guess I want to see where that place is, the place where she hauls off and assaults me. Some people have ant farms. I'm more into people. So now you know what was going on yesterday. And, yeah, I know, something's wrong with me."

Billie pushes her hair back. She says, "Why are you telling me all this?"

He shrugs. "I don't know. You look like you're in a world of hurt. I don't really care. It's just that I get bored. And you look really terrible, and I thought that there was probably something interesting going on. Besides, Aliss can see us in here, from the desk, and this will drive her crazy."

"I'm okay," Billie says. "Nobody hurt me. I'm the bad guy here."

"That's unexpected. Also interesting. Go on," Conrad Linthor says. "Tell me everything."

Billie tells him. Everything except for the part where she pees the bed.

When her tale is told, Conrad Linthor stands up and says, "Come on. We're going to go see a friend of mine. You need the cure."

"For love?" Billie's lame attempt at humor. She was wondering if telling someone what she's done would make her feel better. It hasn't.

"No cure for love," Conrad Linthor says. "Because there's no such thing. Your hangover we can do something about."

As they navigate the lobby, there are new boards up announcing that free teeth-whitening sessions are available in suite 412 for qualified superheroes. Billie looks over at the front desk and sees Aliss looking back. Aliss draws her finger across her throat. If looks could kill you wouldn't be reading this e-mail.

Conrad Linthor goes through a door that you're clearly not meant to go through. Billie follows anyway and they're in a corridor, in a maze of corridors. If this were an MMORPG, the zombies or the giant fruit bats or the gnoles with their intricately knotted, deadly ropes would show up any minute. Instead, every once in a while, they pass hotel cleaning staff; bellboys sneaking cigarettes. Everyone nods at Conrad Linthor, just like the superheroes in the Starbucks in the lobby.

Billie doesn't want to ask, but eventually she does. "Who *are* you?"

"Call me Eloise," Conrad Linthor says.

"Sorry?" Billie imagines that they are no longer in the hotel at all. The corridor they are currently navigating slopes gently downward. Maybe they will end up on the shores of a subterranean lake, or in a dungeon, or in Narnia, or King Nermal's Chamber, or even Keokuk, Iowa. It's a small world, after all. Bigger on the inside.

"You know, Eloise. The girl who lives in The Plaza? Has a pet whale named Moby Dick?"

He waits, like Billie's supposed to know what he's talking about. When she doesn't say anything, he says, "Never mind. It's just this book—a classic of modern children's literature, actually—about a girl who lives in The Plaza. Which is a hotel. A bit nicer than this one, maybe, but never mind. I live here."

He keeps on talking. They keep on walking.

Billie's hangover is a special effect. Conrad Linthor is going on and on about superheroes. His father is an agent. Apparently superheroes have agents. Represents all of the big guys. Knows everyone. Agoraphobic. Never leaves the hotel. Everyone comes to him. Big banquet tomorrow night, for his biggest client. Tyrannosaurus Hex. Hex is retiring. Going to go live in the mountains and breed tarantula wasps. Conrad Linthor's father is throwing a party for Hex. Everyone will be there.

Billie's legs are noodles. The ends of her hair are poison needles. Her tongue is a bristly sponge, and her eyes are bags of bleach.

Two wheeled carts come round the next corner like comets, followed at arm's length by hurtling busboys. They sail down the corridor at top speed. Conrad Linthor and Billie flatten themselves against the wall. "You have to move fast," Conrad explains. "Or else the food gets cold. Guests complain."

Around that corner, enormous doors, still swinging. Big enough to birth a Greyhound bus bound for Keokuk. A behemoth. A white whale. Billie passes through the doors onto the far shores of what is, of course, a hotel kitchen. Far away, miles, it seems to Billie, there are clouds of vapor and vague figures moving through them. Clanging noises, people yelling, the thick, sweet smell of caramelized onions, onions that will never make anyone cry again. Other savory reeks.

Conrad Linthor steers Billie to a marble-topped table. Copper whisks, mixing bowls, dinged pots hang down on hooks.

Billie feels she ought to say something. "You must have a lot of money," she contributes. "To live in a hotel."

"No shit, Sherlock," Conrad Linthor says. "Sit down. I'll be back."

Billie climbs, slowly and carefully, up a laddery stool and lays her poor head down on the dusty, funereal slab. (It's actually a pastry station, the dust is flour, but Billie is mentally in a bad place.) Paul Zell, Paul Zell. She stares at the tiled wall. Billie's heart has a crack in it. Her head is made of radiation. The Starbucks espresso she forced down has burnt a thousand pinprick holes in Billie's wretched stomach.

Conrad Linthor comes back too soon. He says, "This is her."

There's a guy with him. Skinny, with serious acne scars. Big shoulders. Funny little paper hat and a stained apron. "Ernesto, Billie," Conrad says. "Billie, Ernesto."

"How old did you say?" Ernesto says. He folds his arms, as if Billie is a bad cut of meat Conrad Linthor is trying to pass off as prime rib.

"Sixteen, right?"

Billie confirms.

"She came to the city because of some pervert she met online?"

"In an MMORPG," Conrad says.

"He isn't a pervert," Billie says. "He thought I was my sister. I was pretending to be my sister. She's in her thirties."

"What's your guess?" Conrad asks Ernesto. "Superhero or dentist?"

"One more time," Billie says. "I'm not here to audition for anything. And do I look like a dentist?"

"You look like trouble," Ernesto says. "Drink this." He hands her a glass full of something slimy and green.

"What's in it?" Billie says.

"Wheatgrass," Ernesto says. "And other stuff. Secret recipe. Hold your nose and drink it down."

"Yuck," Billie says. (I won't even try to describe the taste of Ernesto's hangover cure. Except, I will never drink again.) "Yuck, yuck, yuck."

"Keep holding your nose," Ernesto advises Billie. To Conrad: "They met online?"

"Yeah," Billie says. "In FarAway."

"Yeah, I know that game. Dentist," Ernesto says. "For sure."

"Except," Conrad says, "it gets better. It wasn't just a game. Inside this game, they were playing a game. They were playing *chess.*"

"Ohhhh," Ernesto says. Now he's grinning.

"Superhero," Conrad says. They high-five each other. "The only question is who."

"What was the alias again?" Ernesto asks Billie. "The name this dude gave?"

"Paul Zell?" Billie says. "Wait, you think Paul Zell is a superhero? No way. He does tech support for a nonprofit. Something involving endangered species."

Conrad Linthor and Ernesto exchange another look. "Superhero for sure," Conrad says.

Ernesto says, "Or supervillain. All those freaks are into chess. It's like a disease."

"No way," Billie says again.

Conrad Linthor says, "Because there's no chance Paul Zell would have lied to you about anything. Because the two of you were being completely and totally honest with each other." Which shuts Billie up.

Conrad Linthor says, "I just can't get this picture out of my head. This superhero going out and buying a ring. And there you are. This sixteen-year-old girl." He laughs. He nudges Billie as if to say, I'm not laughing at you. I'm laughing near you.

"And there I was," Billie says. "Here I am."

Ernesto has to gasp for air he is laughing so hard.

Billie says, "I guess it's kind of funny. In a horrible way."

"So, anyway," Conrad says. "Since Billie's into chess, I thought we ought to show her your project. Have they set up the banquet room yet?"

Ernesto stops laughing, holds his right hand out, like he's stopping traffic. "Hey, man. Maybe later? I've got prep. I'm salad station tonight. You know?"

"Ernesto's an artist," Conrad says. "I keep telling him he needs to make some appointments, take a portfolio downtown. My dad says people would pay serious bucks for what Ernesto does."

Billie isn't really paying attention to this conversation. She's thinking about Paul Zell. How could you be a superhero, Paul Zell? Can you miss something that big? A secret as big as that? Sure, she thinks. Probably you can miss it by a mile.

"I make things out of butter," Ernesto says. "It's no big deal.

Like, sure, someone's going to pay me a million bucks for something I carved out of butter."

"It's a statement," Conrad Linthor says, "an artistic statement about the world we live in."

"We live in a world made out of butter," Ernesto says. "Doesn't seem like much of a statement to me. You any good at chess?"

"What?" Billie says.

"Chess. You any good?"

"I'm not bad," Billie says. "You know, it's just for fun. Paul Zell's really good."

"So he wins most of the time?" Ernesto says.

"Yeah," Billie says. She thinks about it. "Wait, no. I guess I win more."

"You gonna be a superhero when you grow up? Because those guys are way into chess."

Conrad Linthor says, "It's the superhero triangle. Warning signs you might grow up to save the world. Chess is an indicator. Weird coincidences, that's another one. For example, you're always in the wrong place at the right time. Bed-wetting. Plus you have an ability of some kind."

"I don't have an ability," Billie says. "Not even one of those really pointless ones like always knowing the right time, or whether it's going to rain."

"Your power might develop later on," Conrad Linthor says.

"It won't."

"Well, okay. But it might," Conrad Linthor says. "It's why I noticed you in the first place. You stick out. She sticks out, right?"

"I guess," Ernesto says. He gives her that appraising-a-cut-of-meat look again. Then nods. "Sure. She sticks out. You stick out."

"I stick out," Billie says. "I stick out like what?"

"Even Aliss noticed," Conrad says. "She thought you were here to audition, remember?"

Ernesto says, "Oh, yeah. Because Aliss is such a fine judge of character."

"Shut up," Conrad says. "Look, Billie. It's not a bad thing, okay? Some people, you can just tell. So maybe you're just some girl. But maybe you can do something that you don't even know about yet."

"You sound like my guidance counselor," Billie says. "Like my sister. Why do people always try to tell you that life gets better? Like life has a bad cold. Like, here I am, and where is my sister right now? She drove my dad up to Peoria yesterday. To St. Francis, because he has pancreatic cancer. And that's the only reason I'm here, because my dad's dying, and so nobody is even going to notice that I'm gone. Lucky me, right?"

Ernesto and Conrad Linthor are both staring at her.

"I'm a superhero," Billie says. "Or a sidekick. Whatever you say. Paul Zell is a superhero, too. Everybody's a superhero. The world is made of butter. I don't even know what that means."

"How's the hangover?" Conrad Linthor asks her.

"Butter," Billie says. Not even intentionally. The hangover is gone. Of course she still feels terrible, but that's not hangover related. That's Paul Zell related. That's just everything else.

"Sorry about, you know, uh, your dad." That's Ernesto.

Billie shrugs. Grimaces. As if on cue, there is a piercing scream somewhere far away. Then a lot of shouting. Some laughing. Off in the distance, something seems to be happening. "Gotta go," Ernesto says.

"Ernesto!" It's a short guy in a tall hat. He says, "Hey, Mr. Linthor. What's up?"

"Gregor," Conrad says. "Hope that wasn't anything serious."

"Nah, man," the short guy says. "Just Portland. Sliced off the tip of his pointer finger. Again."

"See you, Conrad," Ernesto says. "Nice to meet you, Billie. Stay out of trouble."

As Ernesto goes off with the short guy, the short guy is saying, "So who's the girl? She looks like somebody. Somebody's sidekick?"

Conrad yells after them. "Maybe we'll see you later, okay?"

He tells Billie, "There's a thing tonight up on the roof. You ought to come by. Then maybe we can go see Ernesto's party sculptures."

"I may not be here," Billie says. "It's Paul Zell's room, not mine. What if he's checked out?"

"Then your key won't work," Conrad Linthor says. "Look, if you're locked out, just call up to the penthouse later and tell me and I'll see what I can do. Right now I've got to get to class."

"You're in school?" Billie says.

"Just taking some classes down at the New School," Conrad says. "Life drawing. Film studies. I'm working on a novel, but it's not like that's a full-time commitment, right?"

Billie is almost sorry to leave the kitchen behind. It's the first place in New York where she's been one hundred percent sure she doesn't have to worry about running into Paul Zell. It isn't that this is a good thing, it's just her spider sense isn't tingling all the time. Not that Billie has anything that's the equivalent of spider sense. And maybe room 1584 can also be considered a safe haven now. The room key still works. Someone has remade the bed, taken away the towels and sheets in the bathroom. Melinda's red sweater and skirt are hanging down over the shower rod. Someone rinsed them out first.

Billie orders room service. Then she decides to set out for Bryant Park. She'll go watch the chess players, which is what she and Paul Zell were going to do, what they talked about doing online. Maybe you'll be there, Paul Zell.

She has a map. She doesn't get lost. She walks the whole way. When she gets to Bryant Park, sure enough, there are some chess games going on. Old men, college kids, maybe even a few superheroes. Pigeons everywhere, underfoot. New Yorkers walking their dogs. A lady yelling at a phone. No Paul Zell. Not that Billie would know Paul Zell if she saw him.

Billie sits on a bench beside a trash can and after a while someone sits down beside her. Not Paul Zell. A superhero. The superhero from the hotel business center.

"We meet again," the superhero says.

Billie says, "Are you following me?"

"No," the superhero says. "Maybe. I'm Lightswitch."

"I've heard of you," Billie says. "You're famous."

"Famous is relative," Lightswitch says. "Sure, I've been on *Oprah*. But I'm no Tyrannosaurus Hex."

"There's a comic book about you," Billie says. "Although, uh, she doesn't look like you. Not really."

"The artist likes to draw boobs life-sized. Just the boobs."

They sit for a while in companionable silence. "You play chess?" Billie asks.

"Of course," Lightswitch says. "Doesn't everyone? Who's your favorite chess personage?"

"You mean player? Paul Morphy," Billie says. "Although Koneru Humpy has the best name ever."

"Agreed," Lightswitch says. "So are you in town for the shindig? Shindig. What kind of word is that? Archeological excavation of the shin. Knee surgery. Do you work with someone?"

"Do you mean, am I a sidekick?" Billie says. "No. I'm not a sidekick. I'm Billie Faggart. Hi."

"Sidekick. There's another one. Kick in the side. Pain in the neck. Kick in the shin. Ignore me. I get distracted sometimes." Lightswitch holds out a hand for Billie to shake, and Billie does. She thinks that there will be a baby jolt maybe, like one of those joke buzzers. But there's nothing. It's just an ordinary handshake, except Lightswitch's completely solid hand still looks funny, staticky, like it's really somewhere else. Billie can't remember if Lightswitch is from the future or the eighth dimension. Or maybe neither of those is quite right.

Two little kids come up and want Lightswitch's autograph. They look at Billie as if wondering whether they ought to ask for her autograph, too.

Billie stands up, and Lightswitch says, "Wait. Let me give you my card."

"Why?" Billie says.

"Just in case," Lightswitch says. "You might change your mind at some point about the sidekick thing. It isn't a long-term career, you know, but it's not a bad thing to do for a while. Mostly it's fan mail, photo ops, banter practice."

Billie says, "Um, what happened to your last sidekick?" And then, seeing the look on Lightswitch's face, wonders if this is not the kind of question you're supposed to ask a superhero.

"Fell off a building. Kidding. Sold her story to the tabloids. Used the proceeds to go to law school." Lightswitch kicks at a can. "Bam. Anyway. My card."

Billie looks, but there's nobody around to tell her what any of this means. Maybe you'd know, Paul Zell.

Billie says, "Do you know somebody named Paul Zell?"

"Paul Zell? Rings a bell. There's another one. Ding dong. Paul Zell. But no. I don't think I do, after all. It's a business card. Not an executive decision. Just take it, okay?" Lightswitch says. So Billie does.

Billie doesn't intend to show for Conrad Linthor's shindig. She walks aimlessly. Gawks at the gawkworthy. Pleasurably ponders a present for her sister, decides discretion is the better part of harmonious family relationships. Caped superheroes swoop and wheel and dip around the Empire State Building. No crime in progress. Show business. Billie walks until she has blisters. Doesn't think about Paul Zell. Paul Zell, Paul Zell. Doesn't think about Lightswitch. Pays twelve bucks to see a movie and don't ask me what movie or if it was any good. I don't remember. When she comes out of the movie theater, back out onto the street, everything sizzles with light. It's Fourth of July bright. Apparently New York is afraid of the dark. Billie decides she'll go to bed early. Get a wake-up call and walk down to Port Authority. Catch her bus. Go home to Keokuk and never think about New York again. Stay off FarAway. Concede the chess game. Burn the business card. But: Paul Zell, Paul Zell.

Meanwhile, back at the hotel, Aliss the nemesis has been lying in wait. Actually, it's more like standing behind a flower arrangement, but never mind. Aliss pounces. Billie is easy prey.

"Going to your boyfriend's party?" Aliss hisses. There's only one *s* in that particular sentence, but Aliss knows how to make an *s* count.

She links arms with Billie. Pulls her into an elevator.

"What party?" Billie says. "What boyfriend?" Aliss gives her a look. Hits the button marked Roof, then the emergency stop button, like she's opening cargo doors, one, two. Good-bye, cruel old world. That bomb is going to drop.

"If you mean Conrad Linthor," Billie says, "that was nothing. In the Starbucks. He just wanted to talk about you. In fact, he gave me this. Because he was afraid he was going to lose it. But he's planning on giving it to you. Tomorrow, I think."

She takes out the ring that you left behind, Paul Zell.

Surely you've checked the jeweler's box by now. Seen the ring is gone. Billie found it in the bedsheets that morning when she woke up. Remember? I was wearing it on my big toe. All day long Billie carried it around in her pocket, just like the business card. It didn't fit her ring finger.

I slipped it off and on, on and off all day long.

Billie and Aliss both stare at the ring. Both of them seem to find it hard to speak.

Finally: "It's mine?" Aliss says. She puts her hand out, like the ring's a cute dog. Not a ring. Like she wants to pet it. "That's a two-carat diamond. At least. Antique setting. Just explain one thing, please. Why did Conrad give you my ring? You expect me to believe he let some girl carry my engagement ring around all day?"

"Yeah, well, you know Conrad," Billie says.

"Yeah," Aliss says. She's silent for another long moment. "Can I?"

She takes the ring, tries it on her ring finger. It fits. There's an inappropriate ache in Billie's throat. Aliss says, "Wow. Just wow. I guess I have to give it back. Okay. I can do that." She holds up her hand. Drags the diamond along the glass elevator wall, then rubs at the scratch it's left behind. Then checks the diamond, like she might have damaged it. But a diamond is the superhero of the mineral world. Diamonds cut glass. Not the other way around.

Aliss presses the button. The elevator elevates.

"Maybe you should go to the party and I should just go to bed," Billie says. "I have to catch a bus in the morning."

"No," Aliss says. "Wait. Now I'm nervous. I can't go up there by myself. You have to come with me. Except we can't act like we're friends, because then Conrad will suspect something's up. That I *know*. You can't tell him I know."

"I won't. I swear," Billie says.

"How's my hair?" Aliss says. "Shit. Don't tell him, but they fired me. Just like that. I'm not supposed to be here. Management knew something was up with me and Conrad. I'm not the first girl he's gotten fired. But I'm not going to say anything right now. I'll tell him later."

Billie says, "That sucks."

"You have no idea," Aliss says. "It's such a crappy job. People are such assholes, and you still have to say have a nice day. And smile." She gives the ring back. Smiles.

The elevator opens on sky. There's a sign saying Private Party. Like the whole sky is a private party. It's just after nine o'clock. The sky is orange. The pool is the color the sky ought to be. There are superheroes splashing around in it. That bubble of blood floating above it, like an oversized beach ball. Tango music plays but no one is dancing.

Conrad Linthor lounges on a lounge chair. He comes over when he sees Billie and Aliss. "Girls," he says. He purrs, actually.

"Hey, Conrad," Aliss says. Her hip cocked like a gun hammer. Her hair is remarkable. The piercing is in. "Great party."

"Billie," Conrad says. "I'm so glad you came. There are some people you ought to meet." He takes Billie's arm and drags her off. Maybe he's going to throw her in the pool.

"Is Ernesto here?" Billie looks back, but Aliss is having a conversation now with someone in a uniform.

"This kind of party isn't really for hotel staff," Conrad says. "They get in trouble if they socialize with the guests."

"Don't worry about Aliss," Billie says. "Apparently she got fired. But you probably already know that."

Conrad smiles. They're on the edge of a group of strangers who all look vaguely familiar, vaguely improbable. There are scales, feathers, ridiculous outfits designed to show off ridiculous physiques. Why does everything remind Billie of FarAway? Except for the smell. Why do superheroes smell weird? Paul Zell.

The tango has become something dangerous. A woman is singing. There is nobody here that Billie wants to meet.

Conrad Linthor is drunk. Or high. "This is Billie," he says. "My sidekick for the night. Billie, this is everyone."

"Hi, everyone," Billie says. "Excuse me." She rescues her arm from Conrad Linthor. She heads for the elevator. Aliss has escaped the hotel employee and is crouched down by the pool, one finger in the water. Probably the deep end. You can tell by her slumped shoulders that she's thinking about drowning herself. A good move: perhaps someone here will save her. Once someone has saved your life, they might as well fall in love with you, too. It's just good economics.

"Wait," Conrad Linthor says. He's not that old, Billie decides. He's just a kid. He hasn't even done anything all that

bad, yet. And yet you can see how badness accumulates around
him. Builds up like lightning on a lightning rod. If Billie sticks
around, it will build up on her, too. That spider sense she doesn't
have is tingling. Paul Zell, Paul Zell.

"Ernesto will be so disappointed," Conrad Linthor says.
They're both jogging now. Billie sees the lit stair sign, decides
not to wait for the elevator. She takes the stairs two at a time.
Conrad Linthor bounds down behind her. "He really wanted
you to see what he made. For the banquet. It's too bad you can't
stay. I wanted to invite you to the banquet. You could meet Tyrannosaurus Hex. Get an autograph or two. Make some good
contacts. Being a sidekick is all about making the right contacts."

"I'm not a sidekick!" Billie yells up. "That was a dumb joke
even before you made it the first time. Even if I were a sidekick,
I wouldn't be yours. Like *you* would ever be a superhero. Just
because you know people. So what's your secret name, superhero? What's your superpower?"

She stops on the stairs so suddenly that Conrad Linthor runs
into her. They both stumble forward, smack into the wall on the
twenty-second-floor landing. But they don't fall.

Conrad Linthor says, "My superpower is money." The wall
props him up. "Only superpower that counts for anything. Better than invisibility. Better than being able to fly. Much better
than telekinesis or teleportation or that other one. Telepathy.
Knowing what other people are thinking. Why would you ever
want to know what other people are thinking? Did you know
everyone thinks that one day they might be a millionaire? Like
that's a lot of money. They have no idea. They don't want to be
a superhero. They just want to be like me. They want to be rich."

Billie has nothing to say to this.

"You know what the difference is between a superhero and a supervillain?" Conrad Linthor asks her.

Billie waits.

"The superhero has a really good agent," Conrad Linthor says. "Someone like my dad. You have no idea the kind of stuff they get away with. A sixteen-year-old girl is *nothing*."

"What about Lightswitch?" Billie says.

"Who? Her? She's no big deal," Conrad Linthor says. "Old school."

"I'm going to go to bed now," Billie says.

"No," Conrad Linthor says. "Wait. You have to come with me and see what Ernesto did. It's just so cool. Everything's carved out of butter."

"If I go see, will you let me go to bed?"

"Sure," Conrad Linthor says.

"Will you be nice to Aliss? If she's still up at the party when you get back?"

"I'll try," Conrad Linthor says.

"Okay," Billie says. "I'll go look at Ernesto's butter. Is he around?"

Conrad Linthor levers himself off the wall. Pats it. "Ernesto? I don't know where he is. How should I know?"

They go into the forbidden maze. Back to the kitchen, and through it, now empty and dark and somehow like a morgue. A mausoleum.

"Ernesto's been doing the work in a freezer," Conrad Linthor says. "You have to keep these guys cold. Wait. Let me get it un-locked. Cool tool, right? Borrowed it from The Empty Jar. He's one of dad's clients. They're making a movie about him. I saw the script. It's crap."

The lock comes off. The lights go on. Before I tell you what was inside the freezer, Paul Zell, first let me tell you something about how big the freezer is. It will help you visualize. The freezer is plenty big. Bigger than most New York apartments, Billie thinks, although this is just hearsay. She's never been in a New York apartment.

What's inside the supersized freezer? Supervillains. Warm Gun, The Nin-jew, Cat Lady, Hellalujah, Shibboleth, The Shambler, Mandroid, Manplant, The Manticle, Patty Cakes. Lots of others. Name a famous supervillain and he or she or zhe is in the freezer. They're life-sized. They're not real, although Billie's heart slams. She thinks: Who caught them all? How are they so perfectly still? Maybe Conrad Linthor is a superhero, after all.

Conrad Linthor touches Hellalujah's red, bunchy bicep. Presses just a little. The color smears. Lardy, yellow-white underneath.

The supervillains are made out of butter. "Hand tinted," Conrad says.

"Ernesto made these?" Billie says. She wants to touch one, too. She walks up to Patty Cakes. Breathes on the cold, outstretched palms. You can see Patty Cakes's lifeline. Her love line. Billie realizes something else. The butter statues are all decorated to look like chess pieces. Their signature outfits have been changed to black and red. Cat Lady is wearing a butter crown.

Conrad Linthor puts his hand on Hellalujah's shoulder. Puts his arm around Hellalujah. Then he squeezes, hard. His arm goes through Hellalujah's neck. Like an arm going through butter. The head pops off.

"Careful!" Billie says.

"I can't believe it's butter," Conrad says. He giggles. "Come on. Can you believe this? He made a whole chess set out of butter. And why? For some banquet for some guy who used to fight crime? That's just crap. This is better. Us here having some fun. This is spontaneous. Haven't you always wanted to fight the bad guy and win? Now's your chance."

"But Ernesto made these!" Billie's fists are clenched.

"You heard him," Conrad says. "It's no big deal. It's not art. There's no statement here. It's just butter."

He has Hellalujah's sad head in his arms. "Heavy," he says. "Catch. Food fight." He throws the head at Billie. It hits her in the chest and knocks her over.

She lies on the cold floor, looking at Hellalujah's head. One side is flat. Half of Hellalujah's broad nose is stuck like a slug to Billie's chest. Her right arm is slimy with colored butter.

Billie sits up. She cradles Hellalujah's head, hurls it back at Conrad. She misses. Hellalujah's head smacks into Mandroid's shiny stomach. Hangs there, half embedded.

"Funny," Conrad Linthor says.

Billie shrieks. She leaps at him, her hands killing claws. They both go down on top of The Shambler. Billie brings her knee up between Conrad Linthor's legs, drives it up into butter. She grabs Conrad Linthor by the hair, bangs his head on The Shambler's head. "Ow," Conrad Linthor says. "Ow, ow, ow."

He wriggles under her. Gets hold of her hands, pulls at them even as she tightens her grip on his hair. His hair is slick with butter and she can't hold on. She lets go. His head flops down. "Get off," he says. "Get off."

Billie drives her elbow into his stomach. Her feet skid a little as she stands up. She grabs hold of Warm Gun's gun for balance and it breaks off. "Sorry," she says, apologizing to butter. "I'm sorry. So sorry."

Conrad Linthor is trying to sit up. There's spit at the corner of his mouth, or maybe it's butter.

Billie runs for the door. Gets there just as Conrad Linthor realizes what she's doing. "Wait!" he says. "Don't you dare! You bitch!"

Too late. She's got the door shut. She leans against it, smearing it with butter.

Conrad Linthor pounds on the other side. "Billie!" It's a faint yell. Barely audible. "Let me out, okay? It was just fun. I was just having fun. It was fun, wasn't it?"

Here's the thing, Paul Zell. It was fun. That moment when I threw Hellalujah's head at him? That felt good. It felt so good I'd pay a million bucks to do it again. I can admit that now. But I don't *like* that it felt good. I don't like that it felt like fun. But I guess now I understand why supervillains do what they do. Why they run around and destroy things. Because it feels fantastic. Someday I'm going to buy a lot of butter and build something out of it, just so I can tear it all to pieces again.

Billie could leave Conrad Linthor in the freezer. Walk away. Somebody would probably find him. Right?

But then she thinks about what he'll do in there. He'll kick apart all of the other buttervillains. Stomp them into greasy pieces. She knows he'll do it because she can imagine doing the same thing.

So in a little while she lets him out.

"Not funny," Conrad Linthor says. He looks very funny.

Picture him, all decked out in red and black butter. His lips are purplish-bluish. He's shivering with cold. So is Billie. "Not funny at all," Billie agrees. "What the hell was that? Ernesto's your friend. How could you do that to him?"

"He's not really a friend," Conrad Linthor says. "Not like you and me. He's just some guy I hang out with sometimes. Friends are boring. I get bored."

"We're not friends," Billie says.

"Sure," Conrad Linthor says. "I know that. But I thought if I said we were, you might fall for it. You have no idea how stupid some people are. Besides I was doing it for you. No, really. I was. Sometimes when a superhero is in a really bad situation, that's when they finally discover their ability. What they can do. With some people it's an amulet, or a ring, but mostly it's just environmental. Your adrenaline kicks in. My father is always trying stuff on me just in case I've got something that we haven't figured out yet."

Maybe some of this is true and maybe all of it is true and maybe Conrad Linthor is just testing Billie again. Is she that stupid? He's watching her right now, to see if she's falling for any of this.

"I'm out of here," Billie says. She checks her pocket just to make sure Paul Zell's ring is still there. She's been doing that all day.

"Wait," Conrad Linthor says. "You don't know how to get back. You need help."

"I made a trail," Billie says. All the way through the corridors this time, she pressed the diamond along the wall. Left a thin little mark. Nothing anyone else would even know to look for.

"Fine," Conrad Linthor says. "I'm going to stay down here and make some scrambled eggs. Sure you don't want any?"

"I'm not hungry," Billie says.

Even as she's leaving, Conrad Linthor is explaining to her that they'll meet again. This is their origin story. Maybe they're each other's nemesis or maybe they're destined to team up and save the world and make lots of—

Eventually Billie can't hear him anymore. She leaves a trail of butter all the way back to the lobby. Gets in an elevator before anyone has noticed the state she's in, or maybe by this point in the weekend the hotel staff have dealt with stranger things.

She takes a shower and goes to bed still smelling of butter. She wakes up early.

The bubble of blood is down in the lobby again, floating over the fountain.

Billie thinks about going over to ask for an autograph. Pretending to be a fan. Could you pop that bubble with a ballpoint pen? This is the kind of thought Conrad Linthor goes around thinking, she's pretty sure.

Billie catches her bus. And that's the end of the story, Paul Zell. Dear Paul Zell.

Except for the ring. Here's the thing about the ring. Billie wrapped it in tissue paper and sealed it up in a hotel envelope. She wrote "Ernesto in the kitchen" on the outside of the envelope. She wrote a note. The note said: "This ring belongs to Paul Zell. If he comes looking for it, maybe he'll give you a reward. A couple hundred bucks seems fair. Tell him I'll pay him back. But if he doesn't get in touch, you should keep the ring. Or sell it. I'm sorry about Hellalujah and Mandroid and The Shambler. I didn't know what Conrad Linthor was going to do."

So Paul Zell. That's the whole story. Except for the part where I got home and found the e-mail from you, the one where you explained what had happened to you. That you had an emergency appendectomy and never made it to New York at all, and what happened to me? Did I make it to the hotel? Did I wonder where you were? You say you can't imagine how worried and/or angry I must have been. Etc.

I'll be honest with you, Paul Zell. I read your e-mail and part of me thought, I'm saved. We'll both pretend none of this ever happened. I'll go on being Melinda and Melinda will go on being the Enchantress Magic EightBall and Paul Zell, whoever Paul Zell is, will go on being the Master Thief Boggle.

But that would be crazy. I would be a fifteen-year-old liar, and you would be some weird guy who's so pathetic and lonely that he's willing to settle for me. Not even for me. To settle for the person I was pretending to be. But you're better than that, Paul Zell. You have to be better than that. So I wrote you this letter.

If you read this letter the whole way through, now you know what happened to your ring, and a lot of other things, too. I still have your conditioner. If you give Ernesto the reward, let me know and I'll sell Constant Bliss and the Enchantress Magic EightBall. So I can pay you back. It's not a big deal. I can go be someone else, right?

Or else, I guess, you could ignore this letter. We could pretend I never sent it. That I never came to New York to meet Paul Zell. That Paul Zell wasn't going to give me a ring.

We could pretend that you never discovered my secret identity. We could meet up a couple times a week in FarAway and
play chess. We could go on a quest. Save the world. We could
chat. Flirt. I could tell you about Melinda's week and we could
pretend that maybe someday we're going to be brave enough to
meet face-to-face.

But here's the deal, Paul Zell. I'll be older one day. I may never
discover my superpower. I don't think I want to be a sidekick.
Not even yours, Paul Zell. Although maybe that would have
been simpler. If I'd been honest. And if you're what or who I
think you are. And: maybe I'm not even being honest now.
Maybe I'd settle for sidekick. For being your sidekick. If that was
all you offered.

Conrad Linthor is crazy and dangerous and a bad person, but
I think he's right about one thing. He's right that sometimes
people meet again. Even if we never really truly met each other,
I want to believe you and I will meet again. I want you to know
that there was a reason that I bought a bus ticket and came to
New York. The reason was that I love you. That part was really
true. I really did throw up on Santa Claus once. I can do twelve
cartwheels in a row. May third is my birthday, not Melinda's. I'm
allergic to cats. I love you. I didn't lie to you about everything.

When I'm eighteen, I'm going to take the bus back to New
York City. I'm going to walk down to Bryant Park. And I'm
going to bring my chess set. I'm going to do it on my birthday.
I'll be there all day long.

Your move, Paul Zell.

Valley of the Girls

O nce, for about a month or two, I decided I was going to be a different kind of guy. Muscley. Not always thinking so much. My body was going to be a temple, not a dive bar. The kitchen made me smoothies, raw eggs blended with kale and wheat germ and bee pollen. That sort of thing. I stopped drinking, flushed all of Darius's goodies down the toilet. I was civil to my Face. I went running. I read the books, did the homework my tutor assigned. I was a model son, a good brother. The Olds didn't know what to think.

Hero, of course, knew something was up. Hero always knew. Maybe she saw the way I watched her Face when there was an event and we all had to do the public thing.

Meanwhile I could see the way that Hero's Face looked at my Face. There was no way this was going to end well. So I gave up on raw eggs and virtue and love. Fell right back into the old life, the high life, the good, sweet, sour, rotten old life. Was it much of a life? It had its moments.

"Oh, shit," (Hero) says. "I think I've made a terrible mistake. Help me, ( ). Help me, please?"

She drops the snake. I step hard on its head. Nobody here is having a good night.

"You have to give me the code," I say. "Give me the code and I'll go get help."

She bends over and pukes stale champagne on my shoes. There are two drops of blood on her arm. "It hurts," she says. "It hurts really bad!"

"Give me the code, (Hero)."

She cries for a while, and then she stops. She won't say anything. She just sits and rocks. I stroke her hair, and ask her for the code. When she doesn't give it to me, I go over and start trying numbers. I try her birthday, then mine. I try a lot of numbers. None of them work.

I chased the same route every day for that month. Down through the woods at the back of the main guesthouse, into the Valley of the Girls just as the sun was coming up. That's how you ought to see the pyramids, you know. With the sun coming up. I liked to take a piss at the foot of (Alicia)'s pyramid. Later on I told (Alicia) I pissed on her pyramid. "Marking your territory, ( )?" she said. She ran her fingers through my hair.

I don't love (Alicia). I don't hate (Alicia). Her Face has this plush, red mouth. Once I put a finger up against her lips, just to see how they felt. You're not supposed to mess with people's Faces, but everybody I know does it. What's the Face going to do? Quit?

But (Alicia) has better legs. Longer, rounder, the kind you want to die between. I wish she were here right now. The sun is up, but it isn't going to shine on me for a long time. We're down here in the cold, and (Hero) isn't speaking to me.

What is it with rich girls and pyramids, anyway?

In hieroglyphs, you put the names of the important people, kings and queens and gods, in a cartouche. Like this.

(Stevie)

(Preeti)

(Nishi)

(Hero)

(Alicia)

(Liberty)

(Vyvienne)

(Yumiko)

( )

"Were you really going to do it?" (Hero) wants to know. This is before the snake, before I know what she's up to.

"Yeah," I say.

"Why?"

"Why not?" I say. "Lots of reasons. 'Why' is kind of a dumb question, isn't it? I mean, why did God make me so pretty? Why size four jeans?"

There's a walk-in closet in the burial chamber. I went through it looking for something useful. Anything useful. Silk shawls, crushed velvet dresses, black jeans in the wrong size. A stereo system loaded with the kind of music rich goth girls listen to. Extra pillows. Sterling silver. Perfumes, makeup. A mummified cat. (Noodles). I remember when (Noodles) died. We were eight. They were already laying the foundations of (Hero)'s pyramid. The Olds called in the embalmers.

We helped with the natron. I had nightmares for a week.

(Hero) says, "They're for the afterlife, okay?"

"You're not going to be fat in the afterlife?" At this point, I still don't know (Hero)'s plan, but I'm starting to worry. (Hero) has a taste for the epic. I suppose it runs in the family.

"My *Ba* is skinny," (Hero) says. "Unlike yours, (   ). You may be skinny on the outside, but you have a fat-ass heart. Anubis will judge you. Ammit will devour you."

She sounds so serious. I should laugh. You try laughing when you're down in the dark, in your sister's secret burial chamber— not the decoy one where everybody hangs out and drinks, where once—oh, God, how sweet is that memory still—you and your sister's Face did it on the memorial stone—under three hundred thousand limestone blocks, down at the bottom of a shaft behind a door in an antechamber that maybe somebody, in a couple of hundred years, will stumble into.

What kind of afterlife do you get to have as a mummy? If you're (Hero), I guess you believe your *Ba* and *Ka* will reunite in the afterlife. (Hero) thinks she's going to be an *Akh,* an immortal. She and the rest of them go around stockpiling everything they think they need to have an excellent afterlife. The Olds indulge them. The girls plan for the afterlife. The boys play sports, collect race cars or twentieth-century space shuttles, scheme to get laid. I specialize in the latter.

The girls have *ushabti* made of themselves, give them to each other at the pyramid dedication ceremonies, the sweet sixteen parties. They collect *shabti* of their favorite singers, actors, whatever. They read *The Book of the Dead.* In the meantime, their pyramids are where we go to have a good time. When I commissioned the artist who makes my *ushabti,* I had her make two different kinds. One is for people I don't know well. The other *shabti* is for the girls I've slept with. I modeled for that one in the nude. If I'm going to hang out with these girls in the afterlife, I want to have all my working parts.

Me, I've done some reading, too. What happens once you're a mummy? Grave robbers dig you up. Sometimes they grind you up and sell you as medicine, fertilizer, pigment. People used to have these mummy parties. Invite their friends over. Unwrap a mummy. See what's inside.

Maybe nobody ever finds you. Maybe you end up in a display case in a museum. Maybe your curse kills lots of people. I know which one I'm hoping for.

"(   )," (Yumiko) said, "I don't want this thing to be boring. Fireworks and Faces, celebrities promoting their new thing."

This was earlier.

Once (Yumiko) and I did it in (Angela)'s pyramid, right in front of a false door. Another time she punched me in the side of the face because she caught me and (Preeti) in bed. Gave me a cauliflower ear.

(Yumiko)'s pyramid isn't quite as big as (Stevie)'s, or even (Preeti)'s pyramid. But it's on higher ground. From up on top, you can see down to the ocean.

"So what do you want me to do?" I asked her.

"Just do something," (Yumiko) said.

I had an idea right away.

"Let me out, (Hero)."

We came down here with a bottle of champagne. (Hero) asked me to open it. By the time I had the cork out, she'd shut the door. No handle. Just a keypad.

"Eventually you're going to have to let me out, (Hero)."

"Do you remember the watermelon game?" (Hero) says. She's lying on a divan. We're reminiscing about the good old times. I think. We were going to have a serious talk. Only it turned out it wasn't about what I thought it was about. It wasn't about the movie I'd made. The *erotic film*. It was about the other thing.

"It's really cold down here," I say. "I'm going to catch a cold."

"Tough," (Hero) says.

I pace a bit. "The watermelon game. With (Vyvienne)'s unicorn?" (Vyvienne)'s mother is twice as rich as God. (Vyvienne)'s pyramid is three times the size of (Hero)'s. She kisses like a fish, fucks like a fiend, and her hobby is breeding chimeras. Most of the estates around here have a real problem with unicorns now, thanks to (Vyvienne). They're territorial. You don't mess with them in mating season.

Anyway, I came up with this variation on French bullfighting, *Taureau Piscine,* except with unicorns. You got a point every time you and the unicorn were in the swimming pool together. We did *Licorne Pasteque,* too. Brought out a side table and a couple of chairs and set them up on the lawn. Cut up the watermelon and took turns. You can eat the watermelon, but only while you're sitting at the table. Meanwhile the unicorn is getting more and more pissed off that you're in its territory.

It was insanely awesome until the stupid unicorn broke its leg going into the pool, and somebody had to come and put a bullet in its head. Plus, the Olds got mad about one of the chairs. Turned out to be an antique. Priceless. The unicorn broke the back to kindling.

"Do you remember how (Vyvienne) cried and cried?" (Hero) says. Even this is part of the happy memory for (Hero). She hates (Vyvienne). Why? Some boring reason. I forget the specifics. Here's the gist of it: (Hero) is fat. (Vyvienne) is a bitch.

"I felt sorrier for whoever was going to have to clean up the pool," I say.

"Liar," (Hero) says. "You've never felt sorry for anyone in your life. You're a textbook sociopath. You were going to kill all of our friends. I'm doing the world a huge favor."

"They aren't your friends," I say. "None of them even like you. I don't know why you'd want to save a single one of them."

(Hero) says nothing. Her eyes get pink.

I say, "They'll find us eventually." We've both got implants, of course. Implants to keep the girls from getting pregnant, to make us puke if we try drugs or take a drink. There are ways to get around this. Darius is always good for new solutions. The implant—the Entourage—is also a way for our parents' security teams to monitor us. In case of kidnappers. In case we go places that are off-limits, or run away. Rich people don't like to lose their stuff.

"This chamber has some pretty interesting muffling qualities," Hero says. "I installed the hardware myself. Top-gear spy stuff. You know, just in case."

"In case of what?" I ask.

She ignores that. "Also, I paid a guy for three hundred thousand microdot trackers. One hundred and fifty have your profile. One hundred and fifty have mine. They're programmed to go on and off-line in random clusters, at irregular intervals, for the next three months, starting about ten minutes ago. You think you're the only one in the world who suffers. Who's unhappy. You don't even see me. You've been so busy obsessing over Tara and Philip, you never notice anything else."

"Who?" I say.

"Your Face and my Face," Hero says. "You freak." There are tears in her eyes, but her voice stays calm. "Anyway. The trackers are being distributed to partygoers at raves worldwide tonight. They're glued onto promotional material inside a CD for one of my favorite bands. Nobody you'd know. Oh, and all the guests at Yumiko's party got one, too, and I left a CD at all of the false doors at all of the pyramids, like offerings. Those are all live right now."

I've always been the good-looking one. The popular one. Sometimes I forget that Hero is the smart one.

"I love you, ⬚."

Liberty falls in love all the time. But I was curious. I said, "You love me? Why do you love me?"

She thought about it for a minute. "Because you're insane," she said. "You don't care about anything."

"That's why you love me?" I said. We were at a gala or something. We'd just come back from the men's room, where everybody was trying out Darius's new drug.

My Face was hanging out with my parents in front of all the cameras. The Olds love my Face. The son they wish they had. Somebody with a tray walked by and Hero's Face took a glass of champagne. She was over by the buffet table. The other buffet table, the one for Faces and the Olds and the celebrities and the publicists and all the other tribes and hangers-on.

My darling. My working girl. My sister's Face. I tried to catch her eye, clowning in my latex leggings, but I was invisible. Every gesture, every word was for them, for him. The cameras. My Face. And me? A speck of nothing. Not even a blot. Negative space.

She'd said we couldn't see each other anymore. She said she was afraid of getting caught breaking contract. Like that didn't happen all the time. Like with Mr. Amandit. Preeti and Nishi's father. He left his wife. It was Liberty's Face he left his wife for. The Face of his daughters' best friend. I think they're in Iceland now, Mr. Amandit and the nobody girl who used to be a Face.

Then there's Stevie. Everybody knows she's in love with her own Face. It's embarrassing to watch.

Anyway, nobody knew about us. I was always careful. Even if Hero got her nose in, what was she going to say? What was she going to do?

"I love you because you're you, ⬚," Liberty said. "You're the only person I know who's better looking than their own Face."

I was holding a skewer of chicken. I almost stabbed it into Liberty's arm before I knew what I was doing. My mouth was full of chewed chicken. I spat it out at Liberty. It landed on her cheek.

"What the fuck, ⬚!" Liberty said. The piece of chicken plopped down onto the floor. Everybody was staring. Nobody took a picture. I didn't exist. Nobody had done anything wrong.

Aside from that, we all had a good time. Even Liberty says so. That was the time all of us showed up in this gear I found online. Red rubber, plenty of pointy stuff, chains and leather, dildos and codpieces, vampire teeth and plastinated viscera. I had a really nice pair of hand-painted latex tits wobbling around like epaulets on my shoulders. I had an inadequately sedated fruit bat caged up in my pompadour. So how could she not look at me?

Kids today, the Olds say. What can you do?

I may be down here for some time. I'm going to try to see it the way they see it, the Olds.

You're an Old. So you think, wouldn't it be easier if your children did what they were told? Like your employees? Wouldn't it be nice, at least when you're out in public with the family? The Olds are rich. They're used to people doing what they're told to do.

When you're as rich as the Olds are, you are your own brand.

That's what their people are always telling them. Your children are an extension of your brand. They can improve your Q rating or they can degrade it. Mostly they can degrade it. So there's the device they implant that makes us invisible to cameras. The Entourage.

And then there's the Face. Who is a nobody, a real person, who comes and takes your place at the table. They get an education, the best health care, a salary, all the nice clothes and all the same toys that you get. They get your parents whenever the Olds' team decides there's a need or an opportunity. If you go online, or turn on the TV, there they are, being you. Being better than you will ever be at being you. When you look at yourself in the mirror, you have to be careful, or you'll start to feel very strange. Is that really you?

Most politicians have Faces, too. For safety. Because it shouldn't matter what someone looks like, or how good they are at making a speech, but of course it does. The difference is that politicians choose to have their Faces. They choose.

The Olds like to say it's because we're children. We'll understand when we're older, when we start our adult lives without blemish, without online evidence of our mistakes, our indiscretions. No sexytime videos. No embarrassing photos of ourselves in Nazi regalia or topless in Nice. No footage before the nose job, before the boob job, before the acne clears up.

The Olds get us into good colleges, and then the world tilts just for a moment. Our Faces retire. We get a few years to make our own mistakes, out in the open, and then we settle down, and we come into our millions or billions or whatever. We inherit the earth, like that proverb says. The rich shall inherit the earth.

We get married, merge our money with other money, improve our Q ratings, become Olds, acquire kids, and you bet your ass those kids are going to have Faces, just like we did.

I never got into the Egyptian thing the way the girls did. I always liked the Norse gods better. You know. Loki. The slaying of Baldur. Ragnarok.

None of the other guys showed up for (Yumiko)'s party. It's just their Faces. The guys all left for the moon about a week ago. They've been partying up there all week. I've never been into the space travel thing. Plenty of ways to have fun without leaving the planet.

It wasn't hard to get hold of the thing I was looking for. Darius couldn't help me, but he knew a guy who knew a guy who knew exactly what I was talking about. We met in Las Vegas, because why not? We saw a show together, and then we went online and watched a video that had been filmed in his lab. Somewhere in Moldova, he said. He said his name was Nikolay.

I showed him my video. The one I'd made for the party for (Yumiko)'s pyramid dedication thingy.

We were both very drunk. I'd taken Darius's blocker, and Nikolay was interested in that. I explained about the Entourage, how you had to work around it if you wanted to have fun. He was sympathetic.

He liked the video a lot.

"That's me," I told him. "That's (   )."

"Not you," he said. "You're making joke at me. You have Entourage device. But, girl, she's very nice. Very sexy."

"That's my sister," I said. "She's seventeen."

"Another joke," Nikolay said. "But, if my sister, I would go ahead, fuck her anyway."

"How could you do this to me?" (Hero) wants to know.

"It had nothing to do with you." I pat her back when she starts to cry. I don't know whether she's talking about the sexy video or the other thing.

"It was bad enough when you slept with her," she says, weeping. "That was practically incest. But I saw the video." So: the video, then. "The one you gave (Yumiko). The one she's going to put online. Don't you understand? She's me. He's you. That's us, on that video, that's us having sex."

"It was good enough for the Egyptians," I say, trying to console her. "Besides, it isn't us. Remember? They aren't us."

I try to remember what it was like when it was just us. The Olds say we slept in the same crib. I was a baby, she climbed in. (Hero) cried when I fell down. (Hero) has always been the one who cries.

"How did you know what I was planning?"

"Oh, please, ( )," (Hero) says. "I always know when you're about to go off the deep end. You go around with this smile on your face, like the whole world is sucking you off. Besides, Darius told me you'd been asking about really bad shit. He likes me, you know. He likes me much better than you."

"He's the only one," I say.

"Fuck you," Hero says. "Anyway, it's not like you were the only one with plans for tonight. I'm sick of this place. Sick of these people."

There is a martial line of *shabti* on a stone shelf. Our friends. People who would like to be our friends. Rock stars that the Olds used to hang out with, movie stars. Saudi princes who like fat, gloomy girls with money. She picks up a prince, throws it against the wall.

"Fuck Vyvienne and all her unicorns," Hero says.

She picks up another *shabti*. "Fuck Yumiko."

I take Yumiko from her. "I did," I say. "I give her a three out of five. For enthusiasm." I drop the *shabti* on the floor.

"You are so vile,   ," Hero says. "Have you ever been in love? Even once?"

She's fishing. She knows. Of course she knows.

Why did you sleep with him? Are you in love with him? He's me. Why aren't I him? Fuck both of you.

"Fuck our parents," I say. I pick up an oil lamp and throw it at the *shabti* on the shelf.

The room gets brighter for a moment, then darker.

"It's funny," Hero says. "We used to do everything together. And then we didn't. And right now, it's weird. You planning on doing what you were going to do. And me, what I was planning. It's like we were in each other's brains again."

"You went out and bought a biological agent? We should have gone in on it together. Buy two, get one free."

"No," Hero says. She looks shy, like she's afraid I'll laugh at her.

I wait. Eventually she'll tell me what she needs to tell me and then I'll hand over the little metal canister that Nikolay gave me, and she'll unlock the door to the burial chamber. Then we'll go back up into the world and that video won't be the end of the world. It will just be something that people talk about. Something to make the Olds crazy.

"I was going to kill myself," (Hero) says. "You know, down here. I was going to come down here after the fireworks, and then I decided that I didn't want to be alone when I did it."

Which is just like (Hero). Throws a pity party, then realizes she's forgotten to send out invitations.

"And then I found out what you were up to," (Hero) says. "I thought I ought to stop you. I wouldn't have to be alone. And I would finally live up to my name. I'd save everybody. Even if they never knew it."

"You were going to kill yourself?" I say. "For real? Like with a gun?"

"Like with this," (Hero) says. She reaches into the jeweled box on her belt. There's a little thing curled up in there, an enameled loop of chain, black and bronze. It uncoils in her hand, becomes a snake.

(Alicia) was the first one to get a Face. I got mine when I was eight. I didn't really know what was going on. I met all these boys my age, and then the Olds sat down and had a talk with me. They explained what was going on, said that I got to pick which Face I wanted. I picked the one who looked the nicest, the one who looked like he might be fun to hang out with. That's how stupid I was back then.

(Hero) couldn't choose, so I did it for her. Pick *her*, I said. That's how strange life is. I picked her out of all the others.

Yumiko said she'd already had the conversation with her Face. (We talk to our Faces as little as possible, although sometimes we sleep with each other's. Forbidden fruit is always freakier. Is that why I did what I did? I don't know. How am I supposed to know?) Yumiko said her Face agreed to sign a new contract when Yumiko turns eighteen. She doesn't see any reason to give up having a Face.

Nishi is Preeti's younger sister. They only broke ground on Nishi's pyramid last summer. Upper management teams from her father's company came out to lay the first course of stones. A team-building exercise. Usually it's lifers from the supermax prison out in Pelican Bay. Once they get to work, they mostly look the same, lifers and upper management. It's hard work. We like to go out and watch.

Every once in a while a consulting archaeologist or an architect will come over and try to make conversation. They think we want context.

They talk about grave goods, about how one day future archaeologists will know what life was like because some rich girls decided they wanted to build their own pyramids.

We think that's funny.

They like to complain about the climate. Apparently it isn't ideal. "Of course, they may not be standing give or take a couple of hundred years. Once you factor in geological events. Earthquakes. There's the geopolitical dimension. There's grave robbers."

They go on and on about the cunning of grave robbers.

We get them drunk. We ask them about the curse of the mummies just to see them get worked up. We ask them if they aren't worried about the Olds. We ask what used to happen to the men who built the pyramids in Egypt. Didn't they used to disappear? we ask. Just to make sure nobody knew where the good stuff was buried? We say there are one or two members of the consulting team who worked on (Alicia)'s pyramid that we were friendly with. We mention we haven't been able to get hold of them in a while, not since the pyramid was finished.

They were up on the unfinished outer wall of (Nishi)'s pyramid. I guess they'd been up there all night. Talking. Making love. Making plans.

They didn't see me. Invisible, that's what I am. I had my phone. I filmed them until my phone ran out of memory. There was a unicorn down in the meadow by a pyramid. (Alicia)'s pyramid. Two impossible things. Three things that shouldn't exist. Four.

That was when I gave up on becoming someone new, the running, the kale, the whole thing. That was when I gave up on becoming the new me. Somebody already had that job. Somebody already had the only thing I wanted.

"Give me the code." I say it over and over again. I don't know how long it's been. (Hero)'s arm is green and black and all blown up like a party balloon. I tried sucking out the poison. Maybe that did some good. Maybe I didn't think of it soon enough. My lips are a little tingly. A little numb.

"⬚?" Hero says. "I don't want to die."

"You aren't going to die," I say. "Give me the code. Let me save you."

"I don't want them to die," Hero says. "If I give you the code, you'll do it. And I'll die down here by myself."

"You're not going to die," I say. I stroke her cheek. "I'm not going to kill anyone."

After a while she says, "Okay." Then she tells me the code. Maybe it's a string of numbers that means something to her. More likely it's random. I told you she was smarter than me.

I repeat the code back to her and she nods. I've covered her up with a shawl, because she's so cold. I lay her head down on a pillow, brush her hair back.

She says, "You loved her better than you loved me. It isn't fair. Nobody ever loved me best."

"What makes you think I loved her?" I say. "You think this was all about love? Really, Hero? This was just me being dumb again. And you, saving the day."

She closes her eyes. Gives me a horrible, blind smile.

I go over to the door and enter the code.

The door doesn't open. I try again and it still doesn't open.

"Hero? Give me the code again?"

She doesn't say anything. I go over and shake her gently. "Tell me the code one more time. Come on. One more time."

Her eyes stay closed. Her mouth falls open. Her tongue sticks out.

"Hero." I pinch her arm. Say her name over and over again. Then I go nuts. I make kind of a mess. It's a good thing Hero isn't around to see.

And now it's a little bit later, and Hero is still dead, and I'm still trapped down here with a dead hero and a dead cat and a bunch of broken *shabti*s. No food. No good music. Just a small canister of something nasty cooked up by my good friend Nikolay, and a department store's worth of size four jeans and the dregs of a bottle of very expensive champagne.

The Egyptians believed that every night the spirit of the person buried in a pyramid rose up through the false doors to go out into the world. The *Ba*. The *Ba* can't be imprisoned in a small dark room at the bottom of a deep shaft hidden under some pile of stones. Maybe I'll fly out some night, some part of me. The best part. The part of me that was good. I keep trying combinations, but I don't know how many numbers (Hero) used, what combination. It's a Sisyphean task. It's something to do. There's not much oil left to light the lamps. The lamps that are left. I broke most of them.

Some air comes in through the bottom of the door, but not much. It smells bad in here. I wrapped (Hero) up in her shawls and hid her in the closet. She's in there with (Noodles). I put (Noodles) in her arms. Every once in a while I fall asleep and when I wake up I realize I don't know which numbers I've tried, which I haven't.

The Olds must wonder what happened. They'll think it had something to do with that video. Their people will be doing damage control. I wonder what will happen to my Face. What will happen to *her*. Maybe one night I'll fly out. My *Ba* will fly right to her, like a bird.

One day someone will open the door that I can't. I'll be alive or else I won't. I can open the canister or I can leave it closed.

What would you do? I talk about it with (Hero), down here in the dark. Sometimes I decide one thing, sometimes I decide another.

Dying of thirst is a hard way to die.

I don't really want to drink my own urine.

If I open the canister, I die faster. It will be my curse on you, the one who opens the tomb. Why should you go on living when she and I are dead? When no one remembers our names?

(Hero).

Tara.

I don't want you to know my name. It was his name, really.

Origin Story

Origin Story

"Dorothy Gale," she said.

"I guess so." He said it grudgingly. Maybe he wished that he'd thought of it first. Maybe he didn't think going home again was all that heroic.

They were sitting on the side of a mountain. Above them, visitors to the Land of Oz theme park had once sailed in molded plastic balloon gondolas over the Yellow Brick Road. Some of the support pylons tilted back against scrawny little opportunistic pines. There was something majestic about the pylons now that their work was done. Fallen giants. Moth-eaten blue ferns grew over the peeling yellow bricks.

The house of Dorothy Gale's aunt and uncle had been cunningly designed. You came up the path, went into the front parlor, and looked around. You were led through the kitchen. There were dishes in the kitchen cabinets. Daisies in a vase. Pictures on the wall. Follow your Dorothy down into the cellar with the rest of your group, watch the movie tornado swirl around on the dirty dark wall, and when everyone tramped up the other, identical set of steps through the other, identical cellar door, it was the same house, same rooms, but tornado-tipped. The parlor floor now slanted and when you went out through the (back) front door, there was a pair of stockinged plaster legs sticking out from under the house. A pair of ruby slippers. A yellow brick road. You weren't in North Carolina anymore.

The whole house was a ruin now. None of the pictures hung straight. There were salamanders in the walls and poison ivy coming up in the kitchen sink. Mushrooms in the cellar, and an old mattress someone had dragged down the stairs. You had to hope Dorothy Gale had moved on.

It was four in the afternoon and they were both slightly drunk. Her name was Bunnatine Powderfinger. She called him Biscuit.

She said, "Come on, of course she is. The ruby slippers, those are like her special power. It's all about how she was a superhero the whole time, only she didn't know it. And she comes to Oz from another world. Like Superman in reverse. And she has lots of sidekicks." She pictured them skipping down the road, arm in arm. Facing down evil. Dropping houses on it, throwing buckets of water at it. Singing stupid songs and not even caring if anyone was listening.

He grunted. She knew what he thought. Sidekicks were for people who were too lazy to write personal ads. "The Wizard of Oz. He even has a secret identity. And he wants everything to be green, all of his stuff is green, just like Green Lantern."

The thing about green was true, but so beside the point that she could hardly stand it. The Wizard of Oz was a humbug. She said, "But he's *not* great and powerful. He just pretends to be great and powerful. The Wicked Witch of the West is greater and more powerfuller. She's got flying monkeys. She's like a mad scientist. She even has a secret weakness. Water is like Kryptonite to her." She'd always thought the actress Margaret Hamilton was damn sexy. The way she rode that bicycle and the wind that picked her up and carried her off like an invisible lover; that funny, mocking, shrill little piece of music coming out of nowhere. That nose.

When she looked over, she saw that he'd put his silly outfit back on inside out. How often did that happen? There was an ant in her underwear. She made the decision to find this erotic, and then realized it might be a tick. No, it was an ant. "Margaret Hamilton, baby," she said. "I'd do her."

He was watching her wriggle, of course. Too drunk at the moment to do anything. That was fine with her. And she was too drunk to feel embarrassed about having ants in her pants. Just like that Ella Fitzgerald song. *Finis, finis.*

The big lunk, her old chum, said, "I'd watch. But she turns into a big witchy puddle when she gets a bucketful in the face. Not good. When it rains does she say, Oops, sorry, can't fight crime today? Interesting sexual subtext there, by the way. Very girl on girl. Girl meets nemesis, gets her wet, she melts. Screeches orgasmically while she does it, too."

How could he be drunk and talk like that? There were more ants. Had she been lying on an ant pile while they did it? Poor ants. Poor Bunnatine. She stood up and took her dress and her underwear off—no silly outfits for her—and shook them vigorously. Come out with your little legs up, you ants. She pretended she was shaking some sense into him. Or maybe what she wanted was to shake some sense out of him. Who knew? Not her.

She said, "Margaret Hamilton wouldn't fight crime, baby. She'd conquer the world. She just needs a wet suit. A sexy wet suit." She put her clothes back on again. Maybe that's what she needed. A wet suit. A prophylactic to keep her from melting. The booze didn't work at all. What did they call it? A social lubricant. And it helped her not to care so much. Anesthetic. It helped hold her together afterward, when he left town again. Superglue.

No bucket of water at hand. She could throw the rest of her beer, but then he'd just look at her and say, Why'd you do that, Bunnatine? It would hurt his feelings. The big lump.

He said, "Why are you looking at me like that, Bunnatine?"

"Here. Have another Little Boy," she said, giving up, passing him a wide mouth. Yes, she was sitting on an anthill. It was definitely an anthill. Tiny superheroic ants were swarming out to defend their hill, chase off the enormous and evil although infinitely desirable doom of Bunnatine's ass. "It'll put hair on your chest and then make it fall out again."

"Enjoy the parade?" Every year, the same thing. Balloons going up and up like they couldn't wait to leave town and pudding-faced cloggers on pickup trucks and on the curbs teenage girls holding signs. WE LOVE YOU. I LOVE YOU MORE. I WANT TO HAVE YOUR SUPER BABY. Teenage girls not wearing bras. Poor little sluts. The big lump never even noticed and too bad for them if he did. She could tell them stories.

He said, "Yeah. It was great. Best parade ever."

Anyone else would've thought he was being one hundred percent sincere. Nobody else knew him like she did. He looked like a sweetheart, but even when he tried to be gentle, he left bruises.

She said, "I liked when they read all the poetry. Big bouncy guy / way up in the lonely sky."

"Yeah. So whose idea was that?"

She said, "*The Daily Catastrophe* sponsored it. Mrs. Dooley over at the high school got all her students to write the poems. I saved a copy of the paper. Figured you'd want it for your scrapbook."

"That's the best part about saving the world. The poetry. That's why I do it." He was throwing rocks at an owl that was hanging out on a tree branch for some reason. It was probably sick. Owls didn't usually do that. A rock knocked off some leaves. Blam! Took off some bark. Pow! The owl just sat there.

She said, "Don't be a jerk."

"Sorry."

She said, "You look tired."

"Yeah."

"Still not sleeping great?"

"Not great."

"Little Red Riding Hood."

"No way." His tone was dismissive. *As if,* Bunnatine, you dumb bunny. "Sure, she's got a costume, but she gets eaten. She doesn't have any superpowers. Baked goods don't count."

"Sleeping Beauty?" She thought of a girl in a moldy old

tower, asleep for a hundred years. Ants crawling over her. Mice. Some guy's lips. That girl must have had the world's worst morning breath. Amazing to think that someone would kiss her. And kissing people when they're asleep? She didn't approve. "Or does she not count, because some guy had to come along and save her?"

He had a faraway look in his eyes. As if he were thinking of someone, some girl he'd watched sleeping. She knew he slept around. Grateful women saved from evildoers or obnoxious blind dates. Models and movie stars and transit workers and trapeze artists, too, probably. She read about it in the tabloids. Or maybe he was thinking about being able to sleep in for a hundred years. Even when they were kids, he'd always been too jumpy to sleep through the night. Always coming over to her house and throwing rocks at the window. His face at her window. Wake up, Bunnatine. Wake up. Let's go fight crime.

He said, "Her superpower is the ability to sleep through anything. Origin story: she tragically pricks her finger on a spinning wheel. What's with the fairy tales and kids' books, Bunnatine? Rapunzel's got lots of hair that she can turn into a hairy ladder. Not so hot. Who else? The girl in Rumpelstiltskin. She spins straw into gold."

She missed these conversations when he wasn't around. Nobody else in town talked like this. The mutants were sweet, but they were more into music. They didn't talk much. It wasn't like talking with him. He always had a comeback, a wisecrack, a double entendre, some cheesy sleazy pickup line that cracked her up, that she fell for every time. It was probably all that witty banter during the big fights. She'd probably get confused. Banter when she was supposed to *POW! POW!* when she was meant to banter.

She said, "You've got it backward. Rumpelstiltskin spins the straw into gold. She just uses the poor freak and then she hires somebody to go spy on him to find out his name."

"Cool."

She said, "No, it's not cool. She cheats."

"So what? Was she supposed to give up her kid to some little guy who spins gold?"

"Why not? I mean, she probably wasn't the world's best parent or anything. Her kid didn't grow up to be anyone special. There aren't any fairy tales about that kid."

"Your mom."

She said, "What?"

"Your mom! C'mon, Bunnatine. She was a superhero."

"My mom? Ha *ha*."

He said, "I'm not joking. I've been thinking about this for a few years. Being a waitress? Just her disguise."

She made a face and then unmade it. It was what she'd always thought: he'd had a crush on her mom. "So what's her superpower?"

He gnawed on a fingernail with those big square teeth. "I don't know. I don't know her secret identity. It's secret. So you don't pry. It's bad form, even if you're archenemies. But I was at the restaurant once when we were in high school and she was carrying eight plates at once. One was a bowl of soup, I think. Three on each arm, one between her teeth, and one on top of her head. Because somebody at the restaurant bet her she couldn't."

"Yeah, I remember that. She dropped everything. And she chipped a tooth."

"Only because that fuckhead Robert Potter tripped her," he pointed out.

"It was an accident."

He picked up her hand. Was he going to bite her fingernail now? No, he was studying the palm. Like he was going to read it or something. It wasn't hard, reading a waitress's palm. You'll spend the rest of your life getting into hot water. He said gently, "No, it wasn't. I saw the whole thing. He knew what he was doing."

It embarrassed her to see how small her hand was in his. As if he'd grown up and she just hadn't bothered. She still remembered when she'd been taller. "Really?"

"Really. Robert Potter is your mother's nemesis."

She took her hand back. Slapped a beer in his. "Stop making fun of my mom. She doesn't have a nemesis. And why does that word always sound like someone's got a disease? Robert Potter's just a fuckhead."

"Once Potter said he'd pay me ten dollars if I gave him a pair of Mom's underwear. It was when Mom and I weren't getting along. I was like fourteen. We were at the grocery store and she slapped me for some reason. So I guess he thought I'd do it. Everybody saw her slap me. I think it was because I told her Rice Krispies were full of sugar and she should stop trying to poison me. So he came up to me afterward in the parking lot."

Beer made you talk too much. Add that to the list. It wasn't her favorite thing about beer. Next thing she knew, she'd be crying about some dumb thing or begging him to stay.

He was grinning. "Did you do it?"

"No. I told him I'd do it for twenty bucks. So he gave me twenty bucks and I just kept it. I mean, it wasn't like he was going to tell anyone."

"Cool."

"Yeah. Then I made him give me twenty more dollars. I said if he didn't, I'd tell my mom the whole story."

That wasn't the whole story, either, of course. She didn't imagine she'd ever tell him the whole story. But the result of the story was that she had enough money for beer and some weed. She paid some guy to buy beer for her. That was the night she'd brought Biscuit up here.

They'd done it on the mattress in the basement of the wrecked farmhouse, and later on they'd done it in the theater, on the pokey little stage where girls in blue dresses and flammable wigs used to sing and tap-dance. Leaves everywhere. The smell of smoke, someone farther up the mountain, checking on their still, maybe, chain-smoking. Reading girly magazines. Biscuit saying, Did I hurt you? Is this okay? Do you want another beer? She'd wanted to kick him, make him stop trying to take care of her, and also to go on kissing him. She always felt that way around Biscuit. Or maybe she always felt that way and Biscuit had nothing to do with it.

He said, "So did you ever tell her?"

"No. I was afraid that she'd go after him with a ball-peen hammer and end up in jail."

When she got home that night. Her mother looking at Bunnatine like she knew everything, but she didn't, she didn't. She said: "I know what you've been up to, Bunnatine. Your body is a temple and you treat it like dirt."

So Bunnatine said: "I don't care." She'd meant it, too.

"I always liked your mom."

"She always liked you." Liked Biscuit better than she liked Bunnatine. Well, they both liked him better. Thank God her mother had never slept with Biscuit. She imagined a parallel universe in which her mother fell in love with Biscuit. They went off together to fight crime. Invited Bunnatine up to their secret hideaway/love nest for Thanksgiving. She showed up and wrecked the place. They went on *Oprah*. While they were in the studio some supervillain—sure, okay, that fuckhead Robert Potter—implemented his dreadful, unstoppable, terrible plan. That parallel universe was his to loot, pillage, discard like a half-eaten grapefruit, and it was all her fault.

The thing was, there *were* parallel universes. She pictured poor parallel Bunnatine, sent a warning through the mystic veil that separates universes. Go on *Oprah* or save the world? Do whatever you have to do, baby.

The Biscuit in this universe said, "Is she at the restaurant tonight?"

"Her night off," Bunnatine said. "She's got a poker night with some friends. She'll come home with more money than she makes in tips and lecture me about the evils of gambling."

"I'm pretty pooped anyway," he said. "All that poetry wore me out."

"So where are you staying?"

He didn't say anything. She hated when he did this.

She said, "You don't trust me, baby?"

"Remember Volan Crowe?"

"What? That kid from high school?"

"Yeah. Remember his superhero comics?"

"He drew comics?"

"He made up Mann Man. A superhero with all the powers of Thomas Mann."

"You can't go home again."

"That's the other Thomas. Thomas Wolfe."

"Thomas Wolfman. A hairy superhero who gets lost driving home whenever the moon is full."

"Thomas Thomas Virginia Woolfman Woman."

"Now with extra extra superpowers."

"Whatever happened to him?"

"Didn't he die of tuberculosis?"

"Not him. I mean that kid."

"Didn't he turn out to have a superpower?"

"Yeah. He could hang pictures perfectly straight on any wall. He never needed a level."

"I thought he tried to destroy the world."

"Yeah, that's right. He was calling himself something weird. Fast Kid with Secret Money. Something like that."

"What about you?"

She said, "Me?"

"Yeah."

"Keeping an eye on this place. They don't pay much, but it's easy money. I had another job, but it didn't work out. A place down off I-40. They had a stage, put on shows. Nothing too gross. So me and Kath, remember how she could make herself glow, we were making some extra cash two nights a week. They'd turn down the lights and she'd come out onstage with no clothes on and she'd be all lit up from inside. It was real pretty. And when it was my turn, guys could pay extra money to come and lie on the stage. Do you remember that hat, my favorite hat? The oatmeal-colored one with the pom-poms and the knitted ears?"

"Yeah."

"Well, they kept it cold in there. I think so that we'd have perky tits when we came out onstage. So we'd move around with a bit more rah-rah. But I wore the hat. I got management to let me wear the hat, because I don't float real well when my ears get cold."

"I gave you that hat," he said.

"I loved that hat. So I'd be wearing the hat and this dress— something modest, girl next door—and come out onstage and hover a foot above their faces. So they could see I wasn't wearing any underwear."

He was smiling. "Saving the world by taking off your underwear, Bunnatine?"

"Shut up. I'd look down and see them lying there on the stage like I'd frozen them." *Zap.* "They weren't supposed to touch me. Just look. I always felt a million miles above them. Like I was a bird." *A plane.* "All I had to do was scissor my legs, kick a little, just lift up my hem a little. Do twirls. Smile. They'd just lie there and breathe hard like they were doing all the work. And when

the music stopped, I'd float offstage again. But then Kath left for
Atlantic City to go sing in a cabaret show. And then some asshole got frisky. Some college kid. He grabbed my ankle and I
kicked him in the head. So now I'm back at the restaurant with
Mom."

He said, "How come you never did that for me, Bunnatine?
Float like that?"

She shrugged. "It's different with you," she said, as if it were.
But of course it wasn't. Why should it be?

"Come on, Bunnatine," he said. "Show me your stuff."

She stood up, shimmied her underwear down to her ankles
with an expert wriggle. All part of the show. "Close your eyes for
a sec."

"No way."

"Close your eyes. I'll tell you when to open them."

He closed his eyes and she took a breath, let herself float up.
She could only get about two feet off the ground before that old
invisible hand yanked her down again, held her tethered just
above the ground. She used to cry about that. Now she just
thought it was funny. She let her underwear dangle off her big
toe. Dropped it on his face. "Okay, baby. You can open your eyes."

His eyes were open. She ignored him, hummed a bit. *Why oh
why oh why can't I.* Held out her dress at the hem so that she
could look down the neckline and see the ground, see him
looking back up.

"Shit, Bunnatine," he said. "Wish I'd brought a camera."

She thought of all those girls on the sidewalk. "No touching,"
she said, and touched herself.

He grabbed her ankle and yanked. Yanked her all the way
down. Stuck his head up inside her dress, and his other hand.

Grabbed a breast and then her shoulder so that she fell down on top of him, knocked the wind out of her. His mouth propping her up, her knees just above the ground, cheek banged down on the bone of his hip. It was like a game of Twister, there was something Parker Brothers about his new outfit. There was a gusset in his outfit, so he could stop and use the bathroom, she guessed, when he was out fighting crime. Not get caught with his pants down. His busy, busy hand was down there, undoing the Velcro. The other hand was still wrapped around her ankle. His face was scratchy. Bam, pow. Her toes curled.

He said up into her dress, "Bunnatine. Bunnatine."

"Don't talk with your mouth full, Biscuit," she said.

She said, "There was a tabloid reporter around, wanting to hear stories."

He said, "If I ever read about you and me, Bunnatine, I'll come back and make you sorry. I'm saying that for your own good. Do something like that, and they'll come after you. They'll use you against me."

"So how do you know they don't know already? Whoever *they* are?"

"I'd know," he said. "I can smell those creeps from a mile away."

She got up to pee. She said, "I wouldn't do anything like that anyway." She thought about his parents and felt bad. She shouldn't have said anything about the reporter. Weasel-y guy. Staring at her tits when she brought him coffee.

She was squatting behind a tree when she saw the yearlings. Two of them. They were trying so hard to be invisible. Just dappled spots hanging in the air. They were watching her like they'd never seen anything so fucked up. Like the end of the world. They took off when she stood up. "That's right," she said. "Get the hell away. Tell anybody about this and I'll kick your sorry Bambi asses."

She said, "Okay. So I've been wondering about this whole costume thing. Your new outfit. I wasn't going to say anything, but it's driving me nuts. What's with all these crazy stripes and the embroidery?"

"You don't like it?"

"I like the lightning bolt. And the tower. And the frogs. It's psychedelic, Biscuit. Can you please explain why y'all wear such stupid outfits? Promise I won't tell anyone."

"They aren't stupid."

"Yes, they are. Tights are stupid. It's like you're showing off. Look how big my dick is."

"Tights are comfortable. They allow freedom of movement. They're machine washable." He began to say something else, then stopped. Grinned. Said, almost reluctantly, "Sometimes you hear stories about some asshole stuffing his tights."

She started to giggle. Giggling gave her the hiccups. He whacked her on the back.

She said, "Ever forget to run a load of laundry? Have to fight crime when you ought to be doing your laundry instead?"

He said, "Better than a suit and tie, Bunnatine. You can get a sewing machine and go to town, *dee eye why*, but who has the time? It's all about advertising. Looking big and bold. But you don't want to be too designer. Too Nike or Adidas. So last year I needed a new outfit, asked around, and found this women's co-operative down on a remote beach in Costa Rica. They've got an arrangement with a charity here in the States. Collection points in forty major cities where you drop off bathing suits and leotards and bike shorts, and then everything goes down to Costa Rica. There's a beach house some big-shot rock star donated to them. A big glass and concrete slab and the tide goes in and out right under the glass floor. I went for a personal fitting. These women are real artists, talented people, super creative. They're all unwed mothers, too. They bring their kids to work and the kids are running around everywhere and they're all wearing these really great superhero costumes. They do work for anybody. Even pro wrestlers. Villains. Crime lords, politicians. Good guys and bad guys. Sometimes you'll be fighting somebody, this real asshole, and you'll both be getting winded, and then you start noticing his outfit and he's looking, too, and then you're both wondering if you got your outfits at this same place. And you feel like you ought to stop and say something nice about what they're wearing. How you both think it's so great that these women can support their families like this."

"I still think tights look stupid." She thought of those kids wearing their superhero outfits. Probably grew up and became drug dealers or maids or organ donors.

"What? What's so funny?"

He said, "I can't stop thinking about Robert Potter and your mother. Did he want clean underwear? Or did he want dirty underwear?"

She said, "What do you think?"

"I think twenty bucks wasn't enough money."

"He's a creep."

"So you think he's been in love with her for a long time?"

She said, "What?"

"Like maybe they had an affair once a long time ago."

"No way!" It made her want to puke.

"No, seriously, what if he was your father or something?"

"Fuck you!"

"Well, come on. Haven't you wondered? I mean, he could be your father. It's always been obvious he and your mom have unfinished business. And he's always trying to talk to you."

"Stop talking! Right now!"

"Or what, you'll kick my ass? I'd like to see you try." He sounded amused.

She wrapped her arms around herself. Ignore him, Bunnatine. Wait until he's had more to drink. *Then* kick his ass.

He said, "Come on. I remember when we were kids. You used to wait until your mom got home from work and fell asleep. You said you used to sneak into her bedroom and ask her questions while she was sleeping. Just to see if she would tell you who your dad was."

"I haven't done that for a while. She finally woke up and caught me. She was really pissed off. I've never seen her get mad like that. I never told you about it. I was too embarrassed."

He didn't say anything.

"So I kept begging and finally she made up some story about this guy from another planet. Some *tourist*. Some tourist with wings and stuff. She said that he's going to come back someday. That's why she never shacked up or got married. She's still waiting for him to come back."

"Don't look at me like that. I know it's bullshit. I mean, if he had wings, why don't I have wings? That would be so cool. To fly. Really fly. Even when I used to practice every day, I never got more than two feet off the ground. Two fucking feet. What's two feet good for? Waiting tables. I float sometimes, so I don't get varicose veins like Mom."

"You could probably go higher if you really tried."

"You want to see me try? Here, hold this. Okay. One, two, three. Up, up, and a little bit more up. See?"

He frowned, looked off into the trees. Trying not to laugh. She knew him.

"What? Are you impressed or not?"

"Can I be honest? Yes and no. You could work on your technique. You're a bit wobbly. And I don't understand why all your hair went straight up and started waving around. Do you know that it's doing that?"

"Static electricity?" she said. "Why are you so mean?"

"Hey," he said. "I'm just trying to be honest. I'm just wondering why you never told me any of that stuff about your dad. I could ask around, see if anybody knows him."

"It's not any of your business," she said. "But thanks."

"I thought we were better friends than this, Bunnatine."

He was looking hurt.

"You're still my best friend in the whole world," she said. "I promise."

"I love this place," he said.

"Yeah. Me, too." Only if he loved it so much, then why didn't he ever stay? So busy saving the world, he couldn't save the Land of Oz. Those poor Munchkins. Poor Bunnatine. They were almost out of beer.

He said, "So what are they up to? The developers? What are they plotting?"

"The usual. Tear everything down. Build condos."

"And you don't mind?"

"Of course I mind!" she said.

He said, "I always think it looks a lot more real now. The way it's falling all to pieces. The way the Yellow Brick Road is disappearing. It makes it feel like Oz was a real place. Being abandoned makes you more real, you know?"

Beer turned him into Biscuit the philosopher-king. Another thing about beer. She had another beer to help with the philosophy. He had one, too.

She said, "Sometimes there are coyotes up here. Bears, too. The mutants. Once I saw a Sasquatch and two tiny Sasquatch babies."

"No way."

"And lots and lots of deer. Guys come up here in hunting season. When I catch 'em, they always make jokes about hunting Munchkins. I think they're idiots to come up here with guns. Mutants don't like guns."

"Who does?" he said.

She said, "Remember Tweetsie Railroad? That rickety roller coaster? Remember how those guys dressed like toy-store Indians used to come onto the train?"

He said, "Fudge. Your mom would buy us fudge. Remember how we sat in the front row and there was that one showgirl? The one with the three-inch ruff of pubic hair sticking out the legs of her underwear? During the cancan?"

She said, "I don't remember that!"

He leaned over her, nibbled on her neck. People were going to think she'd been attacked by a pod of squids. Little red sucker marks everywhere. She yawned.

He said, "Oh, come on! You remember! Your mom started laughing and couldn't stop. There was a guy sitting right next to us and he kept taking pictures."

She said, "How do you remember all this stuff? I kept a diary all through school, and I still don't remember everything that you remember. Like, what I remember is how you wouldn't speak to me for a week because I said I thought *Atlas Shrugged* was boring. How you told me the ending of *The Empire Strikes Back* before I saw it. 'Hey, guess what? Darth Vader is Luke's father!' When I had the flu and you went without me?"

He said, "You didn't believe me."

"That's not the point!"

"Yeah. I guess not. Sorry about that."

"I miss that hat. The one with the pom-poms. Some drunk stole it out of my car."

"I'll buy you another one."

"Don't bother. It's just I could fly better when I was wearing it."

He said, "It's not really flying. It's more like hovering."

"What, like leaping around like a pogo stick makes you special? Okay, so apparently it does. But you look like an idiot. Those enormous legs. That outfit. Anyone ever tell you that?"

"Why are you such a pain in the ass?"

"Why are you so mean? Why do you have to win every fight?"

"Why do you, Bunnatine? I have to win because I have to. I have to win. That's my job. Everybody always wants me to be a nice guy. But I'm a good guy."

"What's the difference again?"

"A nice guy wouldn't do this, Bunnatine. Or this."

"Say you're trapped in an apartment building. It's on fire. You're on the sixth floor. No, the tenth floor."

She was still kind of stupid from the first demonstration. She said, "Hey! Put me down! You asshole! Come back! Where are you going? Are you going to leave me up here?"

"Hold on, Bunnatine. I'm coming back. I'm coming to save you. There. You can let go now."

She held on to the branch like anything. The view was so beautiful she couldn't stand it. You could almost ignore him, pretend you'd gotten up here all by yourself.

He kept jumping up. "Bunnatine. Let go." He grabbed her wrist and yanked her off. She made herself as heavy as possible. The ground rushed up at them and she twisted, hard. Fell out of his arms.

"Bunnatine!" he said.

She caught herself a foot before she smacked into the ruins of the Yellow Brick Road.

"I'm fine," she said, hovering. But she was better than fine! How beautiful it was from down here, too.

He looked so anxious. "God, Bunnatine, I'm sorry." It made her want to laugh to see him so worried. She put her feet down gently. The whole world was made of glass, and the glass was full of champagne, and Bunnatine was a bubble, just flicking up and up and up.

She said, "Stop apologizing, okay? It was great! The look on your face. Being in the air like that. Come on, Biscuit, again! Do it again! I'll let you do whatever you want this time."

"You want me to do it again?" he said.

She felt just like a little kid. She said, "Do it again! Do it again!"

She shouldn't have gotten in the car with him, of course. But he was just old pervy Potter and she had the upper hand. She explained how he was going to give her more money. He just sat there listening. He said they'd have to go to the bank. He drove her right through town, parked the car behind the Food Lion.

She wasn't worried. She still had the upper hand. She said, "What's up, pervert? Gonna do a little Dumpster diving?"

He was looking at her. He said, "How old are you?"

She said, "Fourteen."

He said, "Old enough."

"How come you left after high school? How come you always leave?"

He said, "How come you broke up with me in eleventh grade?"

"Don't answer a question with a question. No one likes it when you do that."

"Well, maybe that's why I left. Because you're always yelling at me."

"You ignored me in high school. Like you were ashamed of me. *I'll see you later, Bunnatine. Quit it, Bunnatine. I'm busy.* Didn't you think I was cute? There were plenty of guys at school who thought I was cute."

"They were all idiots."

"I didn't mean it like that. I just meant that they were really idiots. Come on, you know you thought so, too."

"Can we change the subject?"

"Okay."

"It wasn't that I was ashamed of you, Bunnatine. You were distracting. I was trying to keep my average up. Trying to learn something. Remember that time we were studying and you tore up all my notes and ate them?"

"I saw they still haven't found that guy. That nutcase. The one who killed your parents."

"No. They won't." He threw rocks at where the owl had been. Nailed that sorry, invisible, absent owl.

"Yeah?" she said. "Why not?"

"I took care of it. He wanted me to find him, you know?

He just wanted to get my attention. That's why you gotta be careful, Bunnatine. There are people out there who really don't like me."

"Your dad was a sweetheart. Always tipped twenty percent. A whole dollar if he was just getting coffee."

"Yeah. I don't want to talk about him, Bunnatine. Still hurts. You know?"

"Yeah. Sorry. So how's your sister doing?"

"Okay. Still in Chicago. They've got a kid now. A little girl."

"Yeah. I thought I heard that. Cute kid?"

"She looks like me, can you imagine? She seems okay, though. Normal."

"Are we sitting in poison ivy?"

"No. Look. There's a deer over there. Watching us."

"When do you have to be at work?"

"Not until six A.M. I just need to go home first and take a shower."

"Cool. Is there any beer left?"

"No. Sorry," she said. "Should've brought more."

"That's okay. I've got this. Want some?"

"Why don't you leave?"

"Why go wait tables in some other place? I like it here. This is where I grew up. It was a good place to grow up. I like all the trees. I like the people. I even like how the tourists drive real slow between here and Boone. I just need to find a new job or Mom and I are going to end up killing each other."

"I thought you were getting along."

"Yeah. As long as I do exactly what she says."

"I saw her at the parade. With some little kid."

"Yeah. She's been babysitting for a friend at the restaurant. Mom's into it. She's been reading the kid all these fairy tales. She can't stand the Disney stuff, which is all the kid wants. Now they're reading *The Wizard of Oz*. I'm supposed to get your autograph, by the way. For the kid."

"Sure thing! You got a pen?"

"Oh, shit. It doesn't matter. Maybe next time."

It got dark slow and then real fast at the end, the way it always did, even in the summer, like daylight realized it had to be somewhere right away. Somewhere else. On weekends she came up here and read mystery novels in her car. Moths beating at the windows. Got out every once in a while to take a walk and look for kids getting into trouble. She knew all the places they liked to go. Sometimes the mutants were down where the stage used to be, practicing. They'd started a band. They were always asking if she was sure she couldn't sing. She really, really couldn't sing. That's okay, the mutants always said. You can just howl. Scream. We're into that. They traded her 'shine for cigarettes. Told her long, meandering mutant jokes with lots of hand gestures and incomprehensible punch lines. Dark was her favorite time. In the dark she could imagine that this really was the Land of Oz, that when the sun couldn't stay away any longer, when the sun finally came back up, she'd still be there. In Oz. Not here.

Click those heels, Bunnatine. There's no home like a summer place.

She said, "Still having nightmares?"

"Yeah."

"The ones about the end of the world?"

"Yeah, you nosy bitch. Those ones."

"Still ends in the big fire?"

"No. A flood."

"Remember that television show?"

"Which one?"

"You know. *Buffy the Vampire Slayer.* Even Mom liked it."

"I saw it a few times."

"I keep thinking about how that vampire, Angel, whenever he got evil, you knew he was evil because he started wearing black leather pants."

"Why are you obsessed with what people wear? Shit, Bunnatine. It was just a TV show."

"Yeah, I know. But those black leather pants he wore, they must have been his *evil* pants. Like fat pants."

"What?"

"Fat pants. The kind of pants that people who get thin keep in their closet. Just in case they get fat again."

He just looked at her. His big ugly face was all red and blotchy from drinking.

She said, "So my question is this. Does Angel the vampire keep a pair of black leather pants in his closet? Just in case? Like fat pants? Do vampires have closets? Or does he donate his evil pants to Goodwill when he's good again? Because if so then every time he turns evil, he has to go buy new evil pants."

He said, "It's just television, Bunnatine."

"You keep yawning."

He smiled at her. Such a nice-boy smile. Drove girls of all ages wild. He said, "I'm just tired."

"Parades can really take it out of you."

"Fuck you."

She said, "Go on. Take a nap. I'll stay awake and keep lookout for mutants and nemesissies and autograph hounds."

"Maybe just for a minute or two. You'd really like him."

"Who?"

"The nemesis I'm seeing right now. He's got a great sense of humor. Sent me a piano crate full of albino kittens last week. Some project he's working on. They pissed everywhere. Had to find homes for them all. Of course, first we checked to make sure that they weren't little bombs or possessed by demons or programmed to hypnotize small children with their swirly red kitten eyes. Give them bad dreams. That would have been a real PR nightmare."

"So what's up with this one? Why does he want to destroy the world?"

"He won't say. I don't think his heart's really in it. He keeps doing all these crazy stunts, like with the kittens. There was a thing with a machine to turn everything into tomato juice. But somebody who used to hang out with him says he doesn't even like tomato juice. If he ever tries to kidnap you, Bunnatine, whatever you do, don't say yes if he offers you a game of chess. Try to stay off the subject of chess. He's one of those guys who think all master criminals ought to be chess players, but he's terrible. He gets sulky."

"I'll try to remember. Are you comfortable? Put your head here. Are you cold? That outfit doesn't look very warm. Do you want my jacket?"

"Stop fussing, Bunnatine. Am I too heavy?"

"Go to sleep, Biscuit."

His head was so heavy she couldn't figure out how he carried it around on his neck all day. He wasn't asleep. She could hear him thinking.

He said, "You know, someday I'm going to fuck up. Someday I'll fuck up and the world won't get saved."

"Yeah. I know. A big flood. That's okay. You just take care of yourself, okay? And I'll take care of myself and the world will take care of itself, too."

Her leg felt wet. Gross. He was drooling on her leg. He said, "I dream about you, Bunnatine. I dream that you're drowning, too. And I can't do anything about it. I can't save you."

She said, "You don't have to save me, baby. Remember? I float. Let everything turn into water. Just turn into water. Let it turn into beer. Tomato juice. Let the Land of Oz sink. Ozlantis. Little happy mutant Dorothy mermaids. Let all those mountain houses and ski condos go down, all the way down and the deer and the bricks and the high school girls and the people who never tip. It isn't all that great a world anyway, you know? Biscuit? Maybe it doesn't want to be saved. So stop worrying so much. I'll float.

I'm Ivory soap. Won't even get my toes wet until you come and find me."

"Oh, good, Bunnatine," he said, drooling, "that's a weight off my mind"—and fell asleep. She sat beneath his heavy head and listened to the air rushing around up there in the invisible leaves. It sounded like water moving fast. Waterfalls and lakes of water rushing up the side of the mountain. But that was some other universe. Here it was only night and wind and trees and the stars were coming out. Hey, Dad, you fuckhead.

Her legs fell asleep and she needed to pee again, but she didn't want to wake up Biscuit. She bent over and kissed him on the top of his head. He didn't wake up. He just mumbled, Quit it, Bunnatine. Love me alone. Or something like that.

She remembers being a kid. Nine or ten. Sneaking back into the house at four in the morning. Her best friend, Biscuit, has gone home, too, to lie in his bed and not sleep. She had to beg him to let her go home. They have school tomorrow. She's tired and she's so hungry. Fighting crime is hard work. Her mother is in the kitchen, making pancakes. There's something about the way she looks that tells Bunnatine she's been out all night, too. Maybe she's been out fighting crime, too. Bunnatine knows her mother is a superhero. She isn't just a waitress. That's just her cover story.

She stands in the door of the kitchen and watches her mother. She practices her hovering. She practices all the time.

Her mother says, "Want some pancakes, Bunnatine?"

She waited as long as she could, and then she heaved his head up and put it down on the ground. She covered his shoulders with her jacket. Like setting a table with a handkerchief. Look at the big guy, lying there so peacefully. Maybe he'll sleep for a hundred years. But more likely the mutants will wake him, eventually, with their barbaric yawps. They're into kazoos right now and heavy-metal hooting. She can hear them warming up. Biscuit hung out with some of the mutants at school, years and years ago. They'll get a kick out of his new outfit. There's a ten-year high school reunion coming up, and Biscuit will come home for that. He gets all sentimental about things like that. Mutants, on the other hand, don't do things like parades or reunions. They're good at keeping secrets, though. They made great babysitters when her mom couldn't take care of the kid.

She keeps her headlights off, all the way down the mountain. Turns the engine off, too. Just sails down the mountain like a black wing.

When she gets home, she's mostly sober and of course the kid is still asleep. Her mom doesn't say anything, although Bunnatine knows she doesn't approve. She thinks Bunnatine ought to tell Biscuit about the kid. But it's a little late for that, and who knows? Maybe she isn't his kid anyway.

The kid has fudge smeared all over her face and her pillow. Leftover fudge from the parade, probably. Bunnatine's mom has a real sweet tooth. Kid probably sat up eating it in the dark, after

Bunnatine's mom put her to bed. Bunnatine kisses the kid on the forehead. Goes and gets a washcloth, comes back and wipes off some of the fudge. Kid still doesn't wake up. She's going to be real disappointed about the autograph. Maybe Bunnatine will just forge Biscuit's handwriting. Write something real nice. It's not like Biscuit will care. Bunnatine would like to crawl into the kid's bed, just curl up around the kid and get warm again, but she's already missed two shifts this week. So she takes a hot shower and goes to sit with her mom in the kitchen until she has to leave for work. Neither of them has much to say to the other, which is normal, but her mom makes Bunnatine some eggs and toast. If Biscuit were here, she'd make him breakfast, too, and Bunnatine imagines that, eating breakfast with Biscuit and her mom, waiting for the sun to come up so that the day can start all over again. Then the kid comes in the kitchen, crying and holding out her arms for Bunnatine. "Mommy," she says. "Mommy, I had a really bad dream."

Bunnatine picks her up. Such a heavy little kid. Her nose is running and she still smells like fudge. No wonder she had a bad dream. Bunnatine says, "Shhh. It's okay, baby. It was just a bad dream. Just a dream. Tell me about the dream."

The Lesson

The Lesson

The fight starts two days before Thanh and Harper are due to fly out to the wedding. The wedding is on a small private island somewhere off the coast of South Carolina. Or Alabama. The bride is an old friend. The fight is about all sorts of things. Thanh's long-standing resentment of Harper's atrocious work schedule, the discovery by Harper that Thanh, in a fit of industriousness, has thrown away all of Harper's bits and ends of cheese while cleaning out the refrigerator.

The fight is about money. Harper works too much. Thanh is an assistant principal in the Brookline school system. He hasn't had a raise in three years. The fight is about Thanh's relationship with the woman who is, precariously, six months pregnant with Harper and Thanh's longed-for child. Thanh tries once again to explain to Harper. He doesn't even really like Naomi that much. Although he is of course grateful to her. Why be grateful to her? Harper says. We're paying her. She's doing this because we're paying her money. Not because she wants to be friends with us. With you. The thing Thanh doesn't say is that he might actually like Naomi under other circumstances. Let's say, if they were stuck next to each other on a long flight. If they never had to see each other again. If she weren't carrying Harper and Thanh's baby. If she were doing a better job of carrying the baby. They have chosen not to know the gender of the baby.

The point is that liking Naomi isn't the point. The point is rather that she grow to like—love, even—Thanh and, by association, of course (of course!) Harper. That she sees that they are deserving of love. Surely they are deserving of love. Naomi's goodwill, her friendship, her *affection,* is an insurance policy. They are both afraid, Thanh and Harper, that Naomi will change her mind when the baby is born. Then they will have no baby and no legal recourse and no money to try again.

Anyway the cheese was old. Harper is getting fat. The beard, which Thanh loathes, isn't fooling anyone. Thanh has spent too much money on the wedding present. The plane tickets weren't cheap, either.

Naomi, the surrogate, is on bed rest. Two weeks ago a surgeon put a stitch in her cervix. A cerclage, which almost sounds pretty. How did we end up with a surrogate with an incompetent cervix? says Harper. She's only twenty-seven!

Naomi gets out of bed to use the toilet and every other day she can take a shower. Her fellow graduate students come over and what do you think they talk about when they're not talking about linguistics? Thanh and Harper, probably, and how much Naomi is suffering. Does she confide in her friends? Tell them she thinks about keeping the baby? It was her egg, after all. That was probably a dumb idea.

Thanh keeps a toothbrush at Naomi's apartment. Easier than running upstairs. Their building is full of old Russians with rent-stabilized leases. The women exercise on the treadmills in high heels. They gossip in Russian. Never smile at Thanh when he comes into the exercise room to lift weights or run. They see him go in and out of Naomi's apartment. Must wonder. Sometimes Thanh works at Naomi's kitchen table. One night he falls asleep on the bed beside her, Naomi telling him something about her childhood, the TV on. Naomi watches episode after episode of *CSI*. All that blood. It can't be good for the baby. When Thanh wakes up, she is watching him. You farted in your sleep, she says. And laughs. What time is it? He checks his phone and sees he has no missed calls. Harper is probably still at work. He doesn't like me very much, Naomi says. He likes you! Thanh says. (He knows who she means.) I mean he doesn't really like people. But he likes you. *Mm,* Naomi says. He'll like the baby, Thanh says. You should hear him talk about preschools, art lessons, he's already thinking about pets. Maybe a gerbil to start with? Or a chameleon. He's already started a college fund. *Mm,* Naomi says again. He's good-looking, she says. I'll give him that. You should have seen him when he was twenty-five, Thanh says. It's all been downhill since then. Hungry? He heats up the pho ga he made upstairs. His mother's recipe. He does the dishes afterward.

He accidentally saw a text on Naomi's phone the other day. To one of her friends. The short one. I AM HORNY ALL THE TIME. They should have used a donor egg. But that would have cost more money, and how much more money is there in the world? Wherever it is, it isn't in Harper and Thanh's bank account. They went through catalogs. IQs, hobbies, genetic histories. It seemed impersonal. Like ordering take-out food from an online menu. Should we have the chicken or the shrimp? Naomi and Harper have thick, curly blond hair, similar chins, mouths, athletic builds. So they decided to use Thanh's sperm. Harper says once, late at night: he thinks it would be harder to love his own child.

Thanh wants to tell Harper about the text. Maybe it would make him laugh. He doesn't. It wouldn't.

Eventually the fight is about the wedding. Should they cancel? Thanh thinks if they leave town now, something terrible will happen. The baby will come. He can't say this to Harper. That would also be bad for the baby.

At this stage of a pregnancy a fetus's lungs are insufficiently developed. Should Naomi go into labor now, the baby will live or the baby will die. It's fifty-fifty. If the baby lives, the chances are one in five it will be severely disabled. Harper wants to go to the wedding. He won't know anyone there except for Thanh and Fleur, but Harper likes meeting people, especially when he knows he never has to see them again. Harper likes new people. Harper and Thanh have been together now for sixteen years. Married for six. Anyway, when will there be another chance for adventure? The next stage of their life is slouching over the horizon.

Naomi says go. The tickets are nonrefundable. Everything will be fine. Thanh's mother, Han, agrees to fly in from Chicago and stay with Naomi. Han and Naomi have become friends on Facebook. Han doesn't understand anything about Thanh's life, he has understood this for a long time, but she loves him anyway. She loves Naomi, too, because Naomi is carrying her grandchild. Naomi's own mother is not in the picture. Harper's parents are both assholes.

They go to Fleur's wedding.

Fleur was always in charge of parties. Always threw the best parties, the ones that people who have long since moved out to the wealthier suburbs—Newton, Sudbury, Lincoln—still talk about, the parties that took days in darkened rooms to recover from. Fleur was, in her twenties, thrifty, ruthless, psychologically astute. Able to wring maximum fun, maximum exhausting whimsy, out of all gatherings. And now Fleur has not only filthy improvisatory cunning, but money. Who is paying for all of this? Fleur's fiancé David's family owns the island. He does something that Fleur is vague about. Travels. There is family money. His family is in snacks. A van picks up Harper and Thanh, two other couples, and two women from Chula Vista. Friends of Fleur. Fleur moved out to Point Loma a few years ago, which is where she met David doing whatever it is that he does. The women are Marianne and Laura. They say David is nice. Good with his hands. A little scary. They don't really know him. They know Fleur from Bikram yoga. The air-conditioning in the van isn't working. The wedding guests are taken in the van from the tiny regional airport where everyone flew in on tiny, toy-sized prop planes to an equally tiny pier. Everything snack-sized. The boat that goes over to Bad Claw Island has a glass bottom. How cute, Marianne says. The pilot, a black guy with the greenest eyes Thanh has ever seen, is gay. Indisputably gay. Down here the Atlantic is softer. It seems bigger. But maybe that's because everything else is so much smaller. There's a cooler on the boat; in it, individual see-through thermoses filled with something citrusy and alcoholic. In a basket, prepackaged snacks, crackers, and cookies. Fleur spent her twenties as a bartender in various Boston bars. She and Thanh met at ManRay. ManRay has been closed for a long time now. Thousands of years.

Han has sent Thanh a text. Everything is fine. Okay? Fine! Great! She and Naomi are watching Bollywood musicals. Eating Belgian fries. Naomi wants to know all about Thanh and Harper when they were young and dumb. (Not that this is how Han puts it. Nevertheless.) Don't tell her anything, Thanh texts back. I mean it.

Harper is in one of his golden moods. Rare these days. He looks a hundred years younger than this morning when they caught the cab. He solicits information from the two couples. Which side of the wedding party. Where they are coming from.

What they do. Everyone here is a friend of Fleur's, but no one has as long and distinguished a claim as Harper and Thanh. Harper, saying he has a bad back, lies down on the glass bottom of the boat. Everyone has to rearrange their feet. No one minds. He tells a story about the time Fleur, inebriated and in a rage, who knows what brought it on, kicked in the front of a jukebox at an Allston bar. The Silhouette. All of those early nineties alt-rock boys in their dirty black jeans. Legs like toothpicks, jeans so tight they could hardly bend their knees when they sat down. Thanh used to marvel at their barely-there asses. Allston rock butt. A U2 song is playing on the jukebox when Fleur kicks it in. Harper, nimble spinner of the spectacular untruth, improvises a story. Bono once jerked off on her little sister when she fell asleep backstage after a concert. After that, Fleur gets free drinks whenever they go to The Silhouette. She even works there for a few months.

Is this the kind of story you are supposed to tell to strangers on your way to a wedding? Better, Thanh supposes, than the one about the albatross. The best part of Harper's story is that Harper wasn't even at The Silhouette that night. It was just Thanh and Fleur, on some night. Thanh was the one who made up the story about Bono. But there is no story that Harper does not further embellish, does not re-embroider. Thanh wonders if that story still circulates. Did anyone ever tell it back to Bono himself? Maybe Thanh should Google it. You can see the lumpy profile of what must be Bad Claw Island, maybe half a mile away. Tide's out, the pilot says over the intercom. You can wade over from here. Water's maybe three feet deep. You can swim! If you want. Harper jumps up. His back good as new. Absolutely, he says. Who's in? Harper takes off his shoes, jeans, shirt. There's that fat, hairy belly. Leaves his briefs on. He goes over the side and down the ladder. Two men and a woman named Natasha join him. All in their underwear.

Thanh stays put beneath the white canopy of the boat. Little waves slap pleasantly at the hull. There's the most pleasant little breeze. He likes the way the water looks through the glass bottom. Like a magic trick. Why spoil it? Besides, he forgot to collect the laundry out of the dryer before they caught the plane. He isn't wearing any underwear. The boat gets to shore first, but before Thanh steps off onto the dock, Harper swims up under the glass. Presses his lips up. Then, suggestively, his wriggling hips. Here I am, Thanh, having sex with a boat. See, Thanh? I told you we would have a good time.

Fleur is on the dock, kissing her friends. The boat pilot, too. Why not? He's very good-looking. Fleur's wearing a white bikini and a top hat. Her hair is longer than Thanh has ever seen it. She's let it go back to its natural color. I'm the wedding party, she says, still giving those loving kisses. Exuberant kisses! She smells like frangipani and bourbon. Representing both the bride, me, and my groom, David. Because he's not here yet. He's delayed. Look at you, Thanh! Both of you! Has it really been two years? My God. Come up to the lodge. Everyone else has to sleep in a yurt on the beach. Well, everyone except the old people, who are staying over on the mainland. But you and Harper get a bed. A bed in an actual room and there's even a door. Remember the apartment in Somerville? The girl who came over from Ireland to visit her girlfriend and got dumped before she even landed? We put a mattress behind the sofa and she stayed all summer? Have you seen Barb? Is she still in Prague? Do you know if you're having a boy or a girl yet? What's this woman like, the surrogate?

She never stops talking. Kissing, talking, Fleur likes to do both. The other wedding guests are sent off to claim their yurts. Fleur's sister Lenny takes them away. Thanh has never liked Lenny. He hasn't seen her in over a decade, but he doesn't like her any better now. Harper puts his pants back on and they follow Fleur up the beach. Did you ever sleep with her? Harper said once to Thanh. Of course not, Thanh said.

Bad Claw Lodge is an ugly wooden box done up in white gingerbread trim. Two stories. A listing porch, a banging screen door. Little dormer windows tucked under the flaking, papery eaves. The island is probably worth three million, Fleur says. The lodge? Some day it will blow out to sea, and I will get down on my knees and thank God. How big is the island? Harper asks. Two miles. Something like that. You can walk around it in half an hour. It gets bigger after every storm. But then the mainland is getting smaller.

There are buckets and pans set out on the painted floor of the lodge. On counters. On the mildew-stained couch and in the fireplace. It rained all night, Fleur says. All morning, too. I thought it would rain all day. The roof is a sieve. She takes them upstairs and down a hall so low that Harper must duck to get under a beam. Here, she says. Bathroom's next door. The water is all run-off, so if you want a hot shower, take it in the afternoon. The catchtank is on the roof. There's space enough in the room they're sleeping in for one twin bed, shoved up against the window. There's a three-legged table. On the bed is a Pyrex mixing bowl with an inch of rainwater at the bottom. Fleur says, I'll take that. On the little table is a piece of taxidermy. Something cat-like, but with a peculiarly flattened, leathery tail. It has an angry face. A wrinkled, whiskery snout of a nose. What's that? Harper says. A beaver? Fleur says, That thing? It's something native down here. They had poisonous claws, or laid eggs, or something like that. They're extinct. That's worth a fortune, too. They were such a nuisance everyone just eradicated them. Shot them, trapped them, cut them up for bait. That was a long time ago, before anyone cared about stuff like that. Anyway! They never bothered to come up with a name for whatever they were, but then after they were gone they named the island after them. I think. Bad Claw. That thing is definitely worth more than this house. Thanh checks his phone again. There's no signal here, Fleur says. You have to go back to the mainland for that. Harper and Thanh look at each other. Is there a phone in the house?

There isn't.

Thanh and Harper fight about whether or not Thanh should go back to check messages, to call Han and Naomi. Whether they should stay on the mainland. We could have a real bed, Thanh says. Fleur will understand. I want to stay here, Harper says. And we are not going to say one word about this to Fleur. It's her wedding! Do you think she wants to have to pretend to feel worried about something that probably isn't even going to be an issue? Fine. Then I'll go in the boat the next time it's bringing people over, Thanh says. Call and make sure everything is okay, and then come right back. No, Harper says. I'll go. We'll tell Fleur it's a work thing.

It turns out that Harper can swim/wade back to the mainland. The tide will be in later on, though, so he'll get a ride back on the boat. He puts his cell phone, with a couple of twenties, inside two plastic baggies. Fleur takes Thanh aside as soon as Harper is in the water. What's up? she says. Everything okay? We're fine, Thanh says. Really. Fine. Okay, Fleur says. Come help me mix drinks and tell me stuff. I need a quick crash course in marriage. What's sex like? Well, to start with, Thanh says, you need good lube and a lot of preparation. I also recommend two or three trapeze artists. And a marching band. The marching band is essential. They make drinks. People gather on the porch. Someone plays Leonard Cohen songs on a guitar. There are oysters and hot dogs and cold tomato halves filled with spinach and cheese. More drinks. Thanh says to Fleur, Tell me about David. He's a good guy? How am I supposed to answer that, Fleur says. She's gotten some sun. There are lines on her face that Thanh doesn't remember. She's doing what she used to do, back in the old days. Picking up abandoned drinks, finishing them. David has a terrible job. Did you know they had me vetted when we moved in together? To see if I was a security risk. We're at different ends of the political spectrum. But he's good to me. And he's rich. That doesn't hurt. And I love him. Well, Thanh says. He takes the empty glass from her hand.

It's nine at night by the time Harper gets back. People are playing Truth or Dare. Or, as Fleur calls it, Security Risk or Do

Something Stupid Because It's Fun. There are other people on
the boat with Harper. Thank God, Fleur says. He's here. But it
isn't David. It's three men and a woman, all in knife-pleated
pants, white shirts. Are those the caterers? someone asks. Fleur
shshes them. Friends of David, she says, and goes down to the
dock to meet them. No kisses this time. Thanh, Harper says. Let's
go somewhere and talk.

They're at the top of the stairs when Thanh sees a plastic
bowl, rainwater in it, on the landing. Hold on, he tells Harper,
and pukes into it. Takes the bowl into the bathroom, dumps
the vomit and rainwater into the toilet. Rinses it. Rinses his
mouth. Okay. He's okay. Harper is in their room, sitting on the
little bed. They're okay, he says. They're in the hospital. She was
having contractions. They've given her something to stop the
contractions. And something else, uh, Dexamethasone. I looked
it up on the phone. It's a steroid. It increases surfactants in the
lungs. Whatever those are. So if he's born, he'll have a better
chance. He, Thanh says. Oh, Harper says. Yeah. Naomi spilled the
beans. Sorry about that. We need to go back, Thanh says. Thanh,
Harper says. We can't. There are no flights. No seats. Not tomorrow anyway. I called. Han's there. The contractions have stopped.
Tomorrow morning, first thing, you can go over to the mainland
and talk to them. Thanh lies down on the bed. He doesn't un-
dress. There's sand between his toes. He's cold. Harper lies down
beside him. Harper says, It'll be okay. They'll be okay. They're
almost asleep when Thanh says, I don't know about this David
guy. I rode over with some of his work friends, Harper says. Bad
news, those guys. I asked what exactly David did, and they started
talking about the lesson of 9/11. Thanh says, Someone asked if

they were the caterers. Caterers, Harper says. Like you'd want to eat anything they served you.

There are noises in the night. Thanh, Harper says. Do you hear that? Hear what? Thanh says. But then he hears it, too. Little rustling noises, dry leaves' noises. Little scratchings. Harper gets out of bed, turns on the light. The noises stop. Harper turns off the light. Almost immediately the noises start up again. Harper gets up, the light is turned on, the noises stop. When it happens a third time, Harper leaves the light on. The taxidermied Bad Claw watches them with its glassy eyes, lips forever lifted in a sneer. There is nothing in the room except for Harper and Thanh and the Bad Claw, the table and the bed and their suitcases. Thanh checks his phone. There are no messages, no signal. The bed is too small. Harper begins to snore. He didn't used to snore. There are no other noises. Thanh only falls back asleep as the sun is coming up.

In the morning, Fleur and a bunch of other people are making a lot of noise on the porch. There's yelling. Little cries of delight. Has David arrived? They make their way down. Go on, Fleur is saying. Try them on. Everyone gets one. Everyone's a bride today. She is taking wedding dresses out of a set of oversized luggage. Remember these? she says to Thanh and Harper. Remember when I won all that money at the poker game in Somerville? She tells everyone else, I didn't know what to do with it. The next week was the wedding dress sale, Filene's Basement. It's famous, she tells her California friends. Everyone used to go. Even if you never, ever planned to get married. You went to watch grown women fight over dresses, and then there you are, buying a dress, too. So I went and I got kind of fascinated with the dresses that no one else wanted. All of the really horrible dresses. At the end of the day they're practically paying you to take them. I spent all my poker money on wedding dresses. I've been saving them ever since. For a party. Or a wedding. Something. Here, she says to Harper. This one will look good on you. I was saving it just for you.

So Harper takes off his shirt. He steps into the dress, yanks it up over his chest. There are cap sleeves. Fake seed pearls. Fake buttons up the back. Was there really a time when women wore dresses like this and no one thought it was strange and everyone pretended that they looked beautiful and cried? How much did Fleur pay? There's a tag still attached. $3,000. A line through that. More prices, all crossed out. Fleur sees Thanh looking. You *know* I didn't pay more than fifty bucks for any of them, she says. Harper and Thanh were married in a courthouse office. They wore good suits. Red boxers, because red is lucky. Luck is necessary. Here's marriage advice Thanh could give Fleur. Be lucky.

How are the yurts? Thanh asks the woman from the van. Marianne? Or Laura. Whatever. The yurts? Really nice, the woman says. I've always wanted to stay in a yurt. Me, too, Thanh says. He's never entertained a single thought about a yurt in his entire life. Here, the woman says, will you zip me up? He zips her up. You look nice, he says. Really, she says. Yes, he says. It suits you somehow. But she doesn't seem pleased by this, the way she was pleased about the yurt. Maybe because it's such an awful dress. The (un)caterers are playing Hearts on the steps. Harper says to Fleur, I need to go back over to the mainland again. Work. Fleur says, Tide's in. I don't know when the boat is back over. It's already come once this morning, with groceries. Maybe after lunch? First we're going to go on an expedition. Put on a dress. (This to Thanh.) You guys, too. (This to the caterers.) Think of it as information gathering in field settings. Everybody needs coffee, grab coffee.

Everyone is amenable. Wedding guests in wedding dresses grab coffee and fruit and premade breakfast sandwiches. They put on sunblock, or hats, and troop off after Fleur. Thanh and Harper go along. Everyone goes. Even the caterers.

The center of the island, at least Thanh assumes it's the center of the island, is uphill. Laurel and pine. Loamy soil flecked with sand. There's a sort of path, pocketed with roots, and Fleur tells them to stay on it. Poison oak, she says. Sinkholes. Pines crowd in until the procession must go single file. Thanh has to hold up the train of his awful borrowed dress. The path becomes slippery with old needles. There's no breeze, just the medicinal smell of pine and salt. No one talks. The caterers are just in front of Thanh, Harper behind. He bets the caterers have a working phone. If the boat doesn't come soon, he'll figure out how to get it. Why did they sleep so late? Han will be no use to Naomi if things go wrong. She will be no use to Thanh and Harper. But then, what use would Thanh and Harper be? Nevertheless, they shouldn't be here. Here is of no use to anyone. The wedding party emerges into a clearing. At the center is an indentation, a sunken pocket of what Thanh realizes is water. A pond? Hardly big enough to be a pond. There's an algae bloom, bright as an egg yolk. So, Fleur says. We're here! This is where David's family comes every year, so they can each make a wish. Right, Sheila, Robert? She is addressing an older couple. Thanh hasn't even noticed them until now, although they are the only people in the clearing who aren't wearing wedding dresses. This should make them stand out, he thinks. They don't. They could set themselves on fire, and you still probably wouldn't notice them. There's a cairn of pebbles and shells and bits of broken pottery. Fleur picks up a pebble, says, You make a wish and you throw something in. Come on, everyone gets a wish. Come on, come on. She tosses her pebble. Wedding guests gather around the mucky hole. Is it very deep? someone asks Fleur. She shrugs. Maybe, she says. Probably not. I don't know. Someone picks up a shell and drops it in. People make wishes. Harper rolls his eyes at Thanh. Shrugs. Picks up a pebble. People are making all sorts of wishes. A man in a watered silk dress with a mandarin collar, really it's the best of the awful dresses, wishes for a new job. Fair enough. The caterers make wishes, secret wishes. Even caterers get to make wishes. Marianne thinks, Let my mother die. Let her die soon. And Fleur? What did she wish? Fleur wishes with all of her heart, Please let him get here soon. Let him get here safely. Please let him love me. Please let this work. Thanh doesn't want to make a wish. He is suspicious of wishes. Go on, Fleur says. She puts a piece of shell in Thanh's hand. And then she waits. Should he wish that the baby inside Naomi stays inside a little longer? What would be the cost of that wish? Should he wish that the baby will live? If he lives, let him be healthy and strong and happy? He could wish that Naomi will not wish to keep the baby. He could wish to be a good father. That Harper would be a good father. Would that be a good wish? A safe wish? It seems dangerous to Thanh to make demands of God, of the universe, of a muddy hole. How can he anticipate the thing that he ought to wish for? Fleur is waiting. So Thanh throws the bit of shell in, and tries with all his heart not to make any wish at all. Even as he tries, he feels something—that wish, what is it, what is it?— rising up from his stomach, his lungs, his heart, spilling out. Too late! Down goes Thanh's bit of shell with all the other pebbles and bits, the other wishes. Harper sees Thanh's face. He wants that look to go away. What can be done? He wants to get back and see if the boat has come in. He'll go over to the mainland again if Thanh will let him. Harper doesn't believe in wishes, but he drops his pebble anyway. He thinks, I wonder what was making the noise last night? He holds Thanh's hand all the way back down the trail. The dresses are ridiculous. The kind of fun that they used to have is no longer fun. Now it seems more like work. David's parents are just in front of Harper and Thanh. They didn't make any wishes, but perhaps they have everything they want already. Thanh wonders. What kinds of things did they wish for their son? Harper decides that if the boat isn't back, he'll swim over in the ridiculous dress. What a great story that will make. He isn't thinking about Naomi and the baby. He is making every effort not to think about them at all. What a waste it will all be, what a disaster it will be if things go wrong at this stage. Will Thanh want to try again? They won't be able to afford it. Somehow all of this will be Harper's fault. They shouldn't have come to the wedding.

A baby born at twenty-four weeks may weigh just over a pound. The boat is at the dock. David has not come in on it. Thanh says, I should go this time. No, Harper says. You stay. I'll go. You should stay. Have some lunch. Take a nap. Really, Thanh should go, but Harper goes instead. He doesn't wear the dress. Before you are allowed to enter the NICU you must wash your hands and forearms up to the elbows for no less than two minutes each time. There is a clock and you watch the minute hand. This is to keep the babies safe from infection. Fleur suggests various games. Frisbee, Capture the Flag, Marco Polo in the water. The caterers play all of these games as if they are not playing games at all. Your wedding ring will fit around the wrist of a twenty-four-week baby. All of the wedding dresses have been bundled up in a pile on the beach with some driftwood. There will be a bonfire tonight. Lunch has been delivered on the boat. Thanh doesn't want any lunch. In a male baby born at twenty-four weeks, the scrotum and the glans of the penis have not yet developed. The skin cannot hold heat or moisture in. They have no fat. No reserves. They are stuck with needles, tubes, wires, monitors. Astronauts in the smallest diapers you have ever seen. Their ears don't resemble ears yet. They are placed in nests of artificial lambswool. Pink like cotton candy. Thanh doesn't want to play Capture the Flag. Fleur has made pitchers and pitchers of Bad Claw Island Ice Tea, and Thanh downs drink after drink after drink. He sits on the sand and drinks. Fleur sits with him for a while, and they talk about things that don't matter to either one of them. Fleur drinks, but not as much as Thanh. She must wonder. Does she wonder why he is drinking like this? She doesn't ask. David's mother sits down beside them. She says, I always wanted to write a book about this place. A book for children. It was going to be about the Bad Claws, before people ever lived here. But I couldn't figure out what the lesson would be. Children's books should have a lesson, don't you think? You should always learn something when you read a story. That's important. Premature baby girls have better outcomes than premature baby boys. Caucasian boys fare worst of all. Nurses have a name for this: Wimpy White Boys. Fleur says, I'm getting married tomorrow. If David doesn't show up, I'll marry the Bad Claw. The one in your room. Put that ring right around that poisonous little dewclaw. That would be funny, wouldn't it? Just watch. I'll do it. Eventually Thanh is sitting by himself, and then, later, someone is standing over him. Harper. Hey there, Harper is saying. Hey there, buddy. Thanh? What? Thanh says. What. He thinks this is what he says. He is asking a question, but he isn't sure what he is asking. Harper is telling him something about someone whose name is William. The eyes of a twenty-four-week baby will still be fused shut. He can be given around five grams of breast milk a day through a gastro-nasal tube. Every diaper must be weighed. Urine output is monitored. Heart rate. Weight gain. Growth of the blood vessels in the retina. Lungs will not fully develop until the thirty-seventh week. Oxygen saturation of the blood is monitored. Everything noted in a binder book. Parents may look at the book. May ask questions. A high-speed oscillating ventilator may be required. Sometimes a tracheotomy is required. Supplemental oxygen. Blood transfusions. There is a price for all of these interventions. There is a cost. Cerebral palsy is a risk. Brain bleeds. Scarring of the lungs. Loss of vision. Necrotizing enterocolitis. The business of staying alive is hard work. Nurses say, He's so feisty. He's a fighter. That's a good thing. Harper goes away. Eventually he comes back with Fleur. The bonfire has been lit. It's dark. You have to eat something, Fleur says. Thanh? Here. She opens a packet of crackers. Thanh obediently eats cracker after cracker. Sips water. The crackers are sweetish. Dry. Nurses don't necessarily call the pre-

mature babies by their names. Why not? Maybe it makes it easier.
They call the babies Peanut. Muffin. What an adorable muffin.
What a little peanut. Parents may visit the NICU at any hour,
day or night. Some parents find it hard to visit. Their presence is
not essential. There is no vital task. Their child may die. There is
no privacy. Every morning and every evening the doctors make
rounds. Parents may listen in. They may ask questions. Parents
may ask questions. There will not always be answers. There are
motivational posters. Social workers. Financial counselors. A
baby born at twenty-four weeks is expensive! Who knew a baby
could cost so much? Fleur and Harper help Thanh up the stairs
and into bed. Harper is saying, In the morning. We have standby
seats. Turn him on his side. In case he pukes. There. The first
twenty-four hours are the most critical.

Harper is snoring in Thanh's ear. Is this what has woken him?
There's another noise in the room. That rustling again. That cel-
lophane noise. Do you hear that? Thanh says. His tongue is thick.
Harper. Harper says, Ungh. The noise increases. Harper says,
What the hell, Thanh. Thanh is sitting up in bed now. He's still
drunk, but he is piecing together the things that Harper tried to
tell him a few hours ago. Naomi has had the baby. Harper, he
says. Harper gets up and puts on the light. There is movement in
the room, a kind of black liquid rushing. Beetles are pouring—
a cataract—out of the Bad Claw onto the table and down the
wall, across the floor, and toward the bed and the window.
Something urgent in their progress, some necessary, timely task
that they are engaged in. The lively, massed shape of them is the
shadow of an unseen thing, moving through the room. Scurry-

ing night. There will be a night in the NICU, much later, when Thanh looks over at another isolette. Sees, in the violet light, a spider moving across the inside wall. Every year, the nurse says when he calls her over. Every spring we get a migration or something. Spiders everywhere. She reaches in, scoops the spider into a cup. "Christ on a bicycle!" Harper says. "What the fuck?" He and Thanh are out of the room as fast as they can go. Down the stairs, and out of the house. They stumble down the rough beach to the dock. The lumpy yurts silent and black. The sky full of so many stars. God has an inordinate fondness for stars and also for beetles. The small and the very far away. Harper has the suitcase. Thanh carries their shoes. No doubt they've left something behind.

They sit on the dock. Do you remember anything I told you last night? Harper asks. Thanh says, Tell me. We have a son, Harper says. His name is William. Your mother picked that. William. She wanted him to have a name. In case. We'll call when we get to the mainland. We'll get the first flight. If there are no flights, we'll rent a car. We could swim, Thanh says. That's a terrible idea, Harper says. He puts his arms around Thanh. Breathes into his hair. It will be okay, Harper says. It may not be okay, Thanh says. I don't know if I can do this. Why did we want to do this? Harper says, Look. He points. There, far away, are the lights of the mainland. Closer: light moving over the water. The light becomes a boat and then the boat comes close enough that the pilot can throw a rope to Harper. He pulls the boat in. A man steps off. He looks at Harper, at Thanh, a little puzzled. This is the bridegroom. He says, "Were you waiting for me?" Thanh begins to laugh, but Harper throws his arms open wide and embraces David. Welcomes him. Then David goes up the beach to the house. His shadow trails behind him, catches on beach grass and little pebbles. What kind of person is he? Not a good one, but he is loved by Fleur and what does it matter to Thanh and Harper anyway? Even caterers get married. There's no law against it. They get on the boat and ride back to the mainland. Fish swim up under the glass bottom, toward the light. Harper pays the pilot of the boat, whose name is Richard, a hundred bucks to take them to the airport. By the time they are on the prop plane that will take them to Charlotte where they will catch another flight to Boston, Thanh is undergoing a hangover of supernatural proportions. The hangover renders him incapable of thought. This is a mercy. Waiting for flights, Harper talks to Han, and once to Naomi. Thanh and Harper hold hands in the cab all the way to Children's Hospital, and Han meets them in the main lobby. "Come up," she says. "Come up and meet your son."

On an island, Fleur and David marry each other. There is cake. The wedding gift, which cost too much money, is opened. Days go by. Months go by. Years. Sometimes Thanh remembers Bad Claw, the procession of wedding dresses, the caterers, the boat coming toward the island. The place where he picked up a pebble. Sometimes Thanh wonders. Was this it, the thing that he had wished for, even as he had tried to wish for nothing at all? Was it this moment? Or was it this? Or this. Brief joys. The shadow of the valley of the shadow. Even here, even here, he wondered. Perhaps it was.

There is a day when they are able to bring the boy, their son, home from the NICU. They have prepared his room. There has been time, after all, a surplus of time to outfit the room with the usual things. A crib. Soft animals. A rug. A chair. A light.

One day the crib is too small. The boy learns to walk. Naomi graduates. Sometimes she takes the boy to the zoo or to museums. One day she says to Thanh, Sometimes I forget that he didn't die. Things were so bad for so long. Sometimes I think that he did die, and this is another boy entirely. I love him with all my heart, but sometimes I can't stop crying about the other one. Do you ever feel that way? Harper still works too much. Sometimes he tells the boy the story about how he was born, and the island, and the wedding. How Harper's wedding ring fit over his wrist. How Harper, wearing a wedding dress, rode over in a glass-bottomed boat, and was told that their son was born. Han gets older. She says, Sometimes I think that when I am dead and a ghost I will go back to that hospital. I spent so long there. I will be a ghost who washes her hands and waits. I won't know where else to haunt. The boy grows up. He is the same boy, even if sometimes it is hard to believe this could be true. Thanh and Harper stay married. The boy is loved. The loved one suffers. All loved ones suffer. Love is not enough to prevent this. Love is not enough. Love is enough. The thing that you wished for. Was this it?

Here endeth the lesson.

The New Boyfriend

Ainslie doesn't rip open presents. She's always been careful with her things, even the things that don't matter. Immy is a ripper, but this is not Immy's present, not Immy's birthday. Sometimes Immy thinks that this may not be Immy's life. Better luck next time around, Immy, she tells herself.

Ainslie scores under the tape with a fingernail, then carefully teases the pink wrapping paper out from under the coffin-shaped box.

Ainslie's new Boyfriend is in there.

Ainslie's birthday, this year, is just Ainslie and her bestest, oldest friends. Just Ainslie, Sky, Elin, and Immy. No family allowed. No boys.

Earlier there was sushi and cake and lots of pictures to put up online so that everyone will know how much fun they are having.

No presents, Ainslie said, but of course Immy and Elin and

Sky bring presents. No one ever means it when they say that. Not even Ainslie, who already has everything.

It's normal to want to give your best friend something because you love her. Because you want her to know that you love her. It isn't a competition. Ainslie loves Elin and Immy and Sky equally, even if Immy and Ainslie have been friends longest.

Immy's heart isn't as big as Ainslie's heart. Immy loves Ainslie best. She also hates her best. She's had a lot of practice at both.

They're in the sunroom. As if you could keep the sun in a room, Immy thinks. Well, if you could, Ainslie's mother probably would.

But the sun has gone down. The world is night, and it belongs to all of them, even if it belongs to Ainslie most of all. Ainslie's brought out dozens of pillar candles, a small forest of mirrored candelabras, both of her Boyfriends. They both wear little birthday hats, because that's the thing about Boyfriends, according to Elin, who has a lot of opinions and isn't shy about sharing them. You can't take them too seriously.

Of course anyone can have an opinion. Immy has plenty. In her opinion, in order not to take a Boyfriend seriously, you have to have a Boyfriend in the first place, and only Ainslie has one. (Two.) (Three.)

Creatures of the night in silly hats, Vampire Boyfriend (Oliver) and Werewolf Boyfriend (Alan) lounge on candy-striped settees and gaze with identical longing at their girlfriend, Ainslie. Immy decides against having a second piece of cake. One piece of cake really ought to be enough for anyone.

And yet, there on the floor, right under the cake (plenty left, Immy, why not have another piece, really?) and the candelabras, right there under everyone's noses, the new Boyfriend has been waiting all this time. Immy knew, right away, as soon as she came into the sunroom, exactly which Boyfriend it would be.

It's dark inside the box, of course. Night wrapped up in pink paper. Are his eyes open or closed? Can he hear them talking? Love will wake him.

Love, oh love. Terrible, wonderful love.

Ainslie lifts the lid of the coffin, and white rose petals spill out, all over the floor, and— "Oh," Sky says. "He's, um, he's gorgeous."

Real rose petals, real and crushed and bruised. Probably not the best packing material, but oh, what a smell is filling the room.

Not night, after all.

The Boyfriend's eyes are closed. His arms are folded across his chest, but his palms are open and full of rose petals. His hair is dark. His face is very young. Maybe a little surprised; his lips parted, just a little, like he has just been kissed.

"Which one is he?" Elin says.

"The Ghost one," Immy says.

Ainslie reaches out, touches the Ghost Boyfriend's face, brushes a piece of hair back from his eyes. "So soft," she says. "So weird. Fake Boyfriend, real hair."

"I thought they weren't selling those anymore?" Elin says.

"They're not," Immy says. Her chest feels very tight, as if she's suddenly full of poison. You have to keep it all inside. Like throwing yourself on a bomb to save everyone else. Except you're the bomb.

Why does Ainslie always get what she wants? Why does Ainslie always get what *Immy* wants? She says, "They don't. You can't get them now."

"Not unless you're Ainslie, right?" Sky says without a trace of discernible malice. She scoops out handfuls of petals, throws them at Ainslie. They all throw rose petals. When Immy reaches into the coffin, she tries very hard not to let her hand brush against Ainslie's Ghost Boyfriend.

"What are you going to call him?" Elin says.

"Don't know," Ainslie says. She's reading the instructions. "So there are two modes, apparently. Embodied or Spectral. Embodied is just, you know, the usual thing." She waves a hand in the direction of her Vampire Boyfriend, Oliver. He waves back. "In Spectral Mode it's like a movie projection and he floats around. You can hang out with him like that, but it's random or something. Like, he comes and goes."

"Huh," Sky says. "So you can't see him all the time, but maybe he's watching you? What if you're getting dressed or on the toilet or something and all of a sudden he's there?"

"Maybe that's why they did the recall," Elin says. She is tearing a white petal into littler and littler pieces, and smiling, like that's her idea of fun.

"You can customize him," Ainslie says. "If you have a thing that belonged to somebody who died. There's a compartment somewhere. Ew. Inside his mouth. You put something in it. I don't know. That part seems kind of dumb. Like, you're really supposed to believe in ghosts or something."

"That's not supposed to be a good idea," Immy says. "That's the reason they did the recall, remember? There were a lot of stories."

"People are so *impressionable,*" Ainslie says.

"So turn him on already," Elin says. "No pun intended."

"What's the rush?" Ainslie says. "We have to come up with a name first."

They debate names for the new Boyfriend while Ainslie opens friend presents. They take more pictures. Ainslie holding the bottle of absinthe that Sky made from a recipe online. They throw rose petals at her, and so there are petals caught in her hair. It's very pretty.

Oliver and Alan in their hats, Ainslie sitting on Oliver's lap. They change out Alan's boy head for his wolf head. He can't talk with the wolf head on, but he's still very cute in his tuxedo. Cuter than most real boys.

More pictures. The new Boyfriend in his box, Ainslie leaning over to kiss him. Ainslie wearing the red suede boots her grandmother sent. Ainslie holding up the tickets that Elin got her to some show by some band they're both into. Two tickets, one for Ainslie and the other for Elin, of course.

Immy isn't really into music. Sky isn't really into music, either. Music is Elin and Ainslie's thing. Whatever.

Immy's present for Ainslie is a beaded choker with an antique locket to sit right over the hollow of Ainslie's white throat.

The beads are cut glass and jet.

There's a secret in the locket.

The choker is in a little box in a pocket in Immy's purse, and she doesn't take it out. She pretends to search for it and then she says to Ainslie, "Uh oh. I think I left your present at home, maybe?"

Ainslie says, "Whatever, Immy. Give it to me at school on Monday."

She passes around the homemade absinthe and they all drink straight from the bottle. That way, Immy figures, it's harder for everyone else to tell if you're only taking little sips or even only pretending. It's a little bit herbal and a little like toothpaste.

"You could call him Vincent," Sky says. She's looking at baby names on her phone. "Or Bran? Banquo? Tor. Foster, um, maybe not Foster. But it ought to be something old-fashioned, ghost names ought to be old-fashioned."

"Because nowadays no one ever dies," Ainslie says, and swigs from the absinthe bottle.

Fake swigs, bets Immy. Let's all get fake drunk and have fake fun with Ainslie and her fake Boyfriends. Because she's fairly sure that all of this is fake, this whole night, the way she finds herself acting around Ainslie and Elin and Sky tonight, maybe this whole year. And if it's not fake, if it's all real, this fun, these friends, this life, then that's even worse, isn't it?

Immy has no idea why she's in such a horrible mood. Except wait, no. Let's be honest. She knows. She's in a horrible mood because she's a horrible friend who wants everything that belongs to Ainslie. Except maybe Ainslie's mother. Ainslie can keep her mother.

Immy has wanted a Boyfriend ever since they came out, even before Ainslie knew about them. Immy was the one who told Ainslie about them. And then Ainslie had Oliver and Alan, and then you could buy the limited edition Ghost Boyfriend, and then there was the recall and you couldn't get a Ghost Boyfriend anymore, and so that was okay, because then even if Immy couldn't have a Ghost Boyfriend, Ainslie couldn't have one, either. Except now she does have one.

Immy wants a Ghost Boyfriend more than she's ever wanted anything.

"What about Quentin? That's a good name," Sky says.

"What about Justin?" Elin says.

Then they are all looking at Immy. She stares right back at Elin, who says, "Oops." And shrugs and smiles.

"Ainslie can call Ainslie's Ghost Boyfriend whatever she wants," Immy says. She knows what kind of friends she is with Elin. Sometimes a friendship is more like a war.

Ainslie can keep Elin, too.

Anyway, Immy is the one who broke up with Justin. And *Justin* is the one who can't get over it, and anyway *anyway*, Elin is the one who still has a thing for him.

Immy's been there, done that.

Ainslie says, "I'm going to call him Mint."

They all laugh and Ainslie says, "No. Really. His name is Mint. He's my Ghost Boyfriend, I can call him whatever I want."

"Weirdish," Elin says. "But okay."

"Come on," Ainslie says. So they all go over and stand around the box, and then Ainslie leans down and sticks her fingers into the Ghost Boyfriend's hair, moving them around until evidently she's found the right place.

His eyes open. He has really pretty eyes. Long lashes. He looks at them, each in turn. His lips part, just a little, like he is about to say something. But he doesn't.

Immy is blushing. She knows she's blushing.

"Hi," Ainslie says. "I'm your girlfriend. Ainslie. You're Mint. You're my Boyfriend."

The new Boyfriend's eyelids flutter shut. Eyelashes like black fans. Skin just like skin. Even his fingernails are perfect and so real, as real as anything Immy has ever seen.

When his eyes open again, he only looks at Ainslie.

"Okay, so, we'll see you later," Ainslie says.

She straightens up and says to Immy and Elin and Sky, "You guys want to put on some music and dance or something?"

"Wait," Elin says. "What about him? I mean *it*. Are you just going to leave it in there?"

"It takes them a while to wake up the first time," Sky says. Sky has a Biblical Handmaiden. Esther. Sky's parents were kind of religious for a while.

"Oh, yeah," Ainslie says. "There's one other thing. We have to choose a mode. Embodied or Spectral. What do you think?"

"Embodied," Elin says.

"Embodied," Sky says.

"Spectral," Immy says.

"Okay," Ainslie says. "Spectral. Might as well." She reaches back down, runs her fingers through her Boyfriend's hair again. "There. Now let's go out on the deck and dance in the moonlight. Come on, Oliver. Alan. You, too."

Ainslie and Elin DJ. The moon is perfectly round and bright. The night is warm. Ainslie tells Oliver and Alan to dance with Immy and Sky.

Which is the kind of thing Ainslie does. She isn't ever selfish. You have to have things in order to be generous with them. Right?

Immy and Oliver dance. She's in his arms, really, his hand on the small of her back. It's sort of a waltz that they're doing, which doesn't really suit whatever song this is, but Oliver can do either the waltz or the tango—or a kind of sway-y standing-there dance. Sky bounces around with Alan, who still has his wolf head on. Alan is actually more fun to dance with than Oliver is, although the bouncing gets tiring after a while.

"Are you happy, darling?" Oliver the Vampire Boyfriend says, so softly Immy has to ask him to repeat himself. Not that this is, strictly speaking, necessary. Oliver always asks the same questions.

"Sure," she says. Then, "Well, I don't know. Not really. I could be happier. I'd like to be happier." Why not? If you can't be honest with your best friend's Vampire Boyfriend, who can you be honest with? Vampires are all about secrets and unhappiness. Secret unhappinesses. You can see it in their black and fathomless eyes.

"I wish you were happy, my love," Oliver says. He presses her more firmly against his body, nuzzles her hair. "How can I be happy if you are not?"

"Ainslie's your love. Not me," Immy says. She really isn't in the mood. Besides, sometimes it's just really too weird, playing pretend eternal love with a borrowed Boyfriend when what you really want is your own Boyfriend. It would be so, so much nicer to have your own. "So, I mean, don't be unhappy on my account."

"As you wish," Oliver says. "I shall be unhappy on my own account. How happy it makes me, oh delicious one, to be unhappy together with you." He clasps her even tighter in his arms, until she has to ask him to ease up just a little. It's a fine line between being cuddled and being squeezed like a juice box, and Vampire Boyfriends sometimes cross right over that line, maybe without even noticing.

There is also the endless hovering and the endless brooding and all the endless talk about how delicious you are and eternity and they like you to read poetry at them, the old-fashioned rhyming kind, even. It's supposed to be educational, okay? Like the way Werewolf Boyfriends go on and on about the environment, and also are always trying to get you to go running with them.

Immy doesn't get music. She doesn't want to get it. The way it wants to make you feel something. Just because it's a minor chord, you're supposed to feel sad? Just because it goes faster, your pulse is supposed to speed up? Why should you have to do what the music wants you to do? Why shouldn't it do what you want? She doesn't want a soundtrack for her life. And she doesn't want somebody's pretty lyrics getting in the way of what she's really thinking. Whatever it is that she's thinking.

Immy doesn't want a Vampire Boyfriend. Or a Werewolf Boyfriend. Not anymore.

"I want more absinthe," Ainslie says. "Somebody go fetch the absinthe."

"I'll get it, darling," Oliver says.

"No," Immy says. "I'll go get it." If you send a Boyfriend off for a bottle of homemade absinthe, likely as not he'll come back with a bottle of conditioner. Or a lamp.

"Thanks, Immy," Ainslie says.

"No problem," Immy says. But maybe you can't trust a friend, either, because instead of going straight back with the absinthe, she finds herself lingering in the sunroom, looking down at the new Boyfriend. His eyes are closed again. She reaches down and touches his face. Just one finger. His skin is very soft. It isn't actually like skin at all, of course, but it isn't like anything else, either. His eyes don't open this time; he's still not all the way awake. And anyway, Ainslie set him for Spectral Mode. His body will just lie here. His ghost will do whatever it is that ghosts do.

He could already be here, she supposes. He could be watching her.

She doesn't feel as if she's being watched. She feels all alone.

So it's an impulse, maybe, that makes her reach inside her purse and take out Ainslie's present. She rips off the wrapping paper and the ribbon, not carefully.

Inside the locket is a braided ring of human hair. Victorian, according to the online seller. Probably their own kids' hair, but never mind.

Two pieces of the braid of hair are jet black; one is ash blond. Black for Ainslie, blond for Immy.

The ring doesn't fit over any of Immy's fingers. Maybe she has fat fingers. She goes back to the coffin, crouches down beside it. "Hey," she says softly. "I'm Ainslie's friend. Immy."

She puts two fingers on his lips. She takes a breath and holds it, like she's about to jump off a bridge into very deep water. Well, she is. Then she sticks her fingers inside Ainslie's Ghost Boyfriend's mouth. There are the teeth, and, okay, here's the tongue. How weird is this? It's very weird. Immy's not saying that this isn't weird, but she keeps on doing it anyway. Her fingers are where they really shouldn't be.

It's not wet like a real mouth and a real tongue would be. The teeth feel pretty real. The tongue is weird. She keeps thinking how weird this is. She slides a finger under the not-a-real-tongue, and there, underneath, is a place where, when she presses down, a kind of lid thing opens up. She fumbles the hair ring into the compartment there, and then presses the lid back down. Then she takes her fingers out of the Ghost Boyfriend's mouth, studies that face carefully.

Nothing about it seems different to her.

When she stands up and turns around, Elin is there in the doorway. Elin says nothing, just waits.

"I thought I saw him move," Immy says. "But he didn't."

Elin gives her a long look. Immy says, "What?"

"Nothing," Elin says. She looks like she wants to say something else, and then she shrugs. "Just, come on. Oliver keeps on asking me to dance with him, and I don't want to. You know how I feel about Ainslie's Boyfriends." What she is really saying is that she knows how Immy feels about them.

Immy grabs the absinthe. "Okay."

Elin says, "Immy? Can I ask you something?"

Immy waits.

Elin says, "I don't get it. This Boyfriend thing. They're creepy. They're fake. They're not real. I know how much you want one. And I know it sucks. How Ainslie gets everything she wants."

Immy blurts out, "Justin has no sense of humor. And he uses way too much body spray. He kisses like it's arm wrestling, except with lips. Lip wrestling."

"Maybe he just needs more practice?" Elin says. "I mean, Ainslie's Boyfriends don't kiss at all. They're just really big dolls. They're *not real*."

"Maybe I don't want real," Immy says.

"Whatever it is you don't want, I hope you get it. I guess." Elin takes the absinthe bottle from Immy, takes a long slug from the mouth. A real one. Apparently Elin wants real, even if real isn't all that great. Immy suddenly feels very fond of her. Elin isn't always a good friend, but okay, she's a real friend and Immy appreciates that just as much as the way she really, really didn't appreciate it when Justin wanted to lip wrestle.

They go back to the dance party and the real friends and the fake Boyfriends. They leave Ainslie's Mint all alone with the ring of hair in his mouth. Immy doesn't feel guilty about that at all. It was a present for Ainslie and Immy is giving it to her. More or less.

There's only a sludgy oily residue left in the absinthe bottle by the time they go to bed. Oliver and Alan are back in their coffins in the closet downstairs in the rec room, and Ainslie has blown out all of the candles in the sunroom. They've eaten the rest of the cake. Sky is already passed out on a couch in the living room.

Is Mint around? Ainslie says he probably is. "The Ghost Boyfriends are supposed to be kind of shy at first when you put them in Spectral Mode. They don't manifest much right at the beginning. You're just supposed to see them out of the corner of your eye, once in a while. When you aren't expecting them."

"Is that supposed to be fun?" Elin says. "Because it doesn't sound like fun."

"It's supposed to be real," Ainslie says. "Like a real ghost. Like a real ghost is falling in love with you. Like, he could be here right now. Watching us. Watching *me*."

There is something about the way she says this. Ainslie is so sure of being loved.

"On that note," Elin says, "I'm going to go crash on your mom's bed. Your new boyfriend better stay the hell out of there." Elin doesn't like to sleep in the same room as everyone else. She says it's because she snores. "When is your mom getting back, Ainslie?"

"Not until two or three tomorrow. I made her promise to call before she shows up." Ainslie is swaying on her feet. She keeps putting her hand out to balance on things: the side table, the back of a settee, the lid of the coffin. She stumbles and almost falls in, catches herself. "Good night, Mint. God, you're cute. Even cuter than Oliver. Don't you think so?"

The question is for Immy. "I guess," she says, her heart burning for just one beat, with that hatred, that old poison. She watches Ainslie lean over, precariously, and plant a noisy kiss on Mint's forehead.

"I slept in Oliver's coffin once," Ainslie says to Elin and Immy. Immy isn't sure what to say to that, and apparently Elin doesn't know, either.

Immy feels lit up and inside out, her hands and feet heavy and slow as lead, her skull and her rib cage emptied and clean. All that poison dried up. A powder.

Or maybe this is just the way she thinks getting drunk on absinthe should feel. She should probably go drink some water, take some Tylenol.

Immy always sleeps in Ainslie's bed when she stays over. She has her own toothbrush in Ainslie's bathroom, borrows Ainslie's T-shirts to wear to bed. Immy even has a favorite pillow, and Ainslie always remembers which one it is. In the morning, she'll wear Ainslie's clothes home if she wants to. Ainslie never minds.

They brush their teeth and they get dressed for bed, and they turn out the lights and get into bed, and all of that time Immy can hardly breathe, she doesn't even want to blink, because maybe Mint is in the room with them. Maybe he is coming. Perhaps she will look up and Mint will be there. He will be there and then he'll be gone again. She knows Ainslie is thinking the same thing. Ainslie is watching for Mint, too.

"This has been a really, really good birthday," Ainslie says in the dark. "It's everything I wanted it to be. I got everything I wanted."

"I'm glad," Immy says. She means it, too. "You deserve everything you're getting."

Immy doesn't think she'll be able to go to sleep. She doesn't want to sleep, she wants to stay awake. She could wait until Ainslie is asleep and go back to the sunroom. Maybe Mint will go there first. After all, his body is there. She tries to think of what she would say to him, what he might say to her. And soon enough Ainslie's asleep and then Immy's asleep, too.

When she wakes up—she is in the middle of a nightmare, something about a garden—someone is standing beside the bed. A boy. Mint. He's looking down at Ainslie. Ainslie asleep, Ainslie's mouth open, and Mint is touching Ainslie's mouth with his thumb.

Immy sits up in bed.

Mint looks right at her. He looks at her and he smiles. He touches his fingers to his own mouth. Then he disappears.

Immy doesn't see the Ghost Boyfriend again for two weeks. Ainslie says he's around. She thinks he's exploring the house. She sees him, just for seconds at a time, in different rooms, then he's gone. He shows up almost every time Ainslie watches TV. Usually during the commercial breaks.

"He likes to watch commercials?" Immy says. They're at the yogurt place, loading toppings on their frozen yogurt. Blueberries, raspberries, mochi.

"I think he's being considerate," Ainslie says. "He doesn't want to interrupt what I'm doing, so he waits for the commercial breaks. Like, I never see him in the bathroom or when I'm getting dressed for school. So I think it's the same thing with the TV."

Over in the corner of the yogurt shop a middle-aged woman sits and moves a stroller back and forth with one hand while she eats with the other. Immy keeps looking over. She can't tell if it's a real baby in the stroller or a Baby.

"So he's there for a few seconds and he does what, exactly?" she says.

"He watches TV with me. The commercials. He seems to like the commercials where a man and a woman are driving somewhere in a car. You know, those ones where there's a road going alongside the ocean? Or a hill. He looks at the commercials on TV and he looks at me," Ainslie says. "He just looks at me. Like no one has ever looked at me before. And then he goes away."

There's something about the way Ainslie says this, about her face, and so Immy does what the Ghost Boyfriend does. She looks at Ainslie as carefully and as closely as she can. Ainslie looks like she had a very bad night's sleep. Her lips are chapped and there's lots of concealer, poorly applied, under her eyes. As if she's keeping secrets there, under the skin. "Do you ever see him at night? In your bedroom?"

Ainslie blinks. "No," she says. "No, I don't think so."

"Good," Immy says. "Because that would be creepy, if he was there looking at you while you were asleep."

Ainslie's face crumples, just a little. "Yeah. That would be creepy."

School is school. Why can't it ever be something else? Immy can't believe she has two more years of this. Two more years of equations and sad books where bad things happen to boring people and Justin giving her wounded looks. Okay, so maybe he'll get over it faster than that. If she ignores him. Two more years of unflattering gym shorts and Spanish that she's never going to use and having to be the person that she's always been, because that's the person that everyone thinks she is. That everyone assumes she's always going to be. Everyone thinks this is the real Immy. And what if the Immy they see is the real Immy, and the one on the inside is just hormones and chemicals and too many little secrets and weird jumbled thoughts that don't mean anything, after all?

Maybe she should shave her head. Maybe she should take her classes more seriously. Maybe she should give Justin another chance. Maybe not.

She has a dream that night. She's driving a fast car along a curving road. The ocean is far below. The Ghost Boyfriend sits in the passenger seat. They don't say anything to each other. The moon is high overhead.

She texts Ainslie in the morning. *I dreamed about your Boyfi. Weird right?*

Ainslie doesn't text back.

That afternoon Immy and Sky go over to Ainslie's house to study for a Spanish quiz. Elin takes AP Latin because, Elin.

They mostly don't study, though. They ransack the cupboards for the Reese's Peanut Butter Cups and Little Debbie Spinwheels and bags of Oreos that Ainslie's mother hides away in soup tureens and behind boxes of rice and cereal. Once they found a little baggie with weed in it and they flushed it down the toilet.

Ainslie says they're doing her mother a favor eating the Oreos and Reese's. They're teenagers. They have higher metabolisms.

Sky says, "*Dónde está* Mint?"

Ainslie says, "He's downstairs. In the rec room with Oliver and Alan." She's decapitating a Reese's Peanut Butter Cup. Ainslie only eats the insides. Like a spider. Spiders only eat the insides. "I turned him off, actually."

"You did what?" Immy says.

"I turned him off," Ainslie says. "He was kind of freaking my mom out. I can see why they did the recall. It's not romantic, having a Boyfriend pop in and out of existence all the time. And it's not like Mint ever said anything romantic. He just stared. And, you know, after a week it felt like if I was looking in one direction, maybe he was right there behind me. I got a sore neck because I kept jerking my head back to look up at the ceiling because once I looked up and he was there. And once I found him under the kitchen table. So I kept having to look under things, too."

"Just like a real ghost in a movie," Sky says. Sky loves scary movies. No one will go see them with her.

"What about Embodied? Did you try him out in Embodied Mode?" Immy says.

"Yeah," Ainslie says. "And that was also no fun. He said all the right stuff, the stuff Oliver and Alan say, but you know what? I didn't buy it. I don't know. Maybe we're getting too old for Boyfriends."

"Let's go turn him on," Sky says. "I want to see. I want to see him float up on the ceiling."

"No," Ainslie says. Ainslie never says no. They both stare at her. The little pile of emptied Reese's Cups. She says, "Here. You want the chocolate?"

Ainslie wants to show them something online. It's an actor they all like. He's naked and you can totally see his penis. They've all seen penises online before, but this one belongs to someone famous. Sky and Ainslie go looking for other famous penises, and Immy goes back to the kitchen to study. But first she goes down to the rec room.

The rec room is full of Ainslie's mother's abandoned projects. An easel with a smock still draped across it. A sewing machine, a rowing machine, bins of fabric and half-finished scrapbooks with pictures of Ainslie and Immy when they could still run around the yard naked, Ainslie and Immy and Sky when they had their first ballet recital, Ainslie and Immy and Sky and Elin graduating from middle school. Back before Ainslie's parents divorced, and Immy got boobs and Ainslie got Boyfriends. All those Ainslies and Immys, with their dolls and their princess dresses and Halloween costumes and Valentines. Immy's always been the prettier one. Ainslie isn't a dog, isn't hideous, but Immy's much prettier. If Boyfriends worked the usual way, Immy could get one like *that*.

But maybe then she wouldn't want one.

There are three coffins standing up inside the closet of the rec room. No room for a fourth, is Immy's first thought. They used to spend hours playing with Oliver and Alan. Now they hardly ever do. That's her second. And it's not like Immy can just suggest bringing them out. They belong to Ainslie. It's not like playing dolls. It's more like telling your friend you want to hang out with some fake people she keeps in her closet, and anyway they're only nice to you because Ainslie wants them to be nice to you. If Immy had a Boyfriend she wouldn't keep him in a closet in her basement.

The first coffin she opens is Oliver. The second one is Mint. It's a ridiculous name. No wonder he's been acting weird.

"Hi, Mint," she says. "It's Immy again. Wake up."

Then she holds her breath, and turns around to look for him, but he's not there, of course. He's just a fake boy in a fake coffin, right? That's what Ainslie thinks, anyway. What Immy thinks is you shouldn't be able to just turn your Boyfriend off, just because he's not the way you want him to be.

She sticks her fingers into his hair. It's incredibly soft. Real hair, which should be creepy, but it's not. If he were Ainslie's real boyfriend, she couldn't do this.

She finds the little soft place behind the ear and presses down. Once for Embodied, twice for Spectral Mode. She presses down again. She wakes him up.

When she closes the lid of the coffin and turns around, this time the Ghost Boyfriend is perched on an exercise bike. He's staring at her like she's really there. Like he knows her, knows something about her.

Like he sees the real Immy, the one she isn't sure is really there. Right now, though, she's real. Immy is real. They both are. They're making each other realer the longer they look at each other, and isn't that what love should be? Isn't that what love should do?

"I'm Immy," she says. "Imogen."

She says, "I wish you could tell me your real name. Ainslie doesn't know I did this. So be careful. Don't let her see you."

He smiles at her. She puts out her hand, moves it to where she would be touching his face, if she could touch his face. "If you belonged to me," Immy says, "I wouldn't keep you in a box in a closet in the dark. If you were my Boyfriend."

The rest of the night is penis GIFs and Oreos and Spanish vocabulary. When Ainslie's mother gives Immy and Sky a ride home, Immy looks back and she thinks maybe she can see a boy looking out of the window of Ainslie's bedroom. It's kind of a gas to think about Ainslie being home all alone with her Ghost Boyfriend. Immy falls asleep that night thinking about Ainslie, and ceilings, and kitchen tables, and Mint's soft, baby-fine hair. She wonders whose hair it was.

Immy doesn't know if Ainslie knows she's being haunted. She seems out of sorts, but that could just be Ainslie-and-her-mother stuff. Meanwhile, Sky and Elin are having a fight about some boots that Elin borrowed and wore in the rain. All Immy can think about is Mint. She keeps having that dream about the car and the highway and the ocean. Mint there in the dark with her, the moon above them. Maybe it means something? It ought to mean something.

Friday night is Elin's birthday present to Ainslie, tickets to see O Hell, Kitty! play at the Coliseum. Sky and Immy are going to have a movie night without them, except then Elin gets Sky a ticket, too, an apology for ruining her boots.

Whatever, Immy doesn't want to go anyway.

The idea comes to her when she hears about Ainslie's mom, who was going to be the ride to the concert, and who, it turns out, has gotten a ticket for herself after watching some videos on O Hell, Kitty!'s YouTube channel. Embarrassing for Ainslie, sure, but this is Immy's chance to see Mint.

Immy knows where Ainslie's mom keeps a spare house key. She knows the alarm code, too. One of the benefits of a long-standing friendship: it makes breaking and entering so much easier.

She tells her parents she's been invited to dinner at Ainslie's house. She gets a ride from her dad. Her mother might have waited around until someone opened the front door, but that's why she asked her dad.

She waves—*go, it's okay, just go*—and he drives away. Then she lets herself into Ainslie's house. She stands in the hallway and says, "Hello? Mint? Hello?"

It's early evening. Ainslie's house is stuffed with shadows. Immy can't decide whether or not to turn on the lights. She's made peace with what she's doing, it's for a good cause. But turning on the lights? That would be making herself at home.

She looks up at the ceiling, because she can't help it. She goes into the kitchen, and crouches down to look under the table, and is, despite herself, somehow relieved when Mint isn't there, either.

It gets darker second by second. Really, she needs to turn on the lights. She goes into room after room, turns on lights, goes on. She has the sense that Mint is there ahead of her, leaving each room as she enters it.

She finds him finally—or does he find her? They find each other—in the rec room. One minute Immy is alone, and the next Mint is there, standing so close that she takes a step back without meaning to.

Mint disappears. Then reappears. Standing even closer than before. They're nose to nose. Well, nose to chin. He's not much taller than she is. But she can see through him: the couch, the exercise bike, and the sewing table. He shouldn't stand so close, she thinks. But she shouldn't be here.

None of this is okay. But it's not real. So it's okay.

"It's me," Immy says unnecessarily. "I, uh, I wanted to see if you were, um. If you were okay." He blinks. Smiles. Points at her, then extends his arm, so that it goes right through her middle. She sucks in her tummy. He disappears. She turns around, and there he is again, standing in front of the closet.

He disappears again when she reaches out to open the closet. Is there, inside the closet, standing in front of his coffin. Is gone again. She opens the lid, and there is his body. It's pretty clear, now, what he wants her to do. So she reaches into his hair, finds that button.

She's still standing there like a freak with her fingers in his hair when his eyes open. And this is the first thing Ainslie's Ghost Boyfriend, Mint, ever says to Immy: "You," he says.

"Me?" Immy says.

"You're here," Mint says.

"I had to see you," Immy says. She backs out of the closet in a hurry, because she doesn't want to have a conversation in a closet with Ainslie's Ghost Boyfriend, standing next to the coffins of Ainslie's Vampire Boyfriend and Ainslie's Werewolf Boyfriend. Mint follows. He stretches, arms above his head, flexing his neck, the way Boyfriends do—as if they are real boys who have, regrettably, spent too much time stored in coffins.

"I did something to you," Immy says. "The ring."

Mint puts his fingers up to his lips. Opens his mouth in a wide yawn. Can he feel it in there, the hair ring? The thought makes Immy gag. "You did this," he agrees.

Immy has to sit down. She says, "Okay, I did something. I

wanted to do something, because, well, because *Ainslie.* I *meant* to do something. But what did I do?"

"I'm here," Mint says. "We're here. We're here together."

He says, "We shouldn't be here."

"Why not? Because you belong to Ainslie?" Immy says. "Or do you mean we shouldn't be here *here*? In this house? Or do you mean you shouldn't be here at all? Because you're a ghost. A real ghost?"

Mint just looks at her. A real ghost in a fake boy? She did this? That look in his eyes, is that something real? He has the most beautiful eyes Immy's ever seen. And, okay, so they're molded out of silicone or they're bags full of colored gel and microelectronic components, but so what? How is that really any different from vitreous humors and lenses and rods and cone cells?

Boyfriends can even cry, if you want them to.

Immy wants to believe so badly. More than she's ever wanted anything. She says, "Who are you? What do you want?"

"We shouldn't be here," Mint says again. "We should be together." He touches his mouth. "I belong with you."

"Oh," Immy says. "Wait. Wait." Now she's sure that someone is playing a trick on her. Maybe Ainslie knew, somehow, that she was coming? Maybe she booby-trapped Mint, told him to say all of this, is hiding somewhere with Elin and Sky. They're watching all of this, watching Immy make a fool out of herself. Aren't they?

"I love you," Mint says. And then, as if he's agreeing with himself. "I love *you.* I belong with you. Don't leave me. Don't leave me here alone with her."

Everyone who is alive has a ghost inside them, don't they? So why can't there be a real ghost in a fake boy? Why can't a real ghost in a fake boy fall in love with Immy? Justin did. Why can't Immy get what she wants, just for once?

Why can't Mint get what he wants?

Immy comes up with her plan sitting on the couch with Mint, so close that they're practically touching. Immy can hardly breathe. She studies Mint's fingers, those half moons at the base of his fingernails, the ridges on the tips of his fingers. The creases in his palms. The way his chest rises and falls when he breathes. It would be creepy, staring at a real boy like this, the way Immy stares at Mint. A real boy would want to know why you were staring at him.

She wants to ask Mint so many questions. Who are you? How did you die? What's your real name? What is it that made you love me?

She wants to tell him so many things.

They'll have time for all of that later on.

Her dad texts to say that he's about two minutes from Ainslie's house. No time now. When Mint gets back in his coffin, and Immy is about to put him back in Spectral Mode, she can't wait any longer. She kisses him and presses that button. It's her first real kiss, really. She doesn't count Justin. Lip-wrestling doesn't count.

She kisses Mint right on the lips. His lips are dry and soft and cool. It's everything she ever wanted a kiss to be.

Her dad's car is pulling up in the driveway as she comes up the stairs, and before she reaches the door, Mint is there again in front of her in the dark hallway, a ghost this time. This time he kisses her. It's the ghost of a kiss. And even if she can't feel anything this time, this kiss, too, is everything she's ever wanted.

On the ride home, her dad says, "How's Ainslie?"

"Ainslie's *Ainslie*," Immy says. "You know."

"It would be pretty strange if she wasn't," her dad says. "Is she still big on those Loverboy things?"

"Boyfriends," Immy says. "She got a new one for her birthday. I don't know. Maybe not so much anymore."

Her dad says, "How about you? Any boyfriends? Real ones?"

"I don't know," Immy says. "There was this guy Justin, but, uh, that was a while ago. He was, you know. It wasn't serious. Like, we hung out some. Then we broke up."

"True love, huh?"

The way he says it, jokingly, makes Immy so mad she wants to scream. She pinches her arm, turns and leans her forehead against the cool dark of the car window. Shivers and it's all okay again. "Dad? Can I ask you something?"

"Shoot."

"Do you believe in ghosts?"

"Never seen one," he says. "Don't really want to see one, either. I'd like to think that we don't just hang around here after, you know, we're dead. I'd like to think we get to do something new. Go places."

"Can I ask another question? How do you know? If it's love, I mean."

Her dad turns to look at her, then nods as if she's just told him something she didn't even realize she was saying. He looks back at the road. "That kind of night? Who's thinking the big thoughts about love and death? You or Ainslie?"

"Me. I guess."

"You know what love is, Immy."

"I do?"

"Of course you do. You love your mom, you love me and your mom, right? You love Ainslie. You love your friends."

"Sometimes I love my friends," Immy says. "But that's not the kind of love I mean. I mean, you know, boys. I mean love, like the way love is in books or movies. The kind of love that makes you want to die. That makes you stay up all night, that makes you feel sick to your stomach, the kind of love that makes everything else not matter."

"Oh, Immy," her dad says. "That's not real love. That's a trick the body plays on the mind. It's not a bad trick—it's how we get poetry and songs on the radio and babies—and sometimes it's even good poetry, or good music. Babies are good, too, of course, but, please, Immy, not yet. Stick to music and poems for now."

"God," Immy says. "I wasn't asking about sex. I was asking about love. If that kind of love is just a trick, then maybe the whole thing is a trick. Right? All of it. The friend stuff. The family stuff. You and Mom need to love me because otherwise, it would suck to be you. Stuck with me."

Her dad is quiet for a minute. He hates to lose an argument; Immy loves that he never tries to bullshit her. "Some pretty smart people say that it is all a trick. But, Immy, if it's all a trick, it's the best trick I know. Your mom and I love you. You love us. You and Ainslie love each other. And one day, you'll meet a boy or, I don't know, you'll meet a girl, and you'll fall in love with them. And if you're lucky they'll love you back."

"Sometimes I don't love Ainslie," Immy confesses. "Sometimes I hate her."

"Well," her dad says. "That's part of love, too."

It's funny. Immy likes her own house better than Ainslie's house. She wouldn't want to live in Ainslie's house even if she didn't have to live there with Ainslie's mother. But part of Immy is glad that everybody ends up hanging out at Ainslie's house almost all of the time. She doesn't like it when everyone comes over to her house. She doesn't like when her dad jokes with Ainslie, or when her mother tells Sky how pretty she is. She doesn't like the faces Elin makes when she looks through Immy's parents' CDs. Once at dinner Immy asked her parents if they didn't think it would be nice to build a sunroom off the kitchen. Her parents just looked at each other. Her dad said, "Sure, Immy. That would be nice." He didn't even sound sarcastic.

Immy is in love. Immy has a secret. Ghosts exist and the world is magic and there is an unreal boy whose real name she doesn't even know with a ring made of hair in his mouth, and he loves Immy because she put it there. He loves Immy even though Ainslie is the one he is supposed to love. Guess what? Immy finally has a Boyfriend. And guess what? It's exactly as awesome and wonderful and amazing and scary as she always thought it would be, except it turns out to be something else, too. It's real.

Last night she hardly slept at all. The school cafeteria is too loud and the fluorescent lights are too bright and the sandwich she made for lunch leaves her fingers smelling like old lettuce and mayonnaise.

All Ainslie and Elin and Sky want to talk about is the lead

vocalist of O Hell, Kitty! And the hot guy who spilled his beer on Sky's shirt and Ainslie's mom, who is the worst.

"You should have come," Sky says. "They were like, *amazing*, Immy." So Sky is going to be all about music, too, now? Apparently.

Ainslie says to Immy, "And nobody's even told you the really creepy thing! So we get back to the house last night, and I just wanted to kill my mom. Like, what I really want to do is defenestrate her or chop off her head and put it in the microwave for a few hours, okay, but you can't do that and so Elin and Sky and I had this other idea, which was to turn Mint on and I was going to tell him to go scare her. But guess what?"

"What?" Immy says. She knows what.

"He was already on! Spectral Mode! Which is impossible, because I turned him off, remember? I told you that? I did it a while ago, so how was he back on? That's creepy, right? Like real ghost-stuff creepy."

"Maybe your mom did it?" Immy says.

"Maybe it was the butler," Elin says.

Sky bugs her eyes out and says, "Maybe Ainslie's Ghost Boyfriend is a real ghost boyfriend." Sometimes Immy isn't sure about Sky. Are you supposed to take everything she says at face value? Or is she actually the most sarcastic person Immy knows? Unclear.

"So what did *you* do last night?" Elin says. "Anything interesting?"

It might be worrying, this question, except that Justin is eating lunch two tables away from them. He keeps trying to catch Immy's eye. Elin has noticed and you can practically hear her teeth grinding together. Maybe she can sense how happy Immy is? How loved she is? Immy deliberately looks away from Elin as she answers; sends a little almost smile in Justin's direction. "Well," she says. "You know. Not really. Nothing worth talking about."

Ainslie says, "What do they put on this pizza? It's not cheese. I refuse to believe this is really cheese."

Carrying out the plan, rescuing Mint, is actually pretty simple. Spring break is coming up and Ainslie and her mother are going out to Utah to go skiing. The hard part is the waiting.

Immy can't ask her dad to drive her over to Ainslie's house again, because Ainslie has already come over for dinner and couldn't shut up about black diamond slopes and polygamy and bison, and even if Immy's dad forgets, her mom won't. But she's already done the research to find out how much a cab would cost. Definitely affordable. And she can go during the day while her parents are at work.

Or wait, she can bike over. She's done it once or twice. It's doable.

Then call a taxi when she's ready to leave Ainslie's house. Simple plans are good plans. Buy a duffel bag big enough for Mint to fit in, and remember the blankets to pad out the bag. The thing is, Boyfriends don't weigh as much as you think they would, and the taxi driver will help.

Remember enough money for the tip.

Over to the You-Store-It where Ainslie's mother has a storage space big enough to have a circus in. Immy's been there a few times with Ainslie, bringing over lamps or rugs or ugly pieces of art whenever Ainslie's mother redecorates. There's at least one pretty nice couch. There are outlets in the wall so Mint can recharge.

The key to the You-Store-It locker is hanging up in the laundry room at Ainslie's house. All of the keys at Ainslie's house are labeled. (Just like how Ainslie's mother keeps all her online passwords on a sticky on her screen.) It's as if they want to make things as easy as they can.

And the You-Store-It isn't all that far away from Immy's house. A mile or two, which is absolutely bikeable.

It's not a long-term solution, but it will do until Immy figures out something better. She isn't sure how any of this is going to work. She's trying not to let that bother her. Over spring break there will be frozen yogurt and dumb movie nights and thrift stores with Sky and Elin, and then there will be Mint. If he were a real boy, he could come along, too, for all the other, real stuff. But he isn't, and he can't, and that's okay. She'll take what she can get and be happy about it, because love isn't about convenience and frozen yogurt and real life. That isn't what love is about.

Immy sees Mint twice before spring break. It makes the waiting easier. The first time is when Ainslie asks her over to help with her hair. Ainslie's mother has decided that Ainslie can put in a streak of color, just one streak, for spring break. Ainslie can't decide between green and red.

"Stop or go," Immy says, looking at the squeeze tubes of Manic Panic.

"What?" Ainslie says.

"What do you want to say with your hair?" Immy asks her. "Go is green, stop is red."

Ainslie says, "I'm not trying to make a statement here. I just want to know which one looks better, okay? Is green too weird?"

"I like the green," Immy says. "Goes with your eyes."

"I think I like the red," Ainslie says.

While they're waiting for the bleach to work, Ainslie takes

Immy down to the rec room. The whole time Immy has been trying not to think about Mint. And now that's where Ainslie is taking her.

"I just need to check," Ainslie says. "I check every single day now. Sometimes I check a couple of times. He's never on. But I still have to check. Last night I woke up at three A.M. and I had to come down here and check."

She jerks back the coffin lid, as if she thinks she'll catch Mint up to no good. His eyes are closed, of course, because how can he turn himself on?

Where is he when he isn't here? It hurts Immy to see him like this, turned off like he's just some dumb toy.

The bleachy part of Ainslie's hair, wrapped in foil, sticks practically straight up. Immy imagines yanking it. Hearing Ainslie shriek. And Mint still wouldn't wake up. So what's the point?

Ainslie stabs at Mint's head like she's killing a spider. Turns and shrugs at Immy. "I know I'm being an idiot. He's just a semi-defective Boyfriend or something. He's not even that cute, right? Oliver is much cuter. I don't know why I wanted him so much."

Maybe if Immy said something Ainslie would just give her Mint.

Ainslie says, "I asked my mom if we could sell him on eBay and she had a fit. Acted like I was the worst person in the world. Kept telling me how much she paid for him, how hard it was to get him, that I didn't appreciate everything she did to make me happy. So I had to pretend I was just kidding."

Well, then.

Immy says, "Come on. I think it's time for the bleach to come out."

She gets one last look at Mint before Ainslie shuts the lid again. And Ainslie changes her mind, chooses the green, then the red, the green, and then the red again. They both like the way it looks when it's finished, like a long streak of blood.

At school two days later Ainslie tells them about how her mother went and put a streak of red in her own hair. She's so angry she cries. They all hug her, and then Immy helps her cut all the red right out with a pair of scissors in the art room. All Immy wants, at that moment, is for Ainslie to be as happy as Immy is.

The next time she sees Mint it's two days after that. Four in the morning. She's done a stupid thing, biked all the way over to Ainslie's, six miles in the dark. But she did it for love. Call it a trial run. She lets herself into the house. She's a ghost. She almost goes to Ainslie's bedroom, to stand beside Ainslie's bed and watch her while she's sleeping. Ainslie's almost pretty when she's asleep. Immy's always thought so. But she's seen Ainslie asleep before.

She goes down the stairs to the rec room and she turns Mint on in Spectral Mode. He's there immediately, watching her from over by the couch. "Hi," she says. "I had to come. Everything is fine. I just had to come see you. That's all. I miss you. Today is Friday. I'm coming back on Monday and everything is going to be fine. We'll be together. Okay?"

Her Ghost Boyfriend nods. Smiles at her.

"I love you," she says. He says it back silently.

She really ought to turn him off, but Immy can't do it. Instead she goes back to the closet and she opens the lids of Oliver's and

Alan's coffins. She finds their buttons, one with each hand, and she turns them both on, shutting the closet door as quickly as she can so they won't see her, know who's done this. She's back up the stairs and out the door, the key is under the rock again, and she pedals madly away. When she gets home the sun is just coming up.

She thinks with satisfaction, *That's* going to surprise Ainslie.

But Ainslie doesn't mention it. Ainslie is kind of a wreck since the thing with her mom and the hair. Or maybe it's all the Boyfriend stuff. Either way, what Ainslie really needs are her friends. Immy and Sky and Elin take her out for yogurt after school. Tomorrow Ainslie and her mom go to Utah. Immy wants to get up and dance on tables. There's a song on in the yogurt place and it's kind of a good song. Immy really ought to find out who sings it, except if she asks, Elin, or maybe everybody, will look at her like, you like *that* song? Really? But she does. She actually likes it. Really.

She hardly sleeps at all Sunday night. Goes over and over the plan in her head. Tries to work out all the things that might go wrong so she can fix them before they happen. A horrible idea lodges itself in her head: what if after Immy turned on all of the Boyfriends, Ainslie did something crazy? Like, finally get her mom to take them all to Goodwill? Or worse? But all the coffins are right where they should be. Alan and Oliver and Mint are all off. The taxi drops her off at the You-Store-It and she puts Mint in his duffel bag on a pallet mover and the key works just fine and so what if the storage space smells like dust and mold and there are random things everywhere? She unzips Mint and pushes the button for Embodied.

And it's just like it was in the rec room. The first time they were alone together. It's just so easy to be with him. Immy has already cleared off the couch, plugged in one of the nice lamps, put in one of the bulbs she brought from home. She even has a blanket for them in case the storage space is cold. Well, for her. Mint probably doesn't get cold.

That's one of the things she wants to ask him, now that they can finally talk. Not about getting cold. About his name. She doesn't have to be home for hours.

They're facing each other on the couch. Holding hands just like boyfriends and girlfriends do. It isn't really like holding hands, exactly, because he's made out of silicone and plastics and tubes of gel, metal rods, wiring, whatever, and his hand feels weird if she tries to think of it as a real hand, but that doesn't matter.

And of course he can't really feel her hand, she knows, but it must mean something to him, her hand in his. The way it means something to her. Because he's just as real as he isn't real.

It's good enough. Better than anything she ever imagined.

She's asked him about his name. His real name.

"I don't remember," he says. "I don't remember many things. I remember you. Only you."

She's a little disappointed, but doesn't want him to know it. "Is it okay if I keep calling you Mint?" It's just a stupid name that Ainslie came up with, but when she thinks about it, Immy realizes that Mint is how she thinks of him. It would be weird to try calling him by another name.

"Do you remember anything about when you were alive?"

He says, "It was cold. I was alone. And then you were there. We were together."

"Do you remember how you died?"

"I remember love."

Immy doesn't want to know about other girls. Girls he knew when he was alive. Not even if they're dead and gone. She says, "I've never been in love before. I've never felt like this before."

That awful hand flexes, those fingers curl around her own. She wonders how he knows how much pressure to exert. Is it Mint who does that or is it some kind of Boyfriend basic subroutine? It isn't really important which one it is.

"I can stay for a while," she says. "Then I have to go home."

He looks at her as if he never wants her to leave.

"What will you do when I go home?" Immy says.

"I'll wait," he says. "I'll wait for you to come back to me."

She says, "I promise I'll come back as soon as I can."

"Stay," he says. "Stay with me."

"Okay," Immy says. "I'll stay as long as I can."

She says, finally, when he only looks at her, "What do you want to do? You've been stuck in Ainslie's closet for what, a month now? Where were you before that? Before Ainslie turned you on and I put the ring in your mouth? Is it weird, talking about this?"

"I'm yours," Mint says. "You're mine. Nothing else matters. Only you and I."

So Immy tells him everything. Everything she's been feeling this year. About Justin. About Ainslie. About how she's not sure, sometimes, who she is. They hold hands the whole time. And then, before she leaves, she turns Mint back to Spectral Mode.

That way he can investigate the You-Store-It if he wants to while she's gone. Spectral Mode has a range of three thousand square feet, which is one of the cool features of the Ghost Boyfriend. Immy has been reading everything she can find online about Ghost Boyfriends. She's read it all before, but now it's different.

There's a lot of discussion online about the uncanny valley, dolls, how characters are drawn in video games. Things that look too much like real people: that awful gap between the real and the almost real. Vampire Boyfriends and Werewolf Boyfriends and Ghost Boyfriends, supposedly, don't fall in the uncanny valley. People have an average of forty-three facial muscles. Boyfriends have the equivalent of fifty. They're supposed to be more realistic than real people. Or something. Their heads are slightly bigger; their eyes are bigger, too. To make you feel good things when you look at them. Like how you're supposed to feel when you see a baby.

Immy has joined two separate listservs for people with Boyfriends. She imagines what it will be like, posting to the listservs about the cute things Mint says, the fun things they do.

It's the best week of Immy's life. She hangs out with Elin and Sky. Ainslie texts them to tell them all the horrible things her mother is doing. And Immy spends as much time as she can in the storage space with her Boyfriend. Her boyfriend.

The storage space is dark and awful, but Mint doesn't seem to care. Well, he was living in a coffin in a closet before this. He doesn't have much to compare it to. He tells her about the things that other renters have in their lockers. A lot of pianos, apparently. And textbooks. Mint is perfectly happy to list everything he's discovered. And Immy is perfectly happy to sit and listen to him go on and on about empty aquariums and old dentist chairs and boxes of Beanie Babies.

When she and Justin were hanging out he kept talking about video games he liked. She'd played some of them, too, is pretty good at some kinds of games, but it wasn't like they were having a conversation. Justin didn't leave any room for her to say anything.

Immy manages to find that song from the yogurt place and downloads it onto her phone. She plays it for Mint and they slow dance in the extremely small space not taken up by all of Ainslie's mother's crap.

"I really like this song," she says.

"It's a good song," Mint says. "You're a good dancer. I've been wanting to dance with you for so long."

His hand is on the small of Immy's back. He's a good dancer, too, maybe even better than Oliver, and she leans her head against his shoulder.

"Which hair was yours?" she says.

Mint says, "I'm yours. Only yours."

"No," Immy says. "The ring. Which hair was yours? The blond hair or the black hair?"

"The blond hair," Mint says. "The black."

"Never mind," Immy says. She kisses his shoulder, hugs him a little tighter. It's a little weird, how Mint doesn't smell like anything. It's a good thing, probably. If you kept a real boy in a storage locker, you'd need to figure out how he could take showers. Plus you'd have to feed him. Although maybe Mint is starting to smell a little like the storage space, a little bit like mildew. Maybe Immy should buy him some cologne.

He's still wearing the black funeral suit he came in. Maybe she could buy him some T-shirts and jeans at the thrift store. She can't picture Mint in a T-shirt.

Ainslie comes home in two days, and Immy isn't sure what happens after that. It's not as if Ainslie is going to think Immy took Mint, why would she think that? But it's still going to be complicated. And then there's the storage space, which isn't going to work forever. And anyway, when spring break is over, it's not like Immy can just come over and hang out in the storage space all day.

When she tells Mint all of this, he says nothing. He trusts her to figure something out.

He says, "Stay with me. Never leave me."

He says, "I'll never leave you."

That night she decides she might as well go and see Mint. They've never spent the night together. Anyway she can't fall asleep. Maybe the time is right. They can lie on the couch together, and then she can fall asleep with her head on his shoulder. She can wake up in his arms.

It's bitterly cold. Immy, on her bike, coasts down empty streets. No one sees her go by. She could sneak into a house. Cut off a lock of someone's hair while they're asleep. Pour drain cleaner in a fish tank or put salt in a sugar jar. What couldn't she do? She could go places. Have adventures. Cause all kinds of trouble.

The You-Store-It after midnight is a palace. A mausoleum. Gothic, satiny black, full of other people's secrets. But her secret is the best.

When she gets to the storage locker, she hears voices. A voice. Someone is talking. Mint is talking. Mint is talking to someone. She recognizes everything that he's saying.

"I love you. Only you."

"I love only you."

"Stay with me. Don't ever leave me."

"We're together now. I'll never leave you."

"I love you."

It's peculiar, because Immy set Mint to Spectral Mode. And who is he talking to, anyway? Everything that he's saying, it's everything he says to Immy. All of this is wrong. Something is wrong.

She unlocks the door, lifts it up. And something is definitely wrong, because there is her Ghost Boyfriend, standing in the dark, in Embodied Mode, and there is her Ghost Boyfriend in Spectral Mode. Except the ghost isn't her Ghost Boyfriend. It's a girl. Barely there, less there than Mint ever is. The beam of Immy's flashlight pins the ghost girl there in the air. Holes for eyes. Light hair.

The ghost's hand is reaching out to Mint. Her fingers on his mouth.

Immy may be an idiot, but she's not an *idiot*. She knows, instantly, the mistake she has made. The mistake she has been *allowed* to make. Those three lengths of hair, the two black pieces and the yellow. Apparently Immy isn't the one who gave Ainslie's Ghost Boyfriend a real ghost—she's the one who gave Ainslie's Ghost Boyfriend two ghosts.

No one is in love with her. She isn't anyone's girlfriend.

This isn't her love story.

She goes right up to the Ghost Boyfriend, Mint, whoever he is. And that other girl. That dead girl. Who cares who she is, either. It's not like she can do anything to Immy. But Immy can do something to her. Body or no body.

"Immy," Mint says.

"Shut up," she tells him. And she sticks her fingers right into his traitor's mouth.

He bites down. And then his hands are up and someone's fingers are around her throat. Mint's fingers.

She thinks, They aren't supposed to do that! She's so angry she isn't even scared.

Immy's fingers are under that wriggling tongue and in that compartment and she's got hold of the hair ring. She yanks it out of Mint's mouth and like that, the girl ghost is gone and the Ghost Boyfriend is just a *thing* standing there, its hands loose at her neck, its mouth slightly open.

Immy sticks the hair ring in her pocket. Her fingers are really throbbing, but she can bend them, so not broken. They're just a little mangled.

She's alone with the Ghost Boyfriend looming there, like he's just waiting for her to turn him on again. And those two lovebirds? Those ghosts? Are they still around? She gets out of there as fast as she can.

She rides her bike down dark streets, crying the whole time. Snot all over her face. What an idiot. Worst of all, she'll never be able to tell anyone any of this. Not even *Ainslie.*

She washes her hands thoroughly once she gets home. Takes the nail scissors and a pair of tweezers out of the cabinet in her bathroom. She holds the hair ring under the magnifying glass and uses the tweezers to tease out the blond length of hair. *Are they here?* She hopes so. Cuts through the blond hair with the scissors, and tweezes out every last strand. Now she has a ring of black hair, and a very small pile of blond. The black hair goes back into the locket on the choker she got for Ainslie. Next she goes through her jewelry box, looking for the necklace she used to wear all the time last year. A kind of medicine bag thing on a leather strand. The blond hair goes in it. Every bit.

After that, she gets in bed. Leaves the light on. When she falls asleep, she's in that car again on the moonlit road. Mint is in the passenger seat. Someone else in the backseat. She won't look at either of them. Just keeps on driving. Wonders where she'll be when she gets there.

In the morning, she explains things to her dad. Not everything. Just the part about the Ghost Boyfriend and the storage locker. She tells him it's all part of a joke she and Elin and Sky were going to play on Ainslie, but now she's realized what a bad idea it was. Ainslie would have really freaked out. She explains that Ainslie is really fragile right now. Going through a bad breakup.

He's proud of her. They drive to the You-Store-It and retrieve the Ghost Boyfriend. When he's back in his coffin in the closet in the basement in Ainslie's house, her father takes her out for frozen yogurt.

Ainslie comes back from her ski trip with a tan because Ainslie is a multitasker.

At lunch they all sit out in the sunshine in their coats and scarves, because it's hard to be back inside, back in school again.

"Here," Immy says. "Happy birthday, Ainslie. Finally found it."

It's a little tiny box, hardly worth it, but Ainslie does what she always does. Unwraps it so carefully you'd think what she really likes about presents is the wrapping paper. She takes out the choker and everyone oohs and aahs. When she opens the locket, Immy says, "It's probably not true, but supposedly the hair is Bam Muller's hair." Bam Muller is the lead singer of O Hell, Kitty! She checked. He has black hair.

"Kind of gross," Ainslie says. "But also kind of awesome. Thanks, Immy."

She puts on the choker and everyone admires how it looks against Ainslie's long white neck. Nobody has noticed the little bruises on Immy's neck. You can hardly see them.

"You're welcome," Immy says and gives Ainslie a big hug. "I'm so glad you're back."

"Be more lesbian," Elin says. Sky has spilled the beans on Elin and Justin. The weird thing is that Elin doesn't seem that much happier. Probably the whole kissing thing. Although the way it turns out, Elin and Justin are still together when school gets out. They're together all summer long. And when Halloween rolls around and Ainslie has a party at her house, Elin comes as a sexy Red Riding Hood and Justin is a big bad wolf.

Oliver and Alan and Mint are all at the party. Ainslie brings them out for the first time in a long time. Immy dances with all of them. She dances with Mint twice. They don't really have anything to say to each other.

It's a great party.

Sky has made another batch of absinthe. She's a cowgirl. Ainslie's mother is a sexy witch, and Ainslie isn't in costume at all. Or if she is, nobody knows who she's supposed to be. At some point, Immy realizes that Elin is wearing the choker, the one Immy gave Ainslie. So maybe she borrowed it. Or maybe Ainslie got tired of it and gave it to Elin. Whatever. It's not a big deal.

Immy's wearing her medicine bag. She wears it a lot. Take

that, ghost girl. Immy is looking pretty good. She's a succubus. She has to keep explaining what that is, but that's okay. The main thing is she looks amazing.

Justin, for one, can't take his eyes off her. She looks at him once in a while, smiles just a little. All of that practice, she bets Elin has taught him a thing or two about kissing. And he was Immy's boyfriend first.

Two Houses

Two Houses

Wake up, wake up.

Portia is having a birthday party. The party will start without you. Wake up, Gwenda. Wake up. Hurry, hurry.

Soft music. The smell of warm bread. She could have been back home, how many houses ago? In her childhood bed, her mother downstairs baking bread.

The last sleeper in the spaceship *House of Secrets* opened her eyes, crept from her narrow bed. She rose up, or fell, into the chamber.

The chamber, too, was narrow and small, a honeycombed cell. Soft pink light, invisible drawers, chamber and beds, all of them empty. The astronaut Gwenda stretched out her arms, rubbed at her scalp. Her hair had grown out again. Sometimes she imagined a berth crammed with masses of hair. Centuries passing beneath the strangling weight.

Now there was the smell of old books. A library. Maureen was in her head with her, looking at books. Monitoring her heart rate, the dilation of her pupils. Maureen was the ship, the House and the keeper of all its Secrets. A spirit of the air; a soothing subliminal hum; an alchemical sequence of smells and emanations.

Gwenda inhaled. Stretched again, slowly somersaulted. Arcane chemical processes began within her blood, her nervous system.

This is how it was aboard the spaceship *House of Secrets*. You slept and you woke up and you slept again. You might sleep for a year, for five years. There were six astronauts. Sometimes others were already awake. Sometimes you spent days, a few weeks alone. Except you were never really alone. Maureen was always there. She was there with you sleeping and waking. She was inside you, too.

Everyone is waiting for you in the Great Room. There's roasted carp. A chocolate cake.

"A tidal smell," Gwenda said, trying to place it. "Mangrove trees and the sea caught in a hundred places at their roots. I spent a summer in a place like that."

You arrived with one boy and you left with another.

"So I did," Gwenda said. "I'd forgotten. It was such a long time ago."

A hundred years.

"That long!" Gwenda said.

Not long at all.

"No," Gwenda said. "Not long at all." She touched her hair. "I've been asleep . . ."

Seven years this time.

"Seven years," Gwenda said.

A citrus smell. Lime trees. Other smells, pleasant ones, ones that belonged to Mei and Sullivan and Aune and Portia. Sisi. All of their body chemistries adjusted for harmonious relationships. They were, of necessity, a convivial group.

Gwenda threw off her long sleep. Sank toward the curve of the bulkhead, pressing on a drawer. It swung open and in she went to make her toilet, to be poked and prodded and injected, lathered and sluiced. She rid herself of the new growth of hair, the fine down on her arms and legs.

So slow, so slow, Maureen fretted. Let me get rid of it for you. For good.

"One day," Gwenda said. She opened up her log, checked the charts on her guinea pigs, her carp.

This is why you are last again. You dawdle, Gwenda. You refuse to be sensible in the matter of personal grooming. Everyone is waiting for you. You're missing all of the fun.

"Aune has asked for a Finnish disco or a Finnish sauna or the northern lights. Sullivan is playing with dogs. Mei is chatting up movie stars or famous composers, and Portia is being outrageous. There are waterfalls or redwood trees or dolphins," Gwenda said.

Cherry blossoms. The Westminster dog show. 2009. The Sussex Spaniel Ch. Clussexx Three D Grinchy Glee wins. Sisi is hoping you will hurry. She wants to tell you something.

"Well," Gwenda said. "I'd better hurry, then."

Maureen went before and after, down Corridor One. Lights flicked on, then off again so that the corridor fell away behind Gwenda in darkness. Was Maureen the golden light ahead or the darkness that followed behind? Carp swam in the glassy walls.

Then she was in the Galley and the Great Room was just above her. Long-limbed Sisi poked her head through the glory hole. "New tattoo?"

It was an old joke.

Head to toes, Gwenda was covered in ink. There was a Dürer and a Doré; two Chinese dragons and a Celtic cross; the Queen of Diamonds torn in eight pieces by wolves; a girl on a playground rocket; the Statue of Liberty and the state flag of Illinois; passages from Lewis Carroll and the Book of Revelations and a hundred other books; a hundred other marvels. There was the spaceship *House of Secrets* on the back of Gwenda's right hand, and its sister, *House of Mystery,* on her left.

Sisi had a pair of old cowboy boots, and Aune an ivory cross on a chain. Sullivan had a copy of *Moby-Dick;* Portia had a four-carat diamond in a platinum setting. Mei had her knitting needles.

Gwenda had her tattoos. Astronauts on the Long Trip travel lightly.

Hands pulled Gwenda up and into the Great Room, patted her back, her shoulders, ran over her head. Here, feet had weight. There was a floor, and she stood on it. There was a table and on the table was a cake. Familiar faces grinned at her.

The music was very loud. Silky-coated dogs chased flower petals.

"Surprise!" Sisi said. "Happy birthday, Gwenda!"

"But it isn't my birthday," Gwenda said. "It's Portia's birthday."

"The lie was small," Maureen said.

"It was my idea," Portia said. "My idea to throw you a surprise party."

"Well," Gwenda said. "I'm surprised."

"Come on," Maureen said. "Come and blow out your candles."

The candles were not real, of course. But the cake was.

It was the usual sort of party. They all danced, the way you could only dance in micro gravity. It was all good fun. When dinner was ready, Maureen sent away the Finnish dance music, the dogs, the cherry blossoms. You could hear Shakespeare say to Mei, "I always dreamed of being an astronaut." And then he vanished.

Once there had been two ships. Standard practice, in the Third Age of Space Travel, to build more than one ship at a time, to send companion ships out on their long voyages. Redundancy enhances resilience. Sister ships *Seeker* and *Messenger,* called *House of Secrets* and *House of Mystery* by their crews, left Earth on a summer day in the year 2059.

House of Secrets had seen her twin disappear in a wink, a blink. First there, then nowhere. That had been thirty years ago. Space was full of mysteries. Space was full of secrets.

Dinner was beef Wellington (fake) with asparagus and new potatoes (both real) and sourdough rolls (realish). The experimental chickens were laying again, and so there were poached eggs, too, as well as the chocolate cake. Maureen increased gravity, because even fake beef Wellington requires suitable gravity. Mei threw rolls across the table at Gwenda. "Look at that, will you?" she said. "Every now and then a girl likes to watch something fall."

Aune supplied bulbs of something alcoholic. No one asked what it was. Aune worked with eukaryotes and archaea. "I made enough to get us lit," she said. "Just a little lit. Because today is Gwenda's birthday."

"It was my birthday just a little while ago," Portia said. "How old am I, anyway? Never mind, who's counting."

"To Portia," Aune said. "Forever youngish."

"To Proxima Centauri," Sullivan said. "Getting closer every day. Not that much closer."

"Here's to all us Goldilockses. Here's to a planet that's just right."

"To real gardens," Aune said. "With real toads."

"To Maureen," Sisi said. "And old friends." She squeezed Gwenda's hand.

"To our *House of Secrets,*" Mei said.

"To *House of Mystery,*" Sisi said. They all turned and looked at her. Sisi squeezed Gwenda's hand again. They drank.

"We didn't get you anything, Gwenda," Sullivan said.

"I don't want anything," Gwenda said.

"I do," Portia said. "Stories! Ones I haven't heard before."

Sisi cleared her throat. "There's just one thing," she said. "We ought to tell Gwenda the one thing."

"You'll ruin her birthday," Portia said.

"What?" Gwenda asked Sisi.

"It's nothing," Sisi said. "Nothing at all. Only the mind playing tricks. You know how it goes."

"Maureen?" Gwenda said. "What's going on?"

Maureen blew through the room, a vinegar breeze. "Approximately thirty-one hours ago Sisi was in the Control Room. She performed several usual tasks and then asked me to bring up our immediate course. Twelve seconds later, I observed her heart rate had increased precipitously. When I asked her if something was wrong, she said, 'Do you see it, too, Maureen?' I asked Sisi to tell me what she was seeing. Sisi said, '*House of Mystery.* Over to starboard. It was there. Then it was gone.' I told Sisi I had not seen it. We called back the visuals, but nothing was recorded there. I broadcast on all channels. No one answered. No one has seen *House of Mystery* in the intervening time."

"Sisi?" Gwenda said.

"It was there," Sisi said. "Swear to God I saw it. Like looking in a mirror. So near I could almost touch it."

They all began to talk at once.

"Do you think—"

"Just a trick of the imagination—"

"It disappeared like that. Remember?" Sullivan snapped his fingers. "Why couldn't they come back again the same way?"

"No!" Portia said. She glared at them all. "I don't want to talk about this, to rehash all this again. Don't you remember? We talked and talked and we theorized and we rationalized and what difference did it make?"

"Portia?" Maureen said. "I will formulate something for you, if you are distraught."

"No," Portia said. "I don't want anything. I'm *fine*."

"It wasn't really there," Sisi said. "It wasn't there and I wish I hadn't seen it." There were fat-bodied tears on her lower eyelids. Gwenda reached out, lifted one away on her thumb.

"Had you been drinking?" Sullivan said.

"No," Sisi said.

"But we haven't stopped drinking since," Aune said. She tossed back another bulb. "Maureen sobers us up and we just climb that mountain again. Cheers."

Mei said, "I'm just glad it wasn't me who saw it. And I don't want to talk about it anymore. We haven't all been awake like this for so long. Let's not fight."

"No fighting," Gwenda said. "No more gloom. For my birthday present, please."

Sisi nodded.

"Now that that's settled," Portia said, "bring up the lights again, Maureen, please? Take us somewhere new. I want something fancy. Something with history. An old English country house, roaring fireplace, suits of armor, tapestries, bluebells, sheep, moors, detectives in deerstalkers, Cathy scratching at the windows. You know."

"It isn't your birthday," Sullivan said.

"I don't care," Gwenda said, and Portia blew her a kiss.

That breeze ran up and down the room again. The table sank back into the floor. The curved walls receded, extruding furnishings, two panting greyhounds. They were in a Great Hall instead of the Great Room. Tapestries hung on plaster walls, threadbare and musty. There were flagstones, blackened beams. A roaring fire. Through the mullioned windows a gardener and his boy were cutting roses.

You could smell the cold rising off stones, a yew log upon the fire, the roses and the dust of centuries.

"Halfmark House," Maureen said. "Built in 1508. Queen Elizabeth came here on a progress in 1575 that nearly bankrupted the Halfmark family. Churchill spent a weekend in December of 1942. There are many photos. It was once said to be the second-most haunted manor in England. There are three monks and a Grey Lady, a White Lady, a yellow fog, and a stag."

"Exactly what I wanted," Portia said. "To float around like a ghost in an old English manor. Turn the gravity off, Maureen."

"I like you, my girl," Aune said. "But you are a strange one."

"Of course I am," Portia said. "We all are." She made a wheel of herself and rolled around the room. Hair seethed around her face in the way that Gwenda hated.

"Let's each pick one of Gwenda's tattoos," Sisi said. "And make up a story about it."

"Dibs on the phoenix," Sullivan said. "You can never go wrong with a phoenix."

"No," Portia said. "Let's tell ghost stories. Aune, you start. Maureen can provide the special effects."

"I don't know any ghost stories," Aune said slowly. "I know stories about trolls. No. Wait. I have one ghost story. It was a story that my great-grandmother told about the farm in Pirkanmaa where she grew up."

The Great Room grew darker until they were all only shadows, floating in shadow. Sisi wrapped an arm around Gwenda's waist. Outside the great windows, the gardeners and the rose-bushes disappeared. Now you saw a neat little farm and rocky fields, sloping up toward the twilight bulk of a coniferous forest.

"Yes," Aune said. "Exactly like that. I visited once when I was just a girl. The farm was in ruins. Now the world will have changed again. Maybe there is another farm or maybe it is all forest now.

"At the time of this story my great-grandmother was a girl of eight or nine. She went to school for part of the year. The rest of the year she and her brothers and sisters did the work of the farm. My great-grandmother's work was to take the cows to a meadow where the pasturage was rich in clover and sweet grasses. The cows were very big and she was very small, but they knew to come when she called them. In the evening she brought the herd home again. The path went along a ridge. On the near side she and her cows passed a closer meadow that her family did not use even though the pasturage looked very fine to my great-grandmother. There was a brook down in the meadow, and an old tree, a grand old man. There was a rock under the tree, a great slab that looked something like a table."

Outside the windows of Halfmark House, a tree formed itself in a grassy, sunken meadow.

"My great-grandmother didn't like that meadow. Sometimes when she looked down she saw people sitting around the table that the rock made. They were eating and drinking. They wore old-fashioned clothing, the kind her own great-grandmother would have worn. She knew that they had been dead a very long time."

"Ugh," Mei said. "Look!"

"Yes," Aune said in her calm, uninflected voice. "Like that. One day my great-grandmother, her name was Aune, too, I should have said that first, I suppose, one day Aune was leading her cows home along the ridge and she looked down into the meadow. She saw the people eating and drinking at their table. And while she was looking down, they turned and looked at her. They began to wave at her, to beckon that she should come down and sit with them and eat and drink. But instead she turned away and went home and told her mother what had happened. And after that, her older brother, who was a very unimaginative boy, had the job of taking the cattle to the far pasture."

The people at the table were waving at Gwenda and Mei and Portia and the rest of them now. Sullivan waved back.

"Creepy!" Portia said. "That was a good one. Maureen, didn't you think so?"

"It was a good story," Maureen said. "I liked the cows."

"So not the point, Maureen," Portia said. "Anyway."

"I have a story," Sullivan said. "In the broad outlines it's a bit like Aune's story."

"You could change things," Portia said. "I wouldn't mind."

"I'll just tell it the way I heard it," Sullivan said. "Anyhow, it's Kentucky, not Finland, and there aren't any cows. That is, there were cows, because it's another farm, but not in the story. It's a story my grandfather told me."

The gardeners were outside the windows again. They were ghosts, too, Gwenda thought. They would come and go, always doing the same things. Was this what it had been like to be rich, looked after by so many servants, all of them practically invisible, practically ghosts—just like Maureen, really—for all the notice you had to take of them?

Never mind, they were all ghosts now.

She and Sisi lay cushioned on the air, arms wrapped around each other's waists so as not to go flying away. They floated just above the twitching silk ears of a greyhound. The sensation of heat from the fireplace furred one arm, one leg, burned pleasantly along one side of her face. If something *happened,* if a meteor were to crash through a bulkhead, if a fire broke out in the Long Gallery, if a seam ruptured and they all went flying into space, could she and Sisi keep hold of each other? She resolved she would. She would keep hold.

Sullivan had the most wonderful voice for telling stories. He was describing the part of Kentucky where his family still lived. They hunted the wild pigs that lived in the forest. Went to a church on Sundays. There was a tornado.

Rain beat at the windows of Halfmark House. You could smell the ozone beading on the glass. Trees thrashed and groaned.

After the tornado passed through, men came to Sullivan's grandfather's house. They were going to look for a girl who had gone missing. Sullivan's grandfather, a young man at the time, went with them. The hunting trails were all gone. Parts of the forest had been flattened. Sullivan's grandfather was with the group that found the girl. A tree had fallen across her body and cut her almost in two. She was crawling, dragging herself along the ground by her fingernails. There was nothing they could do for her and so she died while they watched.

"After that," Sullivan said, "my grandfather only hunted in

those woods a time or two. Then he never hunted there again. He said that he knew what it was to hear a ghost walk, but he'd never heard one crawl before."

"Look!" Portia said. Outside the window something was crawling through the ruptured dirt. "Shut it off, Maureen! Shut it off! Shut it off!"

The gardeners again with their terrible shears.

"No more old-people ghost stories," Portia said. "Okay?"

Sullivan pushed himself up toward the whitewashed ceiling. "Don't ask for ghost stories if you don't want them, Portia," he said.

"I know," Portia said. "I know! I guess you spooked me. So it must have been a good one, right?"

"Right," Sullivan said, mollified. "I guess it was."

"That poor girl," Aune said. "To relive that moment over and over again. Who would want that, to be a ghost?"

"Maybe it isn't always bad?" Mei said. "Maybe there are well-adjusted ghosts? Happy ghosts?"

"I never saw the point," Sullivan said. "I mean, they say ghosts appear as a warning. So what's the warning in that story I told you? Don't get caught in the forest during a tornado? Don't get cut in half? Don't die?"

"I thought they were more like a memory," Gwenda said. "Not really there at all. Just an echo recorded somehow and played back, what they did, what happened to them."

Sisi said, "But Aune's ghosts—the other Aune—they looked at her. They wanted her to come down and eat with them. What would have happened then?"

"Nothing good," Aune said.

"Maybe it's genetic," Mei said. "Seeing ghosts. That kind of thing."

"Then Aune and I would be prone," Sullivan said.

"Not me," Sisi said. "I've never seen a ghost." She thought for a minute. "Unless I did. You know. No. It wasn't a ghost. What I saw. How could a ship be a ghost?"

"Don't think about it now," Mei said, imploring. "Let's not tell any more ghost stories. Let's have a gossip instead. Talk about back when we used to have sex lives."

"No," Gwenda said. "Let's have one more ghost story. Just one, for my birthday. Maureen?"

That breeze licked at her ear. "Yes?"

"Do you know any ghost stories?"

Maureen said, "I have all of the stories of Edith Wharton and M. R. James and many others in my library. Would you like to hear one?"

"No," Gwenda said. "I want a real story."

Portia said, "Mei, you must know a ghost story. No old people, though. I want a sexy ghost story."

"God, no," Mei said. "No sexy ghosts for me. Thank God."

Sisi said, "I have a story. It isn't mine, of course. Like I said, I've never seen a ghost."

"Go on," Gwenda said.

"Not my ghost story," Sisi said. "And not really a ghost story. I'm not sure what it was. It was the story of a man that I dated for a while."

"A boyfriend story!" Sullivan said. "I love your boyfriend stories, Sisi. Which one?"

We could go all the way to Proxima Centauri and back and Sisi still wouldn't have run out of stories about her boyfriends, Gwenda thought. But here she is, here we are, all of us together. And what are they? Dead and buried. Ghosts! Every last one of them.

"I don't think I've told any of you about him," Sisi was saying. "This was during the period when they weren't building new ships. Remember? They kept sending us out to do fund-raising? I was supposed to be some kind of Ambassadress for Space. Emphasis on the dress, little and slinky and black. I was supposed to be seductive and also noble and representative of everything that made it worth going to space for. I did a good enough job that they sent me over to meet a consortium of investors and big shots in London. I met all sorts of guys, but the only one I clicked with was this one dude, Liam.

"Okay. Here's where it gets complicated for a bit. Liam's mother was English. She came from this old family, lots of money and not a lot of supervision and by the time she was a teenager, she was a total wreck. Into booze, hard drugs, recreational Satanism, you name it. Got kicked out of school after school after school, and after that she got kicked out of all of the best rehab programs, too. In the end, her family kicked her out. Gave her money to go away. She ended up in prison for a couple of years, had a baby. That was Liam. Bounced around Europe for a while, then when Liam was about seven or eight, she found God and got herself cleaned up. By this point her father and mother were both dead. One of the superbugs. Her brother had inherited everything. She went back to the ancestral pile—imagine a place like this, okay?—and tried to make things good with her brother. Are you with me so far?"

"So it's a real old-fashioned English ghost story," Portia said.

"You have no idea," Sisi said. "You have no idea. So her brother was kind of a jerk. And let me emphasize, once again, this was a rich family, like you have no idea. The mother and the father and brother were into collecting art. Contemporary stuff.

Video installations, performance art, stuff that was really far out. They commissioned this one artist, an American, to come and do a site-specific installation. That's what Liam called it. It was supposed to be a commentary on the transatlantic exchange, the post-colonial relationship between England and the U.S., something like that. And what he did was he bought a ranch house out in a suburb in Arizona, the same state, by the way, where you can still go and see the original London Bridge. This artist bought the suburban ranch house, circa 2000, and the furniture in it and everything else, down to the rolls of toilet paper and the cans of soup in the cupboards. And he had the house dismantled with all of the pieces numbered, and plenty of photographs and video so he would know exactly where everything went, and it all got shipped over to England, where he built it all again on Liam's family's estate. And, simultaneously, he had a second house built right beside it. This second house was an exact replica, from the foundation to the pictures on the wall to the cans of soup on the shelves in the kitchen."

"Why would anybody ever bother to do that?" Mei said.

"Don't ask me," Sisi said. "If I had that much money, I'd spend it on shoes and booze and vacations for me and all of my friends."

"Hear, hear," Gwenda said. They all raised their bulbs and drank.

"This stuff is ferocious, Aune," Sisi said. "I think it's changing my mitochondria."

"Quite possibly," Aune said. "Cheers."

"Anyway, this double installation won some award. Got lots of attention. The whole point was that nobody knew which house was which. Then the superbug took out the mom and dad, and a couple of years after that, Liam's mother, the black sheep, came home. And her brother said to her, 'I don't want you living in the family home with me. But I'll let you live on the estate. I'll even give you a job with the housekeeping staff. And in exchange you'll live in my installation.' Which was, apparently, something that the artist had really wanted to make part of the project, to find a family to come and live in it.

"This jerk brother said, 'You and my nephew can come and live in my installation. I'll even let you pick which house.'

"Liam's mother went away and talked to God about it. Then she came back and moved into one of the houses."

"How did she decide which house to live in?" Sullivan said.

"Good question," Sisi said. "No idea. Maybe God told her? Look, what I was interested in at the time was Liam. I know why he liked me. Here I was, this South African girl with an American passport, dreadlocks, and cowboy boots, talking about how I was going to get in a rocket and go up in space, just as soon as I could. What man doesn't like a girl who doesn't plan to stick around?

"What I don't know is why I liked him so much. The thing is, he wasn't really a good-looking guy. He had a nice round English butt. His hair wasn't terrible. But there was something about him, you just knew he was going to get you into trouble. The good kind of trouble. When I met him his mother was dead. His uncle was dead, too. They weren't a lucky family. They had money instead of luck. The uncle had never married, and he'd left Liam everything.

"We went out for dinner. We gave each other all the right kind of signals, and then we fooled around some and he said he wanted to take me up to his country house for the weekend. It sounded like fun. I guess I was picturing one of those little thatched cottages you see in detective shows. But it was like this instead." Sisi gestured around. "Big old pile. Except with video screens in the corners showing mice eating each other and little kids eating cereal. Nice, right?

"He said we were going to go for a walk around the estate. We walked out about a mile through this typical South of England landscape and then suddenly we're approaching this weather-beaten, rotting stucco house that looked like every ranch house I'd ever seen in a depopulated neighborhood in the Southwest, y'all. This house was all by itself on a green English hill. It looked seriously wrong. Maybe it had looked better before the other one had burned down, or at least more intentionally weird, the way an art installation should, but anyway. Actually, I don't think so. I think it always looked wrong."

"Go back," Mei said. "What happened to the other house?"

"I'll get there in a bit," Sisi said. "So there we are in front of this horrible house, and Liam picked me up and carried me across the threshold like we were newlyweds. He dropped me on a rotting tan couch and said, 'I was hoping you would spend the night with me.'

"I said to him, 'Here?' And he said, 'Here is where I grew up. This is home.' And now we're back at the part where Liam and his mother moved into the installation."

"This story isn't like the other stories," Maureen said.

"You know, I've never told this story before," Sisi said. "The rest of it, I'm not even sure I know how to tell it."

"Liam and his mother moved into the installation," Portia said.

"Yeah. Liam's mummy picked a house and they moved in. Liam's just this little kid. A bit abnormal because of how they'd been living. And there are all these weird rules, like they aren't allowed to eat any of the food on the shelves in the kitchen. Because that's part of the installation. Instead the mother has a mini-fridge in the closet in her bedroom. Oh, and there are clothes in the closets in the bedrooms. And there's a TV, but it's an old one and the installation artist set it up so it only plays shows that were current in the early oughts in the U.S., which was the last time the house was occupied.

"And there are weird stains on the carpets in some of the rooms. Big brown stains.

"But Liam doesn't care so much about that. He gets to pick his own bedroom, which seems to be set up for a boy maybe a year or two older than Liam is. There's a model train set on the floor, which Liam can play with, as long as he's careful. And there are comic books, good ones that Liam hasn't read before. There are cowboys on the sheets. There's a big stain here in the corner, under the window.

"And he's allowed to go into the other bedrooms as long as he doesn't mess anything up. There's a pink bedroom with twin beds. A stain in the closet. A really big one. There's a room for an older boy, too, with posters of actresses that Liam doesn't recognize, and lots of American sports stuff. Football, but not the right kind.

"Liam's mother sleeps in the pink bedroom. You would expect her to take the master bedroom, but she doesn't like the bed. She says it isn't comfortable. Anyway, there's a stain that goes right through the duvet, through the sheets. It's as if the stain came up *through* the mattress."

"Uh oh," Gwenda says. She thinks she's beginning to see the shape of this story.

"You bet," Sisi says. "But remember, there are two houses. Liam's mummy is responsible for looking after both houses. She also volunteers at the church down in the village. Liam goes to the village school. For the first two weeks the other boys beat him up, and then they lose interest and after that everyone leaves him alone. In the afternoons he comes back and plays in his two houses. Sometimes he falls asleep in one house, watching TV, and when he wakes up he isn't sure where he is. Sometimes his uncle comes by to invite him to go for a walk on the estate, or to go fishing. He likes his uncle. Sometimes they walk up to the manor house and play billiards. His uncle arranges for him to have riding lessons and that's the best thing in the world. He gets to pretend that he's a cowboy. Maybe that's why he liked me. Those boots.

"Sometimes he plays cops and robbers. He used to know some pretty bad guys, back before his mother got religion, and Liam isn't exactly sure which he is yet, a good guy or a bad guy. He has a complicated relationship with his mother. Life is better than it used to be, but religion takes up about the same amount of space as the drugs did. It doesn't leave much room for Liam.

"Anyway, there are some cop shows on the TV. After a few months he's seen them all at least once. There's one called *CSI,* and it's all about fingerprints and murder and blood. And Liam starts to get an idea about the stain in his bedroom and the stain in the master bedroom and the other stains, the ones in the living room, on the sofa and over behind the La-Z-Boy that you mostly don't notice at first, because it's hidden. There's one stain up on the wallpaper in the living room and after a while it starts to look a lot like a handprint.

"So Liam starts to wonder if something bad happened in his

house. And in that other house. He's older now, maybe ten or eleven. He wants to know why are there two houses, exactly the same, next door to each other? How could there have been a murder—okay, a series of murders, where everything happened exactly the same way twice? He doesn't want to ask his mother because lately when he tries to talk to his mother all she does is quote Bible verses at him. He doesn't want to ask his uncle about it, either, because the older Liam gets, the more he can see that even when his uncle is being super nice, he's still not all that nice. The only reason he's nice to Liam is because Liam is his heir.

"His uncle has showed him some of the other pieces in his art collection, and he tells Liam that he envies him, getting to be a part of an actual installation. Liam knows his house came from America. He knows the name of the artist who designed the installation. So that's enough to go online and find out what's going on, which is that, sure enough, the original house, the one the artist bought and brought over, is a murder house. Some high-school kid got up in the middle of the night and killed his whole family with a hammer. And this artist, his idea was based on something the robber barons did at the turn of the previous century, which was buy up castles abroad and have them brought over stone by stone to be rebuilt in Texas, or upstate Pennsylvania, or wherever. A lot of those castles were supposed to be haunted. Buying a castle with a ghost in it and moving it across the ocean? Why not? So that was idea number one, to flip that. But then he had idea number two, which was, what makes a haunted house? If you take it to pieces and transport it all the way across the Atlantic Ocean, does the ghost come with it if you put it back together exactly the way it was? And if you can

put a haunted house back together again, piece by piece by
piece, can you build your own haunted house from scratch if
you re-create all of the pieces? And idea number three, forget the
ghosts, can the real live people who go and walk around in one
house or the other, or even better, the ones who live in a house
without knowing which house is which, would they know
which one was real and which one was ersatz? Would they see
real ghosts in the real house? Imagine they saw ghosts in the fake
one?"

"So which house were they living in?" Sullivan asked.

"Does it really matter which house they were living in?" Sisi
said. "I mean, Liam spent time in both houses. He said he never
knew which house was real. Which house was haunted. The artist was the only one with that piece of information.

"I'll tell the rest of the story as quickly as I can. So by the time
Liam brought me to see his ancestral home, one of the installation houses had burned down. Liam's mother did it. Maybe for
religious reasons? Liam was kind of vague about why. I got the
feeling it had to do with his teenage years. They went on living
there, you see. Liam got older and I'm guessing his mother
caught him fooling around with a girl or smoking pot, something, in the house that they didn't live in. By this point she had
become convinced that one of the houses was occupied by un-
quiet spirits, but she couldn't make up her mind which. And in
any case it didn't do any good. If there were ghosts in the other
house, they just moved in next door once it burned down. I
mean, why not? Everything was already set up exactly the way
that they liked it."

"Wait, so there were ghosts?" Gwenda said.

"Liam said there were. He said he never saw them, but later

on, when he lived in other places, he realized that there must have been ghosts. In both places. Both houses. Other places just felt empty to him. He said to think of it like maybe you grew up in a place where there was always a party going on, all the time, or a bar fight, one that went on for years, or maybe just somewhere where the TV was always on. And then you leave the party, or you get thrown out of the bar, and all of a sudden you realize you're all alone. Like, you just can't sleep as well without that TV on. You can't get to sleep. He said he was always on high alert when he was away from the murder house because something was missing and he couldn't figure out what. I think that's what I picked up on. That extra vibration, that twitchy radar."

"That's sick," Sullivan said.

"Yeah," Sisi said. "That relationship was over real quick. So that's my ghost story."

Mei said, "No, wait, go back. There's got to be more than that!"

"Not really," Sisi said. "No. Not much more. He'd brought a picnic dinner with us. Lobster and champagne and the works. We sat and ate at the kitchen table while he told me about his childhood. Then he gave me the tour. Showed me all the stains where those people died. I kept looking out the window and the sun got lower and lower. I didn't want to be in that house after it got dark."

They were all in that house now, flicking through those rooms, one after another. "Maureen?" Mei said. "Can you change it back?"

"Of course," Maureen said. Once again there were the greyhounds, the garden, the fire, and the roses. Shadows slicked the flagstones, blotted and clung to the tapestries.

"Better," Sisi said. "Thank you. You went and found it online, didn't you, Maureen? That was exactly the way I remember it. I went outside to think and have a cigarette. Yeah, I know. Bad astronaut. But I still kind of wanted to sleep with this guy. Just once. So he was messed up, so what? Sometimes messed-up sex is the best. When I came back inside the house, I still hadn't made up my mind. And then I made up my mind in a hurry. Because this guy? I went to look for him and he was down on the floor in that little boy's bedroom. Under the window, okay? On top of that *stain*. He was rolling around on the floor. You know, the way cats do? He had this look on his face. Like when they get catnip. I got out of there in a hurry. Drove away in his Land Rover. The keys were still in the ignition. Left it at a transport café and hitched the rest of the way home and never saw him again."

"You win," Portia said. "I don't know what you win, but you win. That guy of yours was *wrong*."

"What about the artist? I mean, what he did," Mei said. "That Liam guy would have been okay if it weren't for what he did. Right? I mean it's something to think about. Say we find some nice Goldilocks planet. If the conditions are suitable and we grow some trees and some cows, do we get the table with the ghosts sitting around it? Did they come along with Aune? With us? Are they here now? If we tell Maureen to build a haunted house around us right now, does she have to make the ghosts? Or do they just show up?"

Maureen said, "It would be an interesting experiment."

The Great Room began to change around them. The couch came first.

"Maureen!" Portia said. "Don't you dare!"

Gwenda said, "But we don't need to run that experiment. I mean, isn't it already running?" She appealed to the others, to Sullivan, to Aune. "You know. I mean, you know what I mean?"

"Not really," Sisi said. "What are you saying?"

Gwenda looked at the others. Then Sisi again. Sisi stretched luxuriously, weightlessly. Gwenda thought of the stain on the carpet, the man rolling on it like a cat.

"Gwenda, my love. What are you trying to say?" Sisi said.

"I know a ghost story," Maureen said. "I know one, after all. Do you want to hear it?"

Before anyone could answer, they were in the Great Room again, except they were outside it, too. They floated, somehow, in a great nothingness. But there was the table again with dinner upon it, where they had sat with one another.

The room grew darker and colder and the lost crew of the ship *House of Mystery* sat around the table.

That sister crew, those old friends, they looked up from their meal, from their conversation. They turned and regarded the crew of the ship *House of Secrets.* They wore dress uniforms, as if in celebration, but they were maimed by some catastrophe. They lifted their ruined hands and waved, smiling.

There was a smell of char and chemicals and icy rot that Gwenda almost knew.

And then it was her own friends around the table. Mei, Sullivan, Portia, Aune, Sisi. She saw herself sitting there, hacked almost in two. She got up, moved toward herself, then vanished.

The Great Room reshaped itself out of nothingness and horror. They were back in the English country house. The air was full of sour spray. Someone had thrown up. Someone else sobbed.

Aune said, "Maureen, that was unkind."

Maureen said nothing. She went about the room like a ghost, coaxing the vomit into a ball.

"The hell was that?" Sisi said. "Maureen? What were you thinking? Gwenda? My darling?" She reached for Gwenda's hand, but Gwenda pushed away.

She went forward in a great spasm, her arms extended to catch the wall. Going before her on the right hand, the ship *House of Secrets*, and on the left, *House of Mystery*.

She could no longer tell the one from the other.

Light

two men, one raised by wolves

The man at the bar on the stool beside her: bent like a hook over some item. A book, not a drink. A children's book, dog-eared. When he noticed her stare, he grinned and said, "Got a light?" It was a Friday night, and The Splinter was full of men saying things. Some guy off in a booth was saying, for example, "Well, sure, you can be raised by wolves and lead a normal life but—"

She said, "I don't smoke."

The man straightened up. He said, "Not that kind of light. I mean a *light*. Do you have a *light*?"

"I don't understand," she said. And then because he was not bad looking, she said, "Sorry."

"Stupid bitch," he said. "Never mind." He went back to his book. The pages were greasy and soft and torn; he had it open at a watercolor illustration of a boy and a girl standing in front of a dragon the size of a Volkswagen bus. The man had a pen. He'd drawn word bubbles coming out of the children's mouths, and now he was writing in words. The children were saying—

The man snapped the book shut; it was a library book.

"Excuse me," she said, "but I'm a children's librarian. Can I ask why you're defacing that book?"

"I don't know, *can* you? *May*be you can and *may*be you can't, but why ask me?" the man said. Turning his back to her, he hunched over the picture book again.

Which was really too much. She had once been a child. She owned a library card. She opened up her shoulder bag and took a needle out of the travel sewing kit. She palmed the needle and then, after finishing off her Rum and Rum and Coke—a drink she'd invented in her twenties and was still very fond of—she jabbed the man in his left buttock. Very fast. Her hand was back in her lap and she was signaling the bartender for another drink when the man beside her howled and sat up. Now everyone was looking at him. He slid off his bar stool and hurried away, glancing back at her once in outrage.

There was a drop of blood on the needle. She wiped it on a bar napkin.

At a table nearby three women were talking about a new pocket universe. A new diet. A coworker's new baby; a girl born with no shadow. This was bad, although thank God not as bad as it could have been, a woman—someone called her Caroline—was saying. A long, lubricated conversation followed about over-the-counter shadows—prosthetics, available in most drugstores, not expensive and reasonably durable. Everyone was in agreement that it was almost impossible to distinguish a homemade or store-bought shadow from a real one. Caroline and her friends began to talk of babies born with two shadows. Children with two shadows did not grow up happy. They didn't get on well with other children. You could cut a pair of shadows apart with a pair of crooked scissors, but it wasn't a permanent solution. By the end of the day the second shadow always grew back, twice as long. If you didn't bother to cut back the second shadow, then eventually you had twins, one of whom was only slightly realer than the other.

Lindsey had grown up in a stucco house in a scab-raw development in Dade County. On one side of the development there were orange groves; opposite Lindsey's house had been a bruised and trampled nothing. A wilderness. It grew back, then overran the edges of the new development. Banyan trees dripping with spiky little air-drinking epiphytics; banana spiders; tunnels of coral reef, barely covered by blackish, sandy dirt, that Lindsey and her brother lowered themselves into and then emerged out of, skinned, bloody, triumphant; bulldozed football-field-sized depressions that filled with water when it rained and produced thousands of fingernail-sized tan toads. Lindsey kept them in jars. She caught wolf spiders, Cuban lizards, tobacco grasshoppers yellow and pink—solid as toy cars—that spat when you caged them in your hand, blue crabs that swarmed across the yard, through the house, and into the swimming pool where they drowned. Geckos with their velvet bellies and papery clockwork insides, tick-tock barks; scorpions; king snakes and coral snakes and corn snakes, *red and yellow kill a fellow, red and black friendly Jack;* anoles, obscure until they sent out the bloody fans of their throats. When Lindsey was ten, a lightning strike ignited a fire under the coral reef. For a week the ground was warm to the touch. Smoke ghosted up. They kept the sprinklers on but the grass died anyway. Snakes were everywhere. Lindsey's new twin brother, Alan, caught five, lost three of them in the house while he was watching Saturday morning cartoons.

Lindsey had had a happy childhood. The women in the bar didn't know what they were talking about.

It was almost a shame when the man who had theories about being raised by wolves came over and threw his drink in the face of the woman named Caroline. There was a commotion. Lindsey took advantage of it and left, in a leisurely way, without paying her tab. She caught the eye she wanted to catch. They had both been thinking of making an exit, and so she went for a walk on the beach with the man who threw drinks and had theories about being raised by wolves. He was charming, but she felt his theories were only that: charming. When she said this, he became less charming. Nevertheless, she invited him home.

"Nice place," he said. "I like all the whatsits."

"It's all my brother's stuff," Lindsey said.

"Your *brother*? Does he live with you?"

"God, no," Lindsey said. "He's ... wherever he is."

"I had a sister. Died when I was two," the man said. "Wolves make really shitty parents."

"Ha," she said experimentally.

"Ha," he said. And then, "Look at that," as he was undressing her. Their four shadows fell across her double bed, sticky and wilted as if from lovemaking that hadn't even begun. At the sight of their languorously intertwined shadows, the wolf man became charming again. "Look at these sweet little tits," he said over and over again, as though she might not ever have noticed how sweet and little her tits were. He exclaimed at the sight of every part of her: afterward she slept poorly, apprehensive that he might steal away, taking along one of the body parts or pieces that he seemed to admire so much.

In the morning, she woke and found herself stuck beneath the body of the wolf man as if she had been trapped beneath a collapsed and derelict building. When she began to wriggle her way out from under him, he woke and complained of a fucking terrible hangover. He called her "Joanie" several times, asked to borrow a pair of scissors, and spent a long time in her bathroom with the door locked while she read the paper. Smuggling ring apprehended by _____. Government overthrown in _____. Family of twelve last seen in vicinity of _____. Start of hurricane season _____. The wolf man came out of the bathroom, dressed hurriedly, and left.

She found, in a spongy black heap, the amputated shadow of his dead twin and three soaked, pungent towels on the bathroom floor; there were stubby black bits of beard in the sink. The blades of her nail scissors tarry and blunted.

She threw away the reeking towels. She mopped up the shadow, folding it into a large Ziploc bag, carried the bag into the kitchen, and put the shadow down the disposal. She ran the water for a long time.

Then she went outside and sat on her patio and watched the iguanas eat the flowers off her hibiscus. It was six A.M. and already quite warm.

no vodka, one egg

Sponges hold water. Water holds light. Lindsey was hollow all the way through when she wasn't full of alcohol. The water in the canal was glazed, veined with light that wouldn't hold still. It was vile. She had the beginnings of one of her headaches. Light beat down and her second shadow began to move, rippling in waves like the light-shot water in the canal. She went inside. The egg in the door had a spot of blood in its yolk when she cracked it in the pan. She liked vodka in her orange juice, but there was no orange juice in the fridge, no vodka in the freezer; only a smallish iguana.

The Keys were overrun with iguanas. They ate her hibiscus; every once in a while she caught one of the smaller ones with the pool net and stuck it in her freezer for a few days. This was supposedly a humane way of dealing with iguanas. You could even eat them, although she did not. She was a vegetarian.

She put out food for the bigger iguanas when she saw them. They liked ripe fruit. She liked to watch them eat. She knew that she was not being consistent or fair in her dealings, but there it was.

men unlucky at cards

Lindsey's job was not a particularly complicated one. There was an office, and behind the office was a warehouse full of sleeping people. There was an agency in D.C. that paid her company to take responsibility for the sleepers. Every year, hikers and cavers and construction workers found a few dozen more. No one knew how to wake them up. No one knew what they meant, what they did, where they came from. No one really even knew if they were people.

There were always at least two security guards on duty at the warehouse. They were mostly, in Lindsey's opinion, lecherous assholes. She spent the day going through invoices, and then went home again. The wolf man wasn't at The Splinter and the bartender threw everyone out at two A.M.; she went back to the warehouse on a hunch, four hours into the night shift.

Bickle and Lowes had hauled out five sleepers, three women and two men. They'd put Miami Hydra baseball caps on the male sleepers and stripped the women, propped them up in chairs around a foldout table. Someone had arranged the hands of one of the male sleepers down between the legs of one of the women. Cards had been dealt out. Maybe it was just a game of strip poker and the three women had been unlucky. It was hard to play your cards well when you were asleep.

Larry Bickle stood behind one of the women, his cheek against her hair. He seemed to be giving her advice about how to play her cards. He wasn't holding his drink carefully enough, and the woman's neat lap brimmed with beer.

Lindsey watched for a few minutes. Bickle and Lowes had gotten to the sloppy, expansive stage of drunkenness that, sober, she resented most. False happiness.

When Lowes saw Lindsey he stood up so fast his chair tipped over. "Hey, now," he'd said. "It's different from how it looks."

Both guards had little conical paper party hats on their heads.

A third man, no one Lindsey recognized, came wandering down the middle aisle like he'd been shopping at Walmart. He wore boxer shorts and a party hat. "Who's this?" he said, leering at Lindsey.

Larry Bickle's hand was on his gun. What was he going to do? Shoot her? She said, "I've already called the police."

"Oh, fuck me," Larry Bickle said. He said some other things.

"You called who?" Edgar Lowes said.

"They'll be here in about ten minutes," Lindsey said. "If I were you, I'd leave right now. Just go."

"What is that bitch saying?" Larry Bickle said unhappily. He was really quite drunk. His hand was still on his gun.

She took out her own gun, a Beretta. She pointed it in the direction of Bickle and Lowes. "Put your gun belts on the ground and take off your uniforms. Leave your keys and your ID cards. You, too, whoever you are. Hand over your IDs and I won't write this up."

"You've got little cats on your gun," Edgar Lowes said.

"Hello Kitty stickers," she said. "I count coup." Although she'd only ever shot one person.

The men took off their clothes, but seemed to forget the paper hats. Edgar Lowes had a long purple scar down his chest. He saw Lindsey looking. "Triple bypass. I *need* this job. Health insurance."

"Too bad," Lindsey said. She followed them out into the parking lot. The third man didn't seem to care that he was naked. He didn't even have his hands cupped around his balls, the way Bickle and Lowes did. He said to Lindsey, "They've done this a couple of times, ma'am. Heard about it from a friend. Tonight was my birthday party."

Then: "That's my digital camera."

"Happy birthday. Thanks for the camera, Mr."—she checked his ID—"Mr. Junro. You keep your mouth shut about this and, like I said, I won't press charges. Say thank you if you agree."

"Thank you," Mr. Junro said.

"I'm still not giving your camera back," Lindsey said.

"That's okay," Mr. Junro said. "That's fine."

She watched the three men get into their cars and drive away. Then she went back into the warehouse and folded up the uniforms, emptied the guns, cleaned up the sleepers, used the dolly to get the sleepers back to their boxes. There was a bottle of cognac on the card table that had probably not belonged to either Bickle or Lowes, and plenty of beer. She drank steadily. A song came to her, and she sang it. *Tall and tan and young and drunken and.* She knew she was getting the words wrong. *A moonlit pyre. Like a bird on fire. I have tried in my way to be you.*

It was almost five A.M. Not much point in going home. The floor came up at her in waves, and she would have liked to lie down on it.

The sleeper in Box 113 was Harrisburg Pennsylvania. The sleepers were all named after their place of origin. Other countries did it differently. Harrisburg Pennsylvania had long eyelashes and a bruise on his cheek that had never faded. The skin of a sleeper was always just a little cooler than you expected. You could get used to anything. She set the alarm in her cell phone to wake her up at seven A.M., which was an hour before the shift change.

In the morning, Harrisburg Pennsylvania was still asleep and Lindsey was still drunk.

All she said to her supervisor, the general office manager, was that she'd fired Bickle and Lowes. Mr. Charles gave her a long-suffering look. He said, "You look a bit rough."

"I'll go home early," she said.

She would have liked to replace Bickle and Lowes with women, but in the end she hired an older man with excellent job references and a graduate student, Jason, who said he planned to spend his evenings working on his dissertation. (He was a philosophy student, and she asked what philosopher his dissertation was on. If he'd said, "Nietzsche," she might have terminated the interview. But he said, "John Locke.")

She'd already requested additional grant money to pay for security cameras, but when it was turned down she went ahead and bought the cameras anyway. She had a bad feeling about the two men who worked the Sunday to Wednesday day shift.

as children they were inseparable

On Tuesday, there was a phone call from Alan. He was yelling in Lin-Lan before she could even say hello.

"Berma lisgo airport. Tus fah me?"

"Alan?"

He said, "I'm at the airport, Lin-Lin, just wondering if I can come and stay with you for a bit. Not too long. Just need to keep my head down for a while. You won't even know I'm there."

"Back up," she said. "Alan? Where are you?"

"The airport," he said, clearly annoyed. "Where all the planes are."

"I thought you were in Tibet," she said.

"Well," Alan said. "That wasn't working out. I've decided to move on."

"What did you do?" she said. "Alan?"

"Lin-Lin, please," he said. "I'll explain everything tonight. When do you get home? Six? I'll make dinner. House key still under the broken planter?"

"Fisfis meh," she said. "Fine."

He hung up.

The last time she'd seen Alan in the flesh was two years ago, just after Elliot had left for good. Her husband.

They'd both been more than a little drunk and Alan was always nicer when he was drunk. He gave her a hug and said, "Come on, Lindsey. You can tell me. It's a bit of a relief, isn't it?"

The sky was swollen and low. Lindsey loved this, the sudden green afternoon darkness as rain came down in heavy drumming torrents so loud she could hardly hear the radio station in her car, the calm, jokey pronouncements of the local weather witch. The vice president was under investigation; evidence suggested a series of secret dealings with malign spirits. A woman had given birth to half a dozen rabbits. A local gas station had been robbed by invisible men. Some cult had thrown all the infidels out of a popular pocket universe. Nothing new, in other words. The sky was always falling. U.S. 1 was bumper to bumper all the way to Plantation Key.

Alan sat out on the patio, a bottle of wine under his chair, the wineglass in his hand half full of rain, half full of wine. "Lindsey!" he said. "Want a drink?" He didn't get up.

She said, "Alan? It's raining."

"It's warm," he said and blinked fat balls of rain out of his eyelashes. "It was cold where I was."

"I thought you were going to make dinner," she said.

"Oh." Alan stood up and made a show of wringing out his shirt and his peasant-style cotton pants. The rain collapsed steadily on their heads.

"There's nothing in your kitchen. I would have made margaritas, but all you had was the salt."

"Let's go inside," Lindsey said. "Do you have any dry clothes? Where's your luggage, Alan?"

He gave her a sly look. "You know. In there."

She knew. "You put your stuff in Elliot's room." It had been her room, too, but she hadn't slept there in almost a year. She only slept there when she was alone.

Alan said, "All the things he left are still there. Like he might still be in there, too, somewhere down in the sheets, all folded up like a secret note. Very creepy, Lin-Lin."

Alan was only thirty-eight. The same age as Lindsey, of course, unless you were counting from the point where he was finally real enough to eat his own birthday cake. She thought that he looked every year of their age. Older.

"Go get changed," she said. "I'll order takeout."

"What's in the grocery bags?" he said.

She slapped his hand away. "Nothing for you," she said.

close encounters of the absurd kind

She'd met Elliot at an open mike in a pocket universe in Coconut Grove. A benefit at a gay bar for some charity. Men everywhere, but most of them not interested in her. By the time Alan's turn came, he was already drunk or high or both. He got onstage and said, "I'll be in the bathroom." Then he carefully climbed off again. Everyone cheered. Elliot was on later.

Elliot was over seven feet tall; his hair was a sunny yellow and his skin was greenish. Lindsey had noticed the way that Alan looked at him when they first came in. Alan had been in this universe before.

Elliot sang that song about the monster from Ipanema. He couldn't carry a tune, but he made Lindsey laugh so hard that whiskey came out of her nose. After the song, he came over and sat at the bar. He said, "You're Alan's twin." He only had four fingers on each hand. His skin looked smooth and rough at the same time.

She said, "I'm the original. He's the copy. Wherever he is. Passed out in the bathroom probably."

Elliot said, "Should I go get him or should we leave him here?"

"Where are we going?" she said.

"To bed," he said. His pupils were oddly shaped. His hair wasn't really hair. It was more like barbules, pinfeathers.

"What would we do there?" she said, and he just looked at her. Sometimes these things worked and sometimes they didn't. That was the fun of it.

She thought about it. "Okay. On the condition you promise me you've never fooled around with Alan. Ever."

"Your universe or mine?" he said.

Elliot wasn't the first thing Lindsey had brought back from a pocket universe. She'd gone on vacation once and brought back the pit of a green fruit that fizzed like sherbet when you bit into it, and gave you dreams about staircases, ladders, rockets, things that went up and up, although nothing had come up when she planted it, although almost everything grew in Florida.

Her mother had gone on vacation in a pocket universe when she was first pregnant with Lindsey. Now people knew better. Doctors cautioned pregnant women against such trips.

For the last few years Alan had had a job with a tour group that ran trips out of Singapore. He spoke German, Spanish, Japanese, Mandarin Chinese, passable Tibetan, various pocket-universe trade languages. The tours took charter flights into Tibet and then trekked up into some of the more tourist-friendly pocket universes. Tibet was riddled with pocket universes.

"You lost them?" she said.

"Not all of them," Alan said. His hair was still wet with rain. He needed a haircut. "Just one van. I thought I told the driver Sakya but I may have said Gyantse. They showed up eventually, just two days behind schedule. It's not as if they were children. Everyone in Sakya speaks English. When they caught up with us I was charming and full of remorse and we were all pals again."

She waited for the rest of the story. Somehow it made you feel better, knowing that Alan had the same effect on everyone.

"But then there was a mix-up at customs back at Changi. They found a reliquary in this old bastard's luggage. Some ridiculous little god in a dried-up seed pod. Some other things. The old bastard swore up and down that none of it was his. That I'd snuck up to his room and put them into his luggage. That I'd seduced him. The agency got involved and the whole story about Sakya came out. So that was that."

"Alan," she said.

"I was hoping I could stay down here for a few weeks."

"You'll stay out of my hair," she said.

"Of course," he said. "Can I borrow a toothbrush?"

more like Disney World than Disney World

Their parents were retired, living in an older, established pocket universe that was apparently much more like Florida than Florida had ever been. No mosquitoes, no indigenous species larger than a lapdog, except for birdlike creatures whose songs made you want to cry and whose flesh tasted like veal. Fruit trees no one had to cultivate. Grass so downy and tender and fragrant no one slept indoors. Lakes so big and so shallow that you could spend all day walking across them. It wasn't a large universe, and

nowadays there was a long waiting list of men and women waiting to retire to it. Lindsey and Alan's parents had invested all of
their savings in a one-room cabana with a view of one of the
smaller lakes. Lotus-eating, they called it. It sounded boring to
Lindsey, but her mother no longer e-mailed to ask if Lindsey was
seeing anyone. If she was ever going to remarry and produce children. Grandchildren were no longer required. Grandchildren
would have obliged Lindsey and Alan's parents to leave paradise in
order to visit once in a while. Come back all that long way to
Florida. "That nasty place we used to live," Lindsey's mother said.
Alan had a theory that their parents were not telling them everything. "They've become nudists," he insisted. "Or swingers. Or
both. Mom always had exhibitionist tendencies. Always leaving
the bathroom door open. No wonder I'm gay. No wonder you're
not."

Lindsey lay awake in her bed. Alan was in the kitchen. Pretending to make tea for himself while he looked for a hidden stash of
alcohol. There was the kettle, whistling. The refrigerator door
opened and shut. The television went on. Went off. Various closet
doors and cabinet drawers opened, shut. It was Alan's ritual, the
way he made himself at home. Now he was next door, in Elliot's
room. Two clicks as he shut and locked the door. Other noises.
Going through drawers, more carefully this time. Alan had loved
Elliot, too. Elliot had left almost everything behind.

Alan. Putting his things away. The rattle of hangers as he made
room for himself, shoving Elliot's clothes farther back into the
closet. Or worse, trying them on. Beautiful Elliot's beautiful
clothes.

At two in the morning, he came and stood outside her bedroom door. He said softly, "Lindsey? Are you awake?"

She didn't answer and he went away again.

In the morning he was asleep on the sofa. A DVD was playing, the sound was off. Somehow he'd found Elliot's stash of imported pocket-universe porn, the secret stash she'd spent weeks looking for and never found. Trust Alan to turn it up. But she was childishly pleased to see he hadn't found the gin behind the sofa cushion.

When she came home from work he was out on the patio again, trying, uselessly, to catch her favorite iguana. "Be careful of the tail," she said.

"Monster came up and bit my toe," he said.

"That's Elliot. That's what I call him. I've been feeding him," she said. "He's gotten used to people. Probably thinks you're invading his territory."

"Elliot?" he said and laughed. "That's sick."

"He's big and green," she said. "You don't see the resemblance?" Her iguana disappeared into the network of banyan trees that dipped over the canal. The banyans were full of iguanas, leaves rustling greenly with their green and secret meetings. "The only difference is he comes back."

She went to get a take-out menu. Or maybe Alan would come down to The Splinter with her. The door to Elliot's room was open. Everything had been tidied away. Even the bed had been made.

Even worse: when they went down to The Splinter, every time someone sat down next to her, Alan made a game of pretending that he was her boyfriend. They fought all the way home. In the morning he asked if she would lend him the car. She knew better, but she lent him the car just the same.

Mr. Charles knocked on her office door at two. "Bad news," he said. "Jack Harris in Pittsburgh went ahead and sent us two dozen sleepers. Jason signed for them. Didn't think to call us first."

"You're kidding," she said.

"'Fraid not," he said. "I'm going to call Jack Harris. Ask what the hell he thought he was doing. I made it clear the other day that we weren't approved with regards to capacity. That's six over. He's just going to have to take those six right back again."

"Has the driver already gone?" she said.

"Yep."

"Typical," she said. "They think they can walk all over us."

"While I'm calling," he said. "Maybe you go over to the warehouse and take a look at the paperwork. Figure out what to do with this group in the meantime."

There were twenty-two new sleepers, eighteen males and four females. The new kid from the night shift—Jason—already had them on the dollies.

She went over to get a better look. "Where are they coming from?"

Jason handed her the dockets. "All over the place. Four of them turned up on property belonging to some guy in South Dakota. Says the government ought to compensate him for the loss of his crop."

"What happened to his crop?" she said.

"He set fire to it. They were underneath a big old dead tree out in his fields. Fortunately for everybody his son was there, too. While the father was pouring gasoline on everything, the son dragged the sleepers into the bed of the truck, got them out of there. Called the hotline."

"Lucky," she said. "What the hell was the father thinking?"

"People your age—" Jason said and stopped. Started again. "Older people seem to get these weird ideas sometimes. They want everything to be the way it was. Before."

"I'm not that old," she said.

"I didn't mean that," he said. Got pink. "I just mean, you know . . ."

She touched her hair. "Maybe you didn't notice, but I have two shadows. So I'm part of the weirdness. People like me are the people that people get ideas about. Why are you on the day shift?"

"Jermaine's wife is out of town, so he has to take care of the kids. So what are we going to do with these guys? The extras?"

"Leave them on the dollies," she said. "It's not like they care where they are."

She tried calling Alan's cell phone at five-thirty, but got no answer. She checked e-mail and played Solitaire. She hated Solitaire. Enjoyed shuffling through the cards she should have played. Playing cards when she shouldn't have. Why should she pretend to want to win when there wasn't anything to win?

At seven-thirty she looked out and saw her car in the parking lot. When she went out, Alan wasn't there. So she went down to the warehouse and found him with the grad student. Jason. Flirting, of course. Or talking philosophy. Was there a difference? The other guard, Hurley, was eating his dinner.

"Hey, Lin-Lin," Alan said. "Come see this. Come here."

"What are you doing?" Lindsey said. "Where have you been?"

"Grocery shopping," he said. "Come here, Lindsey. Come see."

Jason made a don't-blame-me face. She'd have to take him aside at some point. Warn him about Alan. Philosophy didn't prepare you for people like Alan.

"Look at her," Alan said.

She looked down. A woman dressed in a way that suggested she had probably been someone important once, maybe hundreds of years ago, somewhere, probably, that wasn't anything like here. Versailles Kentucky. "I've seen sleepers before."

"No. You don't *see*," Alan said. "Of course you don't. You don't spend a lot of time looking in mirrors, do you? This kind of haircut would look good on you."

He fluffed Versailles Kentucky's hair.

"Alan," she said. A warning.

"Look," he said. "Just look. Look at her. She looks just like you. She's *you*."

"You're crazy," she said.

"Am I?" Alan appealed to Jason. "You thought so, too."

Jason hung his head. He mumbled something. Said, "I said that maybe there was a similarity."

Alan reached down and grabbed the sleeper's bare foot, lifted the leg straight up.

"Alan!" Lindsey said. She pried his hand loose. The indents of his fingers came up on Versailles Kentucky's leg in red and white. "What are you doing?"

"It's fine," Alan said. "I just wanted to see if she has a birthmark like yours. Lindsey has a birthmark behind her knee," he said to Jason. "Looks like a battleship."

Even Hurley was staring now.

The sleeper didn't look a thing like Lindsey. No birthmark. Funny, though. The more she thought about it, the more Lindsey thought maybe she looked like Alan.

not herself today

She turned her head a little to the side. Put on all the lights in the bathroom and stuck her face up close to the mirror again. Stepped back. The longer she looked, the less she looked like anyone she knew. She certainly didn't look like herself. Maybe she hadn't for years. There wasn't anyone she could ask, except Alan.

Alan was right. She needed a haircut.

Alan had the blender out. The kitchen stank of rum. "Let me guess," he said. "You met someone nice in there." He held out a glass. "I thought we could have a nice quiet night in. Watch The Weather Channel. Do charades. You can knit. I'll wind your yarn for you."

"I don't knit."

"No," he said. His voice was kind. Loving. "You tangle. You knot. You muddle."

"You needle," she said. "What is it that you want? Why are you here? To pick a fight? Hash out old childhood psychodramas?"

"Per bol tuh, Lin-Lin?" Alan said. "What do *you* want?" She sipped ferociously. She knew what she wanted. "Why are *you* here?"

"This is my home," she said. "I have everything I want. A job at a company with real growth potential. A boss who likes me. A bar just around the corner, and it's full of men who want to buy me drinks. A yard full of iguanas and a spare shadow in case one should suddenly fall off."

"This isn't your house," Alan said. "Elliot bought it. Elliot filled it up with his junk. And all the nice stuff is mine. You haven't changed a thing since he took off."

"I have more iguanas now," she said. She took her Rum Runner into the living room. Alan already had The Weather Channel on. Behind the perky blond weather witch, in violent primary colors, a tropical depression hovered off the coast of Cuba.

Alan came and stood behind the couch. He put his drink down and began to rub her neck.

"Pretty, isn't it?" she said. "That storm."

"Remember when we were kids? That hurricane?"

"Yeah," she said. "I probably ought to go haul the storm shutters out of the storage unit. We got pounded last summer."

He went and got the pitcher of frozen rum. Came back and stretched out on the floor at her feet, the pitcher balanced on his stomach. "That kid at your warehouse," he said. He closed his eyes.

"Jason?"

"He seems like a nice kid."

"He's a philosophy student, Lan-Lan. Come on. You can do better."

"Do better? I'm thinking out loud about a guy with a fine ass, Lindsey. Not buying a house. Or contemplating a career change.

Oops, I guess I am officially doing that. Perhaps I'll become a do-gooder. A do-better."

"Just don't make my life harder, okay? Alan?" She nudged him in the hip with her toe, and watched, delighted, as the pitcher tipped over.

"Fisfis tuh!" Alan said. "You did that on purpose!"

He took off his shirt and tossed it at her. Missed. There was a puddle of pink rum on the tile floor.

"Of course I did it on purpose," she said. "I'm not drunk enough yet to do it accidentally."

"I'll drink to that." He picked up her Rum Runner and slurped noisily. "Go make another pitcher while I clean up this fucking mess."

do the monster

"He's got gorgeous eyes. Really, really green. Green as that color there. Right at the eye. That swirl."

"I hadn't noticed his eyes."

"That's because he isn't your type. You don't like nice guys. Here, can I put this on?"

"Yeah. There's a track on there, I think it's the third track. Yeah, that one. Elliot loved this song. He'd put it on, start twitching, then tapping, then shaking, all over. By the end he'd be slithering all over the furniture."

"Oh, yeah. He was a god on the dance floor. But look at me. I'm not too bad, either."

"He was more flexible around the hips. I think he had a bendier spine. He could turn his head almost all the way around."

"Come on, Lindsey, you're not dancing. Come on and dance."

"I don't want to."

"Don't be such a pain in the ass."

"I have a pain inside," she said. And then wondered what she meant. "It's such a pain in the ass."

"Come on. Just dance. Okay?"

"Okay," she said. "I'm okay. See? I'm dancing."

Jason came to dinner. Alan wore one of Elliot's shirts. Lindsey made a perfect cheese soufflé, and she didn't even say anything when Jason assumed that Alan had made it.

She listened to Alan's stories about various pocket universes he'd toured as if she had never heard them before. Most were owned by the Chinese government, and as well as the more famous tourist universes, there were the ones where the Chinese sent dissidents. Very few of the pocket universes were larger than, say, Maryland. Some had been abandoned a long time ago. Some were inhabited. Some weren't friendly. Some pocket universes contained their own pocket universes. You could go a long ways in and never come out again. You could start your own country out there and do whatever you liked, and yet most of the people Lindsey knew, herself included, had never done anything more adventuresome than go for a week to some place where the food and the air and the landscape seemed like something out of a book you'd read as a child; a brochure; a dream.

There were sex-themed pocket universes, of course. Tax shelters and places to dispose of all kinds of things: trash, junked cars, bodies. People went to casinos inside pocket universes more like Vegas than Vegas. More like Hawaii than Hawaii. You must be this tall to enter. This rich. Just this foolish. Because who knew what might happen? Pocket universes might wink out again, suddenly, all at once. There were best-selling books explaining how that might happen.

There was pocket-universe spillover, too. Alan began to reminisce about his adolescence in a way that suggested that it had not really been all that long ago.

"Venetian Pools," he said to Jason. "I haven't been there in a couple of years. Since I was a kid, really. All those grottoes that you could wander off into with someone. Go make out and get such an enormous hard-on you had to jump in the water so nobody noticed and the water was so fucking cold! Can you still get baked ziti at the restaurant? Do you remember that, Lindsey? Sitting out by the pool in your bikini and eating baked ziti? But I heard you can't swim now. Because of the mermaids."

The mermaids were an invasive species, like the iguanas. People had brought them from one of the Disney pocket universes as pets, and now they were everywhere, small but numerous in a way that appealed to children and bird-watchers. They liked to show off and although they didn't seem much smarter than, say, a talking dog, and maybe not even as smart, since they didn't speak, only sang and whistled and made rude gestures, they were too popular with the tourists at the Venetian Pools to be gotten rid of. There were freshwater mermaids and saltwater mermaids—larger and more elusive—and the freshwater kind had begun to show up at Venetian Pools at least ten years ago.

Jason said he'd taken his sister's kids. "I heard they used to drain the pools every night in summer. But they can't do that now, because of the mermaids. So the water isn't as clear as it used to be. They can't even set up filters because the mermaids just tear them out again. Like beavers, I guess. They've constructed this elaborate system of dams and retaining walls and structures out of the coral, these elaborate pens to hold fish. Venetian Pools sell fish so you can toss them in for the mermaids to round up. The kids were into that."

"We get them in the canal sometimes, the saltwater ones," Lindsey said. "They're a lot bigger. They sing."

"Yeah," Jason said. "Lots of singing. Really eerie stuff. Makes you feel like shit. They pipe elevator music over the loudspeakers to drown it out, but even the kids felt bad after a while. I had to buy all this stuff in the gift shop to cheer them up."

Lindsey pondered the problem of Jason, the favorite uncle who could be talked into buying things. He was too young for Alan. When you thought about it, who wasn't too young for Alan?

Alan said, "Didn't you have plans, Lindsey?"

"Did I?" Lindsey said. Then relented. "Actually, I was thinking about heading down to The Splinter. Maybe I'll see you guys down there later?"

"That old hole," Alan said. He wasn't looking at her. He was sending out those old invisible death rays in Jason's direction. Lindsey could practically feel the air getting thicker. It was like humidity, only skankier. "I used to go there to hook up with cute straight guys in the bathroom while Lindsey was passing out her phone number over by the pool tables. The good old days, right, Lindsey? You know what they say about girls with two shadows, don't you, Jason?"

Jason said, "Maybe I should just head home." But Lindsey could tell by the way that he was looking at Alan that he had no idea what he was saying. He wasn't even really listening to what Alan said. He was just responding to that vibe that Alan put out. That *come hither come hither come a little more hither* siren song.

"Don't go," Alan said. Luscious, dripping invisible sweetness rolled off him. Lindsey knew how to do that, too, although she mostly didn't bother now. Most guys, you didn't have to. "Stay a little longer. Lindsey has plans, and I'm lonely. Stay a little longer and I'll play you some of the highlights of Lindsey's ex-husband's collection of pocket-universe gay porn."

"Alan," Lindsey said. Second warning. She knew he was keeping count.

"Sorry," Alan said. He put his hand on Jason's leg. "*Husband's* collection of gay porn. She and Elliot, wherever he is, are still married. I had the biggest hard-on for Elliot. He always said Lindsey was all he wanted. But it's never about what you want, is it? It's about what you need. Right?"

"Right," Jason said.

"We'll talk later," Lindsey said. *"Beh slam bih, tuh eb meh."*

"Sure," Alan said. "Talk, talk." He blew her a kiss.

How did Alan do it? Why did everyone except for Lindsey fall for it? Except, she realized, pedaling her bike down to The Splinter, she did fall for it. She still fell for it. It was her house, and who had been thrown out of it? Who had been insulted, mocked, abused, then summarily dismissed? Her. That's who.

Cars went by, riding their horns. Damn Alan anyway.

She didn't bother to chain up the bike; she probably wouldn't be riding it home. She went into The Splinter and sat down beside a man with an aggressively sharp cologne.

"You look nice," she said. "Buy me a drink and I'll be nice, too."

there are easier ways to kill yourself

The man was kissing her neck. She couldn't find her keys, but that didn't matter. The door was unlocked. Jason's car still in the driveway. No surprise there.

"I have two shadows," she said. It was all shadows. They were shadows, too.

"I don't care," the man said. He really was very nice.

"No," she said. "I mean, my brother's home. We have to be quiet. Okay if we don't turn on the lights? Where are you from?"

"Georgia," the man said. "I work construction. Came down here for the hurricane."

"The hurricane?" she said. "I thought it was headed for the Gulf of Mexico. Watch out for the counter."

"Now it's coming back this way. Won't hit for another couple of days if it hits. You into kinky stuff? You can tie me up," the man said.

"Better knot," she said. "Get it? I'm not into knots. Can never get them untied, even sober. This guy had to have his foot amputated. No circulation. True story. Friend told me."

"Guess I've been lucky so far," the man said. He didn't sound too disappointed, either way. "This house has been through some hurricanes, I bet."

"One or two," she said. "Water comes right in over the tile floor. Messy. Then it goes out again."

She tried to remember his name. Couldn't. It didn't matter. She felt terrific. That had been the thing about being married. The monogamy. Even drunk, she'd always known who was in bed with her. Elliot had been different, all right, but he had always been the same kind of different. Never a different kind of different. Didn't like kissing. Didn't like sleeping in the same bed. Didn't like being serious. Didn't like it when Lindsey was sad. Didn't like living in a house. Didn't like the way the water in the canal felt. Didn't like this, didn't like that. Didn't like the Keys. Didn't like the way people here looked at him. Didn't stay. Elliot, Elliot, Elliot.

"My name's Alberto," the man said.

"Sorry," she said. She and Elliot had always had fun in bed.

"He had a funny-looking penis," she said.

"Excuse me?" Alberto said.

"Do you want something to drink?" she said.

"Actually, do you have a bathroom?"

"Down the hall," she said. "First door."

But he came back in a minute. He turned on the lights and stood there.

"Like what you see?" she said.

His arms were shiny and wet. There was blood on his arms. "I need a tourniquet," he said. "Some kind of tourniquet."

"What did you do?" she said. Almost sober. Putting her robe on. "Is it Alan?"

But it was Jason. Blood all over the bathtub and the half-tiled wall. He'd slashed both his wrists open with a potato peeler. The potato peeler was still there in his hand.

"Is he okay?" she said. "Alan! Where the fuck are you?"

Alberto wrapped one of her good hand towels around one of

Jason's wrists. "Hold this." He stuck another towel around the other wrist and then wrapped duct tape around that. "I called 911," he said. "He's breathing. Couldn't or didn't want to do the job properly. Bad choice of equipment either way. Who is this guy? Your brother?"

"My employee," she said. "I don't believe this. What's with the duct tape?"

"Carry it with me," he said. "You never know when you're going to need some duct tape. Get me a blanket. We need to keep him warm. My ex-wife did this once."

She skidded down the hall. Slammed open the door to Elliot's room. Turned on the lights and grabbed the comforter off the bed.

"*Vas poh!* Your new boyfriend's in the bathroom," she said. "Cut his wrists with my potato peeler. Wake up, Lan-Lan! This is *your* mess."

"*Fisfis wah,* Lin-Lin," Alan said, so she pushed him off the bed.

"What did you do, Alan?" she said. "Did you do something to him?"

He was wearing a pair of Elliot's pajama bottoms. "You're not being funny," he said.

"I'm not kidding," she said. "I'm drunk. There's a man named Alberto in the bathroom. Jason tried to kill himself. Or something."

"Oh, fuck," he said. Tried to sit up. "I was nice to him, Lindsey! Okay? It was real nice. We fucked and then we smoked some stuff and then we were kissing and I fell asleep."

She held out her hand, pulled him up off the floor. "What kind of stuff? Come on."

"Something I picked up somewhere," he said. She wasn't really listening. "Good stuff. Organic. Blessed by monks. They give it to the gods. I took some off a shrine. Everybody does it. You just leave a bowl of milk or something instead. There's no fucking way it made him crazy."

The bathroom was crowded with everyone inside it. No way to avoid standing in Jason's blood. "Oh, fuck," Alan said.

"My brother, Alan," she said. "Here's his comforter. For Jason. Alan, this is Alberto. Jason, can you hear me?" His eyes were open now.

Alberto said to Alan, "It's better than it looks. He didn't really slice up his wrists. More like he peeled them. Dug into one vein pretty good, but I think I've slowed down the bleeding."

Alan shoved Lindsey out of the way and threw up in the sink.

"Alan?" Jason said. There were sirens.

"No," Lindsey said. "It's me. Lindsey. Your boss. My bathtub, Jason. Your blood all over my bathtub. My potato peeler! Mine! What were you thinking?"

"There was an iguana in your freezer," Jason said.

Alberto said, "Why the potato peeler?"

"I was just so happy," Jason said. He was covered in blood. "I've never been so happy in all my life. I didn't want to stop feeling that way. You know?"

"No," Lindsey said.

"Are you going to fire me?" Jason said.

"What do you think?" Lindsey said.

"I'll sue for sexual harassment if you try," Jason said. "I'll say you fired me because I'm gay. Because I slept with your brother."

Alan threw up in the sink again.

"How do you feel now?" Alberto said. "You feel okay?"

"I just feel so happy," Jason said. He began to cry.

one boy, raised from the dead

During the summer between third and fourth grade, Lindsey had witnessed the mother of a girl named Amelia Somersmith call a boy back to life when he fell off the roof during a game of hide-and-seek. He fell off when a kid named Martin saw him hiding up there, and yelled his name. David Filgish stood up and just to show he didn't care that he'd been seen, he turned a cartwheel along the garage roof, only he misjudged where the edge was. He had definitely been dead. Everybody was sure about that. Amelia's mother came running out of the house while everyone was standing there, wondering what to do, looking down at David, and she'd said, "Oh, God, David, you idiot! Don't be dead, don't be dead, don't be dead. Get up right now or I'm calling your mother!"

There had been a piece of grass lying right on David's eye. Amelia's mother's shirt hadn't been buttoned right, so you could see a satiny brown triangle of stomach, and she had sounded so angry that David Filgish sat up and started to cry.

Lindsey Driver had thrown up in the grass, but no one else noticed, not even her twin, Alan, who was only just becoming real enough to play with other children.

They were all too busy asking David if he was all right. Did he know what day it was. How many fingers. What was it like being dead.

not much of a bedside manner

Alan went with Jason in the ambulance. The EMTs were both
quite good-looking. The wind was stronger, pushing the trees
around like a bully. Lindsey would have to put the storm shutters up.

For some reason Alberto was still there. He said, "I'd really like
a beer. What've you got?"

Lindsey could have gone for something a little stronger. She
could smell nothing but blood. "Nothing," she said. "I'm a re-
covering alcoholic."

"Not all that recovered," he said.

"I'm sorry," Lindsey said. "You're a really nice guy. But I wish
you would go away. I'd like to be alone."

He held out his bloody arms. "Could I take a shower first?"

"Could you just go?" Lindsey said.

"I understand," he said. "It's been a rough night. A terrible thing
has happened. Let me help. I could stay and help you clean up."

Lindsey said nothing.

"I see," he said. There was blood on his mouth, too. Like he'd
been drinking blood. He had good shoulders. Nice eyes. She
kept looking at his mouth. The duct tape was back in a pocket
of his cargo pants again. He seemed to have a lot of stuff in his
pockets. "You don't like me, after all?"

"I don't like nice guys," Lindsey said.

There were support groups for people whose shadow grew into a twin. There were support groups for women whose husbands left them. There were support groups for alcoholics. Probably there were support groups for people who hated support groups, but Lindsey didn't believe in support groups.

The warehouse had been built to take a pretty heavy hit. Nevertheless, there were certain precautions: the checklist ran to thirty-five pages. Without Jason they were short-handed, and she had a bad hangover that had lasted all through the weekend, all the way into Monday. The worst in a while. By the time Alan got back from the hospital on Saturday night, she'd finished the gin and started in on the tequila. She was almost wishing that Alberto had stayed. She thought about asking how Jason was, but it seemed pointless. Either he was okay or he wasn't. She wasn't okay. Alan got her down the hall and onto her bed and then climbed into bed, too. Pulled the blanket over both of them.

"Go away," she said.

"I'm freezing," he said. "That fucking hospital. That air-conditioning. No wonder people are sick in hospitals. Just let me lie here."

"Go away," she said again. *"Fisfis wah."*

When she woke up, she was still saying it. "Go away, go away, go away." He wasn't in her bed. Instead there was a dead iguana, the little one from the freezer. Alan had arranged it—if a dead frozen iguana can be said to be arranged—on the pillow beside her face.

Alan was gone. The bathtub stank of old blood, and the rain slammed down on the roof like nails on glass. Little pellets of ice on the grass outside. Now the radio said the hurricane was on course to make landfall somewhere between Fort Lauderdale and St. Augustine sometime Wednesday afternoon. There were no plans to evacuate the Keys. Plenty of wind and rain and nastiness due for the Miami area, but no real damage. She couldn't think why she'd asked Alberto to leave. The storm shutters still needed to go up. He had seemed like a guy who would do that.

She threw away the thawed iguana. Threw away the potato peeler all rusted with blood. Ran hot water in the bath until the bottom of the tub was a faint, blistered pink. Then she crawled back into bed.

If Alan had been there, he could have opened a can and made her soup. Brought her ginger ale in a glass. Finally she turned on the television in the living room, loud enough that she could hear it from her bedroom. That way she wouldn't be listening for Alan. She could pretend that he was home, sitting out in the living room, watching some old monster movie and painting his fingernails black, the way he had done in high school. Kids with conjoined shadows were supposed to be into all that goth makeup, all that music. When Alan had found out twins were supposed to have secret twin languages, he'd done that, too, invented a language, Lin-Lan, and made her memorize it. Made her talk it at the dinner table, too. *Ifzon meh nadora plezbig* meant: *Guess what I did? Bandy Tim Wong legkwa fisfis, meh* meant: *Went all the way with Tim Wong.* (Tim Wong fucked me, in the vernacular.)

People with two shadows were *supposed* to get in trouble. Supposed to *be* trouble. They were supposed to lead friends and lovers astray, bring confusion to their enemies, bring down disaster wherever they went. (She never went anywhere.) Alan had always been a conformist at heart. Whereas she had a house and a job and once she'd even been married. If anyone was keeping track, Lindsey thought it ought to be clear who was ahead.

Mr. Charles still hadn't managed to get rid of the six supernumerary sleepers from Pittsburgh. Jack Harris could shuffle paper like nobody's business.

"I'll call him," Lindsey offered. "You know I love a good fight."

"Good luck," Mr. Charles said. "He says he won't take them back until after the hurricane goes through. But rules say they have to be out of here twenty-four hours before the hurricane hits. We're caught between a rock—"

"—and an asshole," she said. "Let me take care of it."

She was in the warehouse, on hold with someone who worked for Harris, when Jason showed up.

"What's up with that?" Valentina was saying. "Your arms."

"Fell through a sliding door," Jason said. "Plate glass."

"That's not good," Valentina said.

"Lost almost three pints of blood. Just think about that. Three pints. Hey, Lindsey. Doctors just let me out of the hospital. Said I'm not supposed to lift anything heavy."

"Valentina," Lindsey said. "Take the phone for a moment. Don't worry. It's on hold. Just yell if anyone picks up. Jason, can I talk to you over there for a moment?"

"Sure thing," Jason said.

He winced when she grabbed him above the elbow. She didn't loosen her grip until she had him a couple of aisles away. "Give me one good reason why I shouldn't fire you. Besides the sexual harassment thing. Because I would enjoy that. Hearing you try to make that case in court."

Jason said, "Alan's moving in with me. Said you threw him out."

Was any of this a surprise? Yes, and no. She said, "So if I fire you, he'll have to get a job."

"That depends," Jason said. "Are you firing me or not?"

"*Fisfis buh.* Go ask Alan what that means."

"Hey, Lindsey. Lindsey, hey. Someone named Jack Harris is on the phone." Valentina. Getting too close for this conversation to go any further.

"I don't know why you want this job," Lindsey said.

"The benefits," Jason said. "You should see the bill from the emergency room."

"Or why you want my brother."

"Ms. Driver? He says it's urgent."

"Tell him just a second," Lindsey said. To Jason: "All right. You can keep the job on one condition."

"Which is?" He didn't sound nearly as suspicious as he ought to have sounded. Still early days with Alan.

"You get the man on the phone to take back those six sleepers. Today."

"How the fuck do I do that?" Jason said.

"I don't care. But they had better not be here when I show up tomorrow morning. If they're here, you had better not be. Okay?" She poked him in the arm above the bandage. "Next time borrow something sharper than a potato peeler. I've got a whole block full of good German knives."

"Lindsey," Valentina said, "this Harris guy says he can call you back tomorrow if now isn't a good time."

"Jason will take the call," Lindsey said.

everything must go

Her favorite liquor store put everything on sale whenever a hurricane was due. Just their way of making a bad day a little more bearable. She stocked up on everything but only had a glass of wine with dinner. Made a salad and ate it out on the sun dock. The air had that electric green shimmy to it she associated with hurricanes. The water was still as milk, but deflating the dock was a bitch nevertheless. She stowed it in the garage. When she came out, a pod of saltwater mermaids was going out to sea. Who could have ever confused a manatee with a mermaid? They turned and looked at her. Dove down, although she could still see them ribboning there, down along the frondy bottom.

The last time a hurricane had come through, her sun dock had sailed out of the garage and ended up two canals over.

She threw the leftover salad on the grass for the iguanas. The sun went down without a fuss.

Alan didn't come by, so she packed up his clothes for him. Washed the dirty clothes first. Listened to the rain start. She put his backpack out on the dining room table with a note. *Good luck with the suicide kid*.

In the morning she went out in the rain, which was light but steady, and put up the storm shutters. Her neighbors were doing the same. Cut herself on the back of the hand while she was working on the next-to-last one. Bled everywhere. Alan pulled up in Jason's car while she was still cursing. He went into the house and got her a Band-Aid. They put up the last two shutters without talking.

Finally Alan said, "It was my fault. I don't think he does drugs."

"He's not a bad kid," she said. "*So* not your type."

"I'm sorry," he said. "Not about that. You know. I guess I mean about everything."

They went back into the house and he saw his backpack. "Well," he said.

"*Filhatz warfoon meh*," she said. "*Bilbil tuh.*"

"*Nent bruk*," he said. No kidding.

He didn't stay for breakfast. She didn't feel any less or more real after he left.

The six sleepers were out of the warehouse and Jason had a completed stack of paperwork for her. Lots of signatures. Lots of duplicates and triplicates and fucklicates, as Valentina liked to say.

"Not bad," Lindsey said. "Did Jack Harris offer you a job?"

"He offered to come hand me my ass," Jason said. "I said he'd have to get in line. Nasty weather. Are you staying out there?"

"Where would I go?" she said. "There's a big party at The Splinter tonight. It's not like I have to come in to work tomorrow."

"I thought they were evacuating the Keys, after all," he said.

"It's voluntary," she said. "They don't care if we stay or go. I've been through hurricanes. When Alan and I were kids, we spent one camped in a bathtub under a mattress. Read comics with a flashlight all night long. The noise is the worst thing. Good luck with Alan, by the way."

"I've never lived with anybody before." So maybe he knew

just enough to know he had no idea what he had gotten himself into with Alan. "I've never fallen for anybody like this."

"There isn't anybody like Alan," she said. "He has the power to cloud and confuse the minds of men."

"What's your superpower?" Jason said.

"He clouds and confuses," she said. "I confuse and then cloud. It's the order we do it in that you have to pay attention to."

She told Mr. Charles the good news about Jack Harris; they had a cup of coffee together to celebrate, then locked the warehouse down. Mr. Charles had to pick up his kids at school. Hurricanes meant holidays. You didn't get snow days in Florida.

On the way home all the traffic was going the other way. The wind made the traffic lights swing and flip like paper lanterns. She had that feeling she'd had at Christmas, as a child. As if someone was bringing her a present. Something shiny and loud and sharp and messy. She'd always loved bad weather. She'd always loved weather witches in their smart, black suits. Their divination kits, their dramatic seizures, their prophecies which were never entirely accurate, but which always rhymed smartly. When she was little she'd wanted more than anything to grow up and be a weather witch, although why that once had been true, she had no idea.

She rode her bike down to The Splinter. Got soaked. Didn't care. Had a couple of whiskey sours, and then decided she was too excited about the hurricane to get properly drunk. She didn't want to be drunk. And there wasn't a man in the bar she wanted to bring home. The best part of hurricane sex was the hurricane, not the sex, so why bother?

The sky was green as a bruise and the rain was practically horizontal. There were no cars at all on the way home. She was only the least bit drunk. She went down the middle of the road and almost ran over an iguana four feet long, nose to tail. Stiff as a board, but its sides went out and in like little bellows. The rain got them like that, sometimes. They got stupid and slow in the cold. The rest of the time they were stupid and fast.

She wrapped her jacket around the iguana, making sure the tail was immobilized. You could break a man's arm if you had a tail like that. She carried it under one arm, walking her bike all the way back to the house, and decided it would be a good idea to put it in the bathtub. Then she went back out into her yard with a flashlight. Checked the storm shutters to make sure they were properly fastened and discovered three more iguanas as she went. Two smaller ones and one real monster. She brought them all inside.

At eight P.M. it was pitch-dark. The hurricane was two dozen miles out. Picking up water to drop on the heads of people who didn't want any more water. She dozed off at midnight and woke up when the power went off.

The air in the room was so full of water she had to gasp for breath. The iguanas were shadows stretched along the floor. The black shapes of the liquor boxes were every Christmas present she'd ever wanted.

Everything outside was clanking or buzzing or yanking or shrieking. She felt her way into the kitchen and got out the box with her candles and her flashlight and her emergency radio. The shutters banged away like a battle.

"Swung down," the radio told her. "How about that—and this is just the edge, folks. Stay indoors and hunker down if you haven't already left town. This is only a Category 2, but you betcha it'll feel a lot bigger down here on the Keys. We're going to have at least three more hours of this before the eye passes over us. This is one big baby girl, and she's taking her time. The good ones always do."

Lindsey could hardly get the candles lit; the matches were that soggy, her hands greased with sweat. When she went in the bathroom, the iguana looked as battered and beat, in the light from the candle, as some old suitcase.

Her bedroom had too many windows to stay there. She got her pillow and her quilt and a fresh T-shirt. A fresh pair of underwear.

When she went to check Elliot's room there was a body on the bed. She dropped the candle. Tipped wax onto her bare foot. "Elliot?" she said. But when she got the candle lit again it wasn't Elliot, of course, and it wasn't Alan, either. It was the sleeper. Versailles Kentucky. The one who looked like Alan or maybe Lindsey, depending on who was doing the looking. A rubber vise clamped down around Lindsey's head. Barometric pressure.

She dropped the candle again. It was exactly the sort of joke Alan liked. Not a joke at all, that is. She had a pretty good idea where the other sleepers were—in Jason's apartment, not on the way to Pittsburgh. And if anyone found out, it would be her job, too, not just Jason's. No government pension for Lindsey. No comfy early retirement.

Her hand still wasn't steady. The match finally caught and the candle dripped down wax on Versailles Kentucky's neck. But if it was that easy to wake up a sleeper, Lindsey would already know about it.

In the meantime, the bed was up against an exterior wall and there were all the windows. Lindsey dragged Versailles Kentucky off the bed.

She couldn't get a good grip. Versailles Kentucky was heavy. She flopped. Her head snapped back, hair snagging on the floor. Lindsey squatted, took hold of her by the upper arms and pulled her down the dark hall to the bathroom, keeping that floppy head off the ground. This must be what it was like to have murdered someone. She would kill Alan. Think of this as practice, she thought. Body disposal. Dry run. *Wet* run.

She dragged Versailles Kentucky over the bathroom threshold and leaned the body over the tub's lip. She grabbed the iguana. Put it on the bathroom floor. Arranged Kentucky in the tub, first one leg and then the other, folding her down on top of herself.

Next she got the air mattress out of the garage, the noise worse out there. She filled the mattress halfway and squeezed it through the bathroom door. Put more air in. Tented it over the tub. Went and found the flashlight, got a bottle of gin out of the freezer. It was still cold, thank God. She swaddled the iguana in a towel that was still stiff with Jason's blood. Put it in the tub again. Sleeper and iguana. Madonna and her very ugly baby.

Everything was clatter and wail. Lindsey heard a shutter, somewhere, go sailing off to somewhere else. The floor of the living room was wet in the circle of her flashlight when she went back in the living room to collect the other iguanas. That was either the rain beginning to force its way in under the front door and around the sliding glass doors, or else it was the canal. She collected the three other iguanas, dumped them into the tub, too. "Women and iguanas first," she said, and swigged her gin. But nobody heard her over the noise of the wind.

She sat hunched on the lid of her toilet and drank until the wind was almost something she could pretend to ignore. Like a band in a bar that doesn't know how loud they're playing. Eventually she fell asleep, still sitting on the toilet, and only woke up when she dropped the bottle and broke it. The iguanas rustled around like dry leaves in the tub. The wind was gone. It was the eye of the storm or else she'd missed the eye entirely and the rest of the hurricane as well.

Light came faintly through the shuttered window. The batteries of her emergency radio were dead but her cell phone still showed a signal. Three messages from Alan and six messages from a number that she guessed was Jason's. Maybe Alan wanted to apologize for something.

She went outside to see what had become of the world. Except, what had become of the world was that she was no longer in it. The street in front of her house was no longer the street in front of her house. It had become someplace else entirely. There were no other houses. As if the storm had carried them all away. She stood in a meadow full of wildflowers. There were mountains in the far distance, cloudy and blue. The air was very crisp.

Her cell phone showed no signal. When she looked back at her house, she was looking back into her own world. The hurricane was still there, smeared out onto the horizon like poison. The canal was full of the ocean. The Splinter was probably splinters. Her front door still stood open.

She went back inside and filled an old backpack with bottles of gin. Threw in candles, her matchbox, some cans of soup. Padded it all out with underwear and a sweater or two. The white stuff on those mountains was probably snow.

If she put her ear against the sliding glass doors that went out to the canal, she was listening to the eye, that long moment of emptiness when the worst is still to come. Versailles Kentucky was still asleep in the bathtub with the iguanas who were not. There were red marks on Versailles Kentucky's arms and legs where the iguanas had scratched her. Nothing fatal. Lindsey got a brown eyeliner pencil out of the drawer under the sink and lifted up the sleeper's leg. Drew a birthmark in the shape of a battleship. The water in the air would make it smear, but so what. If Alan could have his joke, she would have hers, too.

She lowered the cool leg. On an impulse, she lifted out the smallest iguana, still wrapped in its towel.

When she went out her front door again with her backpack and her bike and the iguana, the meadow with its red and yellow flowers was still there and the sun was coming up behind the mountains, although this was not the direction that the sun usually came up in and Lindsey was glad. She bore the sun a grudge because it did not stand still; it gave her no advantage except in that moment when it passed directly overhead and she had no shadow. Not even one. Everything that had once belonged to her alone was back inside Lindsey where it should have been.

There was something, maybe a mile or two away, that might have been an outcropping of rock. The iguana fit in the basket on her handlebars and the backpack wasn't too uncomfortably heavy. No sign of any people, anywhere, although if she were determined enough, and if her bicycle didn't get a puncture, surely she'd come across whatever the local equivalent of a bar was, eventually. If there wasn't a bar now, then she could always hang around a while longer, see who came up with that bright idea first.

Acknowledgments

I wish I knew how to thank, properly, the following people. Thanks to my family: my mother, Annabel Link; my sister, Holly, and my brother, Ben; my father, Bill and my stepmother, Linda Link. Many thanks for their hospitality and encouragement to Gavin's family—Eugene and Rosemary, the MacArthurs, the McClays, and the Grants. I owe Christopher Rowe and Gwenda Bond for their ghost stories. Richard Butner, Sycamore Hill, and the various Clarion workshops for Space! and Time! Kate Eltham and Robert Hoge. Cassandra Clare and Joshua Lewis for an enlightening discussion about evil pants. Fleur and David Whitaker for the use of their names. Ada Vassilovski and Peter Kramer and Jack Cheng and Barbara Gilly. Karen Joy Fowler, Sarah Rees Brennan, Delia Sherman, Ellen Kushner, Libba Bray, Elka Cloke, and Sarah Smith for reading early drafts. Thanks to Sean for suggesting that I try to write a new kind of story. Thanks to Jessa Crispin for the astrological reading. Thanks to Peter Straub for his stories. Thanks to Ray Bradbury, whose work was the inspiration for the story "Two Houses." Thanks to David Pritchard, Amanda Robinson, and Holly Rowland for conversations about television shows. Thanks to the doctors, nurses, and respiratory therapists in the Baystate NICU, and at Children's Hospital in Boston, and at the Franciscan Hospital for Children. Thanks to the all-seeing, all-knowing Holly Black, for her all-seeing eye, her writerly brain, and for rescuing me from holes that I have fallen into. Thanks to my translators, especially the marvelous Motoyuki Shibata and Debbie Eylon. Thanks to the Banff Centre for the Arts for providing a desk, some elk, a bear, and conversation. Thanks to the editors that I've had the good fortune to work with, among them Ellen Datlow, Rob Spillman, Brigid Hughes, Francis Bickmore, Stephanie Perkins, Gwenda Bond, Yuka Igarishi, and Deborah Noyes. Thanks to Taryn Fagerness. Thanks to Renée Zuckerbrot, who is the best agent in the world, and to Molly Bean, the best dachshund. Thanks to my fantastic editor, Noah Eaker, for his care, his insight, and his enthusiasm. Thanks to Caitlin McKenna, Susan Kamil, and the entire team at Random House. And finally: much love and many thanks to Gavin J. Grant and Ursula Grant. I wrote some stories for you.